Jacob's Eyes

Anita Ballard-Jones

CreateSpace-Assigned
ISBN-13: 978-1535154932
ISBN-10: 1535154934

First Edition

Printed in the USA

Acknowledgments

In Memory of My Late Husband
Joseph L. Jones

First and above all I need to thank my Lord and Savior, Jesus Christ for the inspiration and creativity to write. A special thank you to my mother, Alice Parker and my aunt, Shula Davis for their special support. To my fans, I can never thank you enough for your wonderful letters of praise for my previous novels and for the motivation that encourages me to continue writing. I will always do my best to bring everyone the best that I have. I take great pleasure thanking my reading team, Jenina Kearney, Samika Williams, Marvis Day Henderson, Debra Brown and Sophia Jefferson for taking their time to give this novel that, 'eye of an eagle' read and constructive feedback.

Other Books by the Author

Rehoboth Road

The Dancing Willow Tree: The Sequel to Rehoboth Road

Ashes, Ashes, They All Fall Down

Jupiter's Corner (a short story)

The Complete Story: Rehoboth Road through The Dancing Willow Tree

ೞೞ

COMING SOON

Broken Bond: A Memoir

Life is Worth Living: A memoir of short stories

Jacob's Eyes

Chapter 1

Thunder roared and lightning flashed across the distant sky leaving a reminder of the power of the Almighty. On that morning, He would leave behind sunshine after the rain. The earliest light of dawn lifted with the beauty of an amber glow that rested easy on the horizon. The new life of the season had not yet come to the Carolinas, but the rain had given way to an ethereal beauty and aroma of the fertile earth. But first, peace be still for the preparation of travel for a soon to be departed soul. The weeping willows wept harder from their rain soaked branches; the Spanish moss slapped their soaked draped sashes together loosening moisture to the ground. The rooster crowed; the sweet scent of cedar, oak and birch from the chimneys of the slave quarters and the large white mansion rose, bellowed and hovered about like mini clouds. The slaves knew without uttering a word, it was the morning they had expected. It was the morning unlike any other; it was the hush of the critters; every slave had a quiet about them; the birds sang softer; the dogs didn't hurry about, but just lay; the wind blew strong and hard, but only sounded a whisper. This was the first day that would change their lives for the times to come.

A dim light had shown all night in the left corner apartment suite of Master Dillard's quarters. Lester, his man-servant would place his lantern in the right parlor window if Master's physician indicated he was improving and he would move it to the left window for the contrary. This code was the early notification for his slave brethren only, for they had the most need to know. The physician slumbered lightly in a lounge near the Master's bed, his gold pocket watch held loosely in his hand and wearing a stethoscope around his neck. Lester sat in a wooden chair on the other side waiting to serve.

Master Dillard had been ailing for more than three months. He was a tall man, who just wasted away from an unknown malady. It was a powerful illness that first stole the color from his hair before draining the pigments from his skin so that his flesh matched the hue of freshly fallen snow. At the same time, his two hundred and thirty pound frame melted away like he had been feeding a parasite. The seventy nine pounds he managed to keep were the sum total weight of his skeleton, skin, internal organs and bodily fluid.

On that Sunday morning of April 15, 1860, Master Walter Dillard's deep blue eyes faded to gray. He was dead at the age of fifty two. Before the natural light brightened the day Lester moved the lantern to the left window and the soft moans and cries echoed throughout the slave quarters.

Later that afternoon, Master Jackson Dillard, his son, called all the slaves to the front yard of the mansion house. Their sorrow had been stifled and cloaked while awaiting the formal announcement. They shuffled along with the behavioral gait expected of slaves. A hundred and twenty six men, women and children stood looking up at the second floor terrace. The plantation's only two overseers, Danny Moore and Louis Maynard stood a pace behind Jackson, at a position allowing for respect and support. Master Walter Dillard didn't believe he needed more than two overseers; he assigned his slaves as assistants and drivers during the field work details. He had head grounds-men, head housekeepers, head cooks, head liverymen, head chicken men and so on and they all answered to Maynard and Moore. There was a system of rewards and punishments implemented that he oversaw that kept the slaves in line, including, but not limited to imprisonment, loss of positions, status in housing, land plots, pass privileges and the ultimate threat of being sold.

Jackson appeared to be devastated by his father's death, having loss his mother before his fifth year. He truly loved his father and had sought the help of physicians from all of the surrounding towns, but the cause of his ailing remained a mystery. He never married, was the sole benefactor of his father's estate and since there were no other legal heirs, he was alone to operate the 760 acre plantation; he was thankful he had Moore, Maynard and the slaves.

Moore was a young man, a few years older than Jackson at thirty-years and could easily match his strength, but Maynard was an elder man of Jackson's father's choosing, he was in his early sixties. He had been with the plantation before Jackson's birth. His years of wisdom were his most powerful asset; he knew the weather, the condition of the soil, the temperament of the slaves, when to plant, when to harvest and the answers to the questions asked and the ones Jackson had not yet asked. Louis Maynard was like having a private Farmer's Almanac at hand.

Jackson glanced over the terrace rail and quickly turned back to Moore. "Are they all here?" Gloom permeated his voice and his words were scratchy.

"Yes, sur," Moore responded, stepping forward to speak quietly and close to Jackson's right ear. "Would yuh like me tuh tell 'em, sur?"

Jackson took a deep breath and Maynard knew his answer just by observing his eyes; he gave him a reassuring nod. "Yuh gone be okay, Mr. Dillard?"

"Yes, Danny," Jackson whispered. "Ah don't want 'em tuh think Ah'm weak." He turned, placed both hands on the rail, scanned the yard and boldly yelled out. "Is everybody here?" The wind blew his long blond hair into his face. He combed it back with his fingers and settled it in place by putting on his wide brim hat.

"Yessum," and "we's all here, Massa." Slave voices echoed from across the yard. They all knew why they were called out. They had watched Master waste away and when he became too weak to leave his bed the house Negros carried the word about his condition. They had mourned for him all night and in the early morning when the lantern moved; they knew he was dead before Jackson. Tillie sent the young houseboy, Matt, to Gaffney to fetch Jackson when Master's physician pronounced him dead at dawn on that unusually beautiful Sunday morning. But Jackson last greeted his father early the previous Friday evening before leaving for town. As soon as Jackson rode off, Mammy Pearl slipped Jacob into Master Dillard's apartment suite for his last moments with his father. Now, Jackson had called for all the slaves to gather on the front lawn for the formal announcement.

"Master Walter," Jackson began, "is dead." Then he stood as still and tall as he could to keep his composure. He numbed himself to the soul stirring emotions the slaves could now uncloak. But their cries were a harmony of wails only for the white man's ears. They had moaned and cried when the words first came; they cried mostly for the fear of what would come of them. They had prayed for their lot for many weeks, when they first noticed how Master was wasting away. Some thought he had been vexed, but then they all agreed their fate was tied to his longevity. He took their women, but they reasoned that to be the curse of slavery. Then, all of the house servants agreed to protect his soul, less it be trapped in the mansion; they would rather be sold than work in a haunted house. Lester was charged with ensuring that at least one window would be cracked open in the master's apartment suite at all times so at the moment of his death his soul could escape the house. They cried in joy because the window was indeed open when Lester entered the master's chamber. So at the gathering they wailed and prayed Master Jackson would have mercy and not sell anyone or the plantation.

Master Jackson stood strong; to move would mean breaking down in front of the darkies and that would show weakness. Air, fresh, sweet, cool, spring air gave him strength, while Moore kept his place ensuring his support if necessary. To assist Jackson at that time would be the same as being a crutch to him. Jackson willed his strength to return; he could breakdown later, in private. Looking down from the terrace he saw a younger mirror of himself in Jacob; he had the same shoulder length golden hair, the deep blue eyes and creamy pearl complexion. Jackson held to the railing when Jacob tilted his head and stared up at him; he was forced to see his own anger in the face of his younger mulatto brother. None-the-less Jacob stood tall, stared up at him and hid his emotions under his stoic expression. Jackson turned away and took a deep breath before continuing. "Master Dillard's body is being dressed now and he is being setup in the parlor so yuh all can have yuh final viewin' and last moments with him tuh say yuh goodbyes. This was my daddy's wish and Ah'm duty bound tuh honor it. Later, this evening he'll be moved tuh the ice house and placed on the coolin' board. His final settin'-up and funeral will be Tuesday and might Ah say none of y'all are invited. 'Til then yuh all have extra chores preparin' the house and grounds for the family and guest and that includes preparin' the cemetery, too."

The slave's time with the late Master Dillard had ended and the frantic pace of preparation had begun. The house was thoroughly cleaned, linen washed and black drapes and valances were hung over every window. Family and guest were expected to arrive within twenty four hours and many would be lodging at the mansion. Outdoors chores were plentiful whereas the yard required manicuring, trees pruned and the family cemetery groomed. Master's tombstone was cut into a large flat rock and his grave was dug next to Jackson's mother, his late wife, Amanda. Everything for the funeral was completed before Monday night and the 'settin-up (wake)', funeral and repast took place on Tuesday as planned.

෨෧

Before a new normal could come over The Dillard Plantation the reading of Master Walter Dillard's Last Will and Testament was in order. Jackson Dillard had all of the slaves assemble again on the front lawn. As before, he stood on the second floor balcony of the mansion and Danny Moore and Louis Maynard stood a step behind him.

"Master Walter Dillard's lawyer is here for the reading of the Last Will and Testament and it involves many of you," Jackson yelled out. "Now, before my daddy died he asked me tuh tell yuh somethin'. My daddy fathered twenty six of y'all youngungs. Y'all know who yuh are and his lawyer will call out yuh names tuhday."

"Please don't sell us, Massa!" Young Silky cried out. She was only twelve years old. She and her mother had already clung to each other and slid to the ground. Then other cries sang out and the front yard was in a wave of wails from the fear of the unknown.

Jackson yelled out, "The youngungs gone be freed!" The words left his mouth, but even he could not hear them as they faded into the screams and wails of the slaves. Moore lifted his pistol, pulled off three rounds toward the sky and the slaves dropped to the ground still moaning, but quieter.

Maynard leaned against the wall shaking his bowed head. "Damn yuh, Danny!" he called out. "All yuh had tuh do was hold up yuh hands and yell fer dem tuh be quiet. Why yuh such a damn hot-headed youngster?"

"They quiet ain't dey?" Danny replied. He smirked and holstered his pistol.

"Listen!" Jackson yelled. "Nobody gon' be sold. Fact is . . . Ah need all y'all. Master Dillard, my daddy, done freed all his darky chillum. And there are twenty six of y'all."

The slaves began dancing around and praising the Lord, saying, "Halleluiah! Thank Yuh, Jesus!" They were definitely happier that no one would be sold, than the news that twenty six would be freed. The twenty six were all teenagers or younger and most of their mothers and siblings were still slaves. Master Dillard knew what he was doing by freeing his children; they would never leave their families.

శౖత

The next day Jacob's name was called to receive his freedom paper. It had been eleven years since he walked through the front doors of the large mansion. The skylight had been magnificently designed into a large circular pattern in the ceiling of the third level and now cast an enormous sunbeam onto the mansion's foyer. He remembered when the alterations to the mansion were being made, but it was during those days when he preferred to keep his distance from the big house. A long table had been placed in its light and there sat Samuel Wilson, his master's lawyer and Seth Beckerson, the clerk from the Lauren County Court. Beckerson was present to ensure the emancipations were carried forth in accordance with the law. The county office of Lauren had no intention on having so many slaves present in its courthouse. Jackson Dillard was absent, but on either side of the long stable stood his two overseers, Louis Maynard and Danny Moore. Jacob stared at the paper with the beautiful patterned swirled lines and curves. Penmanship he was used to seeing in the early days when he would spend so much time with his father in the mansion. Now, they were just swirls forming words that he could decipher if he followed the lines closely, but the years had dulled his mind to the familiarity of this manner of writing. He stepped from side to side in a nervous dance and held tight to his large Stetson hat, a gift from his father, the brim curled tight in his hands and his eyes shifting from the paper to the lawyer through his peripheral vision. "Please sur, could yuh read the words tuh me and show me where it be sayin' Ah's free?"

"Now, yuh know a slave is not supposed tuh read," the lawyer scolded. When he looked up to make eye contact with Jacob, Jacob shifted his eyes out of range.

"Yessum. But, sur, Ah's no slave now. Ah's a Natty!" Jacob sang out. The ability to read was his secret, but it made him smile a little inside to play this game with a white man.

"But you are still a niggah," the lawyer reasoned. He stared at Jacob for a minute then added, "Now yuh saying yuh not even a Dillard . . . that yuh someone called, Natty?

"Yessum," Jacob responded.

The lawyer smiled and shook his head, "Well," he began, "Ah guess yuh should know what yuh freedom paper say and showing yuh the words is nothing like teaching yuh tuh read."

"Ah thank yuh kindly, sur. And sur . . . can yuh write 'Jacob Natty' on my paper?"

The lawyer laughed, saying, "Boy, but yuh was born a Dillard, with Dillard blood running through yuh veins. Hell . . . yuh look more like a Dillard than Jackson."

Jacob continued to keep his head low and responded, "Meaning no disrespect, sur. But, Dillard's are born free; Ah's born a slave. My mama's name be, Natty. Da only thing Ah have left of hur, be hur name, sur."

The lawyer wasn't laughing anymore. He turned to Beckerson, who had slouched back on his chair with his thumbs tucked in his vest pockets. Impatient, he smirked. Wilson had known Jacob almost all of his life and understood his point. "Okay, if that's what yuh want," He said, before writing his new name on the paper and then he began to read:

❧

Register No. (1043)

South Carolina to wit

Freedom Papers of {Jacob Natty}

I, Seth Beckenson, Clerk of the County Court of Laurens in the State aforesaid do hereby certify that Jacob Natty is a free man of color having been emancipated in accordance with the Last Will and Testament of Walter Dillard of which has been recorded in this office on June 22, 1859 and being now executed after his death and burial, the time of said will directed that he shall be set free. Jacob is known as a male mulatto with a white complexion and yellow hair with blue eyes. He is eighteen years of age and about six feet three inches high and has a very large scar on his left knee. Recorded and registered according to the laws of South Carolina on this 23rd day of April 1860 in Lauren County. The Register of Jacob Natty a free Negro per Register No 1043, was presented to this agent of the Court, examined and ordered to be certified as correct.

In testimony whereof, I have hereunto set my hand of our said Court at Gaffney this 23rd day of April 1860 and attested by Samuel Wilson, Esq.

representative for Walter Dillard. Recorded this day. Lauren County Court Rep.

Seth Beckenson, Clerk: Seth Beckenson
Witness by: Samuel Wilson, Esq. **Samuel Wilson, Esq**

ౚ౷

Jacob turned and stood humbly staring at Beckerson through his peripheral vision, holding tight to the brim of his hat.

"Are yuh done?" Beckerson wolfed. He slammed his chair forward and picked up his quill. It only took a moment for him to sign the documents and record and register them on the county's register log. When he was done, he callously slung the papers across the table toward Jacob before impatiently drumming his fingers on the table.

"Thank yuh, kindly Mister Samuel Wilson. Ah be keepin' 'em safe," Jacob sang out, "Ah thank yuh kindly, Mister Samuel Wilson," he repeated. He accepted his papers and his smile was so bright his mouth began to ache. He bowed several times as he backed away from the table, never thanking or acknowledging Beckerson before leaving the house. He turned and hurried from the mansion, running briskly to the side of the supply shack before sliding down on his haunches. He pulled out the printed paper, put his finger on each word and began tuh read the entire document. After the third reading he concentrated on the special words and repeated them several times, "Jacob . . . Natty . . . Free." The scripted words were difficult to make out, but the printed words were easy to read and reminded him of times spent with his father.

Within minutes Capers and Juke were sliding down next to Jacob. They were each half-brothers to the other, all sons of Master Dillard and products of the violations of their mothers. But unlike Jacob, Capers and Juke had other family members on the plantation.

Jacob needed to put his precious papers away, but he was afraid to let them out of his hands. As far as Capers and Juke were concerned the documents were just pieces of paper, but Jacob convinced his brothers to stash them away in a safe place. He decided to go to the kitchen and get two canning jars and lids, a dry dish cloth and a large spoon. He tore the dish cloth in half and wrapped his papers in one half, placed it in the canning jar and tightly screwed on the lid. Then, he had his brothers do the same.

"Take yuh jar and hide it. Don't y'all tell nobody where yuh papers be," Jacob instructed. He searched all around to make sure no one was watching, before leading them inside the barn. They crouched down in the corner of the empty mule stall and he continued, "Lissen, some of dese here slaves will steal yuh papers and run away from here. Den pretend dey be you. Ah be leavin' dis here place real soon. Ah want yuh tuh come wit' me like we be talkin'."

Juke shot a glance at Capers and shame shrouded them like a cape. "We wanna leave, but we cain't leave our people," Juke whined.

"Yuh mean yuh scared," Jacob taunted.

"We ain't like yuh, Jacob. All yuh ever talked about was bein' free," Capers whispered. "Ev'rything be happenin' so fast, Ah be confused."

"Me too, Jacob," Juke added. "And Ah's scared. Ah don't know nothin' 'bout what be out dere." He waved his arm and twisted his body to dramatize the world outside of the plantation.

"Me 'either!" Jacob yelled out his disappointment before quieting down to a whisper. "Ah don't know what be out dere and Ah be scared, too, but Ah be free now and Ah'm gon' find out what freedom be like. When Ah be safe, Ah be comin' back for yuh. If Ah can come back, yuh can come back too if'n yuh don't like freedom. All Ah know is, Ah wanna git as far away from Jackson as Ah can be."

Juke and Capers nodded. They understood and believed that Jacob's leaving was more about Jackson than freedom. All of his years and more since their fathers illness, Jacob has had to endure the random sting of Jackson's whip just because he existed.

"Ah be going off tuh stash my jar 'til Ah be ready tuh leave. Y'all need tuh find a safe hidin' place too." Jacob gave his brothers a coy smile before leaving the barn. He was disappointed that the three of them wouldn't be leaving together. In that fleeting moment when he bid them farewell, his reality came alive; that burning desire for freedom that they all once shared had eluded them. The freedom they spoke of in their hiding places no longer glowed in their eyes. They had never felt the whip; they had never been persecuted; they had never loss a mother; they weren't like him, only having the whites as kin. They believed they would survive The Dillard; it was their world and it was the only world they knew.

Jacob walked away, his posture dictating his emotion and disappointment. His jaw shifted from grinding his teeth in a clenched mouth that held back the spoken words of his discontent. His eyes welled with tears that dropped freely away from his lowered head; Ah be alone in my new life too, he told himself. With no more time to waste, he tucked the large kitchen spoon in his waistband and held his jar snuggled under his arm. He checked his surroundings for anyone who might be watching him. When he realized the coast was clear, he crawled under the big white mansion and disappeared between the foundation pillars. Using the large spoon, he dug a deep hole in the dry soil and buried his jar two feet deep.

chapter 2

Natty

Jac ob went back to work in the fields and he continued to be the only one who spoke of freedom. For those in bondage, The Dillard Plantation in Gaffney, South Carolina had been known as a good place to be. Slaves were treated better there than on most farms and plantations anywhere in the region. The quarters and food were decent, they weren't beaten, or tortured, but one man was sold when he showed emotion when his woman was taken for the master's pleasure; that's what happen to Jacob's mother's husband.

Jacob was told his mother was a woman as fair skinned as Master Dillard's wife, Amanda. But Amanda had died during childbirth along with their baby girl and Walter Dillard mourned hard for three months. Then he remembered Natty, the mulatto slave woman who favored Amanda in almost every way. Natty was the prize he had just given his favorite buck, Lawrence permission to marry only weeks before. Now he needed and wanted her to sooth his pain, to be his Amanda. He was mesmerized by her fair skin and baby blue eyes. She wore her silky light brown hair in a single thick braid that she pinned up and around the back of her head. Then she covered her head with a long scarf in the same fashion as the other slave women, understanding that her appearance was her curse. Walter Dillard watched her as she went about her duties in the main house. He stared at her when she took the laundry to the clothesline. He feasted his eyes on the even sway of her hips, the curves of her body, her pleasant smile and he allowed his lust to rule over his conscience. The smiles she gave her husband reminded him of those he received from Amanda. Walter Dillard told himself Natty was his Amanda and he needed her to ease his pain.

One evening Master Walter Dillard walked from his home, down to the slave quarters, with a determined stride. He took a direct path and slapped his riding whip against his boots in beat with his steps. When he reached Lawrence and Natty's cabin he pushed the door open and stood in its opening. Natty was preparing dinner over an open hearth while Lawrence sat at the crude table. Instantly, Lawrence stood at attention and was speechless, his eyes shifted between Master Dillard and his wife. Natty turned from her large kettle, her back still slightly bent and her large spoon positioned over her pot. She inhaled and dropped her spoon. "Oh yes, Massa!" she exclaimed, as she stood upright and wiped both hands on the apron covering her brown paisley dress.

"Yes, sur!" Lawrence called out as if responding to an officer. He continued to stand tall waiting for an order.

"Take it easy, Lawrence. Ah come for Natty. She's gone be mine for a while."

"Sur?" Lawrence questioned. His eyes widened and his mouth fell open. He had heard him correctly. He understood his station in life: property, slave, always a boy, never a man, husband, but his love for Natty scrambled that order.

"Yuh heard me. Come, Natty!"

Lawrence hurried across the small shack and stood in front of Natty. "Sur, yuh just give hur tuh me! Yuh cain't take hur! She be mine!" he cried out.

"Boy, you be mine! Ah just took hur back!" Master stepped forward and reached for Natty with one hand and shoved Lawrence aside with the other.

Instantly, Natty recognized her husband's aggressive reflex toward the master. She called out, "No Lawrence!" Her arm stretched out, her hand giving a firm signal for him to stop. It was at that moment she knew their life together would be changed forever.

Lawrence responded with a stronger push that flung his master away from Natty and against the cabin wall. Then Lawrence stopped. "My Lawd!" he cried out. He was not sorry that he defended his wife's honor, but only that he had violated his station in life. He stood for a moment staring at Natty. Her fingers covered her lips while their master was re-establishing his balance and correcting his posture. Lawrence rushed to Natty, but before he could embrace his woman he felt Master Dillard's riding whip across his face.

Natty screamed for her man as he fell to the floor and Master lashed his body again and again, but not before pushing her back so the whip would not touch her.

"Remember who yuh Master is, boy!" Glaring down at Lawrence, he slapped the whip against his boot just to hear the snapping sound, but Lawrence never flinched. He nudged Natty toward the door and followed her from the cabin.

Lawrence leaped to his feet, rushed to the open door and stopped at the threshold. Master Dillard glanced back and saw this massive man standing tall and threatening. At that moment he decided that Lawrence would be shackled and driven to the slave trader that very evening.

Natty was taken into the mansion and all of the beautiful garments that once belonged to Amanda were laid before her. Walter Dillard refused to recognize or accept her objection. He existed within his own fantasy, so when she smiled because he told her to, he believed her feelings for him to be sincere. She cried for Lawrence and in his warped mind he believed her tears to be the happiness of sleeping with him in his luxurious bed. He had the house servants, the same people she had worked beside every day, draw her bath just as they had prepared the scented bubble water baths for Amanda. Her heart wrenching sobs melted their hearts while they bathed and dressed her in Amanda's silk gown. Walter Dillard took her to his bed and her heart sank.

That night she would belong to her master. He had her dressed to be his Amanda and laid her out on his bed like a large doll; her nakedness was covered by Amanda's white silk gown. Walter stood staring at her. He smiled and had a gentle appearance. Natty managed to remain serene, believing she would live through this night and return to her husband. An experience such as this had happen to her before; it was the plight of a slave woman.

The Master stood over the bed staring at her and at that moment being a slave had a benefit; she wasn't expected to make eye contact with him. She didn't have to acknowledge his desire, but through her peripheral vision she saw admiration and affection. He called her Amanda and she was a witness to his fantasy. It didn't matter, he wasn't Lawrence, but it was her duty to please her master because she was his property. She didn't have to like it and she could tell by the way he looked at her that he would be easy on her and then she could go home; rape was a word without meaning between a slave woman and a master.

Master eased himself down on the edge of the bed, pulled her long hair loose from its braid and combed his finger through it. He lifted her gown exposing her nakedness until he had pulled it over her head. He smiled. She remained stoic and continued to monitor his actions within her peripheral vision.

His hands trembled when he massaged her breast. "Smile when Ah touch yuh," he whispered. He smiled a lusty smile; his cheeks flushed deep pink and his lips wet and shiny in a rose red hue. The pupils of his blue eyes were fixed, glaring and startling with intoxication for the moments to come.

Repulsion was cloaked by duty, so she smiled with her lips and held back the tears in her eyes.

He stroked her body. His hands felt like sandpaper moving over her inner most private parts. He touched her in that place where his Amanda always tightened in shame. He glanced up at her; her order was to obey; she smiled. He opened her legs wider, touching her more. He smiled at her; she complied and smiled back; tears rolled down from the corners of her eyes. He kissed her stomach, slowly, affectionately, around and down to her hairline. He looked up, blinked his eyes, smiled and stared in her face. She breathed deeply, closed her eyes and smiled at him. Again, his hand found her most private area; his face went cold; his smile vanished; she was dry. He stopped, stared at her, puzzled. She smiled boldly and glared into his eyes; he could take her body, but she would not surrender. Suddenly his animalistic behavior was unleashed. He stood from the bedside. Fear clouded Natty's eyes, but she didn't cry out or allow her body to go stiff. He dropped his suspendered trousers and they fell over the riding boots he was still wearing. Natty turned away from the sight of his exposed snow white erected tool. Master Walter never got in the bed, but stood at the edge. He spread Natty's legs and pulled her to him, then did his business until he was satisfied; after all she was just a slave woman, not his Amanda. He cried and a sinister laugh escaped from between Natty's smiling lips; while her soul cried out for Lawrence, her physical being felt the pain of his brutality. She continued to smile because she had made him cry.

Walter Dillard was finished with Natty for that moment. He pulled himself away from her, repositioning her on the bed. Her submissive smiling stare was the only response she had for him and that caused him to turn away. "Cover yuhself!" he ordered. He wanted more of her, but not at that moment, later he would come to her again.

"Sleep now," he whispered in a gentler voice. Tears fell from Natty's eyes and she buried her face in the soft down pillow. All she thought about was the moment her master would tire of her and return her to her Lawrence. She would not sleep that night. Sometime later Walter Dillard pressed his naked body against hers and she was his again.

When the dawn came, Natty eased herself from under Master's arm. She covered her body with the silk gown until she found her own dress. Then she slipped from his apartment suite and ran all the way to her cabin. It was early Sunday morning, a day of rest and she wanted and needed to be in her husband's arms. "Lawrence!" she cried out. She turned around in the small space and was quick to realize its emptiness. She felt dirty, too dirty to heat the water before bathing. She wanted to wash away Master's filth before Lawrence returned. The wash basin, lye soap, a burlap rag and two buckets of room tempered water was nothing like the comfortable bubbly tub bath she had the evening before, but it was all she could do to get everything about Master off of her skin. She removed her dress, lathered her body and rinsed off with the shocking cool water. When she reopened her eyes from the rush of the water, Master Walter Dillard was standing in her cabin holding her dress out to her.

She reached for the dress and just held it, covering herself. She stared at her master.

"He's not comin' back, Natty. He's been taken tuh the trader." He stared in her eyes as he spoke and was ready for any reaction from her.

She froze, dropped her dress and her naked body collapsed to the dirt floor of the cabin.

Master Dillard carried her to her bed, wiped the dirt from her body and dressed her. When Natty regained consciousness, she was back in the master's bed.

Natty mourned for Lawrence at a depth far greater than what his death might have caused. Master Dillard had her body, but every day she willed herself dead. Nine and a half months after she was taken from Lawrence, she gave birth to a son and the good Lord granted her wish.

Master Dillard's fantasy world was over. Natty died giving birth, but unlike Amanda, this baby survived and was named Jacob. Pearl, one of his three cooks, who recently loss her child, was sent for and charged with the responsibility of his total care. She was ordered to move from her cabin to a comfortable room in the mansion near the kitchen.

Jackson was Jacob's half-brother. The six year old son of Amanda and Walter Dillard found displeasure in his new sibling from the moment of his birth. During his visits to his father's suite, Pearl was summoned to bring Jacob up to him.

"This is yuh brother," his father announced.

Jackson stared at the infant before turning his attention to the window. He dared to speak and wondered if his father had ever expressed such admiration for him.

Jacob remained in his father's house long after the slave known as Mammy Pearl returned to her cabin. Walter Dillard had begun fathering other children, but he doted on his Caucasian skin, blue eyed mulatto son, Jacob with the golden hair. He read to him daily and as he grew to the age of reason he began teaching him to read and write and the ways of a southern gentleman. Walter couldn't be with Jacob all the time, but Jackson, his son by Amanda could and he tormented Jacob. When Walter was away from the plantation on business, Jackson's abuse was even worst. Most of the time Jacob found himself hiding out in the slave's quarters. Walter Dillard loved Jacob, but he was a slave, so he received his father's apologetic eyes, while Jackson gave his apology and eluded punishment. Before his eight birthday, Jacob begged his father to allow him to live with Mammy Pearl; he even refused to accept work in the mansion

chapter 3

Freedom

On the second Sunday after Master Dillard's death, Jacob was ready to leave the plantation. Most of Walter Dillard's mulatto children had light brown to fair skin complexions with curly, or straight to wavy hair. Jacob was the fairest of all.

Master Dillard never let any of his mulatto children leave the plantation for any reason. The children couldn't want for a world or life they knew nothing about or he wasn't willing to give to them. And as for the women he violated, he believed that to be his business. He did not harbor any sensitivities about the randomness of his activities. Most masters took a slave as a mistress, but Walter Dillard took any slave he fancied, on any day he fancied her. After his love for Natty he never allowed himself to love another slave, he just took them for his sexual pleasure. A real gentleman would simply visit the brothel in town, even though his slaves were his property. On the other hand, Jackson never touched a slave woman.

For Jacob, the world beyond the boundaries of the plantation was as frightening as walking into the abyss. It was the world of the unknown, but he knew he would journey into it. The only constant was the sky above and the ground below. He knew he would take a right turn at the end of the drive and beyond the tall arched crape myrtle trees because he had watched Jackson ride off in that direction every time he left the plantation. He had decided that if he took a wrong turn, freedom allowed him to turn around and select an alternate direction. Tears filled his eyes when he said good-bye to his favorite brothers, Capers and Juke.

Because of Master Dillard, Jacob had a large extended family. Every slave on the plantation stood around him that Sunday morning; many of them begging him to stay except for Sula. She loved him and for that reason she supported his leaving even if it meant losing him forever. He said he would return for her, but her lifetime of bondage made it unimaginable for her to realize that notion. Her man was now a freeman. She dreamed in real colors and her man's dream was now all the colors of the rainbow. It was his time to leave before his colors turned to shades of gray.

ॐॐ

Sula

A trail of dust mingled with the dew of the early September evening from two separate locations: Master Dillard and his acquaintance, Frank Brandon, a British financier rode up the plantation drive in the canopy-topped surrey driven by his trusty slave, Wiley. In the wake of their dust were two wagons heavy with purchases from their shopping visit in Columbia. Behind the mansion a cloud of dust rose from the drudgery of slaves returning from the fields. They moved on to their quarters and the cargo wagons were driven to the storage units near the barn.

The stable boy held tight to the reins while Wiley stepped down from the carriage to hold open its door for Master Dillard and his guest.

"Boy, go fetch Ollie," Master Dillard ordered while waving his hand off toward the other wagons. "Get that lil gal out of that wagon and tell Ollie Ah said tuh settle hur in." He turned and he and Frank Brandon climbed the steps to the mansion and didn't look back.

Wiley had gathered the reins from the surrey team and began leading the hitch to the stable when the familiar wails of a child were heard. Her cries had quieted during their journey from Columbia. He thought she had fallen asleep, but she had only reduced her wails to a whimper. He had first heard her hysterical screams when she was lifted from the auction block and placed in the third and last wagon. The drivers were instructed to maintain a distance of several yards behind Master Dillard's surrey so as to cause him the most limited discomfort. Now, Wiley tied the horses to a tree and hurried to the child. She was hiding behind three cast-iron wood burning stoves that master had purchased for heating the mansion's apartments. Ollie had yet to arrive and the child was hysterical again.

"C'mon chile," Wiley whispered. "Yuh gon' be jes fine." He held out both arms, but she refused to move. He peeked in the wagon and her big glazed eyes peered at him in a frozen stare. She had swaddled herself in blankets and a burlap sackcloth. Perspiration set on her forehead like pearls while the heat of the evening proceeded to suffocate her tiny body.

Ollie and Mammy Pearl followed the stable boy to the wagon in a hurried pace. Inquisitive expressions etched the faces of everyone and the women's thick bodies thumped the earth in unified strides with their every step.

"What's goin' on? Whut yuh doin Wiley?" Ollie called out as she approached the wagon.

"Now, Ah be jes tryin' tuh he'p," Wiley began explaining. He pointed to the child in the wagon and then waved Ollie over to take a look. "See . . . she be jes a baby. Ah say 'bout nine, ten, or so and she be scared 'bout near tuh death. Master . . . he buy hur right off da block. He say no child need'n be on dat block. He bid high and dey be no mo' bidin' fo' hur."

"Sho-nuff?" Ollie smiled and stood on her tiptoes to get a better look. "Oh, shoot now! Ah be needin' tuh git in dere wit' dat baby. Y'all he'p me up dere wit' hur."

Pearl grabbed the large, heavy wash basin and placed it up-side-down at the back of the wagon. Ollie climbed up and between the stoves, then crawled over to the child. She lifted her apron and wiped the child's face, all the time whispering. "It gon' be fine chile. Yuh be mine now." She cupped the child's face in her hand and kissed her on the forehead.

The little girl hiccupped and cried, "Ah . . . uh . . . want . . . uh . . . mah . . . mama!" Her large almond shaped eyes begged and pleaded, but she knew the truth of her circumstances.

"Ah be da one tuh love yuh now, chile." Ollie began removing the hot burlap cloth and blankets from around her. "Can Ah be yuh new mama?" she asked. She didn't wait for her answer. "Yuh ain't never gon' back. So go on git yuh sorrow out now. Chile yuh know how it be."

The child screamed out a howling wail and Ollie pulled her to her bosom.

Tillie hurried up to the wagon. "What be goin' on here?" she muttered. Then she was quiet and surveyed the situation, her attention shifting between Pearl, the child and Ollie.

"Ollie!" Pearl scolded. "Yuh being tuh hard on dat chile."

"We be slaves! We be property! She cain't be wit' hur family, but da Lawd don' smiled down on hur and give hur tuh us 'cause he knowed we can love hur and she be safe here." Ollie held tight to the crying child. "She gots tuh git hur sorrow out."

Pearl, Tillie and Wiley lowered their heads. They knew Ollie was right. Their station in life could never be pampered or sugar coated. The child had to get over her loss and move on.

The child whined like her soul was turning inside-out while Ollie continued to push the blankets away from her hot body. The child had wrapped her arms around Ollie's neck pressing her cheek to her own. After completely freeing the child from her bindings, Ollie wrapped her arms around her again. She kissed her cheeks and head and hugged her with a warm, gentle touch. The little girl continued to cry a while longer and then began to moan as she stood to survey her new home. The whites of her eyes resembled the reddish hue of an Indian summer and her wet face glistened against her chocolate skin. Ollie held her arm around her tiny waist and led her from between the stoves. Tillie and Pearl held out their arms to receive the child from the wagon.

"C'mon baby!" Tillie said, "we's gon' all love yuh."

"C'mon here now. Jump right here in Mammy Pear's arms."

The child sniffled; her wide teary eyes shifted, searching for sincerity in everyone's face.

"Oh, baby girl. Yuh so thin," Tillie chuckled softly, "we's gon' feed yuh real good and Ah gots me some sweet bread tuh git yuh started wit'."

"Now we's gon' all git our hugs in on this here chile, but Pearl, you and Tillie best be gittin' back tuh da kitchen and Wiley yuh know where yuh need'n tuh be. Massa give hur tuh me and y'all still gots work tuh do." Ollie's grin spread across her lower face as she spoke and tears of joy hung in the wells of her eyes.

"Ah be down tuh yuh cabin wit' fresh clothes for yuh chile in a short time. Tillie can watch the pots for a while," Mammy Pearl announced. She headed toward her cabin, then turned and walked backward as she spoke.

"Thank yuh kindly, Pearl," Ollie said. Then she turned and bent over until her eyes were even with the child's eyes, "Whut be yuh name, baby?" she asked.

"Sula," the child whispered.

"Oh, dat be a pretty name. Where yuh be from?"

"Massa Telson . . . Telson Plantation," Sula squeaked out her response. Her breath quivered when she inhaled, but she continued. "Ah don't know where dat be. Ah don't . . . know where . . . Mama be." She began whining again; then stopped and stepped lightly, shaking her hands rapidly as if her misery was escaping from her extremities. "Ah want my mama, my papa, my brothers! Ah wanna go home," she cried, screamed and danced in her misery. Her eyes were wild like she could suddenly transported herself someplace else.

Ollie grabbed her in a bear hug and pulled her to the ground. "Hush baby! Hush baby! We cain't be yuh folk, but we gon' love yuh."

The two of them sat on the grass under the old shade tree; Ollie continuing to hug Sula; the sides of their faces touching. Ollie rocking her trembling body and humming a soft tune. Soon, Sula was still.

"It was just a game." Sula whispered softly. "Ah always let Rosella win da game. She was gon' win, but she fell down and lose da game." Sula pulled back, turned and stared at Ollie. "Ah be jes standin' dere. Rosella fall by hurself, den tell Massa Ah made hur fall and lose da game." She wiped her tears with the back of her hand. "Da next day Ah be taken by the trader man and Ah see'd my mama and two brothers cryin'. Da 'seer be beatin' Papa. Ah knowed Ah be sold fer sure."

"Well, Sula da good Lawd be lookin' over yuh!" Ollie kissed her cheek. "Dis be a good place." Ollie rolled over to her knees before standing.

Sula stood quickly and stared up at her. "Do lil girls git taken by Massa's sons at dis place?"

"Chile . . . Massa don't want no chile. He want da women. Why yuh ask dat?" Ollie stopped and stared down at the child. "What happen chile?"

"Lucas Telson, he be Massa's son. He take sport wit' us girls. He take us all da time. Take us from da fields; he take us from us cabins. Take us from us papas. He be wit' his friends. When Ah cry, he beat me and still take me."

"Oh baby," Ollie whined. "Dat don't go on here. Now c'mon, we's gots tuh get yuh fed and bathed."

❦

Jacob hurried into the kitchen and brushed up to Mammy Pearl hoping to get a snack before dinner. He was one of the few slaves that took their meals in the mansion's kitchen. Just seeing his thirteen year, he was hardworking, unpresumptuous and charming. Every time Pearl looked at him she wanted to envelop him in her arms and hold on tight. He was the child given to her, the child to replace the children she loss in miscarriage; the child she nursed and was allowed to keep when her child was stillborn; the child she loved; the child she thanked the Lord for every day

Mammy Pearl stood against the sideboard wiping her hands on her apron. "Ollie be given a lil gal tuhday," she announced. She stared at Jacob smiling and nodding her head.

He was so busy consuming his snack he missed part of her statement. "Ma'am?" he responded.

"Massa give Ollie a lil gal tuhday. He buy hur off da block and she be mighty scared. Cute lil thang."

"Mammy . . . yuh say Miss Ollie got a lil gal all tuh herself?" Jacob stopped eating to give her his attention. "Ah wanna see hur?"

"Later boy! Ollie be settlin' hur in. Dat chile be dirty, hungry and tired and she be mighty scared. We go dere tuhgether, later."

☙◦❧

Later as promised, after Mammy Pearl finished her duties in the kitchen, she and Jacob headed for Tillie and Ollie's cabin. Sula was sitting at the table. As soon as Ollie heard the noise at the door she hurried to stand in front of Sula in a protective way.

When Jacob opened the cabin door and Sula saw him, she screamed louder than all the crying and wailing she had made since arriving at The Dillard. She dropped to the wood planked floor and crawled into the corner of the room. "Kill me now! Kill me now!" she screamed. She squatted and covered her head with her arms.

Mammy Pearl and Miss Ollie ran to her. "No, honey. Dis here be Jacob. He be a slave like us. He gone be yuh friend."

Sula screamed, stretched out her left arm and waved it blindly while still covering her head and eyes with her right arm. "Mama! Mama!" she cried. "He gone take me yonder tuh da shack den have his way!" Fear set in her eyes like coal nuggets on white snow and piercing screams continued to escape her lips.

"Ah'm gone always keep yuh safe, Sula!" Jacob cried out. He wrapped her in his arms and she fell limp; her fight was gone and she had melted as if she were lifeless; she had simply surrendered to her fear. He rubbed her coco brown arm and rested the side of his face in her thick wooly hair. "Yuh be safe, Sula. Yuh be loved in this place." He gently rocked her as he spoke. He pleaded with her to stop crying. "Ah know yuh miss yuh mammy and pappy. Mammy Pearl be my new Mama and Miss Ollie be yuh new Mama." When she lifted her head, he wiped her face with his open hand. "We got folk dat love us Sula and Ah ain't gone let nobody ever hurt yuh, ever again."

"But . . . yuh . . . yuh . . . be white. Yuh be Massa?" she whined and her eyes searched his eyes for the truth.

"Ah be a slave just lak you," Jacob announced. "Ah be a slave. Ah just look white."

Then Ollie announced in a louder than necessary tone. "He just look lak dat 'cause Massa be his pappy, but he still be a slave." She pointed to Jacob's eyes. "Just look at 'dem crazy eyes he got."

Sula's wailing quieted to sporadic hiccups as she sat back and stared at Jacob for a long while. She twisted her head to examine his face. She held his eyelids open to examine his eyes and then she touched his hair. "Ah's so scared! Ah want my mama! Ah wanna go home!" she whined.

"Yuh be sold, now. We be yuh new family, now. Dis be da best plantation in da whole world. Massa Dillard . . . he be a good massa and he makes sure his slaves don't be hurt none." Miss Ollie sang out. "Chile, he so good tuh us ain't nobody ever run off."

Jacob gave Sula a convincing smile and then he reminded himself that his father would not allow Jackson to harm Sula if he asked for her protection.

The years moved on and now it was the time for parting. Sula and Jacob had loved each other since those early days and she was the only person who could convince him to stay. Jacob promised her he would find his way back and somehow he would buy her freedom. She understood his intentions and smiled. He held tight to her hand and said his good-byes.

"We's all family here," Mammy Pearl said. "We knows Massa Dillard be gon', but Massa Jackson, he be a good man, too."

Jacob's attention was pulled from Sula. *Jackson wasn't a nice boy and he is not a good man*, he thought. He remembered Jackson even if Mammy Pearl didn't. Jackson was the person that made him not want to be a white man. His brother, who was just six years older than he, made every attempt to never leave a bruise on him after a beating. Accidents didn't count; even accidents that resulted after forceful pushes into the scrap pile. The scar of Jacob's knee and the pain and infection associated with it would remain with him for the remainder of his life. And there were the fishing trips that began when he was four years old. That first time Jackson took him to the lake he hugged him and was playful. It was all a scheme to falsely calm his fears. Once in the rowboat and in the middle of the lake, Jackson tied a rope around his waist, lifted him high and tossed him into the water. *"Can yuh swim, boy? Can yuh swim?"* Jackson yelled out; words that flashed back into Jacob's head as he stood in the yard with Sula and Mammy Pearl. He still remembered the wicked sound of Jackson's laugh when he called out for his daddy. *"That's my daddy!"* Jackson taunted. *"Yuh ain't got no daddy."* At other times, Jackson just hogtied and blindfolded him and threw him in the skip. After rowing him out to the middle of the lake, he was just tossed in. Jackson laughed as he gagged and swallowed water before retrieving him, only to bobble him again and again. The memory of his own screams still made him shiver. Whenever their father was away from the plantation, Jackson's abuse was more intense. He would remove him from Mammy Pearl's care and remind him that she would suffer more than he if he told the secrets of his torturous events. These events raced through Jacob's head even at that moment while he stood ready to leave The Dillard. After the swimming lessons ended, Jackson would strip him naked and imprison him for hours in a dark closet in the mansion. Jackson pulled him about by his hair, had pins stuck in the soles of his feet until he limped for days; forced him to eat worms and other insects and had him eat and smear himself with animal feces. As time passed the intense abuse diminished to slaps, kicks, threatening stares. Finally, Jacob stopped returning to his room in the mansion and ran off to Mammy Pearl's cabin. When his father questioned him, he revealed Jackson's torturous activities. His father replied, "Very well, Jacob, yuh may stay with Mammy Pearl. Ah'll find yuh work in the house."

Jackson's cruelty had included verbal abuse and with Jacob's knowledge of his place on the plantation, his father's behavior was of no surprise to him. "Ah thank yuh sur, but may Ah work da fields wit' da other slaves?" he responded. He expected to see anger on his father's face, but instead he saw wrenching pain as Walter Dillard turned and walked away.

Jacob held Mammy Pearl's hands. "Always 'member Mammy, Massa Jackson is not a good man. Beware of him," he whispered in her ear. He knew it wouldn't be long before the beatings would start and slaves would be sold. It wouldn't be long before things changed for the worst.

Mammy Pearl wiped her eyes with the corner of her apron. "Ah still don't want yuh tuh go, Jacob. Yuh jes see eighteen summers and yuh ain't nevah been off dis here land. Dey be waitin' tuh kill yuh dead out dere."

"Mammy Pearl, Ah be da first one Jackson gon' beat or kill if'n Ah stay here; Ah been runnin' and hidin' from him all my life. Ah love yuh. Yuh be de only mama Ah ever had. Ah ain't nevah gon' forget yuh. When Ah git settled and it be safe, Ah be back tuh see yuh! Fer now, jes know how much Ah love yuh." Jacob walked toward his foster mother as he spoke; embracing the porky woman, his arms barely reaching around her when he kissed her cheeks.

He stepped back, taking notice of Lucy Mae and her ten year old twins, Jenny and Simon, who were clutching to each side of her. Her husband, Jimbo was leaning against the oldest oak tree on the plantation. The sun causing him to squint, but the scowl that draped his face expressed his true temperament. He was known to be a malicious man with his wife and the twins that had been fathered by Walter Dillard. A number of issues fueled his anger, but ranking the highest was his inability to father a child with any woman. He blamed his wife for being raped by the master; he blamed the Lord for his being a slave; he hated himself and he was too much of a coward to take his own life. Lucy Mae and the twins were the only people he could rule over and control and they were always in jeopardy of his abuse.

Lucy Mae gently touched Jacob's arm and looked up at him. "Ah's so happy tuh see yuh goin' off tuh freedom, Jacob. Ah be prayin' fer yuh safety. My chillen be free now, too and we don' hid dem papers in a real safe place."

Jacob smiles, "Good. Keep 'em safe," he whispered. "Yuh know where dem papers be?" he asked the twins.

They didn't speak, but nodded, smiled and their eyes were reassuring.

Lucy Mae nodded. "Yeah Jacob, but dat Jimbo, even he don't know where dey be." She smiled before continuing. "Least Ah know Massa Jackson cain't sell 'em 'way from me now." Lucy Mae continued to share her smile between Jacob and her children.

Jimbo strolled closer to the group and leaned into Lucy Mae's space. "Don't mean he cain't sell you 'way from dem," he muttered, and then he snickered before backing up to the oak tree again.

Lucy Mae pulled her children closer. She glanced up at Jacob and Mammy Pearl and clutched the little bag hanging from her neck.

"Ain't so," Jacob responded. "If anybody git sol' it be you, Jimbo. Jackson ain't gone have nobody 'round here meaner den him."

Lucy Mae and her sandy colored twins with the curly hair, smiled. "Yuh please be safe Jacob and yuh come back tuh see us."

"Yes ma'am," he said. He got down on his knees and embraced the twins. "Y'all be good and stay outta Jackson's sight. Yuh know he don't take kindly tuh us. Ah love yuh 'cause yuh my family." He stood and reached for Lucy Mae and they walked a few feet away from the children. "Get 'way from Jimbo 'fore he hurt yuh, bad. He scared of Mammy Pearl, Miss Tillie and Miss Ollie. Dey say y'all need tuh be comin' tuh live in deir cabin. Jimbo scared of dey juju."

"Jacob, he used tuh beat me bad when he took a mind tuh it. He jes looked at Jenny and Simon, den da evil be on his face. He run tuh get dem chillen. Ah run tuh cover dem. Den he beat me. He hates mah babies. Did yuh see dem juju bags hangin' low 'round dey necks? Dey tuck dem in dey clothes when dey not 'round Jimbo."

Jacob turned back toward the children and smiled. Then he waved to the others who were waiting for his attention and nodded, acknowledging them and gesturing for their patience. "Yes, what dey be?" he asked.

Lucy Mae smiled. "Ah got me a juju bag too, but dey ain't for real. Dese bags jes be tricks tuh keep Jimbo 'way from us." Now, Lucy Mae was laughing so hard she had to cover her mouth with her hand. "Ollie tol' me tuh put dis potion in his stew at supper. She say it gon' make him sleep good and da next day da runs gon' start. She say dat as soon as he go tuh sleep Ah's tuh cut a big patch of his hair from da side of his head and Ah did dat too." She smirked and made sure her back was facing Jimbo, who was now squatting at the base of the huge oak, chewing on a blade of straw-grass.

Jacob peeked over at Jimbo and one side of his thick black wooly hair had been cropped close to his scalp, while the other side was more than two inches long. He chuckled quietly and his eyes signaled for her to continue.

Lucy Mae reached for her bag and held it in her hand. She peeked around, looking for Jimbo and he was gone. She smiled and continued. "Now Ollie, she say, 'Skin 'em good so he knowed he be skint.'" Ah done had da bags and dese rawhide straps she gimme 'fore Ah git home. Dey had three kidney beans and crumpled dried grass in each bag. Ah be tol' tuh separate his hair intuh three heaps and put a heap in each bag. Da next mornin', when Jimbo feel his head, Ah be tol' tuh tell 'em he be vexed and sho' 'em da bags. Tell 'em we be wearin' da bags against his evil and dat he be gittin' a warnin' of da power real soon. Ah tell 'em it be a small warnin', but if he come at us, he be dead 'fore night. His face turned ashy like he already dead and he backed away from us. All day long Jimbo had da runs. He messed his pants so bad he go jump in da river two times. When he look at me, Ah hol' up mah bag and he jerk hisself 'way. Day 'for yeste'day, Jimbo tripped me when we get out tuh da plantin' field. Ah keep a small jar o' itchy power in my dress pocket. A lil time after, he be bendin' over, doin' his plantin'. Ah lift his top and put dat powder on his back. He jump up and say, 'Whut yuh do?' Ah say, Ah put my juju bag on yuh back and yuh bettah not tell, or it be worse." Ah backed away from him and say, 'Yuh know why Ah juju yuh.' He lifted his hand tuh hit me and dat powder commence tuh workin'. He pull at his shirt and dat jes spread dat powder mo' and Jimbo start tuh jumpin' lak a rabbit. 'Somethin' git a hol' o' me!' he be yellin' and jumpin. Ever'body git 'way from him, even da boss man. Ah back 'way too lak it ain't nothin' Ah do. Ah be screamin' fo' somebody tuh he'p him lak a good wife should." Lucy May slapped Jacob's arm lightly and they both broke out in a contagious laugh.

Ollie and Mammy Pearl looked at them and knew what they were talking about and they began to laugh, too.

"Yeah Jacob, he still ain't knowed da juju be a trick. Ollie got mo' tricks fer him if'n he git tuh actin' ugly again. So, don't yuh be worrin' 'bout us."

"Well, Ah do feel bettah," Jacob said. "Yuh jes keep dat juju bag 'round yuh neck."

"Ah will," Lucy May replied and she let out another chuckle.

Jacob reached over and kissed her on her forehead before saying, "Ah'll be back tuh visit when Ah can. Yuh know da sistahs be here for yuh."

"Bye Jacob. Ah'm gon' be prayin' fer yuh. Ah love yuh," Lucy May muttered, as she released his hands.

Jacob returned to Miss Ollie. "Thank yuh for takin' care of Lucy May."

"Someone had tuh take care of dat devil," Miss Ollie said, as she stood close watching Mammy Pearl, who had stopped dabbing at her tears. "Looky here, Jacob. Yuh need tuh be still now. Dis here be our life. Yuh be safe here," Miss Ollie whined and held tight to Jacob's hand. "Yuh know yuh lak mah own." She looked over at Sula. "Gal, cain't yuh do somethin' tuh make 'em wanna stay?"

Sula glanced up and didn't take her eyes off Jacob. "No, Mama Ollie. Dis what he want."

"Miss Ollie, yuh know Ah ain't safe here. Yuh know the things Jackson do tuh me. My daddy did one good thing, he freed me. Ah will not make myself a slave and stay here," Jacob preached. "Ah gots me free papers; Ah's a Natty. How's Ah'm gonna be free if'n Ah live like a slave. Ah's got tuh leave here tuh be free."

"Y'all make way!" Tillie's squeaky voice sliced through the crown. "Y'all gotta move an' make way!" She carried a large stuffed burlap knapsack with a heavy rope attached through the bottom and snaked through the top, making a crude shoulder strap. "Make-way, folk!" she screamed out in the highest pitched voice she could and the crowd separated like Moses parting the Red Sea. "Sula, Ah be on yuh side, so let me be wit yuh man fer now. Ah be right back. C'mere, Jacob! Ah got somethin' fer yuh! Ah cain't stop yuh from leavin', but Ah be givin' yuh des vittles tuh he'p yuh a lil' bit."

Jacob's body dipped from the weight of the knapsack that Tillie carried with ease. When he leaned down to kiss her cheek, she wrapped her thin arms around his neck and began to whisper in his ear. "Set dat bag down an' lissen here, boy!" she ordered.

Jacob did as he was told and before he knew it, he was being pulled to the side while Sula and the crowd watched.

"All right now, yuh'll find all kinds of eatin' stuff in dat bag, but Ah don' took Massa Dillard's gun and a box of bullets. Yuh keep dat gun loaded and where yuh can get tuh it real fast, but keep it hidden. Dis be da Misses gun b'fore she go tuh glory. Ah be da one tuh he'p her dress and Ah see'd hur strap dat gun tuh hur leg. So yuh strap it tuh yuh leg and pull yuh britches down over it. Da gun, da gun pouch and straps be in dat sack. Now don't yuh be 'fraid tuh use it tuh keep yuh own life."

Jacob towered over the five foot tall Miss Tillie. Her skin color carried a hint of beige that with a second glance was enough to classify her as a person of color. "Miss Tillie, how can Ah use dat?" Their eyes met and he took a deep breath.

"Yuh'll know how, if'n da time comes. Just kill 'em dead and hide dey body so dey never be found; bury dem deep so da critters don't be diggin' 'em up. If'n yuh cain't do dat, den yuh best be stayin' right here where yuh know yuh be safe." Tillie clenched her lips and a stern expression let him know she was serious. "Promise me yuh be doin' whut Ah say?"

Jacob stared off in the distance to where he would be traveling and then he turned and glanced back at Sula, Capers and Juke, before attending to Tillie again. "Ah ain't got no problem wit' dat, Miss Tillie. Ah kin do it."

Tillie reached up and gave Jacob another hug then sang out, "Ah forgot yuh blanket. Ah had it all rolled up fer yuh." She hurried off behind the row of cabins. At that moment, Sula ran back to Jacob's side.

Old Wiley came over to Jacob. As Master Dillard's driver, he knew the roads. "Go north tuh Ohio," he suggested. "Moss be growin' on the north side of da trees. Let da trees be yuh guide. Yuh be free 'cause yuh got papers. It be da gittin' dere dat be da problem. But, once yuh be dere da slave hunters cain't be catchin' yuh and draggin' yuh back." Wiley placed his hand on Jacob's shoulder. "Lissen boy. Ah hear dey be freedom in da north."

"Much obliged, sur. Ah be considerin' it." Jacob smiled and nodded at Wiley before walking away.

"Well, least Ah know how tuh get tuh da south. Ah be free already. Ah don't need tuh be goin' north where it be cold," Jacob told Sula. They smiled and began to walk back toward Capers and Juke. Before he could ask them to join him again, he read fear and refusal on their faces. They embraced each other believing they would never be together again, but Jacob spoke out, "Ah be comin' back for yuh so be ready and keep lookin' for me." He turned, kissed Tillie and accepted the thick quilted blanket she had tied up in a tight bedroll. He and Sula walked about fifty feet down the slave path and they had their last moments alone, then Jacob was gone, disappearing into the woods.

chapter 4

Jacob understood the dangers of the road, but the forest was too dense to travel through. He had to walk the road and he was thankful he was afraid. Fear heightened his senses; he believed he could feel the vibrations of a bumblebee, the slither of a snake and surely the comings of humans on foot, horseback or wagon. He could slip into the woods when he needed to hide. He camped in the woods and took Tillie's advice to strap the small derringer to his shin. He strung a hammock in the trees for his night's sleep, thanks to the extra rope Tillie packed. Sleeping on the forest floor was something he wasn't accustomed to; he thought he would sleep high up in the trees, rather than worry about snakes or rats crawling over him during the night. When he couldn't' catch a fish or snare a rabbit, he fell back on the cured meat or jars of preserves from Tillie. If he were lucky at hunting or fishing, he made his campfire during the day and prayed no one would see the smoke.

Being a free man wasn't what he thought it would be. Now, he was a slave to his fears. He was lonely and lost; he couldn't return to the plantation even if he wanted to. And having freedom paper didn't mean a thing to any slave hunter, Night Riders or just evil spirited white men. They'd say, "Boy, show me dem words dat say yuh free."

Jacob knew he could read every word on his freedom paper, but he feared the Night Riders would just beat or kill him because he could read. If he pretended to only know the words, 'free' and his name, the men would tell him his papers didn't say nothing about him being a free man. His papers would be destroyed and he would be returned to servitude; he would either be claimed by the whites that discovered him or sold on the auction block. Jacob had lived the way of the slaves for so long he had no concept of his place in the south, or what his capabilities were.

જજ

Ten sunrises, aimless wandering and Jacob believed he had left South Carolina, but he had only traveled south of The Dillard Plantation by one days walk. All he knew was he never seemed to dry off from the spring rains. He was so tired, his legs ached and his feet were blistered from his wet boots. He thanked the good Lord for the tough soles on his feet because he had taken to carrying his badly worn wet boots around his neck by the rawhide laces. Tears crawled down his face leaving dirt tracks on his white skin, while fear and loneliness pounded in his chest. All he wanted to do was return to The Dillard, but he was hopelessly lost.

Dreary and down-hearted, Jacob decided he wouldn't dive into the bushes when he heard or saw another traveler on the road. He was so beaten down he didn't care if it was a slave hunter. He kept his eyes forward and continued walking. He prayed whoever it was would help him, whether it was their intention or not; maybe they would return him to his plantation, even if that meant taking a beating first; he wanted to go home. Freedom wasn't all he thought it would be.

The sounds of wagon wheels were getting closer and he could hear his heart beat with every step he took. "Lawd, he'p me pleaseee!" he cried out softly. *Dey be right behind me. Ah ain't gon' turn 'round,* he thought.

"Whoa horse! Hello, sur. Can Ah give yuh a ride?" The big black man asked.

That be a culud man Ah see? Ah thank Yuh, Lawd! Jacob thought. "G'day, sur!" Jacob spoke with delight. He was never so happy to see another black man. "Yes sur! Ah jes got freed and Ah be mighty lost!"

"Hold on here, boy! Yuh's a culud boy? Yuh jes be free? Well, bust mah britches!" The black man said. "Boy, where yuh be headin'?"

"Ah don' know. Ah jes wanted tuh be free," Jacob answered. His dirt tracked tears were obvious and he fought to hold back a full explosion of his emotions. "Ah be lookin fer work, but Ah's so scared of white folk; Ah's scared tuh go tuh da town. Now, Ah jes want tuh go back tuh my plantation. It ain't never be dis bad back home."

The black man leaned over and stared at Jacob. "Boy, yuh be white! Yuh must got a itty-bitty drop of culud blood, 'cause yuh as white as snowflakes. Boy . . . in all mah days, Ah ain't never see'd no culud man wit' deep blue eyes lak your'n."

"Yessum ... dey tell me Ah look jes lak my daddy, Massa Walter Dillard," Jacob said, "Now, Ah jes wanna go home."

"Well . . . Jesus is mah Lawd! Yuh sure be a Dillard. Yuh be in da likeness of dat son of his, dat, Jackson Dillard; he be a mean one." The black man gave Jacob a sorry expression. "Lissen here boy, yuh ain't wanna go back dere."

"Why not? Ain't nothin' out here." Jacob responded. He waved his arm around in all directions as if presenting the forest and road to the black man.

The black man climbed down from the wagon and stood before Jacob. "Boy . . . dere be mo' tuh da world out here. Yuh jes be hidin' out in dem woods." The black man slapped his leg and laughed out loud. "Yuh sho-nuff act lak a slave. Ah be a slave and yuh act worse'n me. All yuh need is some white trainin' and yuh kin do right good fer yuhself. Yuh say yuh from da Dillard Plantation? Whatcha be known by? Ah be called, Ol' Blue." He stepped around Jacob, inspecting him from all sides. He reached over, held Jacob's chin in his right hand and turned his head from side to side. "Open yuh eyes wide,' he said, "lemme git a good look at 'em. Wow-we, boy! Yuh really some'em tuh see. Now who yuh say yuh be?"

"Ah be, Jacob Natty, sur. Uh . . . Ah took on my mama's name when Ah be freed."

"Yeah, Ah be hearin' 'bout free slaves changin' dere names." He nodded and smiled. "Now dat be da first sign of a free spirit, a new name, Mr. Natty."

Jacob smiled. "Thank yuh, sur," he replies. He nodded and shifted his stance.

Ol' Blue flinched and then paused before he began speaking again. "Ah jes drove my massa, uh, Massa Haynes tuh Massa Dillard's funeral some weeks back. Yuh say yuh been travelin' ten days and yuh only gits jes forty some-odd miles away. Boy, yuh be wanderin'." Then Blue thought for a few seconds. "Boy, yuh's one of dem Dillard mulatto chillen? Ah see'd a mess a dem on da plantation at da funeral."

"Now, Ah be, Jacob Natty!" Jacob stood tall, straightened his shoulders and spoke with a definite tone to his voice. There was no doubt, freedom gave him a new attitude.

"Boy, now yuh sound lak a white man. Yuh held yuh head up and looked me in mah eyes when yuh spoke. Yuh showed no fear. Dat's 'da ticket,' boy!" Ol' Blue grinned and again slapped his right knee when he spoke. "Ah know a family dat got lots of work fer yuh. Dey take yuh on, culud or white. Yuh tell 'em yuh be jes freed from indentured service and been livin' lak a slave since yuh be eight years old. Dey ain't gon' pay yuh 'til harvest and dat ain't gon' be much of nuttin', but yuh have a place tuh sleep and food tuh eat. And most of all, dey treat yuh real good."

"Thank yuh, sur. We gots indentures on da Dillard, but indentures last seven years." Jacob counted to seven on his fingers.

"Well, yuh gots tuh fib boy, a big fib and yuh gots tuh 'member it. Now, yuh say yuh had tuh pay off six years of yuh pappy's indenture 'cause he be dead, den four years of yuh mammy's 'cause she be dead, too. Say, yuh massa had yuh livin' in da quarters and dat be why yuh act da way yuh do." Blue climbed back up on the wagon and looked down at Jacob. "Now, dis be real import'n, so hear me good," Blue continued, "Ah got lots tuh tell yuh an' a lil' time tuh do it. Don't yuh ev'r let a white man hear yuh say thank yuh tuh a culud man lak yuh just did; just give us a wink, a nod or a sly smile if yuh must, but don't let dem whites see yuh. Let dat be yuh first lesson." Blue was still standing and he stared down at Jacob like he was trying to burn his words into his mind before he continued. "Now, don't yuh be bowin' tuh no whites and callin' 'em massa or sur; jes call 'em mister and dey be callin' yuh mister, too. If'n somethin' be happenin' dat yuh don't lak, jes tell 'em tuh stop doin' it. Stand up fer yuhself. Stand up tall and look 'em in the eyes when yuh talk tuh dem; watch how dey talk tuh each other; study dem; study how dey walk and talk and how dey look at each other. Dey may be loud, but yuh be a quiet man; lissen and learn dey ways. Learn how tuh talk lak dem." Ol' Blue gritted his teeth as he spoke. He wished he had more time to give Jacob 'white training,' and he prayed what he said was enough to hold him until they met again. But Jacob remembered his early years. He knew what Ol' Blue was talking about. He knew how his father, Jackson, Danny Moore, Maynard and the other white hands spoke and related to each other. They didn't shy down, shuffle their feet and bow their heads when speaking to each other. This was slave behavior. White people stood tall and still when they spoke, even when the employees spoke to the master and even the white indentured servants were allowed to address the master on more even terms. Jacob had lived in both worlds and the behaviors and manners learned in his early years would now come in useful if he had to observe, practice and rehearse the pristine ways he had long ago put aside.

Jacob listened and nodded his head with every word Ol' Blue spoke. He remembered being white during his early years until Jackson beat it out of him; he never thought about or wanted to be white again. Suddenly, he was thinking, why not. Survival in this white man's world would be a lot easier.

"Lemme see yuh deep blue eyes again," Ol' Blue continued, "Mah Lawd! Dey ain't gon' never think yuh be a culud. Boy . . . right now yuh look pure white, but yuh got more slave in yuh than any slave Ah be knowin'. Ah wish Ah could hide yuh somewhere 'til Ah teach yuh real good, but yuh do what Ah say. Mah massa let me go tuh da Morton place tuh he'p out, so Ah be seein' yuh real soon."

"Yuh massa let yuh be out here by yuhself. Don't he be lookin' for yuh?" Jacob asked.

"Ah gots me a pass dat says Ah b'long tuh da Haynes Plantation and Ah ain't late yet. But, Ah'm gon' drive yuh tuh da road leadin' tuh da Morton farm. It be early and if'n yuh hurry yuh be dere b'fore sundown. Yuh jes tell 'em Ol' Blue sent yuh. Sam Morton just mortgaged his farm fer seeds and supplies fer plantin' a hundred acres a cotton. Den he went and got mule kicked in da head and now he lay wastin' lak wiltin' cabbage. It ain't likely dat his three boys can plant dat crop deyselves. Miles be only seventeen and da other two boys be even younger. If'n dey don't get da crop in da ground and den tuh harvest, dey gon' lose dey whole farm. Tell yuh da truth, dey be needin' a few mo' hands tuh he'p. My massa be sendin' me ov'r tuh help, but Ah is ol' and slow workin'. Dey be needin' some young he'p lak you.

Jacob was thankful Ol' Blue stopped at the Morton's road. He would have never found it. The Morton's, for reasons of their own, had hidden their property's entrance by securing the low growing branches of the young pine trees across the pass with rawhide. Jacob brushed between the hedges and shrubs until he reached the back side of the pass and follow the clearing through the forest.

Miles Morton had a shotgun pointed at Jacob as he walked from the woods surrounding the Morton farm. It was after the dinner hour, a time when the family was relaxing on the front porch before the evening's insects invaded their tranquility. Rusty's nap was interrupted even before Jacob walked down the road that had cut through the forest. He ran off barking, his ears flapping and his tail pointing causing Miles to pick up his shotgun.

Miles held his aim and watched the tall figure of a man walk further away from the forest. Rusty was now circling him and barking at his feet. Cecilia Morton stood behind Miles holding her twin toddler daughters, one on each hip, while eleven year old Robby and twelve year old Evan stood to her side.

Miles waited. At approximately one hundred yards he fired a single blast toward the sky. "Stop!" he yelled out, "Who are yuh?"

"Ol' Blue, from da Haynes Plantation sent me! Say y'all be needin' he'p!"

"Come a little closer so Ah can see yuh face!" Miles yelled again, keeping the shotgun at a dead aim.

Jacob's legs were so weak he thought he would have to use his hands to push them along. "Lawd, please he'p me. Please tell these ol' legs tuh move," he prayed with each step. He took a deep breath and put one foot in front of the other. "Thank Yuh, Lawd! Thank Yuh, thank Yuh, thank Yuh!" he whispered with every step.

Rusty didn't help Jacob's arrival at the Morton's doorstep; his continued barking and running in circles was distracting. Jacob was trying to concentrate and remember his, 'how to act white lesson' and 'the indentured servitude fib.' *Don't bow, look 'em in the eye*, he kept repeating to himself, *oh and stand tall, call 'em mister and don't allow yuhself tuh be mistreated.*

Jacob would have wet his pants if he hadn't just relieved himself before reaching the clearing in the forest. He knew it was the Lord who sent Ol' Blue and he knew he was a smart man. He was going to use what the good Lord gave him to make the best of his freedom. He walked up to Miles and looked him in his eyes. It was the first time he had ever looked a white man in his eyes since he was a child and it felt real good.

"Pardon my comin' without yuh invite, but please take dat gun outta my face. Ah come tuh he'p y'all if'n Ah can. Ol' Blue sent me."

Miles lowered the gun. "Ah'm sorry, sur. But a man can't be too careful."

"Ah understand. My name be, Jacob Natty. Ah been indentured for ten years over in Gaffney. My mama and papa died before they paid dey indenture, so it fell on me. Now Ah be free. Ol' Blue told me 'bout yuh pappy, said y'all folk be needin' he'p." Jacob spoke fast and without shifting his eyes or turning away. He was nervous and he allowed the story that Ol' Blue concocted for him to spill out and mix with the Morton's need. He remembered the impressions his eyes made on Ol' Blue, so he looked directly at Miles and Mrs. Morton. He could tell, there was no doubt, they believed him to be a white man although he never made that claim. He did realize the indenture story, his white skin and blue eyes were misleading, but he managed to tell it in a convincing way.

"Yeah," Miles said. "It's real hard on Mama. She gotta take care of Lisa and Laura and do even more for Papa. That leaves Robby, Evan and me tuh plant the cotton. Ol' Blue does come when he can." He tilted his head and kicked the red clay dirt before looking up sideways at Jacob. "Now . . . we did 'bout twenty acres wit' Ol' Blue's he'p, but we got eighty more tuh go and then thirty acres of soybeans. Then we still have tuh take care of them chickens, two cows, a mule, four goats, six hogs and Red, our horse. Lissen Mr. Natty, we sure do need the help, but we can't pay yuh nothing 'til harvest. And then yuh pay gone depend on the goodness of the good Lawd and His plans for us. But we can let yuh stay in the barn and give yuh some of whatever food we eat."

"That'll be fine," Jacob said. He nodded his head with understanding, "but Ah gots just one problem . . . after ten years of indenture, Ah be needin' decent clothes. What Ah got be good for the fields, but Ah be needin' decent shirts, britches, johns, sox and a pair of shoes."

"Yuh look tuh be the size of my husband," Mrs. Morton said, "Ah think he can spare some clothes and yuh should be able tuh wear a pair of his boots, too."

"Are yuh sure, Mrs. Morton, Ah ain't meanin' tuh be causin' no trouble."

"Oh, Mr. Natty, it's no trouble. My George will not be needin' 'em right now." She smiled and waved her hand, while she continued speaking. "He has other clothes. He'll be happy knowing yuh here helpin' his family."

"Thank yuh, ma'am." Jacob said. He loved being called mister and would continue to allow it. "Mr. Morton, it be yuh call when we get started in the fields."

"How's daybreak?" Miles responded as he extended his hand for the manly handshake.

Mrs. Morton, being thankful and hospitable asked, "Mr. Natty, have yuh had a decent meal tuhday?" She had set the girls down and they were now running around on the porch.

"No, ma'am," Jacob responded and he couldn't hold back the smile pushing to form on his lips. He could almost hear his stomach speaking for him.

"Well, yuh just c'mon in the kitchen while Ah fix yuh up some decent food."

"Thank yuh, ma'am, but if'n it be all the same tuh yuh, Ah'd rather eat out here on the porch." Jacob wasn't ready to eat in the kitchen of a white family; he wouldn't eat in their kitchen no more than he would sleep in their house.

Mrs. Morton gave Jacob a gentle smile. "All right, Mr. Natty, if that's what yuh want tuh do." She turned and entered the house and the twins followed.

"Mr. Natty," Miles said. He pushed the brim of his hat back on his head, held his other hand out in a giving manner and presented a pleasant smiled. "We're gonna be workin' tuhgether and Ah b'lieve we're 'bout near the same age. Can Ah call yuh, Jacob? You can call me, Miles."

Jacob's knapsack rested on the ground and he continued holding the drawstring as if it had some magical connection to the people he had left behind. He smiled and nodded his head to acknowledge Miles's request, but he hoped Miles could understand what he was about to say, "What yuh be sayin' got meanin', but Ah be indentured most of my life and Ah nevah had no-body call me Mr. Natty. So hearin' everybody call me, mister is lak music tuh my ears, because it makes me feel lak Ah ain't no servant no mo . . . lak Ah ain't no boy no mo. Ah is a man. In time that servant feelin' be outta my blood, then it be time, but not yet. Ah be needin' yuh tuh call me, mister for a while."

"Mr. Natty, Ah can't imagine how being a servant musta made yuh feel," Miles responded. He rubbed his hand over his peach-fuzz beard and shook his head.

"Try bein' a servant and growin' up livin' in da slave quarters. But, Ah gotta say dey be da kindest people Ah ever wanna know," Jacob confessed. Then he thanked the Lord and Mrs. Morton for the food she placed of the table. He tried to eat slowly so he wouldn't give an indication of how famished he was; when he looked up Miles and Mrs. Morton were staring at him.

"How could that man put you in with all those darkies?" Mrs. Morton complained while busying herself with the twins again.

"No offense, ma'am. But those people took me in when my people died. Ah be jes eight and Ah woulda died, too. Ah ain't got nut'in' bad tuh say 'bout dem. Ah be just a servant tuh dat massa, jes like dey slaves. Mammy Pearl, she be like mah mama. She be all Ah had. Ah love hur like Miles loves you and Ah'm gone git back tuh hur one day."

"Ah'm sorry for speakin' what Ah don't know 'bout." Mrs. Morton crossed her hands over her heart as she spoke.

Jacob continued eating and smiled up at Mrs. Morton. "Dis here food is real tasty ma'am and Ah cain't thank yuh 'nough fer da work."

"Oh, Mr. Natty, we all need each other. Miles will show yuh where yuh can sleep and Ah'll have yuh clothes tuhmorrow." Mrs. Morton bowed her head and turned to leave the porch and then she stopped. "Mr. Natty . . . thank yuh for comin'. Ah really do believe the good Lawd sent yuh."

Jacob stood, smiled and nodded in her direction. "Ah do believe he did, ma'am. Thank yuh again, ma'am."

Chapter 5

The crops were in the ground and the Morton boys had worked as hard as any slave. Now it was time to get back to their lessons after completing their other farm chores. There wasn't a school house within ten miles of their spread, so it was left to Mrs. Morton to be the teacher as well as her other many talents.

The boys took their places on the front porch with their books, slates and chalk in hand. Miles was already curled up in a barrel chair, engrossed in the adventure of 'David Copperfield.' On the table lay his next book, Melville's exciting, 'Moby Dick.' Evan and Robby shared the same book, taking turns reading and when one missed a word the other made the correction. The two year old twins just played while Mrs. Morton prepared the boy's math lessons.

Jacob stood propped against the wall while the hunger for learning burned in his heart and etched lines on his face. It had been more than ten years since he spent those memorable days taking secret reading lessons from his father. Mrs. Morton was an insightful woman. She didn't have to ask why he was still standing around. The chores had been completed for the day, dinner was over and Jacob certainly had personal chores of his own to complete.

"Have yuh ever been tuh school, Mr. Natty?" Mrs. Morton asked while she continued to write on her large slate. She never turned to look at him for fear of feeling a quiver of his insecurities.

Jacob pushed his hands deep into his pants pocket and allowed his head to hang low. "No, ma'am, not school, but my papa be teachin' me tuh read some. Ah have two books," he answered softly, "Ah read them over and over so Ah don't forgit my teachin'."

"Do yuh still have yuh books?" Mrs. Morton asked.

Jacob nodded. "Yes, ma'am," he replied.

Mrs. Morton smiled. "Well then, it would be my pleasure if Ah may continue teachin' yuh?" She stopped writing on her slate and turned to face him.

The boys sat at attention. "She really is a good teacher, Mr. Natty," Miles announced.

"Ah'd really like that, ma'am," Jacob answered. He gave her a smile and his blue eyes widened. "Thank yuh, ma'am."

"So where should we start?" she asked.

"Ah can read. Ah read my two books over and over again for years. Now, Ah would like tuh read some different books." He removed his hat and looked sheepishly at Mrs. Morton. "Ah ain't much good at writin' and readin' that curly writin'. And Ah sure would like tuh be figurin' wit' numbers; Ah be real bad at knowin' 'bout money."

"Oh my! Yes, Mr. Natty. We will take care of the writing and arithmetic," Mrs. Morton exclaimed. "But what are the names of yuh two books?"

"Uh . . . 'Last of da Mohicans' and 'Oliver Twist,' ma'am," Jacob responded shamefully. "Ah got 'em in mah bag. Ah be sorry, ma'am, they be old and wore out from me readin' 'em so much."

"Sorry!" She said as she pushed a wisp of hair from her face. "Wearing out books from reading them is remarkable and to be commended. It is nothing tuh be sorry about. Ah will do my best tuh get yuh new books tuh read and we will begin tuh study the numbers and improve your handwriting."

Jacob smiled and rolled the brim of his hat in his hand. "Ah thank yuh kindly, Mrs. Morton," he said and he bowed his head gently. He backed up against the side of the house and continued to roll his hat's brim.

Mr. Morton glanced over at him. "Jacob," she began, "Is there something else you would like tuh say?"

He turned from her attention when he noticed Miles and the younger boys staring at him. A coy smile spread his lips. "Well, yes ma'am," he said, now returning his attention to her. "Uh . . . unless yuh ain't gon' be needin' me, Ah ain't got no plans tuh be leavin'. Ma'am . . . Ah'm a man and Ah just can't be sleepin' wit' animals. Ah wanna build me a cabin down near da woods. Ah be workin' durin' my free time if'n yuh say it can be so."

Mrs. Morton clutched her chest, closed her eyes and inhaled deeply. "Oh my goodness, Mr. Natty. Please forgive me. Yes! Yes! Build your cabin." She turned to her boys. What do yuh say boys?"

"Ah'll help yuh," Miles called out, "we'll have that cabin built before harvest."

"Me too!" Robby said and Evan nodded his head.

Jacob smiled.

◈◈◈

The building of the cabin began and the schooling continued, but they came in last to the needs of the farm. The formal classes were placed on hold, but Jacob continued to read by the light of the oil lamps at night. He and the Morton boys had to work the cotton for several weeks longer each day as the daylight grew. They just couldn't allow the weeds to steal the nutrients from the young plants, nor could they have too many plants in a bed environment. The weakest cotton plants had to be discarded along with the weeds so the stronger ones could flourish. By the time they had worked a hundred acres it was time to work it again until the cotton was taller and stronger than the weeds and could thrive on their own. Finally, they could get back to their afternoon cabin building and later, after supper it was time for schooling.

It rained that Monday morning; it rained so hard that most of the chores on the farms were put off except that Jacob milked the two cows and Miles slopped the hogs and pulled dry hay down for the mule and horse. Evan and Robby collected the eggs, fed the chickens and checked the rabbit traps.

Mr. Morton didn't wake up that Thursday morning in June. At 8:00 A.M. Cecilia Morton went in to feed him his breakfast, but he was unresponsive. There were no vapors on the mirror that she held under his nose. His chest didn't rise and fall, the rhythmic beat of his heart or the pulse in his wrist was absent, but his color remained pink like he was still among the living. The doctor was twenty two miles away, a half day's round trip ride for Miles and then there was the ride back without the assurance the doctor would return with him. Mrs. Morton figured she would wait, because one of two things would happen; her husband was in a very deep sleep or rigor would set in and she would know for sure he had gone on to glory. Either way, the doctor had already told her that her husband was beyond his help. Mrs. Morton's greatest fear was that she would bury her husband alive; that was why the signs of rigor were so very important. She sat by his bed reading her Bible and praying while the boys tended to the twins.

"Dear Lawd, these have been difficult times wit' Sam being hurt like this. Lawd, he's a believer in Jesus Christ our Savior, even if he didn't say it out loud. Ah know it tuh be so. He was baptized as a boy and he was a church going man. Please Lawd, Ah know he was a believer. Please Lawd, please take his soul tuh glory. He was a good man. Jesus says in John 3:16, "For God so loved the world that He gave His only begotten son, that whoever believes in Him shall not perish, but have eternal life." If this is Sam's time, then Ah know Your will is being done. My Sam is so hurt . . . he's like a vegetable, Lawd. Ah don't know how much pain Sam is in and he can't say where it's hurtin'. Lawd, that's the worst kind of pain there is. Lawd, Sam knows Jesus is his Savior. Ah love him so much. Lawd, if it is Your will, please work Your miracle on him. Ah ask this prayer in the name of Your Son and our Savior, Jesus Christ. Amen."

❧❦

It was 10:00 A.M. and Mrs. Morton was sure the Lord's Will had been done. Her husband's body had cooled considerably and his lips had a blue tinge to them. She called for Miles and Jacob.

"Ah believe yuh papa is gone." She grabbed Miles' hands and squeezed them gently.

"Oh Mama," was all he said before turning toward his father. His eyes welled with tears and he quickly wiped them away.

"Is there anything Ah can do, Mrs. Morton?" Jacob asked. He stood with his hands dangling at his side waiting to be put to use.

"Could yuh heat up a bucket of water? Ah want tuh bathe and dress him before his body turns stiff and Ah don't know how much time we have," she whispered. "Don't tell the others yet. Ah'll tell 'em after he's dressed."

She glanced at Miles and decided to give him a little time with his father while she hurried off for Sam's new bib coveralls, blue and white striped shirt and navy bowtie. She gathered wash rags, towels, lye soap, his straight edge razor and hair brush. Then Jacob returned with a bucket of warm water and two tin basins and they were ready to prepare Mr. Morton.

"Miles, we have tuh get started. His body could go into rigor in the next hour."

"Don't say that, Mama!" Miles cried out.

"She be right, Mr. Morton," Jacob spoke up as he leaned closer to Miles. "We don't quite know how long he be gone and he won't loosen up for hours. We gotta be hurryin'. Ah be sorry Mr. Morton, but Ah see'd it happen at The Dillard."

"Miles, we have tuh make him look his best before the stiffness come. Ah know it's hard. Ah've talked tuh the Lawd and he knows best. Yuh papa is at peace now. We'll be seein' him in the hereafter." Mrs. Morton held Miles' hands and spoke softly.

"Why don't y'all folk go on wit' the chillen and let me take care of Mr. Morton. Ah done dis befor'," Jacob announced. "Yuh got a bedspread yuh want me tuh lay 'em out on?"

Surprised, Mrs. Morton glanced around at Jacob, "Yuh gonna do that for us, Mr. Natty?"

"Yes ma'am. Ah'll call yuh when Ah be done. It be my pleasure." Jacob forgot himself and took a gentle slave like bow.

"Lemme help yuh, Mr. Natty. This is my papa."

"Yes, Mr. Morton, but dis be yuh time tuh mourn. Dis be da duty for someone else," Jacob spoke as he escorted them to the door. "Ah be callin' yuh when he be ready.

കൈ

Forty five minutes later Mr. Samuel Morton had been bathed, shaven, hair brushed, dressed and positioned on the homemade quilt his mother had made for him when he was a youngster. Jacob cleaned up the room and bundled up the soiled clothing and linen. He opened the bedroom door and Mrs. Morton and the boys turned in his direction. One by one they stood and slowly walked in. Samuel Morton's arms were crossed over his chest and Jacob had waited for the right moment to set a gentle smile on his face. Mrs. Morton no longer had to worry; her Sam lay in his peaceful position, his complexion and skin tone now free of the fleshy hue of the living. Very soon she knew his muscles would have the feel of the beginning stages of rigor mortis; her final confirmation that she would indeed be burying her husband who had departed this life.

"Mr. Natty, thank you. He looks like he is only sleeping." Cecilia Morton cried as she leaned over and kissed her husband's forehead. She had left the sleeping twins in their crib; there would be time for them to say goodbye to their father and as time passed she knew they would never remember the moment.

The boys stood around the bed sobbing while Jacob quietly backed out of the room. He had one more thing to do. Slavery taught him no job was impossible; Samuel Morton was in need of a proper coffin. The need was definite and he had found a solution, but it required a great deal of work. The stables in the barn were made with flat boards of lumber. Jacob went to work cutting young trees and making post that he used to replace the stable boards.

"Old blue eyes . . . Ah see yuh been workin' hard," Ol' Blue sang out as he stomped into the barn. His large frame cast a mighty shadow over Jacob who was shaving the rough edges off the newly constructed coffin.

Jacob turned with a jerk and looked up. "Blue . . . how'd yuh get here?" he said.

"Miles bought da news tuh da plantation," Ol' Blue began, "Ah be tuh town taken da notice tuh da train depot in Morton's Depot. We ain't got no telly-graph up here yet. Next line be down in Columbia. Den Massa say come here and he'p wit' Massa Morton, but yuh don' did most of da work. Mr. Morton, he be needin' tuh be moved tuh da ice house on da plantation. Massa got a coolin' board. Misses say she spec da settin'-up and funeral be Sat'day. Misses say Ah's tuh tell yuh dat."

"Dat be good news. There still be so much tuh do. Ah gots tuh finish da coffin and stain it, then dig da grave, but dey ain't got no graveyard," Jacob said. He had stopped working, wiped the sweat from his brow and stood looking at Blue.

Ol' Blue squatted down next to Jacob and patted his shoulder. "Well, we's gon' do it tuhgether now. Ah's here tuh he'p, Jacob."

"Ah gots tuh speak tuh da Mortons about a burial place." Jacob stood and walked to the door of the barn and stared out across the western field where the sun was just setting. "Ah'll be back." He headed out toward the house.

Miles, Evan and Robby were sitting quietly on the front porch when he approached. "Mr. Morton," Jacob said. "Can Ah ask yuh somethin'?"

"Anythin'," Miles responded. A day without his father and a day without work to drive his misery away seemed to compound his mourning.

"Where would yuh want me and Ol' Blue tuh build da family burial ground?"

"Ah don't care," Miles whispered. He closed his eyes and rested his head against the side of the house.

Jacob nodded, turned and stared out toward the forest. He toyed with the brim of his hat and wondered if he should pose the question to Mrs. Morton.

"Ah know Ol' Blue is down there wit' yuh and y'all haven't had yuh supper," Mrs. Morton said as she stood behind the screen door. "Ah put some stew in a pot for y'all. Ah was gone have Robby tote it down tuh yuh."

Jacob turned, "Yes ma'am." Ol' Blue, be gittin' on soon. Say he be back in da mornin'. Ah 'pose he can eat befo' he leaves."

"Ah'll be right back wit' yuh supper."

Minutes later Mrs. Morton returned and handed Jacob the covered tin pot of stew and a sack with tin plates and spoons. Jacob thanked her, but before leaving the porch he asked about the burial place. She smiled, but while Jacob waited for a response, he only watched her smile fade. She sighed and for a minute Jacob believed he was reminding her that her husband died that morning.

"Ah don-know, Jacob," she whined, "Ah don-know!" She lifted her apron and caught her tears, turned and hurried in the house as though she were hiding her sorrow from her sons.

"Yes ma'am," Jacob whispered. Carrying the food, he returned to the barn.

ॐॐ

Blue returned to the Morton's farm Friday morning about an hour after sunrise. He was on foot and appeared from the forest that separated the Morton's spread from his master's plantation. He said it was a shorter route than the road since the wagons and mules were all needed for the fields so walking was his only option. There was still a lot of work to do before Samuel Morton's funeral. He and Jacob had to complete the coffin, build the cemetery, carve a head marker and dig the grave.

While Ol' Blue stained the coffin, Jacob worked on a temporary wooden cross that would be used as a grave marker. Later he would search for a large flat rock that could tolerate the chisel while carving a permanent marker, one that wouldn't crack against the deep grooved and that could withstand time. He had seen markers at The Dillard that were smooth and only told that remains of a person rested in that place, but age and weathering had returned the stone to nature. He knew he had time to carve the stone and it would be set in place once it was completed to his satisfaction. After the burial, they would place the temporary wooden cross marker on the grave.

A moderately aged oak tree stood tall and strong, about sixty feet west of the far end of the garden. The tree would be the major cornerstone and provide shade over them as they dug Mr. Morton's grave. Ol' Blue thought it was an ideal place to layout The Morton's Family Cemetery. They stacked large rocks at a distance of fifty paces, squaring off the three remaining corners, each stack to be painted white at a later time.

The sun had already peeked over the horizon while the men dug the grave. When they looked up Evan was standing over them. "Is that for my papa, Mr. Natty?" he asked.

"Yessum, Evan," Jacob answered. He placed his shovel on the ground, crawled out of the grave and reached down to help Ol' Blue climb out. Brushing his hands on his pants, he gave Evan a gentle smile. "We wanted yuh Papa tuh have a nice restin' place close tuh his family."

Evan wiped the tears from his cheeks with the back of his hands and took a deep quivering breath. "Yes sir," he whined. He sniffled, then took a deep breath. "Mama said come git some breakfast."

"Thank yuh, Evan," Jacob said.

Old Blue worked the kinks out of his back and watched Evan run off toward the house. Jacob stood tall and stared off in the distance. At that moment he felt like he was back at The Dillard on the morning he dug Master Dillard's grave. He thought of Sula; *she is the only person who could've convinced me not tuh leave. She thinks she'll never see me again. Ah really want tuh see hur. Ah need tuh be with hur. Ah miss hur and Ah don't know where home is.*

"Jacob! Jacob!" Ol' Blue called out. "What gotcha thinkin' hard lak dat? C'mon, let's git some grub, we kin finish da plot aftah we eat." He grabbed Jacob's elbow and nudged him to move along.

"Yeah Blue," he whispered. "Say do yuh think yuh massa will give yuh time off tuh drive me tuh da Dillard. Ah got a gal back dere Ah be missin' a powerful lot."

"She be a slave?"

"Yessum and Ah be missin' hur. Ah want hur tuh know Ah be safe."

"Boy, don't be doin' dat!" Ol' Blue sang out.

"What?"

"Yuh called me, 'sur.' And 'nother thing . . . yuh said, 'yessum' tuh dat boy. Yuh be a man, a white man. Don't yuh be sayin', 'yessum' tuh no white boy . . . yuh hear me?"

Jacob's eyes brightened as if a new lesson had been learned. He strutted along several paces in front of Ol' Blue and his head nodded ever so slightly. Ol' Blue smiled and they walked toward the farm house.

Then Jacob stopped. He turned and spoke up, "Well, Ah got yuh meaning. Now don't yuh call me, 'boy'."

"Ah recon we both got tuh be careful," Ol' Blue surrendered. He hung his head low and allowed his arm to hang in a sluggish droop as he walked, while Jacob held his head up and tucked his thumbs in his belt. They took to their pace and position again and Ol' Blue smiled. "We's got tuh work out a plan tuh git yuh home for dat visit," Blue whispered.

"Thank yuh, Blue."

◈

Cecilia Morton planned the settin-up (wake) to begin at 12:00 P.M. The preacher arrived for the graveside funeral at 4:00 P.M. with the 'repast' to follow immediately. June days were long and the darkness of night wouldn't arrive until 9:00 P.M.

It didn't matter to Jacob or Old Blue what arrangement Cecilia Morton made, however this was a summer death. That meant Samuel Morton's remains should to be in the ground before sundown. He had expired three days earlier; the cooling board helped to preserve him, but he was not in a frozen state, it was time for him to be buried.

◈

Old Blue and Jacob stood outside the confines of the cemetery, back and away from the oak tree during the service. When the time came for the actual burial two men and other friends of the family stepped forward to help and using heavy twine rope they lowered the coffin into the grave. Ol' Blue kept his head bowed so low he actually bent his back, while Jacob only gave a gentle bow to Mrs. Morton and the boys as they walked back to the house. Blue and Jacob waited until all the mourners were out of sight before they filled in the grave and set the wooden cross in place.

chapter 6

There was no time for mourning; the Mortons said their goodbyes to family and friends. The crops and farm needed tending, the cabin construction needed to continue and their schooling was most important to everyone. Mrs. Morton insisted that in addition to Jacob's arithmetic and penmanship lessons, he needed to improve his speech. She drilled him constantly in an attempt to remove the vernacular of the slave's colloquial dialect. Jacob practiced when in her presence and allowed himself the time for mental rudimentary practice while working or among other white men, but when relaxed he reverted to his more comfortable slave jargon.

Pressing issues plagued Jacob, but his purpose had several justifications. A hundred acres of cotton and only five pickers, including Mrs. Morton seemed an arduous task. It was just July, not yet the time for cotton picking, but Jacob was thinking ahead. As he worked at chiseling Samuel Morton's headstone, he thought of his brothers, Capers and Juke. Hopefully, he could convince them to leave the plantation and perhaps they would enjoy their taste of freedom. This would also be just the excuse he needed to visit with his beloved Sula.

Another month passed, the headstone was completed and set in place, the cotton was higher, August was hotter than July and Jacob never stopped thinking of how to get back to his Sula and The Dillard. He and Miles were sitting on the front porch having breakfast when Jacob pushed his plate aside and walked out to the side of the house. He placed his hands on his hips, dropped his head and kicked at the dry red soil. Miles was soon to follow especially when he suspected Jacob was doing some heavy thinking. He admired him; he was the older brother he always wanted. Whenever Jacob appeared troubled, Miles felt a need to be near him.

Jacob looked at Miles, "Yuh know Mr. Morton," he began, "Yuh got a hundred acres of cotton out there dat we need tuh be pickin' soon. Yuh mama don't need tuh be workin' dem fields and tryin' tuh care for da twins, da house and da cookin'. So dat leaves you, me, an' da boys. And we's got other chores, too. We's got tuh make several passes to git all dat cotton in and we need some cheap farm hands tuh he'p."

"What can we do?" Miles asked. "He stared out over the cotton field like he had never seen it before.

"Well, Ah know where there be two freed slaves. When my indenture was over Ah tried tuh git them tuh leave da plantation wit' me, but they be scared. Now dat Ah be safe, Ah can go back tuh fetch 'em and maybe they will come. Ah don't spec my old massa gone be tuh happy tuh give up his free labor, but they got freedom papers and can leave if they want tuh. But they might have tuh steal away so dere won't be no trouble. The only problem be, Ah don't know how tuh git back tuh The Dillard, but Ol' Blue, he knows da way."

"Why does Ol' Blue know?"

"Cause he don' drove his massa there. Massa Haynes be friends with Massa Dillard befo' he died. Ol' Blue even took his massa tuh Massa Dillard's funeral," Jacob explained. He picked up a dry clump of rock-dirt and crushed it back to dirt-dust. "If Ah could git Ol' Blue tuh take me tuh The Dillard, Ah might be able tuh git dem two freed slave tuh come wit' me and help us work dis place. Ah know they got freedom papers, they just ain't have no place tuh go. They 'bout our age, they hard workin' and we won't have tuh kill ourselves workin' them fields alone. We could start workin dat field soon as dem bolls pop open."

"Mama can talk tuh Mr. Haynes. She can ask for Ol' Blue tuh take yuh tuh get the boys. Ah'll drive hur over there tuhday."

Jacob nodded his head. He didn't smile or appear overjoyed. He didn't want Miles to know it meant that much to him. "Well, if'n it works out it gonna be good for all of us." Was all he said and he patted Miles on the back before walking off toward the barn.

❧

Excitement swept over Jacob like a cloak and filled his body with the kind of energy he had not felt since the day he received his freedom papers. All the while his thoughts were with Sula. He had to get back to her if just for a day. His body ached to be near her and to feel her soft body next to his. Each day the urge became more powerful, but he was still lost and needed Ol' Blue; The Dillard Plantation was as far away from him as a dream. He not only longed for Sula, but he longed for home, not for the life of a slave, but for family. He missed Mammy Pearl. Every slave around him was his family; they were like him and he had nothing to hide. So what, his skin was white, his eyes sky blue and his hair a golden blonde; no one ever made the distinction, it didn't matter. As for Jacob, he believed he was as much a Negro as his chocolate, Sula, with her dark brown eyes and spongy, kinky black hair. He loved her with all his heart; he loved her more than his freedom and once he found his way back to her, he knew he would steal back to the plantation as often as he could.

෨෧

Two days later, just about daybreak on Saturday morning, Ol' Blue road up on the Morton farm in the buck wagon pulled by two young mules. Mrs. Morton had been assured he would be able to drive Jacob, but Mr. Haynes couldn't tell her when he would be available.

Jacob came running out of the barn pulling straw out of his hair and adjusting his coveralls. "Just give me a few minutes tuh git cleaned up and Ah'll be ready," he called out. He was so excited his feet were almost dancing.

Miles stepped out on the front porch, waved and yelled out, "Hey, Ol' Blue!"

"Hey, Massa Miles," Ol' Blue called back just as he climbed down from the wagon. "Well Jacob, yuh got me 'til tuhmorrow night."

"Let me fix yuh some food tuh take on the road," Mrs. Morton called out from the front door. "It's a long ride and y'all gon' get real hungry. Oh . . . Mr. Natty, if yuh bring me that knapsack yuh got, Ah'll put the food in it so y'all won't get hungry when yuh travel back tuhmorrow."

"Ah thank yuh kindly, Mrs. Morton." Jacob hurried back into the barn for the bag and his two quilts.

෨෧

It was early afternoon when Blue pointed in the direction down a dark tree shaded road that was surrounded by a thick forest as far as they could see. "Dat be da road tuh da town of Gaffney," he said. "It starts out dark, but it opens up tuh farmland a ways down."

Jacob pointed up at the roadside sign, "Gaffney," he read. "Seem like they write too many 'fs'. Ah only read one 'f'."

"How yuh readin'?"

"Ah always could read. My pa learned me, but Ah had tuh hide it."

Ol' Blue smiled, nodded his head with so much pride one would think he could read and for a few moments his thoughts seem to take him someplace else. Jacob looked over at him and understood his emotions. He knew what he was thinking, he knew Blue was in a place of pride.

Breaking his silence, Blue smiled. "Yuh home be comin' up shortly," he said, "it be right down da next turnoff."

"We be dat close?"

"Yessum, we's only got a short ride now," Blue announced.

Jacob noted the road to Gaffney on his map, then turned to Blue, "Yuh know . . . Ah been drawing dis map of how yuh gettin' me dis far and Ah b'lieve Ah can get back faster than dese here slow trottin' mules."

Blue had been watching him draw lines and making his letters and marks on his crude map and he figured that was what he was doing.

"We need tuh stop here," Jacob announced. "Ah'm gone bury da knapsack down in da woods 'cause Ah ain't got no need tuh tote it; it'll be here when we come back this way; Ah'm gone leave da shovel, too." Jacob could see confusion on Ol' Blue's face as he spoke. He reached for Tillie's homemade knapsack that Mrs. Morton had packed with baked bread, can preserved vegetables and peaches and beef jerky. He even squeezed in a couple of small quilts that he might need.

"Ah'm gone explain, Blue. But right now Ah just want tuh bury da bag 'fore someone comes up on da road. Ah's got tuh bury it deep so da critters don't get tuh it."

Blue waited quietly in the wagon for about a half an hour, until Jacob returned from the forest.

"Thank yuh, Blue," Jacob said. He climbed onto the wagon. "Ah'm ready."

Blue slapped the mule's ass with the reins and spat on the ground. "Gitty-up," he yelled out. "What yuh up tuh, Jacob?" Blue's voice was suspicious and fearful. Jacob was the most exciting and unusual man he had ever met.

"Ah want yuh tuh go home when we git tuh the turn off. Ah'm gone steal on da plantation after dark," Jacob's voice was serious, but Blue knew his plan was well thought out. "Lissen Blue, if Jackson Dillard sees me, he'll know why Ah be here. He might hurt Sula and he might just shoot me if he thinks Ah be tryin' tuh talk Capers and Juke intuh leavin'. Ah don't want tuh pull yuh intuh dis mess. Ah just want tuh thank yuh for showin' me da way home."

"Ah see yuh point. If'n Ah hurry Ah kin be at da Haynes place b'fore nightfall. Good luck Jacob. Look me up when yuh git back," he said and he gave Jacob a wink and a nod.

"Sho-nuff." Jacob smiled and hurried down the road.

Blue remained at the turnoff until Jacob was out of sight. He breathed a sigh of disappointment and slapped the reins against the mule's asses. He didn't like it one bit, he knew what he had to do and when he pulled one rein to the right, both mules began their u-turn and headed back in the direction they had come.

❧❦

Jacob still had two miles to go before he would reach the plantation. Nothing was familiar; he had only passed that way one time before, when leaving. Suddenly he heard the hooves of a horse coming up fast behind him and at the same time he could see the lights of the big white plantation mansion in the distance. He leaped in the bushes, scrambling to hide behind a large fallen log and he watched as Jackson Dillard raced by. Only then did he raise his head, but he waited until Jackson was out of sight before climbing up on the road again.

By the edge of darkness, he reached the slave's path and hurried to the cabin Sula shared with Miss Ollie and Miss Tillie. Miss Ollie opened the door and quickly covered her mouth with the palm of her hand to stifle her joy. "Tillie, Sula . . . it be Jacob!" The joy of seeing him squeaked from Ollie's mouth and her arms waved in a hurried manner for them to come to the door.

"May Ah come in, Miss Ollie? Ah don't want nobody tuh know Ah'm here." Jacob was pushing pass her, hugging her as he spoke. "Ah need tuh see Sula, Capers and Juke."

"Yuh don't need tuh see me, Jacob?" Tillie asked as she pushed passed Sula and Ollie.

"Oh, Miss Tillie, Ah always need tuh see you." He picked her up, holding her in a hug and spun her around. "Yuh knapsack kept me goin' for ten days 'til Ah found my way."

"Where yuh be now, Jacob?" Tillie questioned. Her hands had locked on to his and her heart told her to hold on for a while even as she felt his gentle tug to escape.

"Just a day's walk from here," he smiled as he responded, "Ah be workin' on a farm." Jacob didn't want to be too specific in case Jackson or Moore tried to find him.

His eyes fixed on Sula, but Miss Tillie was still holding him tight. "Ah be thinkin' 'bout yuh all da time, Sula." It was as though the cabin was empty except for the two of them. He had managed to free his hand from Miss Tillie because he only saw Sula. "You be what keeps me goin'. We only got tuhnight. Ah gots tuh leave early tuhmorrow mornin', but Ah'll be back real soon."

Tillie dropped her hold and stood next to Ollie. "Yuh thought he be talking tuh yuh, didn't' yuh?" Ollie said. Both women laughed.

Then Jacob blushed, remembering Miss Ollie and Miss Tillie were staring at him. "Please don't tell anyone Ah be here. Ah'll explain later. Would yuh please fetch Capers and Juke and Mammy Pearl? Please y'all, tell 'em tuh be real quiet."

They nodded and hurried out the door.

Finally, Jacob and Sula were alone, but they knew the ladies would return very soon and that only left time for them to embrace and kiss each other passionately.

"Ah was so worried 'bout yuh. Ah didn't know if'n yuh be alive or dead," Sula whined.

"Ah knew you'd be worried and that be why Ah had tuh get back, but Ah can't stay long this time. Ah ain't far from here, but it be ten days of wanderin' tuh find this place dat be only a day's walk away."

"Yuh be only a day from here?" Sula whispered excitedly.

Jacob nodded, but he could see how this was upsetting her. He knew she was wondering what took him so long to come back. "Oh Sula, don't think

Ah didn't want tuh come back tuh yuh." He pulled her close to him and held her head to his chest. "Don't cry. Ah wanted tuh come back. Ah thought about yuh every day." He held her head back, kissed her forehead and then he looked in her eyes. "Ah was lost and didn't know how tuh find my way back. I just found my way tuhday and Ah drawed me a map." He reached in his pocket and retrieved the heavy bond paper and quickly unfolded it to show her his charcoal letters and drawings that connected the Morton farm to The Dillard Plantation.

"See, Ah gotta follow dis map tuh get back, but soon Ah won't need a map. But it be da fear of da road, too"

"Yuh gon' leave me again, so soon?" Sula cried.

"Ah have tuh, but Ah'm gon' buy yuh freedom and we's gon' be tuhgether forever."

"Suppose Massa Dillard won't sell me tuh yuh? He be real mad when yuh leave. He be evil. He be lettin' the overseers beat people and have dey way with the young gals. Dat Moore, he beat Sally real bad and put hur in da hot box fo' three days 'cause she bite his private. Massa Jackson let dem do what dey want tuh do." Fear of The Dillard brought tears to her eyes. Jacob could feel her trembling as she spoke. "Dey took Benji' and tie his hands and legs. Dey hung him to a tree and make him stand on tiptoe, hangin' over da ant hill wit' his feet touching it. Dem ants crawled all over Benji 'til we cain't see him no mo' . . . we only see dem ants coverin' him. Dem white folk be laughin' and Benji be screamin' and squirmin'. He be dead two days later. Jackson set up dere on his porch and watched everythin'. He be laughin', too."

Jacob held Sula tight and rubbed her back and arms. "Don't worry, Ah be gettin' yuh away from here if'n Ah have tuh kill Jackson." He wiped away her tears with his fingertips.

"No, Jacob! Den dey just gon' kill you." She stared up into Jacob's eyes praying if he didn't hear her words he would see how she feared for him.

"Don't worry. Ah ain't gon' do nothin' stupid. Ah gots my ways." Jacob held Sula with a gentle touch and her trembling subsided. *Dear Lawd, he'p me keep my promise*, he thought. He felt his heart skip and he inhaled sharply. *Please Lawd.*

Mammy Pearl entered the cabin calling out Jacob's name. Jacob and Sula dropped their embraced and stood beside each other.

"Shush, Mammy Pearl. Ah don't want nobody tuh know Ah be here. But can Ah get a hug from my mama?"

"Yuh sure can darlin'!"

Before Jacob knew it, he was pulled from Sula and smothered in Mammy Pearl's soft fleshy arms. "Is yuh back tuh stay?"

"No ma'am. Ah come to visit tis all and tuh show Capers and Juke a way outta here. Ah be leavin 'fore sun up." Jacob was now holding her hands and he leaned over and kissed her cheek.

Just then Ollie and Tillie came through the door with Juke and Capers.

"You boys had 'nough of slavery yet?" Jacob sang out quietly just as the three of them embraced. "See, Ah be still alive. Now it be yuh time tuh come wit' me."

Capers and Juke stood staring at each other. "Now? . . . Now, Jacob? Ah ain't say nothin' about leavin' dis here pl-place," Capers stammered.

"Me neither," Juke added. His eyes opened wide, giving Jacob a frightful stare.

"Lissen, y'all is free men. Ah only want tuh take yuh tuh a farm that be a day's walk." Jacob swiped his hand over his face before taking a deep frustrating breath. "Now, they be decent white folk and they gon' pay yuh after da harvest. If yuh don't like it, yuh can come back here. Ah'm sure Massa Jackson like havin' yuh wit' yuh free labor."

"When y'all gotta go?" Sula asked again and she held on to Jacob's arm.

"Before daylight. Ah wanna be far away from here before Massa or Moore know y'all be gone." Jacob stared at his brothers as he spoke. "Ah want y'all tuh get yuh freedom papers and stuff and meet me at da end of da slave path befo' daylight." He placed both hands on his hips and paced the floor of the small cabin. He didn't look at his brothers this time because he wanted them to believe he was sure they would leave. He continued pacing as he spoke. "It be Sunday and Ah know they be sleepin' late, so it be a while 'fore they miss yuh. Ah ain't gone beg yuh tuh come. If yuh ain't there, then Ah'll know yuh wanna be a slave all yuh life. Just don't tell nobody yuh see'd me. Ah don't wanna make trouble for Sula, Miss Ollie, Miss Tillie and Mammy Pearl. As far as Massa and Moore know, y'all just run off. And y'all free tuh do dat, but yuh know Massa Jackson ain't like our daddy. Yuh know he gonna try tuh get rid of y'all's freedom papers and make yuh his slaves again."

"Yuh right Jacob. He ain't like his daddy," Tillie broke in. "Freedom be yuh right. Yuh got tuh take it while Jacob be here tuh he'p yuh, or lose it forever. Yuh know Massa done commenced tuh beatin' and torturin' folk. Soon he be sellin' folk off. Go-on now!"

The boys nodded and hurried out the door to gather their things.

৵৵

It was a beautiful moonlit night and Sula and Jacob desired to be alone. Butfirst Miss Tillie and Ollie insisted on Jacob eating a meal of chicken and dumplings, with biscuits that were left over from their supper.

"Now dis only gon' take a minute fer yuh tuh eat somthin'," Miss Ollie demanded.

"Go-on and eat boy. Ah don't know where yuh been, but yuh must be missin' dis down home cookin'," Mammy Pearl sang out. She wasn't going to leave that cabin until Jacob and Sula left; she wanted to soak in as much of Jacob as she could.

Jacob couldn't turn it down; he was practically starving. The excitement of going home had prevented him from touching any of the food in the knapsack and he had not eaten since early that morning. All he could do was thank the women, sit and enjoy their food.

Sula smiled at him while pulling the quilt from her bed and folding it into a neat bundle. Before Jacob could take his last mouthful of food she was pulling him from the makeshift chair. "We gon' see y'all later. It be a beautiful night. We gon' be down at da lake," she announced.

"Thank yuh kindly for da food. Ah guess Ah be seein' y'all later." Jacob took a gentle bow as Sula pulled him toward the door. He reached for his hat and was trying to speak to the ladies at the same time.

Tillie and Ollie smiled. "Love sure make yuh do crazy thangs," Tillie said and she shooed them out the door.

"See yuh when Ah come back home again, Mammy Pearl," Jacob announced.

৵৵

Sula and Jacob spread their quilt out over the grassy clearing, twenty feet back from the water's edge. Absence had made their hearts ache and just kissing and hugging no longer satisfied their longing for each other. Fear of an unwanted pregnancy had prevented them from consummating their love. Jacob knew if Sula got pregnant, Jackson would know it was his baby and to punish him, he would sell the child, or even sell them both. He would surely know it was him that came this night to fetch Juke and Capers. Sula, Tillie, Mammy Pearl and Ollie would be held responsible, only because he would need someone to punish; it was the only way Jackson could hurt him.

Jacob also knew he needed the Lord's help for discipline on that night. He had wanted her from the time he came into his manhood. He had had other girls, but he never made an advance to Sula because of her traumatic past; he wanted to let her come to him. Now she was there before him in her nakedness and he had no control. His eyes caressed Sula and his manhood grew. Sula was the only woman he desired, so he called on the Lord and he was removing his clothes as if he were in a trance. The sensuality of each other's nakedness heightened their arousal and Jacob cried aloud, "Please Lawd, he'p me."

His hand covered Sula's firm breast while his lips moved from her neck to where his hands once were. *He'p me Lawd*, his mind cried out, but he was so hungry for her. He touched her moist spot and she sighed and jerked with pleasure, relaxing and opening her legs to receive him. Her heart pounded in sync with his and she moaned again as he entered her. In the next moment, the experience was over for Jacob; he rolled over and lay next to her side and they held each other. "Ah'm sorry, Sula," he whispered.

"Ah knew it would be like dat for yuh, it be yuh first time wit me, but we have da rest of da night." Sula kissed his lips and then rested her head on his chest.

That night Jacob realized his love for Sula on a higher plain.

chapter 7

Capers and Juke arrived at the main road and had been sitting on a fallen log since 4:00 A.M. It was always possible for them to tell the time on a moonlit night.

By the time Jacob arrived the moon was lower to the horizon and it was like a joyous family reunion. Capers held the jar containing their freedom papers and he carefully tucked it under his arm when he reached to pick up the small bundle containing his meager belongings. Juke followed his movements and the three young men stepped out onto the main road. Jacob glanced back at his brothers to see their reaction at stepping off the plantation. They had turned around and were standing still staring at the glow of the balcony's lanterns from the big house. On a work day and an hour later, they would be marching off to the fields to work until dusk. But on that Sunday morning they were running off to their new life; now, they were free men and they would work as free men.

"All right brothers, it's still dark. We gon' walk on da road an' let our ears be our guide. If we hear anybody comin' we gon' jump in da bushes," Jacob instructed.

"But, we be free. We kin walk da road. We's got papers," Capers announced, as he held up the jar.

Jacob took a deep breath, *oh Lord they just don't understand that they can't trust da white man,* he thought. "Ah understand how yuh feel," Jacob said, "but yuh still too close tuh The Dillard Plantation. Jackson or Moore don't b'lieve in none of dem papers. They'll take yuh back tuh slavery."

Juke's eyes stared at Jacob and then he shifted his gaze toward Capers. They didn't say a word to each other, but Juke's fear spoke for him. *Let's go back befo' Jacob gits us killed!*

"Ah see yuh fears. Yeah, Capers Ah know yuh feel da same as Juke. Yuh just got a different way of showin' it. Ah was afraid too and Ah was on da road for ten days. We have only got tuh travel one day. We's gone make it. Ah'm gone take good care of y'all, but y'all gots tuh do what Ah say. Yuh off da home place now so let's keep movin'." Jacob broke into a steady trot and the brothers picked up their pace and followed.

෨᰼෨

Twenty five minutes later and still moving at a moderate trot, the brothers had cleared The Dillard Plantation Road. Jacob led them into the woods to dig up the knapsack and then he headed off to relieve himself. Juke and Capers were so excited about freedom they allowed carelessness to take them by surprise.

Danny Moore first heard the boys talking and laughing before he crept up on them. "Whatcha doing way down here, boys?" Moore yelled out. He held his rifle uncocked and pointed toward the forest floor.

"We's free, Massa Moore!" Juke's voice trembled as he spoke. "We's got freedom papers."

"Yuh niggers are some dumb boys. Dem papers don't mean nothin'. Now y'all just be good boys and git on back tuh da quarters."

"But, we's free and we's got papers! We's leavin' now!" Capers' sarcastic voice instantly angered Moore. He seemed to completely forget what Jacob said about the papers or he just didn't believe him.

Jacob heard Moore and Capers' talking and hid behind a large oak tree. He reached for the small derringer that was holstered to his leg, but he was too far away for his pistol to do any damage. Somehow he had to get closer without attracting Moore's attention.

Moore cocked his rifle and waved it in the direction of the small hole where the knapsack had been unearthed. "You boys been diggin'. Well, Ah think that's a real good idea, but we gone move deeper intuh the woods. Yuh boys need tuh dig a nice deep hole, so git tuh walkin' and bring that shovel with yuh."

"Where yuh want us tuh go Massa?" Capers asked.

"Just keep walkin' 'til Ah tell yuh tuh stop."

The men walked deeper into the woods. Fright blanketed their faces and they wondered where Jacob was. They left their belongings and Jacob's knapsack at his hiding place. Moore held the reins of his horse and led him into the woods behind him, before finally tying him to a tree.

"We's sorry, Massa Moore!" Juke whined. "We's ready tuh go back now!"

Moore stepped back, cocked his rifle and pointed it at Capers and then at Juke. "Boys! Ah think Ah will blow both of yuh heads off!" Moore said and his words caused Jacob to hold his breath.

"Shut-up and start diggin'! Ah'm 'bout tuh send y'all home. Jackson don't need yuh. Yuh say yuh free. Ah'm 'bout tuh really set yuh free, but Ah ain't diggin' yuh grave, too. So dig that hole nice and deep."

"Massa, we's only got one shovel!" Capers whimpered.

"Then one of yuh gone have tuh dig with yuh hands!"

"Oh Lawdy!" Juke wailed and he cried out with more anguish, asking the Lord for help.

Capers saw Jacob hiding behind the tree. He had followed them and was gesturing for him to cry and wail. To make a ruckus so he joined Juke in his yowling and screaming. Moore took great pleasure in their behavior and began to laugh hysterically. During those moments, the forest was a commotion of sounds.

Jacob rushed up behind Moore. Pap! It was a sound resembling the snap of a branch breaking; it was the sound of Jacob's small caliber pistol. The small bullet hit Moore in the back of his head almost at the same time it left the gun and before the young men could take a breath, Moore fell forward, dead on the ground.

Capers stood as still as a statue, in shock and wondering if he had also been shot since Moore had been pointing the rifle at him.

Jacob collapsed to a squatting position; the smoking pistol dangling off the fingers of his right hand and his left hand pulling his head into his chest. "Oh! . . . Oh! . . . Oh!" he huffed out in whispery wails.

"Oh Lawdy, Jacob! Oh Lawdy! Oh Lawdy!" Juke, still in the shallow hole, held his fist to his head and danced around in circles in a state of confusion. "What we gon' do? What we gon' do, Jacob?" he cried. He stopped circling but started pulling his long wavy hair.

Miss Tillie's voice filled Jacob's head. *Use dat gun if'n yuh life be threatened; Kill 'em dead! Ah did right he was gone shoot Capers,* he told himself. He knew he did what he had to do and his brothers depended on him to be strong. He leapt to his feet. "Get yuhselves tuhgether!" he scolded. "Drag his body way back in dem woods."

Capers exhaled and fell to his knees, almost fainting. Beads of perspiration covered his face.

"You okay, Capers?" Jacob asked while tucking the gun back in the leg holster.

"Yeah . . . Ah thought he shot me." He threw himself prone to the forest floor as if he were asking Mother Earth to help him regain his strength.

"Well, he woulda," Jacob said, before giving his brothers a few seconds of comfort and the dead Moore a final kick in the head. "But, Ah shot him first. Miss Tillie give me dis here gun just for dis reason. Yuh see now, freedom ain't free. Dey give it tuh yuh and dey take it back."

Capers flipped over and took a deep breath before sitting up.

"Okay, see here. We's gon' bury him deep so nobody gone ever find him. You boy's gotta dig da grave while Ah get rid of his horse. Yuh got a shovel, so all yuh need is a good flat rock tuh help wit' da diggin'." Jacob held tight to the reins of Moore's horse for fear it would run back to Moore's home without him.

"How deep we's gotta dig, Jacob?" Juke whined.

"How tall yuh be, Juke?" Jacob replied. "He gotta be so deep the critters don't be diggin' 'em up. Moore gotta just disappear."

"Where yuh goin', Jacob?" Juke asked. He and Capers were still carrying Moore's body deep into the wood.

"Ah'm gonna ride his horse intuh Gaffney and tie it up behind a building, then come back here. Ah want people tuh think he never left town. My friend, Blue said Gaffney be a couple of miles from here. Ah'll be back real soon."

Juke and Capers started digging, taking turns switching between the shovel and the flat rock. Fear kept them silent; they could only nod their heads when Jacob spoke. Their eyes shifted, but they didn't question him; they knew he was right. They only wanted him to hurry back so they could get as far away as possible.

☙❧

Jacob mounted Moore's horse and rode until he saw the sign pointing to Gaffney. He turned right on the road and prayed he wouldn't meet up with anyone. 6:00 A.M. Sunday morning was in his favor and there were no homes or churches on the road.

Riding at a steady pace allowed him to arrive in Gaffney in thirty minutes without causing fatigue to the horse. There wasn't a soul or beast on the main street, but he didn't know one building from another. He dismounted and walked the horse behind the buildings where he saw a stable midway of the back street. Within minutes, the horse was in the corral with other horses and the saddle had been positioned over the stable fence.

When Jacob approached the town he noticed a path through the woods that might keep him off the main road. He assumed the path was a shortcut because he had detected another path a ways up, just off the main road as he was riding in. He didn't know if he would save time, he just wanted to get back to his brothers without being seen. After leaving the horse he casually walked to the path, but as soon as he was under the cover of the forest he took off with the pace of a sprinter. He was back with his brothers before they had dug the grave five feet deep.

Casper jumped out of the grave and wrapped his arm around Jacob. His stomach ached with the fear of never seeing him again. He was his brother, he had freed him, he had killed a man that had brutalized him all of his life and in the moments before Moore's death, he thought it would be him that would die instead.

Juke was quiet with anger and fear, but his expressions spoke for him. He didn't like being mixed up in a murder. The day had caught up with them and they were only a couple of miles away from The Dillard Plantation Road. He was ready to turn back and pretend he never saw Jacob or buried Moore, but if anyone found out what happened he knew he would be boiled in oil. His only hope was to get as far away as possible.

"It's gonna be okay, Juke. Ah know whatcha feelin'. Ah think dat graves deep enough, it's up tuh yuh shoulder. Let's get 'em in it," Jacob said as he picked up Moore's hat and rifle and threw it in the hole.

Moore was rolled into the grave and with indignity he landed face down. The brothers stared at each other before covering him with large rocks, and then pushing and shoveling in the dirt. They allowed a small mound to form over the grave that would flatten the burial site level when the earth settled. Large rocks were stacked over the grave that was then camouflaged with dried leaves and tree branches. They stood over the grave and prayed, not for Moore's soul, but for the forgiveness of their sin and the restoration of their souls; they prayed for their safe travel and that no one discover Moore's body. "And Dear Lawd," Jacob prayed, "let no one suspect us in this deed. Ah pray this in our Savior, Jesus' name. Amen."

"Amen," the brothers sang out.

Jacob patted the brothers on their backs. "Let's git," he instructed. And they hurried back to their possessions. He had done what he had to do. Miss Tillie's words played over and over in his head, telling him how to stay safe and free and he knew it was his responsibility to keep his brothers free. He did what he had to do and his brother's eyes laid heavy on him. They had been slaves, but they were safe. Now he had placed them in another kind of hell, but he knew it wouldn't be long before their burdens would fall away. His last mission was to warn them to never speak a word of what had been done, not even to each other.

Capers and Juke nodded.

&

Jacob had said he was a day's walk away from The Dillard Plantation, but he didn't want anyone to know he was so close just in case they were questioned and had to tell what they knew. But now it was 10:00 A.M. and it had been his plan to be walking down the Morton's Road. Of the five hour journey, he and his brothers had just passed the road to Gaffney and were only one hour from the plantation. Although he could pass for white, his brother could not. If they were seen on the road, questions would be asked. Why would a white man who owned slaves be walking? If he were rich enough to own two bucks, he would at the very least own a horse.

The forest was hot and thick with the growth of late summer, but still cool and damp from the night's dew. The nocturnal creatures had taken their leave and the woods were safer to walk through except for the variety of snakes, insects and occasional bears or wild cats. All three agreed that was nothing compared to the dangers of walking the road in daylight.

Fear heightened their senses and of the three, Capers' senses were the sharpest. "Did yuh hear dat? Ah hear a wagon. Get down, get down," he whispered and he dove into the underbrush.

Jacob and Juke squatted and searched in both directions of the road. "Ol' Blue. Well, Ah'll be, Ol' Blue be comin' for us. C'mon," Jacob ordered and waved his brothers to follow. "Blue be comin' back for us even after Ah told him tuh go home, but he be comin' from da way we just come."

The brothers followed, threw the knapsack on the wagon and climbed aboard.

"Blue, Ah's so glad yuh don't lissen." Jacob spoke out between deep breaths.

"Dat's 'cause yuh be young and dumb and yuh don't know what real danger be. Yuh need a slave tuh drive da wagon wit' slaves so yuh kin be da white overseer. Boy, don't yuh 'member all Ah done taught yuh? And yuh 'member Massa Haynes say Ah ain't gotta be back 'til tuhnight." he scolded.

"Ah just be glad tuh see yuh!" Jacob said and he was happy to relinquish control to Ol' Blue.

"Don't be so glad yuh ferget tuh be smart, Mr. Natty, sur!"

Jacob smiled and nodded. "So where did yuh go?" he asked.

"Ah jes be at da colored sleep house in town."

"Yuh be in Gaffney?" Jacob nodded his head. He knew Blue didn't see him or he would have said something. "So that be why yuh come up behind us."

"Ah huh. Ah mean tuh be waitin' fer yuh at the Gaffney road turnoff at daybreak, but Ah over sleep. Ah hurry tuh catch yuh 'fore yuh git yuhself in trouble."

Jacob and his brothers spoke to each other with their eyes. They all knew it was only the Lord that kept Blue sleep that morning, slaves don't oversleep. If Blue was at the Gaffney Road, he would have surely met up with Danny Moore and anything could have happened.

Jacob's white skin blushed with gratitude for Old Blue. "Thanks yuh, Blue. Thank yuh for knowin'."

"Well Jacob, yuh gone be jes fine. Now, tell me 'bout dese two young bucks." He slapped the mule's asses with the reins and turned in his seat.

"These be my brothers." Jacob nodded at Juke and called his name and did the same for Capers. "They be free and they got papers tuh prove it."

The brothers smiled and nodded at Blue then smiled at Jacob.

"Juke and Capers yuh say?" Blue repeated. He glanced over his shoulders again and witnessed the young men's response to their names.

Jacob smiled.

Then Blue announced, "Y'all be da brothers, but y'all ain't white lak Jacob. Now, Ah taught 'em how tuh pass fer white, but y'all tuh dark fer dat. While we's on dis here road y'all act lak slaves and let Jacob do all the talking if'n we be stopped. Now, Ah don't want y'all tuh be scared 'cause he can sound jes lak dem white folk when he wanna talk proper!"

Jacob turn to talk to his brothers and the sullen expression on their faces concerned him. "Look, Ah had tuh learn tuh talk like dem and we only gone act that way when we leave the Morton's farm and when we are on the main road or in town. White men don't bother Negroes when they be wit' another white man. It be lak dey be botherin' private property. Look here, Ah be the white foreman at the Morton farm and y'all be the property." Jacob searched his brother's faces for signs of understanding. They had never been off the plantation and the concept of human property on a dirt road may have been difficult for them to comprehend, but when he noticed the slightest sign of trust or understanding he smiled.

"We's gone be safe brothers. The funny thing be, da Morton's don't believe in slaves. Dey hired me 'cause Ah tell 'em Ah be a freed indenture and Ah be goin' tuh get y'all tuh come work for them 'cause y'all be freed slaves dat Ah growed up wit'. So when we be on da farm, y'all don't have tuh act like Ah be yuh master, but don't act like Ah be yuh bother either. Ah still be passin' for white."

"Why yuh passin'?" Juke yelled out. He covered his mouth with his hands and waited for Jacob to defend himself.

"Juke, Ah'm here for y'all. When Ah set out, dere be no one for me. Ah was so scared and lost, Ah wandered in da forest for ten days 'til Ol' Blue found me. Our life be hard so yuh use what yuh got tuh survive. If Ah can pass, then pass Ah will, but Ah know who Ah am. When the time comes Ah'll be a Negro man."

"Look-a-here boy," Blue scolded, "dis man don't be needin' tuh explain his doin's tuh yuh. He be givin' yuh a chance tuh live free and yuh questionin' him? If'n yuh don't want tuh be here Ah kin have yuh back in time tuh be a slave in da mornin' b'fore yuh even missed.

"Naw, go on Blue," Capers spoke out. He held up his hand agreeing with Blue and nodded. "Ah know yuh meanin'. Juke is jes scared dat be all. He be comin' 'round soon."

Juke sat in the back of the wagon holding his head in his hands and occasionally wiping tears with his index fingers. He weighed his life of slavery against his few hours of freedom. *Jacob killed a white man and we helped bury him.* His fear was robbing his breath. His prediction of his future left him with a blank empty feeling; then worst of all, Jacob was acting like a white man. He wanted to disappear, to hide, to go home where he was always safe even if he was a slave; to the place without questions, unpleasantries abound, but stability had been assured for him all of his life. But now, with the events of the last few hours, he knew Jacob and Capers would never allow that to happen. He pulled a quilt from the knapsack, crawled into a fetal position and covered himself completely to escape his reality.

Capers didn't say anything, but tugged at Blue and Jacob and gestured for them to look at Juke. They nodded and took a deep breath. They knew what fear was and they knew that Juke believed if he could hide, fear couldn't find him.

కా

Miles Morton was standing on the front porch when the wagon cleared the forest. Rusty ran, barking up the road and Mrs. Morton hurried from the house wiping her wet hand on her apron. It was early afternoon and Juke emerged from under the quilt feeling safer.

Evan and Robby ran up the road and climbed on the back of the wagon with Capers and Juke. "Y'all the free slaves Mr. Natty went tuh fetch?"

Jacob was reading Capers' lip movement, *Mr. Natty?*

"Yes sur," Capers bellowed out and Juke just shook his head.

"Okay boys, yuh gonna have time tuh meet the new men. Y'all go on now."

"Yes sir, Mr. Natty." They sang out as they jumped off the wagon and ran back toward the house.

"See . . . yuh free. Yuh have last names now. The man wrote Dillard as yuh last name." Jacob instructed. "Capers, yuh be Capers Dillard and Juke, yuh be Juke Dillard. Ah be Jacob Natty 'cause Ah didn't want tuh have nothin' tuh do wit' da Dillard's."

Blue drove the wagon right up to the front of the house and everyone got off. Miles, Mrs. Morton and the boys were introduced to Juke and Capers, who stood straight and tall like they were being inspected at a slave auction.

Blue laughed. "'Lax … des friendly folk."

"Did yuh eat anything from the knapsack or are yuh hungry," Mrs. Morton stood in the door ready to bring some food out to them.

"No ma'am. All we wanted tuh do was get back here." Jacob said and then he began to rub his stomach. "Now that we are here, Ah do feel a lil' weak." He turned to the other fellows and smiled and took special care to speak proper to Mrs. Morton.

"Ah hope y'all like ham hocks, beans and cornbread for now," she sang out as she entered the house. Then she reappeared at the door. "But this is a special day. We gon' have fried chicken, cream corn and green beans for dinner. Evan and Robby, help Miles get some cold lemonade for the men."

Juke and Capers stared at each other.

"Yes! White people gone wait on yuh! Dese here be real nice people, so relax!" Jacob whispered as he scolded his brothers. They watched as the Mortons disappeared into the house.

శ్రఃఄ

Jacob sat on the porch with Miles and his mother, while Capers and Juke sat on the steps. Blue had quickly finished his meal and headed back to The Haynes Plantation.

Jacob decided to give Mrs. Morton and Miles a bit of information about Jackson Dillard and how Capers and Juke had to steal away from The Dillard Plantation. They explained how they were freed when Master Walter Dillard died, but his son, Jackson made them afraid to leave. Capers handed Mrs. Morton the jar containing their freedom papers.

"Well, Ah want tuh thank you men for riskin' yuh lives and comin' tuh work for us," Mrs. Morton said. Tears rolled down her cheeks at seeing the young men and she wiped her entire face, pretending she was wiping away perspiration from the summer heat. "Mr. Natty told yuh we can't pay yuh 'til harvest, but Ah promise tuh give yuh good food and a place tuh stay. Mr. Natty is building himself a cabin and yuh welcome tuh do the same, but 'till then, Miles done fixed yuh a place in the barn. My husband went on tuh glory a little while ago, so Ah may have some clothes yuh can use; Miles has enough and Ah think y'all need it more. So again, thank yuh for comin' and welcome. Y'all can wash out back and Mr. Natty will show yuh around the farm."

"Thank yuh, ma'am." Jacob said. Then he nudged his brothers who stood frozen.

"Thank yuh, ma'am," they both sang out together.

"Ah'll bring the clothes and stuff down in a while," Miles said as he turned to enter the house.

"See yuh later, Mr. Morton and thank yuh for everythin'." Jacob called back at him.

"Is this a real place?" Juke whispered. "Is this freedom?"

Capers only nodded as Juke spoke.

"This only be a small corner of freedom for a colored man, but Ah be hearin' there be a war comin'. Blue say white folk be talkin 'bout war b'tween the white folk up north and dem here in the south. The north folk want tuh end slavery. Ah sure hope they have that war and Ah sure hope them folk up north win," Jacob said. "Yuh know white folk got a newspaper that they print out once a week. It be tellin' 'em 'bout stuff. Ah'm gon' have Miles get me a paper when he goes tuh town."

chapter 8

"Mr. Dillard! . . . Mr. Dillard!" Ellen Moore called from the steps of the big house. She held a smooth rock and used it to tap hard on the door because the door knocker had long broken away. Then she called out louder than before, "Jackson Dillard!" It was 8:15 P.M.; still light, but dark enough that her small frame didn't cast a shadow across the front yard when she stepped away from the house. Now Sunday evening, it had been more than thirty four hours since her husband and Jackson rode off together.

"Who belongs tuh that lovely voice summoning me?" Jackson called out from his second story balcony.

"Don't yuh speak tuh me like Ah'm one of those wicked Gaffney women. Where is mah husband? He left here with yuh yesterday morning and Ah ain't seen him since?"

"Ah beg yuh pardon, Mrs. Moore. Ah'll be right down." Jackson pulled on his boots and adjusted his suspenders while hurrying through his apartment, down the central stairs and across the massive foyer. "Mrs. Moore!" he addressed her with concern as he stepped through the front door. "Yuh say Dan didn't come home yet? Ah left him playing cards in the saloon yesterday afternoon. He didn't want to leave . . . he was winning."

"Yuh left him there?"

"Yes ma'am. Ah was home before dark; about six or seven." Jackson walked over to the twin wicker chairs. "Please," he said, while waving his open hand toward the empty chair.

Mrs. Moore pulled her lacey handkerchief from her sleeve and held it in her right hand as if waiting for her first tear to appear. She returned to the porch and sat on the edge of the chair praying Jackson would take pity on her and offer to look for her husband.

"Mr. Dillard, Ah simply don't know what tuh do! Ah mean . . . Ah don't know how tuh go 'bout locatin' mah husband," she whined and dabbed at her tearless eyes.

Jackson stood, walked down into the front yard and looked toward the sunset. "Ma'am, if he has not returned by morning, Ah'll be at yuh service."

"Thank yuh kindly, Mr. Jackson." She offered her hand to him and took a small curtsey before climbing up and into buggy and was driven away.

&

The next morning, Jackson informed Louis Maynard of Moore's absence before riding off to search for him. Maynard was left to supervise the new three man crew of subordinate overseers. Two hundred acres of tobacco was being worked and strung and the legume fields had to be harvested and turned. Moore had hired three new men to work the slaves more efficiently on Jackson's orders; he claimed his father's ways had allowed them to become too lax. Maynard rode the water wagon with his horse tied and trailing behind.

Jackson wasn't as kind as his father; he didn't spare the lash, but he had not turned into a complete monster and was still providing a fair living for his slaves. Families were allowed to remain whole, land was provided for personal gardens, a pregnant woman was given a month before and after the birth of her child before returning to the fields. The living quarters were spacious and very large families were allowed to add on to their cabins. Master Jackson, like his father, raised livestock; chickens, eggs and pork and healthy portions were given to the slaves regularly. The slaves were also allowed to fish and hunt for venison, raccoon, rabbit and squirrel. Jackson believed a healthy slave would live long, work hard, bear many children and would be less likely to run away and he was right. Not one slave had run away from The Dillard in his lifetime. It would be some time before he would miss Capers and Juke, but they were free.

&

Jackson rode his horse in a slow trot down The Dillard Plantation Road. The urge to scan the forest on both sides of the road was heavy, but so was the forest, nonetheless, he continued to do so until he reached the turnoff to Gaffney. He had plenty of time, although Gaffney would be alive with business, the saloon would be closed until noon and it was barely 9:00 A.M. He decided to ask around about Moore; someone had to have seen him. The mercantile was as good a place to start as any; Danny Moore enjoyed his chewing tobacco and because he stayed out the whole weekend he was sure to need a pretty gift for Mrs. Ellen.

Jackson secured his horse to the post outside of Oliver's Mercantile and stepped hard on the wooden plank sidewalk. The double hung screen doors covered the entrance and Jackson opened both of them to gain entry. "Hey Oliver!" he called out. The colored woman standing at the counter picked up the basket of canning jars, bowed in a hunched manner and was careful not to make eye contact as she scooted back and across the aisle. Jackson ignored her while taking his place at the counter. "Oliver! Can't you hear me talkin' tuh you?"

"Year, Ah hear yuh." Oliver responded in a jovial manner.

"Then why don't yuh answer me?" Jackson continued boisterously.

"B'cause it's too damn early for all that noise." Oliver leaned over the counter whispering, "Calm down, boy. Yuh killin' mah tranquility."

"HA! HA! HA!" Jackson laughed as loud as he could. He had to have the last laugh especially in front of the colored woman. "Okay, yuh win," he said in his serious voice. "Listen Oliver, Ah ain't seen my man, Danny Moore since Saturday afternoon. It ain't like him tuh go missin'. Have yuh seen him?"

"Ain't been in here, Jackson."

"It's kinda strange for him tuh go missin', so if you hear somethin' could yuh tell the sheriff?"

"Sho-nuff," Oliver continued to whisper.

Jackson gave Oliver a nod and a tip of his hat. He caught sight of the colored woman again when he turned to leave the store, but believed her not to be worthy of his acknowledgment. He pushed open the screen doors and stood across the threshold, scanning the traffic up and down the main street. The First Citizens Bank had just unlocked its doors and the two men waiting on the sidewalk entered. Jackson knew Moore didn't visit the bank because it was closed over the weekend, but he could question the customers. One man remembered seeing him in the saloon on Saturday, but he didn't remember when he left.

"Thank yuh. If yuh remember anything else would yuh give the information tuh the sheriff?" Jackson tipped his hat as he left the bank.

His next stop was Cantor's Black Smith Shop. An unshaven, three hundred pound, Benny Cantor spent his days sitting in his large rocker, smoking his pipe and drinking ale, while the freed slave, Cole Nelson was now the master iron crafter. Jackson approached, walking pass the hammer slinging Cole and stood over Benny. "Ah'm looking for my man, Danny Moore. He's been missing since Saturday. Have yuh seen him or his horse?"

Benny pulled a dingy-gray, frayed handkerchief from his back pocket and wiped it over his face and neck before tucking it away again. "Ah ain't seen him," was all he had to say. He didn't care much for the wealthy gentlemen of the county, with their knee high leather boots, prancing stallions and clean finger nails.

Jackson glanced at the black man and decided his questions were for white men only. What he didn't know was Benny was too lazy to walk around his own property. Moore's horse had been moved from the corral Sunday before noon to spare it from the heat of the day. It had been watered and placed in one of the inner stalls of Benny's barn by Cole. Cole didn't know it was Moore's horse, but if Jackson had asked him, he would have told him he had an unclaimed horse in the stall. But speaking to a Negro man other than his own slaves was far beneath Jackson and Cole had learned to never speak to a white man unless he was spoken to first. So Cole slung his hammer against the anvil supporting the hot iron rod and stuck to his own business. A moment later he shifted his stance to secretly stare at Jackson as he led his horse away from him.

Jackson stood in the middle of the main street and placed his hands on his hips. He surveyed the buildings to his left and then to his right. *The brothel*, he thought. *If Ah know Moore, he spent Saturday night with Sue Mae.* Ah hate tuh wake the fine ladies up so early, but Ah know they'll want tuh help if they can. He walked over to the building that was attached to the back of the saloon and knocked on the door hard enough to wake up anyone still sleeping. When no one responded after a reasonable period, he called out several times for Luanne.

"Doesn't anybody sleep in this crazy town?" A scratchy voice yelled out from the window beside the door.

"Luanne! It's me, Jackson. It's important. Ah need tuh talk tuh you. Lemme in!"

"Let yuhself in!" She tossed the key out the window. It hit the brim of his hat and bounced to the ground before he heard the window slam shut. He opened the door and looked up the stairs. Luanne stood on the landing tying the sash of her short satin robe around her. Jackson's eyes followed her shapely legs from her ankles up to where her robe met her knees and then up further to the shadow of her red bush. Luanne was the house madam and she was his woman exclusively; he paid her well for the privilege. When he reached the landing, one hand was already massaging her private spot while the other was loosening the tie of her robe.

"I thought you needed to ask me something," Luanne swooned.

Jackson led her toward her room grinning. "It'll wait," he said. He began unbuttoning his shirt and pants along the way. He pushed the bedroom door closed with his foot.

࠾ᄼᅠᄼ

Two hours later, Jackson was dressed, in the dining room and enjoying a brunch prepared by Annie, the hired Negro cook. After informing Luanne about Moore, she left the room to wake Sue Mae and she promised to meet Jackson in the parlor.

Jackson finished eating, pushed his plate away, stood and belched. He wiped his entire face with his napkin before throwing it on his plate. He turned, walked into the classic red parlor of the brothel, with its room size imported Persian rug, red velvet loveseats and chase lounges. The red velvet drapes were still drawn keeping out the daylight. *Why not?* Jackson thought, *these are ladies of the night.* He flung the drapes open and a large ray of light filtered in disturbing particles of dust that floated lightly on the bright sunbeam.

"Mah goodness, Jackson," Luanne chimed, "Ah ain't seen daylight in this room in years."

"Well, you and Sue Mae need tuh get use tuh the light, 'cause Ah like it. Come on in and sit with yuh back tuh the window if yuh have tuh and let's talk." He searched the room for a regular chair, but then he remembered seeing them in the dining room. "Just a minute," he said before hurrying off. Seconds later he returned, placed the chair backward in front of the women and straddled it as he sat. "Sue Mae," he began, "Ah guess Luanne told yuh Danny Moore is missing. Was he with you Saturday night? Ah left him playin' poker and he was winning."

"He sure was!" Sue Mae sang out, giggled and straightened her posture. "But before he was with me he was with the boys at the poker table. That's when Ah was with him. By ten o'clock, he had won almost a hundred dollars. Jack Harris, Lue Gant and Larry Smith folded and Danny went 'all in' with a hundred and ten dollars. Ah thought Stan Cellers was gonna fold, but then he called his bet and put up his farm. Danny told him to put it in writin' and he had Jack write out a note for him. Yuh know he can't write." Sue Mae stopped talking and sat looking at Jackson.

Luanne glanced at Jackson and then turned to face Sue Mae. "Well Damn, Sue Mae! Don't stop now. What happened?" Luanne said.

Jackson stood, pushed the chair back and began to pace in front of the women.

"Now, Stan had called with four fours and a deuce and he smiled at Danny," Sue Mae continued. "Danny sat stone faced like he had loss, then he put down a nine high straight flush. That's when Stan tried to turn over the table, but the other guys held him down. Danny told him he could have his farm back for two hundred and thirty dollars or he would start renting it to him in sixty days. Now, Ah thought that was real fair seein' that how he loss it and all, but Stan was real messed up in the head. Ah recon Ah would be, too."

Jackson stopped and stared at Sue Mae, wondering if Stan had anything to do with Moore's disappearance. But at the same time Luanne was really seeing her tall, dark man in the day time. She had held him in her arms and felt his hard body. He was beyond handsome, with golden hair, chiseled features and crystal blue eyes. She loved him, but she knew he would never be her claim. Her breed was wrong, but when he found his Mrs. Dillard, she would always be there for him on those nights when she turned him out.

Jackson snatched the chair, spun it around before pulling it up and sitting close to Sue Mae. "What did Cellers do next?" he questioned.

Tears filled Sue Mae's eyes. "Yuh think he did something tuh Danny?"

Luanne handed her a handkerchief.

Jackson took hold of Sue Mae's hands. "Listen honey, Ah'm tryin' to find Danny. Ah need tuh piece things together, so if you can just tell me what Cellers did next . . ."

"Nothin'," she interrupted him, "he didn't do nothin' 'cept get a drink and leave the saloon in a big angry hurry. Danny picked up his winnings and we came back here. He stayed wit' me 'til 'bout 4:00 A.M." Sue Mae turned to Luanne. "Yuh think Cellers waited all night for him?"

Jackson picked up his hat before reaching the door. "Thanks for the information ladies. Ah don't know if Stan Cellers knows anythin' and Ah can't go questionin' him. Ah'm just gonna get me a good stiff drink and then turn this information over tuh the sheriff."

Luanne clapped her hands once and walked over to her private bar. "C'mon Jackson," she said, "Lemme give yuh a drink before yuh leave."

☙❧

12:15 P.M., the saloon's doors were open when Jackson walked from Luanne's place up to Main Street and made the left turn. Al Halsey was positioning a fresh keg of ale on the sidebar and turned around with a startled after hearing Jackson call out his name.

Al stood frozen and then he half turned to face Jackson. "Hey Jackson, never seen yuh in town on a Monday."

Jackson pushed his hat back on his head and elbowed the bar. "Yeah . . . well, Ah been tryin' to git some information 'bout my overseer, Danny Moore. Last Ah saw him was Saturday afternoon. Ah heard from the ladies that he won some pretty big poker hands."

"Sho-nuff! Took them boys money like they was his chillen, but he didn't get what he thought he got when he won Stan Cellers' farm." Al reached for a couple of bottles of whisky and placed them on the shelf in front of the large wall mirror.

"How so?" Jackson asked, as his eyes caught Al's reflection.

Al leaned in close to Jackson. "Now listen, yuh know a bartender is like one of them religious men. Yuh know them priest-monk types. Men tell us stuff that we're s'pposed tuh keep. Ah'm doin' wrong, but Ah gots tuh tell yuh this and you gots tuh promise not tuh tell."

Jackson sucked on the inside of his bottom lip and nodded his head.

"Okay." Al whispered. He took a few seconds to search the saloon for other customers. Then he leaned in over the bar to get closer to Jackson before beginning. "Well, earlier Saturday morning Cellers was crying in his brew. It was the second day he'd been in here. Friday afternoon he bought a fifth of whiskey, sat alone in the corner and did that bottle in. His wife come a lookin' for him and the guys hid him out in the back of their buck wagon. The next morning, Saturday, he was back when Ah opened the doors. He was messed up in the head. Said the bank give him one week tuh come up with three hundred dollars or get off his land."

Jackson removed his hat, combed his blond hair back with his fingers and repositioned his hat. "That's what that was about. That dirty cheating rat! Well, that lets Cellers off the hook."

"What's yuh meaning?"

"Ah thought Cellers was sore 'cause he loss tuh Moore. Thought maybe he knew something about his being missing, but if Ah were Cellers, Ah'd be hidin' out from Moore."

"Yeah, Jackson. Ah ain't never known no one tuh welch on a bet like that."

"What about the other men who loss tuh Moore?"

"Hey Jackson, it's early, but how about it man? Let's have a seat."

Jackson nodded, headed for the table closest to the bar and sat waiting for Al to arrive with the whisky and two glasses. Al sat heavy and poured the liquor before speaking. "Yuh know, you and Moore came in around noon. Moore sat at the poker table and he didn't move until twelve or one in the morning." Al chugged his whisky and huffed out a deep breath of air before he continued. "Ah watched a lot of men sit, lose a few bucks and then rise. Moore won a lot of money from most of them and that added up."

Jackson took a small sip of whisky and twirled the rest around in his glass. "Any of the men could've waited around to rob Moore, even Cellers. Seemed like he won more money that day than most of them men made in a year."

"Yeah," Al said as he poured himself another drink. "Yuh know, if Cellers did rob him, he could take that deed he gave Moore and all of his money and then pay the note at the bank."

"That would be a bit obvious and major stupid," Jackson said. He downed his shot of whisky and clapped his glass on the table upside down. "Yuh know Al, it would help if yuh got up a list of the men who gambled with Moore and who knew how much money he won." He stood slowly and tipped his hat. "Ah'm gonna talk with Sheriff Stem before Ah go home. Ah got a plantation tuh run. Ah thank yuh for yuh time."

"Yuh welcome, Jackson. Ah'll be seeing yuh. Ah hope Ah was helpful."

Jackson stopped to visit Ellen Moore before heading home. He would weigh his words, but no matter what he said his news was far less comforting than she had prayed for.

Mrs. Moore sat on her front porch rocker surrounded by her two pre-teen boys and younger daughter. They were all leaning on each other with the same prayer on their hearts. Her eyes settled on Jackson's approach; she rose from her seat and waited for him on the lowest porch step, allowing the banister to be her support. It was of little comfort that Danny wasn't with him. She closed her eyes and listened to the single sound of Jackson's horse as it trotted up her road.

"Ma'am," Jackson spoke.

She opened her eyes and her handkerchief was ready to catch her tears. She knew from the tone of his voice and his forlorn appearance that the news wasn't good. "Danny?" she whined.

"Ah couldn't find him," Jackson confessed.

"You couldn't find him? What do yuh mean? He can't just disappear."

"Yes ma'am. Ah understand, but no one has seen him since Saturday night. Ah have Sheriff Stem investigating. Right now, all we can do is wait. Don't yuh worry none, Ah'm gone take care of you and the children 'til Danny comes home."

chapter 9

The cotton was in and Jacob and his brothers had made it possible for the Morton family to be the first to bring their yield to market. Raw cotton sold at a record high that fall. The south was on edge, believing their state's rights and laws were being eroded by Federal laws. Even before the presidential election, South Carolina's bigwigs were rallying should Lincoln or any abolitionist come into power and alter their way of life. The European nations, the largest consumer of cotton, purchased and stockpiled more of the crop that season for fear of what the future would bring.

It wasn't long before a great unrest blanketed the south with the election of Abraham Lincoln as the sixteenth president of the United States. It was a fact that Lincoln's name never appeared on the southern ballot. He was a northern Republican, who had gain notoriety for his opposition toward the expansion of slavery for new states joining the Union. It appeared southerners only heard the word slavery and took that to mean they were going to lose their slaves. However, at that time, Lincoln's position was a political strategy to perpetuate the balance of power between the free states and the slave states in the congress and senate. But the reality remained that from the moment of the presidential election the threat of secession from the Union for South Carolina became the rallying call. Men seeking southern political power campaigned throughout the south for other slave states to join them in forming a new nation and the lazy south began to bellow and cry out for war.

ॐॐ

The Morton's income tripled even after paying Jacob, Juke and Capers and Mrs. Morton was more than grateful to them.

Now that the crops were in and the garden gleaned, it was time for Mrs. Morton to set up the preserves for the winter. Enough firewood had been cut and stacked to service everyone's needs until spring and the hogs had been fattened for the slaughter. By early December, Jacob's two-room cabin had been completed and he and his brothers were finishing up the second shelter. Mrs. Morton was now schooling Juke and Capers and continuing to drill Jacob on the proper use of the English language; she appeared to take delight in this, her most personal challenge.

Freedom allowed Juke and Capers to decide if they wanted to work or not, but they always worked. They knew they could take a break in the shade, or not work at all during the heat of the day. Now, it was fear that enslaved them, pinning them to the Morton farm and the Moore situation continues to be their haunt.

For the first time in their lives they had money and Miles took Jacob and the brothers into the small town of Clinton, South Carolina for a shopping trip. Mrs. Morton had taught Jacob about money, how to make a purchase and count change so he didn't appear to be an ignorant white man. He only wanted a new Stetson hat and a new pair of work gloves, but he decided to save his money for Sula. He had ample clothes and a good pair of boots, a gift from Mrs. Morton. He had shared the clothes with his brothers so they only needed to buy longjohns, sox and brogan boots for themselves. They kept their old slave clothes for working in the fields and pocketed the rest of their earnings.

෧෧

They worked the winter crops, conditioned the land and continued to labor on the second cabin. The days were shorter and the time Jacob and his brothers spent at the cabins were longer. During the evening they sat in their homemade chairs outside of their cabin doors. A fire flickered a few feet away adding warmth to the cool evening air and taking them back to The Dillard, to the love of home and families and then they reminded themselves of the oppression of slavery.

"Ah wanna go home, if'n jes fer one night." Juke announced. "Ah be so lonely fer mah family. Dis ain't freedom . . . dis be loneliness." His voice cracked as he spoke and his sadness was impossible to dismiss.

"Ah be lonely too, Jacob." Capers whined. "We's been here four months and Ah feel lak Ah be trapped."

"Well, yuh boys ain't trapped like yuh was when yuh be a slave. Do yuh remember how that used tuh be?" Jacob asked sarcastically. He picked up a twig and doodled in the dirt. Tears welled in his eyes and settled there. The light from the fire flickered across his face and he prayed his brothers wouldn't see his sadness. He understood their loneliness. They missed their mothers, they had mothers and brothers and sisters; the love of family overshadowed slavery and oppression. Jacob missed his Sula and Mammy Pearl; he understood why they wanted to return to The Dillard. Just like he needed the comfort of Sula, they needed the comfort of women too. He thought about Danny Moore, then closed his eyes and allowed the flutter of pain and fear to pass. Tillie had said, "Burry 'em deep so nobody can find dey body." Ain't nobody ever gon' find 'em, he thought. "Listen, now," he spoke directly to his brothers, "Blue say we should stay put. Ain't no time tuh be goin' tuh The Dillard."

"Whatya be meanin', Jacob?" Juke squealed and he leaped from his stool.

"He be talkin' 'bout Moore?" Capers whispered. "We can't go back."

"Shusss!" Jacob scolded and sprang from his chair. "We never, ever talk 'bout that. It never happened, yuh hear?" He was so close to Capers face, Capers turned away from his hot breath. He stood and looked at Juke, but he was speaking to both of them. "What he know 'bout Moore? Ol' Blue say it ain't safe for us to be on that road 'cause white folk been actin' crazy 'bout da new president." He kicked the dirt and straddled his chair. "Blue is tellin' it right. Ah been readin' 'bout this white folk craziness."

Remembering Moore, Juke stood and walked near the fire. "Now, goin' home ain't so important. You go on alone, Jacob. See how things be. Then we go next time."

"Shut yuh mouth!" Capers yelled. He jumped from his chair with his arms waving at Juke. "Yuh be bitchin' since we left The Dillard. Yuh put pressure on Jacob every day we be here, now yuh wanna stay here?"

Jacob stood and ran his fingers through his hair. "We can't spend our lives bein' scared tuh live. Juke be right. We be puttin' ourselves back in slavery."

"Yeah," Juke agreed. "Well . . . we sho-nuff be slaves again if dem slave hunters catch us." He was too embarrassed to raise his head as he spoke, even to look at Capers. Jacob, yuh can pass for white. Yuh can go anywhere, but we can't."

Juke stood and glanced up at the moonless sky; he knew Capers understood. "It be da road, Jacob. The Dillard don't scare me. We be stealin' tuh da cabins and ain't nobody gone talk. We be safe den; Massa ain't gon' catch us."

Capers stared at Juke and spoke. "He be right, Jacob. Yuh go without us. Yuh tell em we's just fine and we love 'em. Nobody gone bother yuh when yuh walk da road."

Jacob returned to his chair. The fire flickered against the side of his face while the creosol from the pine logs sprayed sparks in random directions. He wanted to kick the fire logs that were popping, crackling and spitting angry sparks. He was hot and wanted to spit angry words, but he knew the brothers made a good point. "Ah 'member how da road made me feel. Da road ain't safe. Everything be real bad now."

"What yuh be sayin. How can it be worser?" Juke squatted and stared up at Jacob as he spoke.

Jacob sat back in his chair. "Get up Juke! Don't yuh ever squat for no man! He spoke through angry teeth. "Now listen! Dem whites be all fired up 'bout that new president who say he gon' free all da slaves. Da newspaper that Ah be readin' say they might have a war between da southern states that got slaves and da northern states that don't. And Blue say, dem Night Riders be attackin' any darkies they find on da road."

"What dey massa's say when da Night Riders hurt dey property?" Capers ask.

Jacob's glance shifted between his brothers. "They massas be keepin' they negras off the road, or they give 'em a pass. One thing fo' sho', dem white men respect property. Ah be goin' tuh The Dillard . . . and real soon."

Quiet filled the space they shared while their thoughts filled their heads. Earlier, they all wanted to return to The Dillard, then it was all right that Jacob return alone and finally Juke and Capers couldn't image being on the road.

"Ah got me a plan," Jacob announced. "Yuh see, the white man . . . he rides a horse. Ah may look white and Mrs. Morton may be teachin' me white folk ways, but if Ah go a walkin' out on that road, Ah be just like a darkie. Them white men out there gone stop me and make trouble. Ah be needin' me a horse. White men ride horses. Ah be askin' Mrs. Morton 'bout a loan of Red for two days."

"Two days!" Juke yelled out and then he turned to see Capers reaction.

Capers just waved his hand signaling him to be quiet before returning his attention to Jacob.

"It be still early." Jacob stood and stared at the Morton's house. It was only six thirty and the lantern glowed brightly in the living room window. "Ah'm gon' see 'bout the horse loan. They still have the mules and if Mrs. Morton say so, Ah be leavin' next Saturday morning."

"Next Saturday? Why next Saturday?" Juke asked.

"'Cause this week we be slaughterin' and curin' them hogs," Jacob answered. He fetched his lantern from the cabin, lit the wick and began walking across the large field. He held back any sign of excitement so he wouldn't risk the depression that accompanied disappointment if he didn't receive the loan of the horse.

ॐ

Caper stood when he saw the small beam of light waving in rhythm with the stride of Jacob's gait. "He be comin' back! It be Jacob," he announced.

Juke picked up a burning log from the fire and used it as a torch before running toward Jacob. "Well . . . is yuh got Red?" he called out as he neared.

"All be well, brother." Jacob spoke softly and smiled.

"Ah love freedom!" Juke proclaimed. He jumped up and the flame from his log torch spit sparks.

"Well it does my heart good tuh hear yuh say that," Jacob announced.

In a few minutes they were back at the cabin where Capers waited and sat quietly without inquiring about Red.

Jacob blew out the flame on his lantern and sat in his chair. "What be eatin' at yuh? Ah got one brother jumpin' 'round and another deep thinkin'. Y'all sure be confusin'."

"Ah jes be thinkin'. How yuh gon' ride a horse up tuh The Dillard and be safe?" Capers didn't look at Jacob when he spoke, but held his head down and stared off toward the forest.

"Look at me!" Jacob yelled. "Damn it! Both of yuh look at me and hear me. Y'all got tuh get it tuhgether. Y'all be opposite. When one of yuh say, 'go,' da other say, 'come back,' when one of yuh show strength, da other be weak, when one of yuh laugh, da other be cryin'. We gots tuh be a team. We gots tuh work tuhgether. We do what we gots tuh do tuh be strong and tuh survive. Now Ah done said Ah gots me a plan. Y'all ain't never ask 'bout dat. When y'all gon' start thinkin' for yuhself. White man been thinkin' for yuh all yuh life, yuh don't know how tuh think for yuhself. White man give yuh freedom and yuh stayed a slave. Brothers, don't be afraid tuh plan, tuh think things out, tuh think for yuhself and b'lieve in yuhself."

Capers and Juke stared at Jacob and then at each other. They knew he was right. They had always been the left and right sides of each other, but they never had anyone tell them what they already knew; they were each other's external conscience. Their checks and balances were fun when they were boys, but now they were men. Men had to be whole and capable of making decisions they were willing to live and die by. Jacob was the only person who ever told them to think for themselves. Their shoulders snapped back and the chests of proud men protruded outward, their necks straightened and they held their heads high. The curve that slavery placed in their spine had been erased by Jacob's words and examples.

"Sorry Brother," Capers said, "we ain't been actin' lak men." He nodded at Juke and stood tall for Jacob. "Sorry Brother. Thank yuh fer showin' me my failin's."

"All right now, y'all work on it. It ain't gon' happen just like dat." Jacob placed his arms around his brother's shoulders to reassure them that all was well. "Now for da plan." He turned, pulled his chair up to the fire and threw a few small logs on the smoldering embers. Juke and Capers positioned their chairs and waited for Jacob to speak. "Lissen brothers. Ah know y'all be as lonely as me. Ah was thinkin' and this is just a suggestion. Ah hear Ol' Blue's massa is a fair man and he has a lot of colored people on his plantation. Maybe yuh could ask Ol' Blue tuh get permission for y'all tuh visit with his people. Yuh might make 'quaintance with some fine women."

"What yuh say?" Juke asked while shooting a sideways glance at Jacob.

Capers leaped from his chair so fast he knocked it backward. "Massa Haynes holds slaves!" he yelled.

"Oh . . . so now yuh better than slaves?" Jacob said sarcastically. "Yuh better hope he say, yes. He might not want no free men 'round his slaves given 'em ideas."

"Dam you, Jacob, yuh know what Ah be sayin'!" Capers stared Jacob down.

Jacob laughed. "Ah know, but think about it. Talk tuh Ol' Blue. It would be good if y'all spent some time wit' our kind. Yuh can get tuh da Haynes

Plantation through dem woods and across da field. Yuh don't have tuh travel da road. Maybe yuh could start by going tuh church wit' dem."

Juke looked at Capers and they smiled. "Won't it be best if Miles spoke tuh Massa Haynes?" Juke asked.

"Maybe," Jacob said. "Ah be askin' Miles tuhmorrow."

"Thanks, Jacob," Capers said. He and Juke smiled and hope came alive in their eyes.

Ah never saw anyone so eager tuh return tuh a plantation. Ah wish Ah had left dem at The Dillard, Jacob thought. Jacob leaned in from his sitting position and motioned for his brothers to do the same. He continued explaining his plan and assuring his brothers of his safety.

chapter 10

The next afternoon Miles and Jacob rode the carriage over to the Haynes Plantation. Just as they drove up in the front yard, a young, polished, slave boy ran up to Red and grabbed hold to the side of the rein. He wore a black three corner hat, black suit with knickered britches, his white lacy shirt matched his stockings and his large buckled shoes coordinated his total attire. Mr. Haynes stepped out on his front porch carrying a cane carved from teak wood and adorned with a gold tip. A smooth round golden ball was fashioned into a handle. He wore a black suit, black boots, white shirt with a simple collar and cuff. His wide silk breasted tie was held in place by a gold stud that matched his gold studded cufflinks. He reminded Jacob of his father, although opposite in physical appearance, their resemblance was more in temperament and charm. Mr. Haynes was an older man, having a thick frame and round protruding belly. His youthful face was smooth except for a few crow's feet at the corners of his eyes. He was of medium height and slightly bronze from not having shed his summer tan. Jacob was taken by his charming disposition.

The Haynes plantation was smaller than The Dillard, but it was every bit meticulous. Mr. Haynes was courteous. "Come. Sit," he offered. Expecting followers, he began walking to the far end of his porch. "Ah tell yuh, Ah really must take advantage of this lovely day. We don't get many warm days like this in early December." He stopped and shared his attention between Miles and Jacob. "Oh forgive my manners. Ah been going on so, Ah haven't given Mr. Morton here an opportunity for a proper introduction of his companion."

"Yes sir." Miles gave him a head nod. "This is our trusted man, Mr. Jacob Natty."

Jacob looked directly in Mr. Haynes' eyes, nodded and offered his hand.

Mr. Haynes returned the gestures and spoke out, "Yes, yes. Yuh the young man Ah sent Ol' Blue with tuh fetch the field hands."

"Yes sur." Jacob replied.

Ah'm gon' have my tea out here. Please join me," Mr. Haynes said as he glanced at both of the young men before sitting at the small round table.

"Ah thank yuh kindly, sir," Miles responded and gave him an acknowledging nod.

Jacob nodded immediately, "Yes," he said imitating Miles. "Thank yuh, sur." As soon as Mr. Haynes turned, he rubbed his sweating palms against his trousers. *Grete day*, he thought, *white folk sure nod a lot. It's like they be salutin' each other.*

Mr. Haynes slammed his cane against the side of the house and pulled a bright red cord that had a gold colored tassel attached and a loud bell rang off in the distance.

Jacob sat and looked down toward the front yard; the carriage boy was still standing there as still as a statue holding Red's reins. When he turned around a beautiful honey colored Negro woman was hurrying from the side door to their seating area. "Yessum, Massa," her voice was soft and subservient.

"Oh, my darling Annabelle," Mr. Haynes addressed her, not because she was his lover. He addressed all of his female house servants in that manner, believing it softened them and made them to be more trusting. "Take note. We have two more guests for tea."

Annabelle curtsied lightly. "Yessum, Massa," she replied. She gave a sincere smile to all before turning and disappearing through the door.

"My . . . my . . . my . . . Mr. Haynes. She is a beauty," Miles said.

"Yes, she certainly is and she is part of a pair," Mr. Haynes laughed as he spoke because his guests' expressions amused him in their perplexity.

"Ah don't understand?" Miles replied.

Jacob smiled and watched Mr. Haynes' expression; he waited to see what the white men would do or say next.

Mr. Haynes smiled and his right eye twinkled. He leaned into the table and elbowed it. "Well, that beauty is Annabelle," he began, "and she has a twin sister named, Anna Sue. Ah can only tell them apart by the blue or red ribbons they wear in their hair. When she returns notice that she will be wearin' the blue ribbon. Sometimes one of them will take my order and the other will return, but they have strict instructions tuh always wear their proper color ribbons." He sat back in his chair and rubbed the side of his face.

Miles leaned in and spoke excitedly, "Yuh mean yuh have two of them."

"Sho' do!" Mr. Haynes replied. "That family has been slaves on my land for three generations. My great grand-pappy bought hur great grandmother from the traders down in Charleston. Ah've known hur line all my life. Hur mother is my Mrs. Haynes' special handmaiden. She really is family." He seemed to be daydreaming while speaking of their bloodline and he could have gone on about them for hours. He caught himself, cleared his throat and repositioned himself to sit taller in his white wicker armed chair. "What brings yuh fellers tuh my home spread?"

"Well, we have two young hands, free slaves from The Dillard Plantation who work for us," Miles said. "They got papers. These are the two boys, Ol' Blue fetched with Mr. Natty." Miles turned toward Jacob.

"Yes, sur," Jacob began to speak. He took special care to speak in his most proper white man's English. "When it came time for the harvest Ah knew we needed help. Ah knew the fields were no place for Mrs. Morton, so Ah ask the boys tuh leave." He took a deep breath because he knew the lie he told the Mortons was about to beget another lie. "Yuh see, sir, befo' Ah come tuh the Morton's farm, Ah had just been freed of my parents ten year indenture. Some people use tuh say Ah was a mulatto 'cause Ah was forced tuh live in the slave's quarters, but it was a long term indenture. Ah just wanted yuh tuh know that; Ah wanted tuh start out speakin' wit' yuh wit' an honest heart. So Ah do understand if yuh don't wish tuh hear me further."

"Well . . . Mr. Natty, yuh didn't have tuh tell me yuh business, but because yuh did, Ah have tuh ask yuh one question."

"Yes, sur," Jacob responded.

"Are yuh a white man?"

Jacob stared in Mr. Haynes eyes without blinking and wearing a face of stone he answered, "Ah'm as white as Ah could ever be."

Mr. Haynes burst out into a boisterous laugh and slapped both hands down on the lace pattern wrought iron table. "Ah like yuh, Mr. Natty. Yes sirree, Ah sure like you young man. Now, how can Ah help yuh?"

Jacob's stone face graduated to a broad laugh and quickly Miles joined in.

Annabelle stood to the left of Mr. Haynes holding all the fixings for the tea on a large silver tray. Haynes leaned to the side. "Thank yuh, darling," he said. "Ah believe we can fix our own tea."

Annabelle curtsied, took a step backward, before turning to return to the kitchen door. Her steps were so quiet that when Miles turned to look for her, she was gone again. He turned back to face Mr. Haynes and found him smiling broadly.

"She is a quiet one, isn't she?" Haynes commented with a chuckle.

"Yes sir. She's like a whisper," Miles said, reacting with surprise.

Everyone laughed in a gentlemanly fashion before quickly re-establishing their composure.

Miles spoke first saying, "Mr. Haynes, Ah am at a dilemma. Mr. Natty and Blue acquire Juke and Capers Dillard tuh help on the farm. This year we had the highest yield of cotton ever and the hands seemed tuh be very happy with their wages. They have their freedom. They have built their own cabin. They are free tuh find odd work during the off season, but they are unhappy with loneliness. All they want is tuh return tuh The Dillard Plantation. However, sir, word has it that Jackson Dillard will take their freedom away and return them tuh servitude if they do."

Mr. Haynes sat back in his chair and frowned when he heard Jackson Dillard's name. "Loneliness is a powerful emotion," he began. "Walter Dillard was my friend. He told me of his plan tuh free all of his mulatto slaves upon his death." He leaned forward and continued speaking. "He was a kind man. Ah never did take a liken tuh that son of his. He asked tuh court my Cindy and Ah flat out told him, 'No'."

"Sur, may Ah add somethin'?" Jacob asked.

Mr. Haynes nodded.

"Well, sur," Jacob continued, "Them boys may be free, but they are still slaves tuh their fear of freedom. They dare not leave the Morton farm unless they are with a white person. They are afraid tuh walk on the road . . . afraid slave hunters will steal them away and intuh servitude tuh some cruel master."

"How may Ah help?" Haynes asked, "Yuh came here for my help didn't yuh?"

Miles and Jacob glanced at each other and then Miles posed the request. "Sir, Ah wonder if Ah may impose on yuh tuh allow the Dillard boys tuh visit with yuh slaves when they are not engaged in labor?"

Mr. Haynes was quiet for a while. He stared at the untouched teapot and cups. "Let me think on it a while. Let's have our tea before it picks up a chill." He nodded for them to turn over their teacups and prepare to receive the hot teapot to serve themselves. "There are sugar cubes and lemon wedges, but Ah like mine straight and strong," he said.

"Ah'll take the sugar and lemon," Miles said. "Got a bit of a sweet tooth myself."

"Ah'm like you, sur. Ah take my tea straight, just like my coffee," Jacob announced. He held his teacup up saluting Mr. Haynes and Miles before taking a sip.

"Ah ain't much for havin' free colored minglin' with my darkies. But it seems like yuh boy will give a convincin' argument against seekin' freedom. Ah'm offerin' them an invitation tuh visit, but Ah need tuh meet them first. Ah'll be sending Ol' Blue for them in time."

҈

Juke and Capers were as giddy as school children and as nervous as expectant fathers about meeting Mr. Haynes. Jacob had instructed them to address him as Massa Haynes and give to him the same respect they had given Massa Jackson.

"Ah know yuh not tellin' us how tuh be slaves," Capers said.

The three men laughed.

"Yuh right. Ah guess Ah'm more nervous than y'all," Jacob surrendered. He went on to explain his circumstances and the story told to Mr. Haynes about himself. "Y'all gotta burn this lie in yuh heads and tell it the same way each time anybody ask yuh about it. Okay? Right now all Ah can think about is gettin' tuh Sula. If passin' for white will help me do that, then so be it."

"Ah see Blue comin' through the pass!" Juke yelled out. "Wait . . . he's gettin' off the wagon." Juke turned to Jacob and he was still pointing in the direction of the wagon. The wagon driver turned around and returned back through the pass.

All three men began walking toward Blue. Miles came out to the porch and told his mother it was only Ol' Blue coming to fetch Juke and Capers. Evan and Robby stood in the yard with Rusty.

"Hey Blue, what's going on?" Capers called. He ran ahead to meet up with him.

"All be well!" Blue hollered back. He took deep strides and his arms swung in rhythm. It was only minutes before he met up with Capers and they marched on to the Morton's front yard.

Jacob approached. "Good evening, Blue. Are yuh still takin' da men tuh meet Mr. Haynes?" he asked. He stood with his hands in his pockets.

Blue let out a big chuckle. "If all y'all could see yuh faces. Y'all act lak Ah can't walk. Well, Ah be let off 'cause Ah be showin' dese here youngin's how tuh travel tuh the plantation by way of dem woods."

"Da woods?" Capers asked.

"Yessum. Dem woods and cross dat plantin' field. It be more safer and faster dan da road. Dat be why Ah come so early so y'all can learn da way by daylight, but Ah still want yuh tuh tote yuh lamp just fer sure. Now, Ah got my big cane knife, could use a shotgun tuh put down a cougar or bear, but Ah ain't seen none lately." Blue looked in the brothers' eyes and bent over laughing. "Just foolin' yuh boys. Just foolin' yuh." He patted both of their backs at the same time.

Jacob held his head down because he didn't want his brothers to see him laughing. Miles laughed openly while Evan and Robby stood looking at each other with the wide eyes of innocence.

Blue addressed Jacob and Miles. "Ah be leadin' dem back through da woods, but dey gon' find dey way home by huntin' fer dem scraps of rags tied on dem bushes. So now we just gon' need a mess o' rags, two oil lamps and it be mighty good tuh have some large cane knives. Dey be leavin' dem knives by da edge o' da woods. Cain't take it tuh da Massa's house."

Jacob stood before his brothers. "Do yuh want tuh do this? It could still be dark when yuh come back through dem woods." He could see how their nerves were surfacing.

Capers nodded. "Soon dat path we make gon' be wide and clear. Ah just pray Massa Haynes let us visit," he said.

Juke agreed. "Uh . . . Mr. Miles, can we use those big knives in da barn?"

"Sure can and Ah know Mama has some old rags yuh can rip up."

The men freshened up and changed into clean clothes. A few minutes later, Ol' Blue, Juke and Capers entered the woods behind the cabins and disappeared.

Jacob's eyes stayed with them until they were swallowed by the forest. He could hear their knives slashing and cutting away at the undergrowth in their attempt to clear the path long after losing sight of them. His body heaved a gulp of air; he smiled and wondered if he was holding his breath just as he exhaled. *Grete day in da mornin'*, he thought, *loneliness sure be powerful.*

The fireplace warmed the cabin while Jacob tried to read by the remaining daylight from his window. The words were deciphered in his head, but they were just words; his mind was on his brothers. Later, as the sun set and Juke and Capers had still not returned, Jacob became worried and anxious enough that he grabbed his coat and headed off through the woods carrying his lantern. He followed the rag-ties deep into the forest. The daylight was fading faster than his comfort would allow, but just as he was about to strike his flint to light his lantern he heard the jovial laughter of his brothers off in the distance and the heat of his embarrassment flushed his face. He turned and squinted against the fading light to locate the rag-ties and to escape the forest.

He was laughing hard at himself by the time he reached his cabin; so hard he found it difficult to remove his jovial expression. He could only share his brother's happiness privately because he had thought of them as incompetent to find their way home. He was happy because he believed he had finally eased some of the miseries he had levied on them. He sat at his table with his lantern lit, holding his book, waiting and working on hardening his expression of surprise. Time played tricks on him making the wait appear longer than usual, making him hold his composure longer, while he continuously glanced up in anticipation. When the brothers finally arrived they brought with them the loud noise of gladness and Jacob leaped from his seat and was at their side as soon as they had cleared the door.

"It's not The Dillard, Jacob, but it will be so nice tuh be with our people again," Juke swooned.

Capers stood at the side of the table as he spoke. "First, Ol' Blue took us tuh Massa. He met us in the front yard. Said we be welcome tuh come tuh church on Sunday and stay as long as we want if we had an invitation from any of his people tuh visit 'em."

"That be what he say," Juke repeated. "He say so long as we don't cause no trouble we can come tuh visit on Sat'day evening and anytime on Sunday, even to church."

"Now lissen tuh what yuh sayin', cause these be the rules. Haynes said, 'yuh can come tuh church on Sunday, yuh need an invitation tuh visit his people, yuh can visit 'em on Saturday evening and all day Sunday and yuh better not cause no trouble.' Y'all got tuh remember the rules. If yuh see a women yuh take a liken tuh, make sure ain't no one else got eyes for hur cause that be when trouble come. Know when trouble for one of yuh comes, it be trouble for yuh both," Jacob said.

"Ol' Blue and his misses say we be their invite whenever we come," Capers announced.

"We gon' be up at daybreak choppin' back dat forest and paintin' white marks' on da trees. We gon' work on da path every day of da week so it be wide and clear and won't overgrow come spring," Juke announced.

"Well y'all got yuh work cut out for yuh. Ah must say paintin' them trees is a great idea, but yuh got almost two miles of choppin' tuh do before plantin' time."

Capers and Juke both smiled at Jacob as they moved toward the door and then Juke added, "We'll see yuh tuhmorrow, brother."

Chapter 11

The familiar harmonious gospel singing of Rock of Ages had reached Juke and Capers' ears before they cleared the forest. Instead of hurrying along, it held them still as if melting them in their tracks. It was like sopping up the last of the gravy from their mama's chicken and dumplings, then topping it off with that sweet apple pie. When the song ended, they inhaled simultaneously and set out in a steady jog to reach that place where their people had breathed life back into their souls.

Finally, they reached the white washed wooden structure where a cross had been carved through the solid oak door. Everyone that intended to be present for the worship service was already in attendance. There were more slaves on that Sunday morning than usual because of the two free men wishing to unite with them, the people who were forced to remain in bondage.

Juke opened the door and was first to step into the small wood frame structure. He stood to the side, before Capers entered and stood beside him. A coy smile graced their faces and their nervous fingers crumbled and crinkled their caps. The church, the people, the welcoming stares and their excitement were overwhelming and brought tears to their eyes. It wasn't home, but they were home.

The church had twenty benches that served as pews, ten placed on each side of the aisle. There was a makeshift pulpit that stood in front of another set of five benches that were positioned to accommodate the choir. A hush came over the church and all eyes remained on Juke and Capers. Most of the women were seated on the pews and the men had taken their position in the available standing room along the walls.

On the third Sunday of every month, Master Haynes had the white preacher, Pastor Lupper deliver spiritual guidance to his slaves. On all other Sundays, Deacon James was in charge. Without knowledge of the written word he preached the gospel as it was passed down to him with such accuracy, it surprised Master Haynes' preacher. Still, Master Haynes refused him his God-given title as pastor. Simply put, to be pastor was just too powerful for a slave; the title of deacon would just have to do.

Deacon James was dressed in worn bib coverall and a gray long sleeve shirt. He stood behind the lectern and stretched out his arms. "Welcome friends. We been waitin' fer yuh." His broad smile cut through the bush of gray facial hair and broadcasted his spatially toothed mouth. "C'mon up here, young fellers." He walked from behind his lectern and into the aisle.

Juke and Capers grinned like scared children; their eyes were wild with joy as they stepped down the aisle like young chickens.

"Blue . . . c'mon up here and quaint dese here boys wit' us," he said as he nodded in Blue's direction. Deacon James, a tall, thin man, stretched his lanky arms across both Juke and Capers shoulders.

Old Blue moved from his position against the wall with his arms ready to embrace both Juke and Capers at the same time. He smiled and pulled the young men into a bear hug. "So happy tuh have yuh hear wit' us. Yuh be always welcome," he said loudly. He turned and stood next to Juke and addressed the congregation. "Dese here be good men."

The women stood and the men shouted. "Welcome, welcome!" "Here, here!" "We's all brothers here!" A man called out. "Yeah, dat be right," someone else called out.

Juke and Capers smiled and bowed in gratitude toward everyone and then they shifted, grinned and embraced each other.

"Hold on!" A bass-baritone voice vibrated through the church. "What yuh boys really want? Don't no free man want tuh be wit' slaves!"

Deacon James quickly hurried forward. He flung his arm up and pointed at the large husky man in one swift movement. "What be yuh trouble, Rollo?"

Rollo pranced from the back corner wall to the center aisle of the church. "What dey really want, Ah say?" he bellowed again. "Dey got what we all want! Dey be free men! Why dey want tuh be here wit' us slaves?"

Deacon James walked down the aisle until the top of his head was equal to Rollo's shoulder. He stopped. Rollo took two steps backward and stared down at him; his arms drooped limp at his side. Deacon James raised his head and his eyes met with Rollo's eyes.

"We's all done seen dem trees on yuh back. We's all know about yuh missin' big toe. We know how yuh used tuh run for freedom. Dat be 'till yuh come tuh da Haynes. Seem lak now yuh be still. Why dat be, Rollo? Why dat be?"

Rollo's eyes searched the small church. "Massa Haynes . . . he . . . he . . . he be a good massa. Dis place like family tuh me. Don't wanna run no mo'.""

"Yuh ride wit' me tuh town and yuh still don't run. Why dat be?"

"Ah be loved here. Got me family here. Mah people here." Rollo sounded like the wind had been knocked out of him.

Deacon James turned and walked back to the young men while Rollo remained standing down the aisle. "Mah people . . . yuh hear dem things Rollo say. Yeah . . . if we all be free, den we all have each other. But, when just one or two of us be free, den we be alone. Loneliness be a worser prison den slavery. Dese boys been free since April last. Dey work as hard as us, den dey alone da rest of da time. Dey can't walk da road 'cause dey 'fraid da slave hunters gone sell 'em back tuh a worse slavery den dey come from; freedom papers don't mean nothin' in the south. Now, all dey want is da company of dey kind; dey want family and friends."

Rollo raised both of his arms over his head. "Amen Deacon. Fam'ly!" he wolfed out. "Ah understand!"

Everyone stood and applauded. Smiles and hugs were contagious. Capers and Juke were accepted into the fold.

∂∞⌐

Juke and Capers worked on clearing and marking the path for the next six days. Then it was Saturday, Jacob's turn for his journey back to The Dillard. He packed his saddlebags with a four inch carving knife, beef jerky and biscuits and filled his canteen with cool spring water. A thick blanket was folded and then tightly rolled before placing it in the knapsack that Tillie gave him. His small pistol was strapped in place and he wore another gun holstered at his hip in the fashion worn by most white men. He knew he would encounter other folk on the road on a Saturday afternoon, but Old Blue's lessons would finally be put to the test. "Sit tall, command respect and keep yuh business tuh yuhself. Most of da time all yuh gots tuh do is tip yuh hat and say, 'Howdy do,' then keep ridin'." Blue always said, "Look 'em in da eye and don't be bowin' yuh head when yuh talk . . . a gentlemen's nod be all yuh be needin'. And fer da good Lawd's sake, Jacob, don't be a sayin', 'yessum' tuh 'em. If'n dey ask yuh where yuh from? Tell 'em yuh be from Jacksonville, Florida. Ah heard the Morton's got people down dere. If'n dey say where yuh headin'? Tell 'em yuh be headin' tuh Gaffney or yuh be off tuh Columbia. You could tell 'em the truth, but taint none of dey business. Yuh could tell 'em it be none of dey business, but dat be surely a way tuh rile 'em up."

Juke and Capers walked with Jacob up to the main road and double checked his bedroll, food sack and saddle.

Jacob stood back with his hands on his hips and watched his brothers. "Y'all think Ah don't know how tuh fix my stuff?"

"Just yuh be hurryin' back, yuh hear?" Capers murmured.

The brothers had given each other one last group hug before Jacob mounted Red. "Ah'm gon' do my best tuh get back here Sunday before sundown. Y'all have a good weekend." He smiled, kicked his heels into Red's hind quarters and road off in a trot.

ঌৣ৽

Jacob reached Gaffney just after the sun fell below the horizon and while its glow continued to light the sky. The corral came into view and he walked Red to the front of the barn off Main Street where the blacksmith was dousing the blaze under his anvil. Red was tired, hungry, needed water and wiping down.

Jacob walked toward the large dark Negro and before he could speak, the man's deep baritone voice sang out, "She be needin boardin', sur?"

Jacob froze. *Sur?* he thought before saying, "Sho do. Yuh got an empty stall for da night? Will yuh wipe hur down and give hur food and water?" Jacob gave the Negro man a direct look and jerked his head back when he noticed the man's peripheral attention toward him. This was the first time he experienced the Negro/white relationship. He wanted to tell the blacksmith to look him in the eyes like a man, but then he realized he was staring at himself, the slave.

"Yessum," the man replied and he took a slight subservient bow.

As much as he hated the deception, Jacob stood tall and spoke abruptly to the blacksmith, "What's yuh name?" He refused to address the man as, boy.

"Ah be Cole, sur . . . Cole Nelson." The man continued to look away when he spoke to Jacob.

"Well, yuh listen tuh me, Mr. Cole Nelson. Yuh be a free man?" Jacob stood tall with his hands on his hips and smiled.

Cole began a little happy stepping, rocking from side to side. He continued to hold his head down and it bobbed a little up and down. He grinned when he announced quietly, "Yessum . . . Ah be free."

Jacob knew how he felt, he knew he was bursting with wanting to shout, to raising his arms over his head and dance in circles, but he was beating back his joy. His joy was in his heart, his head, his soul and he wasn't going to allow any white man to enslave his spirit and his being again.

"Mr. Nelson, Ah know how yuh feel. Ah hate slavery. All people need tuh be free. Ah am, Jacob Natty."

Cole tilted his head up until his eyes met with Jacob's and nothing else had to be said. They smiled and then Cole took Red's reins and led him to the stall. "Ah'll be taken good care of hur. No charge."

"Yes, Mr. Nelson, there is a charge. A free man works for pay." Jacob unpacked the saddle bags and put the contents in the knapsack. He flipped a quarter across to Cole. "Uh, Mr. Nelson, Ah'll be back tuh fetch my horse in the mornin'. Now, Ah know that's Sunday, will yuh be open?"

"Yessum. Ah'll be here fer yuh."

"Then good evening, man," he said, as he winked and walked off.

The crescent moon did little to light the road from Gaffney and made the path completely unusable. Jacob didn't think to bring a lantern and now he wondered how to make it to The Dillard in the pitch blackness. He slung the knapsack over his shoulder and walked beyond the edge of town and into the darkness of the road. Only seconds had passed before he returned from the abyss. He set his knapsack by the entrance to the road and returned to the stable.

"Mr. Nelson, he called out. He opened the stable door and saw the large Negro appearing from Red's stall.

"Yessum."

"Mr. Natty . . . you can call me, Mr. Natty," Jacob demanded.

Cole stood holding a lantern, his eyes full and fixed and his head nodding.

"Mr. Nelson, do yuh have another lamp Ah might use for the night?"

"Yessum, hear take dissum. Ah'll get da one over dere." He picked up a stem of straw from the barn floor and lifted fire from one lantern to the other.

He smiled when he handed the lantern to Jacob and his smile grew wider when Jacob replied, "thank yuh, man," for the second time before leaving the barn.

"Oh, Mr. Natty," Cole called out, "do yuh got some flint tuh light da lamp later?"

Jacob felt his pockets, before glancing over at Cole. He smiled, knowing he really needed some and shook his head.

Cole had two chunks in his extended hand. "Dese be good when yuh be needin' dem."

"Yuh be a good man, Mr. Nelson." Jacob tipped his hat and was on his way again.

Cole bowed, smiled and then turned to see if anyone was looking or had heard the exchange. He didn't want any trouble later after Mr. Natty's absence. He didn't want folk to say he was getting too uppity or believing he thought he was as good as a white man.

છ∼ન્

The path was safer than the main road and the lantern lit the way only by a few feet. He was a free man passing for white, his whiteness confirmed by his blue eyes. But all his years of living in bondage had oppressed his body and mind. Jacob slung the knapsack over his shoulder and walked on. All the trees, except for the pine were barren. The forest floor rustled and crunched from the noise of dried twigs and dead leaves, but this was a good thing; it was a warning of a traveler on the path or of a large critter. He knew the lantern could only be useful until he reached the slave path, then he would have to hide it along with his knapsack before moving on.

It wasn't long before the lights of The Dillard were visible. While the slave quarters were dark from the rationing of oil, The Dillard mansion had lanterns hanging from the decorative porch brackets on every pillar of the lower level, as well as every pillar on the second level.

"That's good," Jacob whispered to himself, referring to the lights. He knew the brightness at the mansion made everything beyond its glow appear pitch black. He made his way to Mammy Pearl's cabin anticipating warmth, food and comfort. Twice he tapped lightly on the cabin door and each time he waited several seconds before tapping again. He held himself, dancing and shivered against the cold that seemed deeper in his bones while waiting to enter this, his home, the warmest place he remembered. Finally, he opened the door only to find the outside chill more prominent inside. The burnt wood in the fireplace continued to hold its ashen shape under the empty, dusty black kettle. He wanted to call out for Mammy Pearl, but he feared being discovered. He knew only one of two things could have happened; she was dead, or sold off and he prayed for the latter.

The dim light from Miss Ollie and Miss Tillie's cabin flickered in Jacob's face. The door opened and Tillie snatched his arm, quickly pulling him in without uttering a sound. She threw her arms around his neck and hugged him like she had fear in her body. "Oh Jacob! Yuh come. Massa done gone crazy," she whined.

"Where be Mammy Pearl?" Jacob whispered his dialog now more relaxed.

"It be bad, Jacob. Sit. Sit." She pulled the chair away for the table and she sat in another chair. Jacob sat and inhaled the thick cabin air. Tillie continued, her whines turning into mild sobs. "Maynard, he be too old tuh take Massa Moore's place when he go missin', so Massa Jackson hire on three mo' overseers. Dey don't know Juke and Capers, so dey don't know dey gone."

"Massa Moore be missin'?" Jacob bent over to face Tillie directly and expressing his surprise.

Tillie dabbed her eyes with her face rag before saying, "He be missin' right near time yuh left wit' Juke and Capers. Ain't been seen since dat time." She shifted her eyes up and back at Jacob.

"Miss Tillie, why yuh put yuh eyes on me like dat?"

"It just be da timin', tis all."

Jacob shook his head saying, "Where be Mammy Pearl?" His eyes scanned the small cabin and fell upon a burlap drape. "Where be Miss Ollie? Sula be sleep?" He stood, reached and pulled back the curtain. "Where be Sula? Why Simon and Jenny here wit' you?"

"Oh Jacob . . . so much done happened. Yuh need tuh come back and sit." Tillie stopped talking to Jacob and turned to the children. "Take da ash-pail and scoop out dem ember. Take it up tuh Pearl's cabin and make a fire. Der be covers and wood up dere. Y'all stay dere tuhnight; Jacob gone be here wit' me. Go-on, get goin'," Tillie waved her arm at them. "Y'all done ete supper; now, take dese here cakes wit' yuh." She watched them leave the cabin and then she turned and eased herself back into the chair next to Jacob. "Ah be talkin' tuh yuh now."

Jacob returned to his chair. He was frightened and confused. He didn't know what Tillie was going to tell him, but he knew it wasn't going to be good news. Tillie had so much to say she decided to give him the light news first, because she knew when she gave him the heaviest information, he wouldn't hear anything else.

"Ah been carin' for Jenny and Simon, but dey can really take care of deyself. Dey mama died dis September. Be snake bite dat take hur. It be right down dere by da river. Lucy Mae and da chillen be tryin' tuh stay far away from dat Jimbo as possible tuh find some peace. Chillen say dey all be sittin' on da grass and Lucy Mae pushed her foot against dis here rock. Dat be when she get snake bit by that lil rattler. Simon push the snake away wit' a long stick, den smash da head of dat snake, but Lucy May, she died quicker den when she be born and da po' chillen seed it all," Tillie said her words quickly, closed her eyes to hold back her tears and she squeezed Jacob's hands.

Jacob had so many questions; he knew he would allow Tillie to continue telling him about Lucy Mae. He knew she would tell him everything. He rubbed the back of her hands and nodded his head. "Tell me mo', Miss Tillie. Ah be here . . . talk tuh me. Tell me everythin'." His voice was soft and his appearance forlorn.

Tillie used her rag to dab away the sadness collecting in her eyes. There was so much to tell Jacob, so she continued. "We buried her down yonder wit' all our folk. Oh Jacob ... it be a mighty sad time. She be so young. She died so fast da fear of hur sufferin' stay burnt on hur face. Da chillen . . . dey cry and carry on so, it breaks my heart, but dat Jimbo, he just smile. He snatch dem juju bags from dem chillen's neck, but befo' he get hol' of dem chillen, dey run off tuh Pearl's place. We tell Jimbo he be conjur'n' fer sure if'n he come 'round us." Tillie bent over laughing, but her tears flung from her face like rain drops and escaped her cloth. She looked across at Jacob. "Boy . . . yuh know yuh Mammy Pearl . . . she hold out hur hand and blow dat cold fire-ash in Jimbo's face and tell 'em he be blind till she say 'it be done' and Jimbo turn and run into da side of the cabin. Dat ash be stingin' his eyes real bad, but Pearl, she know his tears gon' wash away da fire-ash, so she yell out,

'It be done!' real loud. Jimbo start yellin', 'I ain't blind! Ah ain't blind!' Now Jimbo hide or be running when he see us be near."

Jacob chuckled lightly because he needed to laugh. He was worried because of what Tillie had not said and Tillie worried because of what remained to be said. She chuckled lightly along with Jacob and read his pleading eyes before she continued. "Everybody thinks our juju don' Massa Dillard in, but we ain't got no juju. Ah take da chillen tuh Jimbo's cabin when he be gon' and dey get dey freedom papers and dey clothes." She placed her hand on Jacob's arm and took a deep breath. She closed her eyes and her lips turn into a clenched frown. "Da chillen, dey be stayin' wit' Pearl. But she be gone now."

Jacob stared at her; Miss Tillie had slipped bad news in with the information about the children The situation and circumstances were clear. "Please tell me what happened, Miss Tillie?"

Tillie murmured, "White folk been actin' and talkin' crazy; been talkin' bout dat new president from up north and dat dey gone have a war. It be makin' dem meaner den hell. Things 'round here be real bad. Our days be longer and our food amount be shorter. Ah be gettin' mo' cause Ah work in da kitchen. And, oh, da whippings, Jacob! And dem new overseers be taken da young gals and beatin' our folk. Dey stripped folk naked, den beat 'em and den tied 'em tuh da trees out in da cold all night and dey be mo' dat dey do too. Da bad things dey been doing, Ah ain't see since befo' Ah come here when Ah be little. Massa Jackson don't nevah be here. Massa Maynard s'pose tuh be head man, but he cain't stop dem new overseers. It be real bad, Jacob."

"Ah been hearin da talk, but where be Sula?" Jacob asked.

"He be crazy, dat Massa Jackson. Dey gone. Dey all sold." Tillie grabbed Jacob's hand and held it tight. "He sell Pearl and Ollie and Sula."

"Sold!" Jacob's eyes bulged wide when the word passed his lips. He tried to pull his hand from Tillie's hand, but she held tight. "Massa Jackson never sold a slave. My Daddy never sold a slave."

"Massa Jackson be yuh half-brother, not yuh daddy!" Tillie reminded him, "and . . . Ah 'member one slave he sold." Tillie sucked up her tears and her strength returned.

Jacob managed to free his hands from Tillie's and tried to stand, but he slumped back into the straw bottom chair. His arms wrapped before him protecting his head from the course table. "Oh Lawd!" he cried out, "why'd yuh make 'em tuh hurt us? Yuh be da Massa. Why dey be da massa over us? Why can't we be free?" He sobbed until he felt empty, weary, exhausted and his defenses were down. He feared for the only mother he had ever known, he feared for Sula, the only woman he ever loved. He lifted his head and his eyes were still filled with tears while the veil of helplessness weakened him. Slumping deeper into the straw bottom chair and resting his head on the table seemed to be his only refuge.

Tillie stared at him, nervously nibbling at her bottom lip and wringing her hand. "Ah got mo' tuh tell yuh." She sat next to him and held his hand. "Honey, Sula be four months along wit' yuh chile."

His eyes saw Tillie's lips move and he heard the words she spoke, but he had to hear them from his own lips. "Sula be wit' my chile?" he whispered before leaping from the chair and waiting for confirmation of the words he had just spoken.

Tillie nodded and nervously hugged herself. "Whut yuh be up tuh, Jacob?"

"Ah don' know, but Ah'm gon' do somethin' tuh get my family back." Tears filled his eyes and at the same time hunger was robbing his strength. He cried out, "Do yuh know who got Mama and Sula?"

"And Ollie," Tillie added, "don't yuh be leavin' out my Ollie. She be mah family, too."

"Yes, Ollie too," Jacob surrendered.

"Wiley be told to drive Maynard wit' dem to Jonesville. He say da massa from the Bell Farm down dere took 'em."

"So da sale be arranged? Jackson didn't put 'em on da block?"

"Maybe so, maybe not. Dey been gone 'bout a week," Tillie murmured.

"Den, Ah be needin' tuh talk tuh Wiley." Jacob took a deep breath and a sternness covered his face, "Ah be gettin' dem back," he said. "Got me a plan for tuhnight and yuh don't know nothin' 'bout me being here and make sure dem chillen don't be talkin' non' too. Yuh be needin' tuh go tell da chillen dey ain't see me here." He pointed to the two biscuits wrapped in a cloth in a bread basket.

Tillie stood, almost frozen as she absorbed his words, then she nodded before saying, "Mah Lawd, where be mah manners. Let me fix yuh somethin' while Ah be tellin' yuh all Ah know." She reached for a small side of smoked pork in the press, cut off slices to place in her flat pan and set it on the fire grate. "Me and Ollie," she began. She took a deep breath, wiped her eyes with the back of her wrist and continued, "Yeah and Pearl and Sula, we be workin' in da kitchen when Massa Jackson come in. He see Sula's swollen belly and commence tuh yellin'. Massa say dat's Jacob's baby, but Sula, she don't tell da Massa who da baby's pap be." Tillie scooped stew into a wooded bowl, placed the pork and biscuits into a wooden plate and handed Jacob a spoon. "Boy eat. Ah get yuh some tea tuh calm yuhself. It be made from chamomile blossoms, blackberry leaves and rose petals."

Jacob began to eat and listen to Tillie. He already had a plan and any information she had would be helpful.

"Yessum, chile . . . Massa be hot like hell's fire; he be mad cause he ain't da one tuh pick hur mate. He say she be too uppity. Ah be sure he knowed it be your'n, but Sula don't say. He be mad 'cause yuh left The Dillard. He sell Pearl 'cause he knowed she be like yuh mama. He sell Ollie 'cause he think she be Sula's mama. He leave me here wit' no family and a lonely pain deep in my bones, 'cept Ah got da chillen now." Tillie's sorrow froze her in a trance staring into the flickering fire. A crackling spark snapped her to attention and she turned glancing up at Jacob's staring eyes. "Go on now, yuh keep a eatin' 'cause yuh be thinkin' better on a full belly," she ordered.

"Yessum," Jacob replied. He leaned over his plate, holding a large wooden spoon in his right hand and wiping tears and mucus from his face with the back of his sleeve.

"Den there was dem boys."

"What did Massa say when he found Juke and Capers gone?"

Tillie shook her head and weariness seemed to pull her back into the chair. "Oh chile, Lawdy, Lawdy! Took near three moons 'fore he find dat out. He be madder den a wet cat. He give deir daddies' fifty lashes wit' the cat-o-nine-tales. He say dey shoulda told when dey be gone. Massa say, dey not dey real daddies, so dey shoulda told. Now, don't yuh go tellin' dem boys dat. Some things best left unsaid, yuh hear?" Tillie checked Jacob's expressions for confirmation.

A nod of his head and a deep breath was all Jacob could do to communicate his intention. He felt responsible for everything that had happened. It all started because he came back, but he was going to make it right, or brother Jackson was going to regret living.

Confirmation received, Tillie continued, "Chile, Massa Jackson be so mad 'cause dem new overseers don' know nothin' 'bout his slaves dat he made us all come tuh da yard. Den he made da free chillen go tuh da side and he counted twenty three slaves. Dat be when he knowed Juke and Capers be gone. Juke's pappy say dey run off two weeks earlier. Dem boys be free and Massa Walter Dillard be their real pappy, but Massa Jackson say he ain't got no free slaves on The Dillard Plantation. He say ain't nobody free no mo', but he don't take the papers back. Ah got the chillen's papers, but dey ain't no good now."

Jacob stopped eating again and raised his head. "He can't do dat. Dey freedom is written in da lawyer's book and recorded at da courthouse. All da freed slaves still be free. It be so written in da law book. Ah truly hope dey don't destroy their papers. Tell 'em Miss Tillie . . . tell 'em dey freedom is recorded in the courthouse record book and Jackson can't take it away. Tell 'em tuh keep dey papers safe."

"How yuh know dat?" Tillie questioned.

"Ah saw the lawyers write it in the law book."

"Yuh cain't read!" Tillie said angrily.

"Dat's where yuh wrong. Massa Dillard be teachin' me when Ah be little and be with him all da time. Ah just pretended Ah can't read 'cause Massa say a slave ain't suppose tuh read. Ah let da lawyer think he be teachin' me my name and da word, 'free' when he write it in his law book just tuh make him think he be doin' somethin'. People talk more when dey b'lieve yuh don't know what dey be talkin' 'bout. He said all records are in his legal book. Da freedom paper he give us with da red wax on it be our copy. Another copy with dat wax be at da county courthouse, too," Jacob explained. "Dat be why Jackson can't really take dem papers back. He be trickin' dem chillen."

Tillie smiled. "Yuh tellin' me dem babies still free?"

Jacob smiled, "Yes ma'am. Da lawyer's name be Samuel Wilson and he be in da town of Gaffney. He got a record of dem papers, but Ah don't know how much good it be to da chillen. Da law gone always side wit' da white man. And yes, Ah can read most anythin' now, Miss Tillie and cipher numbers, too. Juke and Capers be learnin', too. Yuh just tell 'em dey still free." He pushed the chair back and stood. "Ah'm gon' do somethin' now. Yuh may see me soon, Ah don' know. Ah be workin' my plan tuh get my family. Ah just need tuh know one thing. Who be in da mansion at night?"

"Just Massa Jackson. Da house workers come in at four in da mornin' and be gone when Massa leave or after he bed down. Maynard and dem new overseers and dey families got da apartment in da back of da house near da kitchen and dere be one who stay in a room near da pantry." She stood, met Jacob's eyes sternly and continued with her response. "Massa Jackson gots his daddy's apartment upstairs in the front of da house." She shifted her stance, turned and sucked in her breath when she realized Jacob was about to be daring. "Whut yuh gon' do, Jacob?" she uttered.

"Yuh don't know nothin', so don't ask." He kissed Tillie and slipped from the cabin.

chapter 12

A dim light flickered in Wiley's cabin so Jacob used a stick to tap on his door. The black man with silver hair and broad features pulled his door open. When he recognized Jacob, he quickly snatched him inside his cabin by his shirt sleeve. He took a quick search of the surrounding darkness before closing the door. "Good tuh see yuh, boy," he said, his voice hushed.

"Good tuh see yuh, too, Wiley."

"How'd yuh know tuh come?" Wiley asked.

"Ah didn't know, Ah just came tuh visit. Ah just found out. Can yuh tell me how tuh get tuh the place where yuh took 'em?"

"Sho-nuff. But whut yuh gone do?" Wiley stared unblinkingly at Jacob.

"Well, Ah been working hard and da harvest paid real good. Ah can't get 'em all, but maybe Ah can buy Sula's freedom. At least Mammy Pearl and Miss Ollie will be together 'til Ah can get them."

"Dat Jackson . . . he sol' all dem fer six hund'ed dollars. It be lak he givin' 'em away. Ah be makin' yuh a map da best Ah can. When yuh get tuh Jonesville, yuh ask fer da Bell Farm."

Jacob watched as Wiley used the hot fire poker to burn a map on a piece of burlap potato sack. It came to Jacob that he passed the crossroad that led to the small area called Jonesville when he travel from Gaffney to the Morton's place outside of Clinton.

He hugged Wiley, thanking him. "Jackson gone pay for hurtin' us. Yuh don't know nothin'. You ain't see me, ever."

"Whut yuh gone do, Jacob?"

"Yuh ain't see me! Hear?" He gave Wiley another hug and disappeared into the night.

Jacob stayed in the shadows until he reached the barn. He pulled at the large barn door, opening it just enough to slip inside, and then closing. After checking each stall for Jackson's horse, he left through the corral area, securing the rear barn door before climbing between the fencing. Jackson was known to spend his Saturday evenings in Gaffney and Jacob had to be sure his horse was not in the barn or corral before entering the house.

The exterior of the mansion glowed from the lanterns hanging from the ornamental beams and they removed most of the shadows Jacob needed for cloaking. Scaling the post to the balcony in the rear of the mansion was risky, but revenge was a strong motive. Knowing if he were not successful it would be his undoing. He had some money, but he knew where he could find more. If Jackson was anything like their father, he kept a large sum in his apartment. Jacob knew if he were lucky it would be in the same wooden box their father used. Old man Dillard always made it clear in his boisterous tone, "Only my personal servants come into my apartment and they don't dare steal from me. For if one dollar goes missing, Ah will not spare the lives of any of them." Old man Dillard never loss a dollar. Jacob knew about his money box because he was his father's oldest and favorite mulatto son and he was the only one to spend private time with him.

Jacob crawled along the balcony floor and entered the nearest window without being notice. The large house was quiet and he made his way to Jackson's apartment by way of the lantern beams that illuminated through the windows of the mansion. He peered over the interior terrace and crouched down to the floor after seeing shadows of whites and Negroes moving about on the lower level. A warning, he thought and he moved against the back wall, crawling until he reached Jackson's apartment. He lay on his belly and slithered back to the railing to peek over and make sure no one was in the rotunda that might see Jackson's door opening. Feeling safe, he slithered back and made his way into Jackson's quarters and began searching for the box. He searched under the bed, in the wardrobe, in his bureau and under the bay window seat. There it was, the box filled with thousands of dollar in gold coins and $3510.00 in paper money. Jacob removed his neckerchief and spread it open on the floor. Three times he snatched up a handful of gold coins and placed them in the center of the cloth, before tying the neckerchief in a tight knot and shoving it in his trouser pocket. He left a heap of gold coins in the box because he knew it would melt into a clump and Jackson wouldn't know how much was missing. He could hear their father bragging as he counted his money, "Gold, my boy! Gold is always more valuable than that paper stuff. Keep yuh gold safe and yuh never be poor!" He patted the large bulge of gold coins in his right pocket and the roll of paper money in his left pocket. Then he began ripping pages from a nearby book; tearing them to resemble the monetary thievery and placing them in the box. He needed to cover the theft so no slave would be punished for his crime.

Jacob's plan was suddenly clear when he looked out of the window at the lantern hanging on the decorative brackets of the support beam. It pitched and swung lively, its oil gushing against the glass container well from the force of the gusty wind. He first reached for the lantern sitting on the end table and poured its oil over the paper and gold in the box and all around the window seat. He closed the window box and threw the remainder of the oil across the room. Remembering the flint rocks in his pockets, he struck them together, generating sparks that ultimately ignited a blaze across the floor. Jacob quickly opened the second window in the apartment and climbed down from the room. With haste, he pulled down the balcony lantern and flung it back through the window. Jackson's suite went up in an explosive blaze. Then Jacob ran to the back of the mansion and escaped into the forest. When he turned back to look, the front top half of the mansion was up in flames. The loud voices of the slaves mingled with that of the whites in their efforts to establish water lines. Jacob smiled knowing it would be difficult getting water up to the second floor; he knew Jackson's apartment would certainly be destroyed.

The gusty wind spread the fire across the front of the mansion and then Jacob believed the good Lord said enough and sent a down pouring rain before the fire burned the pillar on the balcony where the broken bracket could give a clear understanding of how the fire might have started.

Jacob remained in Tillie's cabin while the mansion burned. It was too early to return to Gaffney, too cold and wet to sleep in the woods and he wanted Tillie to tell him the words spoken about his deed. Hours slipped away and he hid in the shadow behind the drape that once provided privacy to Sula. Tillie returned to the cabin and lit her lantern.

"Miss. Tillie," Jacob whispered. He had peeked from his space before speaking, but waited for her response before slightly holding back the drape.

Tillie held her lantern high and slowly moved it in front of her. "Where yuh be, Jacob?" She was soft spoken as she moved into the center of the cabin. She set the lantern on the table and lowered the flame, dimming the cabin's light. "Come out, chile."

"Ma'am, yuh know how our people will burst through doors 'cause there be a little excitement," Jacob whispered. "Well, there sure be a lot this night. Can yuh come back here and tell me what happened?"

Tillie left the lantern on the table and walked behind the drape where in an even fainter light she saw Jacob sitting on the floor propped against the corner walls.

"Boy, why ain't yuh sittin' on da bed?"

"No, that's for you. Can yuh tell me what's goin' on out there?"

"Did yuh do dat, Jacob?" She leaned down into his space and whispered.

"Never mind. Can yuh tell me whut happened?"

"Don't yuh know?"

"Ah know there be a fire. Ah don't know how much of da house be burnt or if it be put out."

Tillie sat back on the bed, bewildered; her arms folded across her chest and her head tilted downward so Jacob might catch the fix of her eyes. "Da fire be mostly out. Ah be so tired, Ah be 'bout tuh drop. Ah ain't no use dead. Ah be slowin' down da waterline, so Ah had tuh move and go sit on da ground. Ah watched da front of da top of da house burn. Ain't nothin left up dere, but da porch and da pillars." Tillie hugged and rocked herself as she spoke. "All da lanterns, dey blowed up. Ol' Wiley hear dat overseer say da bracket brake and da lantern fall and start da fire."

"Was Jackson there?"

"Yuh mean Massa Jackson?"

"Ah mean, Jackson. He ain't my massa. He be yuh massa. Was he there?"

"Yessum," Tillie responded while nodding her head. "He be screamin' 'bout puttin' da fire out. Massa . . . he come ridin' up and Wiley be tryin' tuh hold his horse when da explosion sound. The wind be blowin' up a mess. Dead branches be flyin' and a lantern near da right corner of da mansion blowed down. Thanks da Lawd dat lantern only make a little fire, it be out of oil or all da house be gone."

"Thanks be tuh You, Lawd. Yuh made a way when Ah didn't know there be one," Jacob prayed, "Amen!" Jacob didn't care about the house. He only cared that Jackson might blame a slave for the fire and he might be the cause for someone else's misery.

Tillie stared at Jacob, "What yuh prayin' fer?"

"For y'all, if da Lawd don't step in, Jackson gonna say a slave started da fire."

Tillie reached over and kissed Jacob on the forehead. "Ah love yuh, chile."

"Ah love yuh, too, Miss Tillie. But with all da craziness 'round here, Ah better be leavin' at first light. Ah have a horse at da stable in Gaffney. And anyway, Ah promise Juke and Capers Ah'll be back by high noon on Sunday. Are yuh all right?"

"Shucks chile, Ah be da head cook now dat he don' sold off Pearl and Ollie. Ah be fine. Yuh get yuh some rest now. Yuh only gots a 'lil time. Sleep here in Sula's bed." Tillie stood and patted the cot like bed before wrapping her arms around Jacob.

That night Jacob slept in a twilight. Before first light he wrapped a blanket over his head, then hiding in the thickets, he made his way close enough to get a good view of the mansion. His flesh crawled at his first look. He felt the palpitation of his heart from his chest to his chin and tingle down his arms. *Ah wonder if Jackson has enough money to repair the mansion without sellin' any slaves. Oh Lawd, let no other suffer from my doing. Please Lawd.* He turned and slipped back to Tillie's cabin.

"Boy, Ah thought yuh be gone. It be time fer me tuh get tuh da kitchen." Tillie gave Jacob another hug and they left out together.

Tillie stood in her door and watched Jacob run behind the cabins and disappear into the forest.

Chapter 13

The road between the quarters and the mansion had become mud slick from the runoff of the waterline. Tillie strutted up the cold, soggy road with her feet wrapped in strips of burlap cloth and she carried her precious rundown shoes in her arms. As soon as she reached the well, she cleaned her feet, re-wrapped them in a softer fabric and slipped them into her shoes. Looking up, she saw the mansion in the light of the early dawn and it caused her legs to weaken. She stumbled backward and leaned against the aged magnolia tree. The entire second floor on the right front side of the mansion was gone. It reminded her of a hollowed out decayed tooth that had to be yanked from the sufferer's head to relieve the pain. "Oh Lawdy," she mewed, "whut kind o' pain Massa be feelin'? Whut slave gon' bear dis pain tuh make 'em be better?" She held her breath and exhaled slowly before continuing with a solemn walk behind the mansion to the kitchen. With all she had seen it didn't surprise her that the kitchen held the scent of charred wood. She propped the door open and hurried to push the two swing hinged windows aside. Her eyes closed when a gust of wind blew the curtains into her face. Wondering where the other kitchen slaves were, she told herself they would be along. Suddenly she remembered seeing them on the bucket-line the night before. She lit the lantern on the large table and turned to reach for the water buckets, but they weren't on the bench near the door. *Dey be used fer da fire. Ah'll fetch 'em shortly,* she thought. For a moment, she stood frozen at the water bench; all she knew had changed. She stepped backward until she felt the edge of the table. Her trembling hand felt for the chair and tears welled in her eyes. "Oh Lawdy, oh Lawdy . . . why did dis happen?" She sobbed and mumbled incoherently. Her body vibrated with fears of what would come next. "Oh Lawd, settle dis place and make it lak new again. Ah be da last tuh question why, but please Lawd, heal dis land!" She rested her head in her hands and softly wailed.

Jackson sat quietly on the floor, in the dark corner of the kitchen, in the shadow, in a place where Tillie would never expect him to be. He wasn't there to spy on her, but to be alone, to gather himself, to cry for his loss. His sadness was overbearing. He was asleep until Tillie came in. He had almost loss the mansion that had been in his family for more than a hundred and fifty years. The fire wasn't completely out until after three that morning. A quarter of the second floor was gone and the first floor was water drenched. The rain helped to bring the fire under control, but it was the several bucket-lines that put it out completely. He wondered why Tillie cried for his home, she was just a slave. What did it matter to her? She didn't lose anything; she didn't own anything to lose.

Tillie sat up and used her apron to wipe her face. She remained at the table casting a blank stare between the cupboard and corner of the wall and into the same shadowed area where Jackson was resting.

Slowly, Jackson stood and stepped out of the shadow.

Tillie leaped from her chair and this time she wiped her face with her hand. She bowed three times and with each bow she took a step backward. "Ah's sorry, Massa! Ah's sorry! Ah's sorry!" she whined, but it was more than sorrow; she was apologizing; she was afraid.

Jackson stood staring, puzzled by her actions. "Whut yuh so sorry for? This ain't yuh house." His tone was soft and sad, nothing like the angry man he had turned into since his father's death.

Tillie lowered her head in a submissive posture and was careful not to make eye contact him. "Yessum, Massa Jackson," she whined, twisting her apron as she spoke. "Dis be da only home Ah know. Ah be here fifty six years dis spring."

"Ah know who you are, Tillie. How old are yuh?"

"Ah be told, sixty one, Massa." Tear fell against her cheeks again and she continued twisting her apron.

"Ah understand why yuh so sad," Jackson said. He sat down at the table and pointed to the empty chair. "Sit," he made a special effort to make a request and his eyes lowered to the waiting chair.

Tillie's legs bent to sit in the chair then straightened up while her hands trembled and bounced off the table. She tried to sit a second time only with the same reaction. She held the table and gave Jackson an apologetic glance. She never sat at the same table with a master and her body didn't know how to behave.

Jackson understood fear was the cause of her confusion. "It's okay. Ah'm not gonna hurt yuh. Ah just need tuh ask yuh somethin'. So sit!" He said it to her as an order to be obeyed, knowing that would make it easier for her to be compliant.

Tillie maintained her submissive posture and sat in the chair. Jackson smiled.

"If yuh were free tuhday where would yuh go?" Jackson looked directly at Tillie to see her reaction when she answered his question.

"Nowhere, Massa. Ah ain't got nowhere tuh go!"

"Why Tillie, why would yuh want tuh be a slave?"

"Ah don't want tuh be no slave, Massa. Ah want tuh be free, but Ah be wantin' tuh stay at da only home Ah know. If Ah be free, Ah cain't be sold off."

Jackson sat back in his chair and interlocked his fingers behind his head. "What about yuh family?"

"Ah ain't got no husband; he died some years back and no chillen ever come. All Ah had left was Pearl and Ollie. Yuh grand-pappy bring us here tuhgether, we be just 'lil chillens." She stopped talking and curled her lips inward because she knew she was talking too much.

Jackson stared at her, "Yuh have more tuh say?" he asked.

"Yessum." She nodded and positioned her head so as to attend to Jackson through her peripheral vision. "Yessum Massa," she said again, "Ah b'lieve Pearl and Ollie be my sisters, my real family. But, dey gon' now." Tillie was a strong woman, but she couldn't hold back her tears even if it meant being punished. Her tears dropped to the table and fear held her too still to wipe them away, so she let them lay.

Jackson sat forward and covered his face with his hands. He was tired and weary. A twinge of remorse caused him to shiver. He spent the early morning hours sitting in the shadow of his kitchen wondering what was happening to him. He had been raised by a good man to be a good master. His father never had a problem with the slaves or had major damage to the plantation. He was a prosperous man, turning a substantial profit every year. His father only sold one slave in his lifetime.

It had been different for Jackson. He had revoked granted freedoms, beat slaves and sold three slaves in less than a year of being their master. He believed a lantern system that had lit the mansion for years suddenly caused enormous damage. And he continued to wonder why Danny Moore ran off when he, his wife and children needed him so desperately. He removed his hands from his face and folded them on the table. "Tell me something, Tillie," he said. "What is yuh greatest fear right now?"

Tillie dared to stare quizzically at Jackson. Bravely, she wiped her tears with the corner of her apron and strengthened the tone of her voice, but she maintained her submissive posture. "Yuh be selling slaves tuh get da money tuh rebuild da house." She lowered her head.

Jackson laughed out loud. "Is that what yuh think?"

Tillie nodded.

"Look at me, Tillie," Jackson order. "Ah'm tellin' yuh tuh look me in my face. It's just you and me here, so hold yuh head up."

Tillie eased her head up and her eyes searched the room before settling on Jackson. "Yessum," she whispered.

"Ah'm a very rich man. Ah'm not gonna sell anyone."

The submissive posture returned, "Thank yuh, Massa," Tillie said. "Massa Jackson, kin Ah speak 'bout my family?"

"What do yuh have tuh say?"

"Will Ah ever see my sisters again?"

"It's possible, Tillie, but Ah'm not gonna speak on that now."

"Yessum," Tillie whined. Even more sadness filled the cavity of her heart with his empty words.

"Yuh may get tuh yuh work now, Tillie." He waved his hand shooing her away from her seat at the table.

Tillie's tears ran down her face as she stood and reached for the pail to shovel the ashes from the stove.

Pauly, the curly-headed mulatto house boy ran into the kitchen followed by a cold burst of unwelcomed air. Worried that he was late on such a traumatic morning, he cried out, "Sorry Massa! Dere be somethin' Ah can do fer yuh?"

"Stop yuh whining boy and go saddle my horse."

"Massa . . . Ah's a house boy. Ah don' know how tuh do dat!" the boy whined. He watched Jackson walk out into the front yard.

"Time yuh learned, Pauly. Wiley gon' he'p yuh," Tillie whispered. She wiped her face on her apron, before placing her hands on his shoulders and nodding. "Just go, Pauly, he be he'ping yuh, den wait wit' da horse 'round front," she whispered. She guided him out the door and returned to making the stove fire.

Jackson returned to the kitchen with two buckets of water and set both on the water bench. Tillie stood in amazement. "Massa . . . dat be mah work. Ah be just gettin' da stove fire goin'." She went running across the kitchen with the tea kettle.

"Ah know Tillie. Ah could ring the bell and have all the folk up and workin, but they did save the mansion, didn't they? Ah can bring two buckets of water this mornin'." He stood at the door with his hands on his hips. "Ah need some of yuh calmin' tea and finger cakes," he asked in an unusually kind voice before turning to use the water ladle to dip water into a wash basin which he placed on the stove to warm. A few minutes later he was using his hands to wash the ash from his face and he was sitting down to his tea and finger cakes.

Suddenly he left the table without a word to Tillie. Pauly had been standing in the front yard holding tight to the reins of his horse when Jackson mounted him and rode away, again without uttering a word.

All of Jackson's clothes at The Dillard had been destroyed, but he had a complete outfit at Luanne's brothel. That early December morning was cold and damp; he was cold and his skin felt clammy, his clothes were still damp and gritty with soot. He wanted a bath, fresh clothes and he needed to wash away his misery and sadness. The only cash he had was in his pocket; the cash in his apartment had gone up in flame, but the gold had melted and then hardened into a heap. He told himself he would have his banker replace the value equal to its weight.

It was Sunday and the mercantile was closed, but in light of the situation he knew he could convince Lemon Oliver to give him a private session for personal items. A new wardrobe, building supplies and the employment of contractors to rebuild the mansion were the main reasons to make the journey to Columbia. He planned to leave early Monday morning and it would be a pressing three day round trip railroad excursion, including a full day strictly for business.

He rode his horse hard, punishing it for his frustration and loss. Plumes of mist burst from his nostrils like its lungs were on fire, all while its coarse black mane danced on the wind's current; still the stallion continues to obey its master's grueling pace. Jackson leaned forward and dug his heels in the horse's hind quarters and rode like he had to be in Gaffney for a specific time or reason.

chapter 14

Jacob had just entered the stable when Jackson rode up. As Cole Nelson stepped from the large livery stable doors, Jacob slipped back into Red's stall and remained out of sight, but not before Jackson caught a glimpse of him.

"Hey boy!" Jackson called out. "Take care of my horse!" He leaped off the stallion and left the reins hanging as he stood in the stable entry and stared at the stall. "Ah'll be damned!" his agitated voice sang out. "Did Ah see a white man in that stall?"

Cole hurried to capture the reins of Jackson's horse before the stallion spooked. "Cain't rightly say, sur."

"Hump!" he grunted and pushed passed Cole, walking off towards the brothel.

The stallion panted and whinnied; its muscles quivered and released pearls of perspiration. It reared up, shook its head, stood on all four again and its damp skin continued to shiver. "Okay, boy. Ah'ma gonna cool yuh down. Ah see yuh had a bad time," Cole whispered, soothing him with his touch.

The stallion blew mist from his nostrils like a bull and in an agitated state he pranced with high steps. Cole led him back to the corral and then he walked and talked to the horse until he stopped panting. Jacob remained in the stall with Red and watched until Cole returned the horse to the stable. They walked into the stall nearest the stove where Cole began to wipe the moisture from the stallion's hide before covering him with a thick blanket.

Jacob approached Cole. "Yuh a good man, Mr. Nelson. Thank yuh for tellin' that man yuh didn't see me. Ah don't want no one tuh know Ah was in town."

Cole took a submissive stance and nodded his head. "Yessum," he mumbled.

Jacob lifted his hat and ran his fingers through his hair. "Mr. Nelson," he began, "yuh wouldn't know where Ah could buy a good horse and saddle?"

"Well, da boss man done won a quarter horse . . . a mare in a poker game a few nights back. She come wit' a buck wagon and rig and be 'bout five years strong. Ah recon she be a good ridin' horse and fast, too. He say he sell da lot fer seventy five dollars. She be dat gal rite dere." Cole pointed to the horse in the next stall from Red.

Jacob removed the horse from the stall and walked her out to the corral where he could see her in the early morning light. "Ah need the buck wagon, but Ah'll be needin' a saddle, too."

"Ah gots me an old saddle Ah could sell yuh. Yuh jes give me whut yuh want. All da straps and stirrups be good."

"How's five dollars?"

"Dat's a lot, sur."

"It be a deal if the horse is good . . . five dollars." After riding the mare around the corral, Jacob was satisfied. He walked back into the stable counting out all the money as he approached Cole. "Mr. Nelson," he called out, "Ah'll be takin' that mare, but Ah need a bill of sale. Don't want it bein' said Ah stole hur."

Cole's eyes brightened. "Ah got dat. Boss man, he made da sale note. Said don't sell dat horse and rig fer less." He reached in a tin box and handed Jacob the only piece of paper in it.

It was a simple note and read like a proper receipt.

☙❧

Bill of Sale
Gaffney Blacksmith and Livery Stable
Gaffney, South Carolina
Sold to _____ in December __ 1860.
A five year old mare. A brown quarter horse with a
white patch on her belly. A buck wagon and rig for $75.00
D Canti

☙❧

"Mr. Nelson, Ah need a quill." Jacob printed his name, 'Jacob Natty' then filled in the number '8' for the date on the receipt, before counting the money out in Cole's hand.

"She be a fine horse, Mr. Natty."

Jacob held out his hand for a gentleman's handshake. Cole wiped his hand on his coverall before obliging.

"Mr. Nelson, that man who left his horse, did yuh see where he went?" Jacob asked.

Cole walked to the front of the stable and looked in both directions. "Where he always go. Tuh da ho' house," he answered, "but Ah never see 'em be dirty lak dat and he sure be mean tuhday. 'Bout ride dat horse tuh death."

"Which way did he go?" Jacob asked.

Cole pointed toward the whorehouse.

Jacob hitched the brown horse to the buck wagon and threw Red's saddle and the old saddle in the wagon's bed, before tying Red to the wagon's rear right panel. He left Gaffney at 7:00 A.M., traveling on the street behind the livery stable. It wasn't long before he had turned onto the road leading to Clinton.

Jacob had a purse of $3510.00 in paper money, which did not include the money he earned from the harvest. His mind raced with thoughts of his sudden wealth and he realized it wasn't wise to carry such a large amount openly. He found a small money purse in the old saddlebag and decided to place the gold and cash in it, hiding it under the wagon, near the seat and tying it more securely with additional straps.

Jacob's solitary ride and the rhythmic trot of the horse's prance allowed his mind to wander. *Ah want tuh stop and try tuh buy Sula's freedom, but where would we go. Ah can't just bring hur onto the Morton farm without an invitation and Ah can't leave hur on the Bell Farm. Juke and Capers got money, too. If we can't stay at the Morton's, then we'll leave. Juke and Capers can stay, but Ah'll take Sula and move on.*

The sign read "Jonesville Plantation" and tingles crawled down Jacob's spine like giant spiders. He forgot to breathe until his body took over and inhaled for him. He stared at the road ahead and held the reins tightly while looking to his left. Tears filled his eyes. *All the more reason tuh go on and get one of da brothers tuh drive me,* he thought. *A white gentleman would never drive hisself tuh pick up his slave woman. This would give me time tuh get things right wit' Mrs. Morton and tuh put on my good church goin' clothes.* He took another deep breath, nodded his head and slapped the horse's ass with the reins. "Getty-up!" he yelled. The horses resumed their traveling trot until reaching the turn off for the Morton Farm. After taking the turn onto the private road, Jacob drove the horses at a cool down pace through the forest pass.

Once at the stable, Jacob leaped from the wagon, hurriedly unhitched the horses and led them to the water trough. While they quenched their thirst, he entered the barn and placed fresh hay in the stalls. Holding a large sackcloth, he stood at the barn door and turned when he heard Juke calling him.

"Brother, I believed yuh to be at the Haynes on this wonderful Sunday afternoon. Is Capers here, too?" He yelled out

"Oh, Jacob!" Juke ran toward him stumbled over the hard chunks of soil in the plowed field.

A few seconds later Capers began to run across the field.

Jacob stopped what he was doing and watched as his brothers approached. He thought about how fragile they were and although he preferred to lie to them, he knew one lie would only lead to another.

"Brother, yuh back," Juke's voice was jubilant. He gave Jacob a manly hug. "Thank da Lawd yuh ain't late and yuh didn't make us worry." He glanced over at the stable. "Is dat yours?" He said pointing to the horse and buck wagon.

"Ah jes thought of a name for that horse . . . Nutmeg. Yeah, Ah'm gone call hur, Nutmeg, that be good name," Jacob said as he tossed the cloth to Juke. He reached in the barn for another cloth and tossed it to Capers. "Y'all help me wipe them down and put the blankets over 'em. We gotta take care of the horses first and then Ah'm gon' tell y'all everythin'. Ah already put hay in da stalls."

As soon as the horses were taken care of Jacob latched the stall gates and the men took seats on a makeshift bench near the barn door. "Hey . . . what y'all doin' here, anyway? Ain't this be visitin' day at da Haynes?" Jacob asked.

"We jes be back a short time 'fore yuh get here," Capers answered. His eyes glittered as he spoke.

Juke blushed.

"Okay, what's goin' on?" Jacob stared each brother down and all he got back were sheepish grins. "C'mon, Ah ain't no fool."

"Yeah," Capers mewed. "There be some nice gals dat be unspoken fer. But Ol' Blue say Massa Haynes be needin' tuh see us this afternoon. It got somethin' tuh do wit' courtin'."

"Laura, she be Blue's daughter," Juke quietly announced. "She be kinda pleasin' tuh look at and dey be so many fine lookin' gals."

"And you, brother?" Jacob placed his hand on Capers shoulder when he spoke.

"Dem gals and dey mama's be lookin' at us real hard. Kinda put me off guard fer now."

Jacob rubbed the new growth of hair on his chin, "Well brothers, don't go settlin'. Dere be lots of good women on a plantation. Master gots two beauties dat live up dere in da big house. Seems like dey be his favorite. Dey be identical twins and dey sure be beautiful. Ah seed 'em."

Jacob just stared at his brothers and smiled. *Ah hope Ah never see loneliness in their eyes again*, he thought.

"Anyway," Capers said, while extending his hand in a gentleman's manner; his eyes and broad smile speaking for him. "Ah be happy yuh back, brother."

"Ah am, too," Juke added.

"We have tuh talk," Jacob announced. He stood and squeezed the back of his neck with his left hand to relieve the tension. He paced in front of them and began telling the brothers all that happened, including the fire and his part in it. He spoke of Jenny and Simon and their mama's death, Mammy Pearls, Miss Ollie and Sula's sale, the paper money, but most of all he spoke of Sula, her pregnancy and his need to buy her freedom. He told them about Nutmeg, the wagon and the rig and why it was necessary to make the purchases. The gold and the beatings their parents endured because of their absence were the only two things he held back from them.

As usual, Juke was shiftless and unreliable. He jumped to his feet and staggered away from Jacob; he began to whine, "Ah . . . don-know 'bout all dis." He ran his hands over his face. "Yuh . . . yuh gone get us mixed up in crazy stuff! Oh Lawdy! Yuh gone get us kilt foolin' wit yuh!" His hands trembled at his side and he stomped around kicking up a dust cloud in the stable. "Just when Ah see where Ah might can make a new life for myself yuh gon' get us kilt!"

"Shet up and sit down, Juke 'fore Ah put yuh down!" Capers yelled. He gave him an angry push before he could say another word. His head hit the back of the six-by-six support beam and he crumbled to a sitting position on the dirt floor. Dazed, his arms went limp at his side and his legs were stretched and splayed out. "Ah be so tired of his whinin'!" Capers complained as he stepped back and stood by Jacob's side.

Jacob looked on without flinching. He clenched his lips and nodded his approval to Capers before saying, "Ah'll talk tuh him when he comes around." They leaned against the stall and waited a few minutes and then Juke came to his senses.

"Whut yuh do dat fer?" Juke sat forward and rubbed the back of his head.

"Sorry brother. Ah ain't be meanin' tuh push yuh dat hard. Let me he'p yuh up," Capers offered, but his position remained stoic.

Jacob leaned over to give Juke a hand. "Let's go tuh the cabin tuh talk." He gave Juke a strong yank to his feet and followed with a coy smile all while brushing hay from his shoulders.

As soon as the cabin door was closed, Jacob grabbed Juke and pinned him across the crude table, face down. Capers stood back. He had never seen this side of Jacob and was unsure of what to expect.

Jacob twisted Jukes right arm behind his back and held him in place. When Juke tried to wiggle free, Jacob jerked his arm up until he gasped in pain. "Okay brother, yuh can go home if yuh want. Ah brought yuh here and Ah'll put yuh on da right road to The Dillard. Now, if Ah turn yuh loose will yuh sit and lissen, 'cause Ah ain't through wit' my talkin'?"

"Yeeaah!" Juke moaned.

Jacob slid off of him and into a chair. "Sit, don't talk, just sit!" he demanded.

Capers sat near Jacob and Juke sat across the table rubbing his arm.

"Yuh have three choices, Juke. Yuh can stay here in these cabins and do nothin' tuh help our folk, yuh can do whatever we can do help them, or yuh can go back tuh The Dillard. Now Ah know yuh workin on a new life, but yuh ain't through with da old one yet. Lissen brother, freedom don't come without a cost."

"Ah . . . Ah," Juke mumbled.

"Shet up! Ah ain't done talkin'!" Jacob slammed his open hand down on the table then pointed his finger toward Juke's face. "Yuh hear me good! If yuh go back, yuh better not say nothin' 'bout Moore or da fire, or where we are. They gone probably whip yuh tuh make yuh talk 'bout us but that gone be when yuh die. 'Cause if it comes back on me or Capers, Ah'm gone say Capers weren't there and you did it all. Yuh know they gone believe me 'cause Ah look most like them." Jacob watched the fear rise in his brother's face and smiled at his own thoughts, *this fool don't know white folk say Ah'm just a niggra tuh them, but it's gone put 'nuff fear in him tuh keep him with us and his mouth shet.*

Juke wiped the tears that were smeared across his face. "Ah be sorry, Jacob. Ah be just so scared all da time."

"Yuh need tuh get out more. Yuh a free man, but yuh mind is still back in slavery. The first thing Ah want tuh do is see 'bout gettin' our own place. Mister Allen Haynes owns over five hundred acres of land. Mrs. Morton's farmland was once owned by Mr. Haynes. Ah would like it if he would sell us 'bout ten acres, then we could raise our own hogs, chickens and vegetables and still work for Mrs. Morton."

Capers shook his head. "He ain't gone do dat. A niggra ain't 'lowed tuh own land."

Jacob smiled saying, "Yeah, but that's da glory. Ah'm gone keep playin' their game. They think Ah'm white." He placed his hands on both brothers' shoulders. Ah just have tuh live this life so we can survive. Ah practice all their moves, Ah study 'em, da way they talk, da way they walk, Ah stand taller, Ah practice my school learnin'. It's all for y'all."

"Got-dog . . . dat's some good thinkin', Jacob!" Capers leaped from his seat and slapped his leg. "Yuh think he sell?"

"Blue say he might sell. Say he got so much land he don't even farm it. He thinks Ah'm white and he like me 'cause Ah he'p Mrs. Morton. Ah'm gone ask Miles tuh ride over tuh his spread wit' me tuhday."

"What yuh gone do 'bout Sula?"

"Nice tuh know yuh care, Juke," Jacob smiled as he spoke. "First, Ah'm gone see about the land. Then Ah have tuh ask Mrs. Morton if Sula can stay wit' us. Ah don't know what she gone say, but Ah will be goin' after Sula in the mornin' and Ah want Juke tuh go wit' me as my driver."

Juke cowered down and turned away from Jacob.

"Why cain't Ah go? Just look at him! He be too scared," Capers reasoned.

"Only one driver will be needed and Juke needs tuh get the jitters out." Jacob stood and stared at his brothers who now appeared so peaceful. He was just as tired and scared as they were. He knew how they felt. And now they felt better because he said things that made them feel that way. But there was no one to make him feel better. He needed honesty and truth. He didn't like what was happening to him. Only honesty and truth with people he had come to trust could give him the foundation he needed or he would just move on. He had money now; he could afford to move on. He had not told the brothers about the more than five thousand dollars in gold. It would be buried in his cabin before he went to sleep that night. He would only spend the paper money and save the more valuable gold for an emergency.

Suddenly, Jacob remembered the appointment his brothers had with Mr. Haynes. "Don't yuh think yuh need tuh be changin' yuh shirts for yuh meetings wit' Mr. Haynes," Jacob said.

Juke looked out the door and up at the sky. "Yuh right, it be getting' late. Ah do wanna go wit' yuh tuh get Sula. Thank yuh fer pickin' me," he said.

chapter 15

"Ah need a bath," Jackson moaned as soon as he saw Luanne. He appeared to be pulling himself up her stairs by his arms, his head hung low and weary and his legs took each step as deliberate as a man twice his age. The scent of charred wood circled him while ash lay on his clothing, in his hair and like fine dust on his new growth beard.

Luanne stood on the top landing with her silk robe covering her nakedness. Jackson approached, kissing her cheek before throwing himself across her red settee. "My goodness Jackson, what happened tuh you?"

He lifted his head, but his eyes only opened to slits. "My house almost burned down last night. Ah need a bath, sleep and clean clothes. All my clothes are gone," he groaned as he fought back his tears and tried to control his breathing. Within seconds he had drifted off to sleep.

An hour passed before Jackson's bath was ready. Luanne's Negro cook and her housekeeper heated and hauled buckets of water to fill the large porcelain bathtub. After his bath, Luanne tucked him in her soft bed and Jackson slept until two o'clock that afternoon. When he woke he found his riding boots polished and standing tall by the side of the bed. His hat had been brushed free of ash and was hanging on the coat stand and a complete set of clothes was hanging from the back of the door. He stood and admired his nakedness in Luanne's cheval floor mirror and a mild streaming breeze bathed his body. He shivered lightly and then smiled when a familiar, internal warmth filled him and his man part rose; he forgot the urgency of his purpose. He opened the bedroom door and met Luanne just as she reached to enter the bedroom.

"Oh!" she said with a startle. "Where yuh goin like that, Jackson? Ah was just gonna see if yuh were awake and hungry."

He smiled. His first smile of the day. "Ah was just gonna call yuh," he whispered.

Luanne smiled, "Oh!" she mewed. And all she had to do was drop her white silk robe and she was ready. She was a professional, his professional; always on the ready, loving him with more love than an ideal wife. Crying for him all of her nights and with him she dreamed of living her ideal life. She accepted the little part of him that he was willing to give and was being thankful he had selected her for his exclusive, only to wonder if he would have loved her in a different life. He wanted lust, she wanted love. He was non-committed and she wanted commitment. He didn't dream, she only dreamed. He never cried, she always cried.

He would only have her for the moments that he needed her and never would she have him for enough time. She felt the flap of the sheet when it sliced through her false reality, as he pulled it away from himself. "Yuh leaving now?"

"Thank yuh, but Ah'll be back later. Ah have tuh see Bill Paterson. Ah must be off tuh Columbia; there's a train out of Yorkville in the morning. Ah need to purchase new clothing and I need to have fittings for my formal wardrobe."

Luanne, still in the bed, rested on her elbow and watched him dress. Then she reached for her robe, moved to her bedroom door and stood with her arms folded. That session of her world had ended and it was time for him to return to his world, but she was happy knowing she would have him again for the entire night.

"Ah must employ a contractor, order lumber and supplies and make arrangements to have the mansion rebuilt, all before leaving to return home." He placed his hat on his head and kissed Luanne on the cheek, "Thank yuh honey for takin' such good care of me. Ah'm gonna love yuh forever." He left the room and Luanne's eyes followed him. "Ah'll be right back," he said again as he hurried down the steps.

"But the bank is closed tuhday!" Luanne yelled down after him.

"Ah know! Ah'm gonna have Paterson open it for me, it's an emergency. Ah found my gold melted down into a clump. It was in the ruins of the house. Ah can get the return value when it's weighed. Ah believe it was more than $9,000. And Ah do need tuh make a cash withdrawal. Ah can't go off tuh Columbia penniless. Paterson will do what Ah say. Ah've got so much money in that bank, Ah practically own it!"

The Morton family was returning from Sunday morning service at the small Baptist Church near Clinton. Rusty always tailed along and settled himself on the church's grassy lawn to wait for their journey home. As the family stepped down from Mr. Haynes' carriage and his driver drove off, Rusty ran directly to the barn door, tail wagging, sniffing around barking and pacing in a frenzy. He was trying to alert the Morton boys to the visitor, Nutmeg. Jacob had returned to the barn and shooed him away, bribing him toward the farm house with a strip of beef jerky.

Miles, hearing the noise, left the house to investigate and found Jacob standing near the front porch. All Jacob could think about was Sula, his own land and how he could be with her.

"Good afternoon, Miles," he said as he continued teasing Rusty with the jerky.

"Ah'm happy tuh see yuh're back."

"Walk with me Miles," Jacob continued. "Ah need tuh talk tuh yuh and Ah want tuh show yuh something."

Miles came out to meet him and Jacob inquired about Mr. Haynes selling a small section of land adjacent to the Morton property.

"Does that mean you and the boys won't be working for us anymore?" Miles held his head down with his hands stretched deep in his pocket.

Jacob had a lot to think about when riding back from Gaffney. He was a man caught between two worlds. The Mortons were the only white people he liked, the only white people he really knew, but he would have to take a chance on trusting them. "Miles, don't call 'em boys," he said in an annoying tone. "They're men just like you and me. Now, tuh answer yuh question, Ah ain't goin' nowhere. Juke and Capers seem tuh be happy here, but that's all the speakin' Ah can do for 'em."

"Sorry Jacob. Ah didn't mean no harm."

"Ah know yuh didn't," he replied, but he had made his point. He patted Miles on his shoulder as they walked back toward the barn. "C'mon Miles, Ah was just thinkin' 'bout a few acres Ah can call my own. Y'all been good tuh me. Ah'm gone always be there for you and yuh mama. Ah was prayin' for a few acres near yuh land so me and the men won't have tuh travel far tuh get tuh work."

"But yuh building yuh cabins so yuh can have better houses. Ain't you all happy here?"

"We are. But Ah really need tuh talk tuh yuh mama. Then yuh'll understand," Jacob responded.

Evan and Robby ran ahead with Rusty.

"Robby, don't y'all open that barn door 'til Ah get there!" Jacob yelled out just as Robby touched the large slide latch. "C'mon Miles, Ah have tuh show yuh what Ah have."

The boys were jumping and skipping with excitement while Rusty barked and ran in circles. Jacob swung the barn doors open and there stood the deep brown, muscular, tall, quarter horse. "Ah named hur, Nutmeg. Ain't she a beauty?"

Miles stared at the large horse that made his Red look like a pony and Evan struggled to hold on to Rusty's collar.

"Uh . . . Evan . . . yuh gonna have tuh really hold tight tuh Rusty so he don't spook Nutmeg," Jacob instructed. Then he glanced up at Robby who was climbing up in the hayloft for a better view. "It's gonna take some time for them tuh get tuh know each other." He opened the stall gate.

"C'mere boy!" Evan picked up Rusty and held tightly to his rope like collar. He wiggled, barked and tried to get out of his arms.

Nutmeg whinnied and stamped the ground when she saw Rusty, but Jacob entered the stall and spoke softly to her while rubbing her head and neck. As soon as she was quiet he had Evan come closer with Rusty. Jacob rubbed Nutmeg and Evan rubbed Rusty. Then, Evan put Rusty on the ground where he sat and stared up at Nutmeg. Nutmeg lowered his neck until she almost kissed Rusty and they were instant friends.

"Damn, Jacob! A love made in heaven," Miles sang out.

"Wow! That's some horse yuh got there, Jacob," Robby yelled down from the hay loft.

"Yep! Bought hur at a livery stable. The owner won hur, the wagon and rig in a poker game.

Jacob and Miles closed the stable door and watched Rusty, Evan and Robby run towards the house. Jacob smiled, hooked his thumbs into his pockets and kicked at the hard, dry dirt. "Miles, Ah need tuh talk tuh you and yuh mama," Jacob said. "Everything wit' me and the men might be changin', dependin' on how y'all take what Ah'm gonna tell yuh. Yuh think Ah can meet yuh in the kitchen and say my peace. It be real important?"

Miles felt goose bumps rise on his arms at the same time the tiny hairs on the back of his neck tingles. "Is somethin' wrong, Jacob?"

Jacob didn't make eye contact with him. He threw his head back and took a deep quivering breath before nodding.

"Well, now seems like a good time," Miles said. "Ah'm sure Mama will meet wit' yuh."

The young men walked side by side from the barn and neither spoke. When they reached the house Jacob continued walking around to the back door.

"We do have a front door, Jacob. Ah don't understand why yuh won't use it."

Jacob stopped and smiled at Miles, then disappeared behind the house. Miles spoke to his mother when he entered the living room and they hurried into the kitchen. Jacob was outside leaning on the back porch railing when Miles opened the kitchen door.

Mrs. Morton was standing at the counter. "Jacob," she called out, "why don't yuh come in and tell me what's botherin' yuh." She walked over and took a seat at her round table and clasped her hands on its top.

Both men sat at the table. Jacob's heart beat with an uneven rhythm. The whites of his eyes were now streaked pink from holding back his misery. Mrs. Morton and Miles stared at him before glancing at each other.

"Ah have always feared white people," Jacob began. He dropped his head and took a deep breath.

"Well darling, that's because yuh own people haven't been kind tuh yuh in yuh whole life." Mrs. Morton responded.

"That be partly true, but please don't hate me. If yuh want me tuh leave, Ah will. Ah have not been truthful," Jacob confessed.

"Jacob, deceitful? My Lord, yuh like family!" Mrs. Morton declared. "Why in the world would Ah want yuh tuh leave?"

Jacob massaged his face with his hand. "That doesn't mean Ah've been truthful. They say if a person has just one drop of Negro blood, they ain't white." He scanned the faces of Miles and his mother for a reaction, but they just stared at him. Their heads slightly bowed and eyes widened, peering up at him as though they were telling him to explain himself. But, he was waiting for them to scream, to call him a nigger, or to throw him from the kitchen.

Mrs. Morton raised her head and spoke first. She inhaled deeply, made a disconcerting eye contact, but kept a stern face. "Jacob, are yuh tellin' us yuh a Negro man?" Mrs. Morton asked. She sat back in her chair and crossed her arms under her medium size bosom, while her shawl hung loosely over her shoulders.

"Yes ma'am," Jacob whispered and he nodded his head.

"Well, yuh white enough for me," Miles responded, believing he needed to ease the tension. He had never experienced his mother's confusing disposition.

"Ah don't care, Jacob. Ah will always love yuh like a son," Mrs. Morton said. "Yuh saved us from starving. Now, Ah understand why yuh only came in the back door and why you always ate on the porch. Jacob, yuh could have such an easy life. Yuh could pass all of yuh life. Why don't yuh just pass?"

"My world is a Negro's world . . . my love is for a slave woman. She is carryin' my child," He waited again to gauge her reaction, but Mrs. Morton just gave him her understanding eyes. He didn't look away or express regret. His face fell soft and gentle when he spoke of his Sula. "Ah know yuh don't approve of a baby before marriage, but life is different and hard for slaves. Now Ah have a chance tuh buy hur freedom and marry hur, but a white man can't marry a slave. This time last year Ah was a slave and so were my half-brothers, Juke and Capers. Ah have twenty three other half brothers and sisters, all the mulatto children of Massa Walter Dillard, of Gaffney, South Carolina. When he died last April, we all got our freedom. Juke, Capers and me were the only freed slaves that left the plantation. Ah came here ten days later. Ah'm sorry Ah lied tuh yuh 'bout that indenture stuff, but Ah was afraid and lost until Ah met Blue on the road and he told me y'all be needin' help."

"Ah understand, Jacob." Mrs. Morton said. She reached over and placed a reassuring hand on top of his hand.

"Yes ma'am. But there are a few more things Ah'd need tuh ask yuh." Jacob just waited to read the acknowledgment on their faces before he continued.

Mrs. Morton smiled gently. "Continue Jacob."

"Yes ma'am. Yuh see, Sula is my love, but she be sold last week. Ain't no slave ever been sold from Da Dillard Plantation in my lifetime." He stood and turned away from Mrs. Morton just in time to use the back of his hands to catch the tears that escaped his eyes. He removed his neckerchief and used it to wipe his face. "Please excuse me, ma'am," he said.

"Take yuh time, Jacob," Miles whispered sympathetically.

More uncontrollable tears fell. Jacob held to the countertop to support himself through the next moments, until he regained his composure.

"Yuh gonna be all right, Jacob." Mrs. Morton's soft voice touched his ears like cotton.

Jacob took another deep breath, "Thank yuh ma'am and you too, Miles. Ah love y'all like family." He turned back to addressing Mrs. Morton and then returned to his seat at the table, his face still creased with anxiety and insecurity. "Well ma'am, my father is dead now and his other son, Jackson has sold three slaves. Two are old women who are sistahs and my Sula. He sold Sula 'cause he is mad at me for leavin', then comin' back and gettin' Juke and Capers. Sula is Juke's kin. She is seventeen years old. Ah'm not worried about the women, they have each other, but one of them is my Mammy Pearl, da only mama Ah ever knowed. She raised me, but she is safe." He stop talking for a moment, wiped his face, inhaled and his breath quivered. He smiled apologetically and stared directly at Mrs. Morton. "Sorry . . . but, yesterday, Ah won some money at a horse race." He gave Mrs. Morton a sheepish look. "And Ah bought me a quarter horse and rig. Ah got enough for some land and me and my brothers hope to buy Sula's freedom and still have a good amount left over." He spoke fast, hoping she would understand his lie of gambling and that the winnings would be put tuh good use. But now, it was time for him to ask the bigger question, so he continued. "Ah need yuh okay tuh bring Sula here until we get our own land. Ah will give hur my cabin and move in wit' my brothers 'til we get married."

Mrs. Morton nodded her head rapidly and then stood from the table turning her back to Miles and Jacob. She raised her apron to her face and began to sob. She tried to hold back her sorrow, but dropped it all into her apron. Her shoulders shook and she made slight howling sounds. Jacob and Miles rushed to comfort her, but she pushed them away. "Ah'm okay!" she whispered as she pulled at her shawl. "Give me a minute. Ah just need a little air." She left through the kitchen door, sat on the porch rocker and cried out the pain of man's inhumanity.

Jacob and Miles returned to their seats at the kitchen table and sat quietly for some time.

"Jacob, how come yuh last name ain't Dillard like yuh brothers?" Miles asked as he broke the silence.

"We had a chance tuh pick any name we wanted for our freedom papers. Ah didn't want my last name tuh be Dillard, so Ah picked my real mother's name. Natty. She died when Ah was born."

"So, Mammy Pearl took care of yuh from birth?" Mrs. Morton spoke up from the kitchen door. She walked back to the table pulling her shawl tighter over her shoulders.

Miles and Jacob suddenly turned around. They smiled. Mrs. Morton stood over them composed and appearing ready to continue. "Okay Jacob, tell me more."

"Uh . . . yes and no, ma'am. Uh . . . Mammy Pearl cared for me like a mother, but Ah stayed wit' my father in da mansion 'til Ah was about eight."

"And he was the one who taught yuh how tuh read?" Mrs. Morton asked.

"Yes ma'am." Jacob replied.

"What happened, Jacob?" Why did yuh leave the mansion?" She asked.

Jacob knew this wasn't about him, but she asked and he had to tell her something. He gave her a short version and later, if she asked for more details, when there weren't more pressing issues, he vowed to tell her more. "Well . . . big brother, Jackson used tuh beat and torture me when our father was out so Ah hid in da quarters with Mammy Pearl. Father never believed what his white son was doing tuh me, so Ah begged him tuh let me stay with Mammy Pearl and he did."

Mrs. Morton's hands covered her mouth. "That's horrible," she cried out. She lightly pinched the bridge of her nose and shook her head. "Oh my Lord!" she whispered.

"Mrs. Morton, Ah want tuh stay near you and my brothers feel the same." He was now completely composed and ready for his last request. "One day they gone want tuh marry and have families of their own. They gone need a place tuh bring their wives. Well, Ah need a little land of my own. Ah know Mr. Haynes will sell me about ten acres as a white man, but not as a black man. If Ah pass for white then, Ah ain't free tuh marry Sula. We will have tuh live in sin. Ah will have tuh pretend she be my housekeeper and my chillen be bastards. Mrs. Morton, if the law say Ah'm a Negro, then Ah'll be a Negro and be happy wit' my lovely Sula and my chillen. The only other thing Ah can do is go north and pray for a little better life. Ma'am, if' Ah give yuh the money will yuh buy the land for me? After a while yuh could quietly deed it over to me. Ah don't ever want tuh be far away from you or yuh family. Y'all be a part of my family."

Mrs. Morton smiled. "Ah'll meet with Mr. Haynes this afternoon."

chapter 16

That Saturday and Sunday appeared to be two of the longest, task filled days Jacob had ever experienced. He returned to his cabin and fell onto his bed. Sleep covered him like a blanket as soon as he closed his eyes. He didn't dream. Weariness pulled him so deep under, he was beyond his dream state; he had drifted into his near death state; that place we all enter into when we are so exhorted our brain, muscles and bodily functions go into hibernation and our willpower surrenders to the nothingness.

He could feel the pull. At first it sounded like music. The layers of his sleep were lifting and the singing was louder, more repetitious. *Go away, shush, be quiet, be quiet*, he whispered at the darkness, but the singing was now noise. It was his name; they were calling his name. Someone was touching him and calling his name. "What! What!" he thought he was yelling, but he was saying nothing. He sprang up and flung his legs over the edge of the bed. "What! Who," he whispered between deep breaths of air.

"Jacob! It's us, Juke and Capers. It's all right, Jacob! Wake up!" Juke said. He had his hand on Jacob's shoulder and he could tell by the far away stare in Jacob's eyes that he was still in a sleep state.

"Leave him alone. He be needin' the rest. What we be wantin' tuh tell him can wait." Capers whispered.

The young and neatly dressed stable boy hurried from his station at the side of the mansion and captured the reins of the horse as soon as they arrived in front of the massive house. Mrs. Morton was always impressed with the formality of the greetings at the Haynes plantation, however not at the price of slavery.

Daniel, a neatly dressed Negro man, met Mrs. Morton and Miles at the front door. He greeted them in a most proper manner; his dialect and attire closely resembling that of a white southern gentleman wearing a black-tailed suit, white shirt and bow tie. He was as black as coal, about sixty years old, pure white eyebrows and his pearly white wavy hair topped off his tall frame.

Miles stood tall and escorted his mother, gently guiding her by her elbow. "Good afternoon, Daniel. We would like tuh speak wit' Mr. Haynes," Miles said.

"Yes sur, Mr. Morton. Y'all follow me please, sur." Daniel led them to the library where every wall was lined with books except where the windows cut through the building and the long burgundy velvet drapes hung. "Please make yuhself at home," Daniel said. He took a bow, turned and left the room, closing the large French doors behind him.

Moments later, Mr. Haynes eased through the same doors and closed them behind himself as he greeted Mrs. Morton.

She remained seated, nodded and offered her hand to Mr. Haynes. He gently touched her gloved hand with his fingertips, nodded and smiled as his formal greeting. He was no stranger to them, a blessing during their time of need. She would consider him a good man, but he was a large holder of slave property and a horse held more value for him than a Negro.

Miles had jumped to his feet as soon as Mr. Haynes entered the library. "Good afternoon, Mr. Haynes. It is a pleasure seeing yuh again," Miles said as he offered his hand.

"Same here . . . same here, young man," Mr. Haynes replied, giving Miles a hardy handshake. "What do Ah own the honor?"

"Well, Mr. Haynes," Mrs. Morton began. "Ah'm asking if yuh would sell me 'bout ten more acres of land tuh border the edge of my property? Yuh know Ah can never thank yuh enough for all the land yuh have already sold me. With the help of the Negro workers Ah have, Ah would like tuh expand my farm."

Haynes sat up in his chair. "Ah thought yuh was building cabins for them on yuh land?"

Miles took a deep breath and glanced at his mother. "Yes sur. But we want to move them onto the purchased land, hire more help and farm more land. Jacob will run the project."

"What about the Negro workers? Will they go to this land?" Haynes asked.

"Ah 'spec' they will," Mrs. Morton said. "They say they are happy workin' for us. They work well and they work hard. They know if the crop is good, they will be paid well. Ah will accommodate them, by allowing for building space and land for a small vegetable garden and a few domestic animals. Ah will work out their expenses later."

Haynes sat back and rubbed his belly. "Mrs. Morton, wouldn't it just be easier tuh take on some slaves?"

"Oh my Lord, no, Mr. Haynes! Ah don't cotton tuh owning another human being. Now, think about it. Ah do better to hire them, rent them a place to live and pay them tuh work for me. Ah won't be responsible for nothing else in their lives and my farm will grow."

Haynes chuckled and twirled the tip of his mustache. "Okay, yuh do it yuh way and Ah'm gone do it my way. Ah did meet two of yuh boys. Seem like fair chaps. Well, Ah do like them. Ah had 'em come see me again tuhday so Ah could formally introduce 'em tuh my beauties, Annabelle and Anna Sue. Ah think yuh boys were smitten; Ah know my gals ain't stopped gigglin' yet."

"Is that so? That would be Capers and Juke. Ah want tuh thank yuh for allowing 'em tuh visit the quarter tuh spend time with their own kind. They were mighty lonely. Ah was afraid Ah was going tuh lose their employ," Mrs. Morton said.

"Well, Ah don't believe they will be going anywhere. They are welcome as long as they stay in line. So now, let's get down tuh business. Ah do have some timber lined bottomland on the edge of yuh property. The problem is six acres of pine and oak timber," Haynes stopped talking, raised his eyebrow and bit down on his lip. "Yes, Ah understand." He smiled "Not good for farming, but good for building. Ah guess I could throw in an extra acre of farm land. Tell yuh what? How's 'bout two dollars an acre for five acres of timberland and four dollars for five acres farm land?" Haynes leaned back in his easy chair and laced his fingers over his round belly. He gave Mrs. Morton a satisfying smile believing he had struck a great deal.

Miles's eyes shifted between Haynes and his mother.

Mrs. Morton smiled, leaned forward in her chair and then spoke with more confidence than Miles knew she had. "Why . . . Ah thank yuh very much for yuh generosity, Mr. Haynes. Now, perhaps Ah could put upon yuh for a few more acres of farmland in addition tuh yuh great offer. Yuh see, Mr. Haynes, my boys gone be so busy workin at my place there will not be much time for clearin' land. Perhaps five more acres of farm land?"

Haynes sat tall and cleared his throat. "Yuh drive a strong bargain, Mrs. Morton." He stared at Miles without blinking, Yuh learning from yuh mama, young man?"

Miles took a deep breath and slowly nodded his head. "Yes sur."

Haynes stood, shook Miles' hand and he kissed the back of his mother's hand before she stood from her seat. "That will be fifty dollars for fifteen acres and Ah will give yuh a receipt and a preliminary deed," he announced. "You can go tuh the land office in town and get yuh final deed on Tuesday. Ah will ride the land boundary wit' yuh tuhday and you and Miles can stake the land. Do yuh have a horse?"

Mrs. Morton paid Mr. Haynes. "If it is all right wit' you, Ah'll wait here while you and Miles ride the land boundary. Ah am just not up tuh that."

Mr. Haynes smiled. "That will be just fine, it is getting late."

"Very well Mr. Haynes. Thank yuh and may the Lord continue tuh smile upon yuh."

"Yuh so very welcome." He turned to Miles. "Son, will yuh have Daniel prepare a mount for you and ready my mare for the task while Ah wait here with yuh mama?"

"Yes sur, Mr. Haynes." Miles disappeared from the room.

Mr. Haynes sat back in his easy chair. He was quiet only for a moment. "Have you heard about the unrest sweeping the south? Ah been hearing serious talk of a war between them northern Yankees and us southern gentlemen."

"War was all a buzz even in the house of the Lord. And for what ungodly reason? The thought of my boys dying in a war scares me tuh death." Mrs. Morton's perpetual smile turned sour as she spoke.

"It seems this country's republican president is a nigger lover who believes Federal laws should be enforced over state laws. He even says he will free all the slaves," Haynes scowled.

"Oh my! That will be a problem for you," Mrs. Morton replied. "Ah guess yuh will have tuh put yuh slaves on yuh payroll. But yuh gonna be just fine Mr. Haynes, 'cause Ah'll be prayin' for yuh. As for me, Ah can't lose my sons to war when we believe all people should be free."

"So, what will yuh do if war comes? Yuh won't be supportin' the south?" Mr. Haynes sat forward in his chair; there was no doubt he believed he needed to reduce the space between them before receiving his answer.

She smiled. "Why, Mr. Haynes, Ah have a very strong relationship with my Lord. He will make a way for me and my family. He will give me guidance in all things that are right and good."

Mr. Haynes slid back in his chair and smiled. "Ah know why Ah love yuh Ms. Morton. Yuh have such a pure soul. Ah believe yuh could convert this old sinner if yuh had the chance."

Mrs. Morton smiled and nodded her head.

"Ah must leave yuh now, Ah believe my horse is ready." Haynes wiggled out of his chair and left the room leaving Mrs. Morton alone to examine all the interesting books in his library.

ॐ◌ॐ

"Hur name be Annabelle. That be da one Ah want," Juke specified. He sat staring at the flickering fire smiling as if he could see her image even there.

"Brother, does it matter; Annabelle, Anna Sue, they be identical," Jacob reminded them.

Juke turned to his brother. "They don't be needin' dem ribbons. Ah know Annabelle. Ah know hur eyes. We speak wit' our eyes."

Capers smiled at his brother. He smiled for his happiness. He saw the connection he made with Annabelle. He was so taken by their connection he neglected to attend to Anna Sue. But he was happy too. Mr. Haynes had given Anna Sue to him and he was a happy man.

Jacob stood in his cabin door wiping his face with his hand. Capers was first to notice him.

"Jacob, come! We need tuh tell yuh about Annabelle and Anna Sue," Juke called out.

Jacob staggered over to his seat and sat. He had not seen such delight on his brother's faces since they were children. He explained that he had seen Annabelle and was happy for them. Just then Miles rode up and informed them that his mother had purchased fifteen acres of prime land from Mr. Haynes. All the brothers gave each other manly hugs. However it was written, they knew it was their land Miles was talking about; suddenly Juke and

Capers believed life was being good to them. However, Jacob's mission was still incomplete.

"Jacob, Mama would like tuh speak with yuh. Could yuh come now?"

"Sure!"

Miles extended his hand and hoisted Jacob up onto Red. "Ah think she can carry both of us across the field," Miles suggested.

"Thank yuh, Miles." His voice was shaky and unstable; then he was quiet for the remainder of the ride.

Miles understood. While Jacob wiped tears away from his cheeks with his fingers, Miles gave him his gift of silence.

Jacob had done all he could to hold back his tears; his cheeks were an explosion of blush pink, his chest hurt and the back of his throat ached. He wanted to scream out his joy and cry out his emotions and sorrow. Less than a year ago he was a slave living the only lifestyle he knew. His universe was the plantation where he had never ventured beyond its boundary. Now he had led his brothers into this new world where they experienced real fear for the first time in their lives. He alone had murdered, stole, nearly burned down the plantation house, got Mammy Pearl, Miss Ollie and Sula sold, lied and he knew he would kill again to get his beloved Sula back. He wondered just how easy everyone's life would have been if he had just remained a slave on the plantation. All he wanted was to be a free man, to love Sula, live, work and take care of his family.

"Ah'll be leavin' early in the morning tuh get Sula," Jacob told Miles. He kept his head bowed and stated his intention in a matter of fact way. "Ah want tuh thank yuh mama before Ah leave."

Mrs. Morton was waiting quietly in the kitchen for them to return. When they stepped through the door, she pushed herself away from the table smoothing her skirt as she stood. "Jacob, Ah was thinkin', Ah should cut away fifteen acres of my land so yuh land boundary won't be near Mr. Haynes. You will have ample timberland, including the land yuh currently building on and at least ten acres of farming land. If that be tuh yuh likin' Ah'll have a surveyor cut out fifteen acres of property and we'll think of someway tuh deed it tuh yuh."

"Ah don't know how tuh thank yuh." His emotions broke the silence as he struggle to gulp air. He swallowed and wiped at a tear while pretending it to be a speck in his eye.

Mrs. Morton smiled and rubbed his arm. Her heart ached and weakness covered her like a wet blanket. Jacob's emotional struggle only served to delay her ability to give him more comforting words. She wanted to reassure him that everything was going to be all right, but she was so overcome and weakened by the oppression of his situation, she didn't have the strength to tell him or Miles of the south's discontent with the northern president. He would find out about that soon enough. She couldn't imagine her family being torn apart; it almost brought her to her knees and the thought of war was so frightening she didn't dare speak of it until she had an opportunity for pray. In a twilight like daze, she tipped around her kitchen tapping everything like a blind person seeking to find their way. When she was standing in front of Jacob, she took her apron and wiped his tears, then whispered, "Are yuh sure yuh have enough money?"

Tears rolled down Jacob's face; he couldn't hold back his sobs. He stood, taking Mrs. Morton's right hand in his. "Thank yuh, ma'am. You are truly a Godly woman and yuh surely gone continue tuh receive his blessings. Ah'm gonna be fine. The Lord has provided me wit' a quarter horse that Ah named, Nutmeg and a buck wagon. Ah am sorry tuh say Ah used my earnin's tuh gamble on a horse race, but Ah did win. Ah b'lieve that was the Lord's plan."

"When yuh leavin'?" she asked.

"Sun up tomorrow. My travels are only 'bout twenty miles yonder, over in a place called Jonesville, tuh the Bell Farm. Ah'm gone take Juke wit' me."

"Can Ah go, Jacob?" Miles asked. He stared at Jacob and then his face begged his mother.

Jacob believed two white men were better than one. He nodded to Mrs. Morton.

"Anytime one of mine can witness goodness, Ah won't stand in the way."

"Me and Juke gonna take the buck wagon. Miles, you ride Nutmeg."

"Mrs. Morton asked, "Is there gonna be somethin' soft for hur tuh sit on?"

"Yes ma'am. Ah got a thick straw bed in the wagon and warm blankets," Jacob responded and he smiled.

chapter 17

Early Monday morning Jackson rode into Yorkville and banged on the livery barn door. When no one answered he left his saddled horse in the corral and nailed a letter to the door that explained his circumstances. He was very careful to mention that he would be returning on Wednesday morning on the 6:00 A.M. train and would need his horse at that time: payment of all charges was promised, an apology was made and a gratuity was assured. A brisk walk took him to the train station and ten minutes later he was seated with his hat pulled down to cover his face. He wanted to sleep; he was exhausted, but the events of the past two days haunted him. It wasn't the house; it was as if an evil had come to The Dillard Plantation. Every time he closed his eyes he imagined another possible evil and then his eyes popped open fleeing another premonition.

The train's whistle sounded before it jerked forward and was steady on its way. Jackson settled down. He thought of Luanne and how she relaxed him. He loved her more than she would ever know, but he could never make her the Lady of The Dillard. If they could go away where no one knew her, he had no family, no heirs to the plantation. *Why do Ah continue to think of Luanne in my future. We could go tuh England or Paris. We could really be happy.* Suddenly Paterson sliced into his thoughts. *"The value of your melted gold is $3876.00."* He wondered how over $5000 in gold disappeared. *Could it have melted and seeped through the floor or into the ashes . . . or . . . maybe someone stole my money and the gold and started that fire as a cover-up. It's possible that some of the gold was loss in the fire, but not that much.* Jackson sat up and while the rush of alertness stiffened him his hat slipped back on his head. "The gold," he whispered. "The fire . . . Jacob?" Suddenly he didn't want to go to Columbia. Columbia could wait, but it was too late, the train was moving at full steam. He wanted to return home. He wanted to find out if Jacob had been at The Dillard looking for Sula. He knew he could ask and he knew he would have to torture his slaves before they would tell him if they had seen Jacob. It would be better if he just visited the Bell's farm when he returned to make sure Sula was still there. If Bell sold Sula to Jacob, the bill of sale would be registered at the courthouse. He knew he could find Jacob.

Jacob and Sula and gold and hatred and anger and revenge consumed him, while loving Luanne was pushed so far inside of him it would take her presence for him to remember loving her.

ॐ∽๑

Jacob, Juke and Miles rode out of Clinton at 6:00 A.M. and were in Jonesville by nine that morning. Juke drove the wagon and Jacob sat on the seat next to him. Miles rode Nutmeg and traveled along the side of the wagon. It was a cold December morning. One hour in the elements and the cold was biting at their bones. Jacob had placed three blankets in the wagon for Sula and he offered one to Juke, who didn't own a coat, mittens or hat. Jacob didn't have gloves or ear muffs, but he had placed the woolen scarf over his head, tied it under his chin, tucking the ends inside his heavy jacket. His wide brim Stetson hat was pulled down over the scarf and he tucked his hands inside his jacket to keep them warm.

"As soon as Ah get Sula Ah'm gone get you and Capers some winter stuff."

"Sho wish Ah had it now," Juke whined. The cold chattered his words and nearly stole his breath.

"Take another blanket." Jacob reached for the reins while Juke got settled. "How yuh doin' Miles?"

"Fair, just fair, but Ah'm going in that store and ask where the Bell Farm is," Miles pointed to a shack of a store off in the distance.

"Ah'm going wit' yuh." Jacob turned to Juke. "Yuh Okay?"

Juke pulled the blankets tighter and nodded.

A few minutes later they returned to the wagon. Travel a half a mile ahead and then take the second road on the left were the directions given at the roadside store. Jacob passed the directions on to Juke, climbed onto the wagon and handed him a hat and a pair of work gloves. Juke shivered as he lowered the two blankets from his head to put on the hat and then he re-wrapped them around his body before slipping on the work gloves.

"Thank yuh, Jacob." Juke huffed from the shivering cold that had brought tears to his eyes.

Jacob was first to see her. "Look over there, Miles. Now Ah know this is the right place."

"Damn, Jacob. That porky woman is Juke's sister?"

"No! That be the woman who raised me. That be my Mammy Pearl."

Mammy Pearl stood to the left side of the large two-level house with the white peeling paint; she was holding two water buckets. The well was nearby, but judging by the way the buckets swayed against the motion of her movement, she was going to the well, rather than returning with her load. She noticed the approaching wagon and the man on horseback trailing several feet behind. She stopped and stared down the road until she made out the faces of Juke and Jacob and then the buckets flew in separate directions and she began screaming for Ollie. She raised such a commotion that Ollie came running from the house. All of their body fat went into motion as they jumped for joy for their loved ones and Juke and Jacob leaped from the wagon like grasshoppers. The women took Jacob and Juke in their embrace and were kissing them all over their heads and faces by the time Master Bell, his wife and four huge teenage boys reached the front yard, each carrying their hunting rifles. Miles had caught up to the wagon, dismounted and stood quietly near his horse.

"Whut's goin' on out here?" Master Bell yelled out. He was holding a shotgun with the barrel pointed toward the ground and waving his left hand to emphasize his words.

Pearl and Ollie stopped immediately and dropped their heads while Jacob spoke up. "Sorry, Mr. Bell. Uh, sur . . . yuh gals were so happy tuh see us, we just got a little carried away. Ah was indentured, inherited a ten year work load from my dead parents and Pearl here," he nodded toward her, "raised me until Ah was free. And yuh Ollie is kin tuh Juke here. Ah know these women are from The Dillard Plantation and that's why we come." His common dialog disappeared and suddenly he sounded like a white man. He stood tall and looked directly in Mr. Bell's eyes.

"Well, they mine now!" Mr. Bell bellowed.

"Yes sur, Mr. Bell and Ah see yuh are a good master. They sure look happy and that makes me feel good. Ah want tuh thank yuh for that," Jacob said. He gave Mr. Bell a large, gratuitous smile and extended his hand for a manly shake.

Mr. Bell switched his rifle to his left hand and accepted Jacob's hand. "Yes sir Mr. . . . uh . . . what did you say your name was?"

"Natty . . . Jacob Natty. Oh and let me introduce you to my two companions." He pointed to Juke. "This is Juke Dillard, a freed slave from The Dillard Plantation. We grew up together."

Juke, still holding the blankets, bowed and mumbled, "Howdy." He never made eye contact with Mr. Bell.

"Say, you wouldn't have an extra warm coat that Ah could buy from yuh. Juke could sure use a warm coat 'round 'bout now. Ah'll pay yuh handsomely," Jacob announced.

"Whut yuh say, boys? Any of yuh got a warm coat yuh done growed outta?" Mr. Bell called out while partially looking over his shoulder at them.

"Yes sur, Papa," two of the boys responded simultaneously and ran off to the house.

"Ah thank yuh kindly, Mr. Bell. Now, this other young man is Miles Morton. He's one of my true blue friends." Jacob walked over and patted him on the back and Mr. Bell gave him a hardy handshake.

Before Jacob could mention Pearl or Ollie again, Mr. Bell's conscience kept him on the subject of his new slaves. "Well, Ah'm a God fearing man. And they are a blessing tuh my wife. Ah never had slaves before. Ah have the boys tuh help me in the fields and when Ah need an extra hand or two, Ah just hire on a few negresses."

"Mr. Bell, may Ah ask what happened tuh the young slave gal? The one they called, Sula?" Jacob questioned. "Yuh see ... she is Juke's half-sister."

"Ah sold hur yesterday. The pregnant wench; Ah didn't want no gal like that 'round my boys."

Jacob held to the buck wagon and caught himself just as he felt his knees buckle. His mouth was so dry he couldn't push out a word and he took to having dry heaving coughs.

Mr. Bell's boys returned with three coats in varying degrees of disrepair and placed them in the wagon's bed.

Mammy Pearl quickly delivered a pitcher of cool well water to Jacob. "It's gone be okay, baby," she whispered. She stood between Jacob and Mr. Bell so he couldn't hear her.

Jacob gave her a big hug, "Thank yuh, Mammy Pearl," he said loud and clear.

Mr. Bell grunted. "Whut yuh think about these coats, Mr. Natty?" He spread them out over the side of the wagon.

"Juke, look at the coats." Jacob held them up and inspected the three, three-quarter length wool coats with the sheepskin linings. "Yuh boys musta growed like weeds. Those coats look like yuh boys grew outta them before they could wear 'em out." He tossed a coat to Juke. "Looka here, Juke."

"Now, dese some coats." Juke grinned and put one on. He rubbed the sleeves and hugged himself, then looked directly into Jacob's eyes.

"What yuh asking for the lot?" Jacob asked. He stood with his hands on his hips and Miles stood beside him smiling.

"How 'bout two dollars?"

"Ah can do that." Jacob announced and he extended his hand for a shake. He excused himself and turned to count out the money. He turned back to Mr. Bell and paid him. "Now Mr. Bell," he said, "would yuh kindly tell me 'bout the gentleman who bought the gal?"

"Well, Mr. Natty, that be Ol' Peabody and he's a mean one. Ah needed the money. She was given tuh me and Ah made a five hundred dollar profit. Ol' Peabody said he was gettin' two slaves."

Miles pushed his hat back and tilted his head. "Two slaves?" he questioned.

Jacob kicked the red dirt. "He's talkin' 'bout the baby. Ah 'spec he'll sell it as soon as it's weaned."

Mr. Bell's body language confirmed Jacob's statement before he quickly changed the subject. "Ol' Peabody and his woman got a small spread. Got, maybe ten, 'leven, field slaves. He said he was tryin' tuh build up his land and he was needin' workin' niggers, not pickaninnies."

Jacob used all of his emotional strength to maintain his composure. "Where can Ah find this Peabody?" He turned away from Bell.

Miles watched Jacob's color fade to a sickening pale and when he took the one step required to reach the wagon, Miles thought Jacob would collapse and he almost ran to his side. Suddenly Jacob took a deep breath and appeared to recover. He stood tall, searched his surroundings and Miles looked away pretending he didn't notice his period of weakness.

"Oh, it ain't far from here," Mr. Bell was saying, "'bout three miles or so. Now, yuh go tuh the crossroad and turn left. Go on yonder 'til yuh get tuh the third road on the right. Take that road and yuh'll come tuh the Peabody spread 'bout a mile down."

Jacob listened intensely and burned the directions into his mind. "Thank yuh Mr. Bell," he said. "Now, may my friend Juke and me say a proper farewell tuh Pearl and Ollie?"

"Sure, take yuh time."

Jacob turned toward Ollie and Pearl and then he turned around to face Mr. Bell again. "Mr. Bell," he said, "may we come to visit Pearl and Ollie from time tuh time and if yuh ever have a need tuh sell 'em, will yuh notify my friend, Mr. Miles Morton in Clinton?"

"Ah sure will," Mr. Bell said.

Miles removed a crumpled piece of paper from his pocket and scribbled his information down. As Jacob walked by he handed the paper to Mr. Bell. Mr. Bell and his sons watched in amazement at the tenderness Jacob and Juke had for Pearl and Ollie. Pearl hugged Jacob and whispered in his ear, "Have yuh seen Simon and Jenny?"

"Yes ma'am. Don't worry. Ah'll take care of them."

chapter 18

Ann Peabody stood on her front porch with a rifle cocked and pointed at the trio as they traveled up her road. The men stopped about three hundred feet away from the house and Jacob removed his hat as he climbed down from his wagon.

"Whut y'all want?" the woman yelled out in a slow drawl while still holding the rifle in place.

"Ah come tuh speak tuh yuh husband on business," Jacob called out.

"Well, he ain't here, so get on yonder!"

"Ma'am, Ah got an opportunity for him tuh double his money on that investment he made just yesterday," Jacob called out again. "It's a lot of money."

The middle-aged woman with the wild hair lowered the rifle. "You!" she hollered out, "come closer! Just you and don't yuh be tryin' nuthin'!"

"Yes ma'am," Jacob responded.

"Lemme get a good look at yuh," the woman said and she squatted. Her eyes were uncontrollably fixed on Jacob. "Yuh sure be a pretty man. Why, yuh hair be lak golden threads. Yuh skin lak cream and those blue eyes should only belong tuh angles. Whut yuh say yuh name be and whut yuh want wit' my husband?"

The woman's clothes were as raggedy as that of a field slave. But what was most shocking to Jacob was Mrs. Peabody herself. She was dirty; her clothes were dirty, the age lines in her skin were filled in with filth, her hands and nails were chunked with dirt. Her hair should have been as golden as his, but it was thick with muck and was a mess of matted locks. What shocked Jacob most were her missing, stained and rotted teeth and all of her emitted an odor that made his nose burn even in the cool December air.

"Sorry ma'am, my business is wit' yuh husband," he managed his response after gathering himself and taking a backward step.

Mrs. Peabody looked over his head and Jacob turn to see what had snatched her attention. A slight-build man riding a large brown quarter horse was galloping up the road and approaching Miles and Juke. The horse was so large the man appeared to be a child, but evidently he was intimidating enough to frighten his woman into hiding. When Jacob turned to speak to her again, she was gone. The little man rode around Miles and Juke and up to the porch before pulling his horse to a halt.

"Who are you?" the little man wolfed at Jacob while still straddling his horse. "Who are they?" He turned and swung his arm in the direction of Juke and Miles, who were now standing by the buck wagon.

"Jacob Natty is my name and they are my business. Ah come tuh make yuh a business proposition." Jacob had his thumbs hooked in his pockets as he looked up at Peabody and refused to say another word until the little man dismounted his horse.

Peabody just stared down at him for a few seconds, "Yeah . . . whut yuh got," he barked before he spat a squirt of tobacco juice on the opposite side of the horse and away from Jacob.

Jacob tilted his head to the left and glanced up at Peabody before walking over to a large fallen log and sitting on it. It wasn't long before the barely five foot little man slid down from his horse and joined him, but he sat on a stump of a fallen oak tree. He shared the same putrid odor that his wife emitted, but his hands and face appeared to be free of visible dirt and his attire was more presentable. Jacob had assessed the condition of the Peabody Farm and he could see these were poor people and would do anything necessary to make a dollar. Peabody's wife was dressed worse than a slave, but soap was cheap and water was free and only laziness prevented them from bathing. This creature of a man was too cheap to buy clothing for his wife or himself. Slaves on The Dillard Plantation lived in smaller, but cleaner and more suitable quarters than the Peabody house and he feared the conditions for the slaves on this grubby steak of land had to be horrendous. He prayed Peabody would need the money more than he wanted Sula.

"Now tell me whut yuh want!" Peabody scowled.

Jacob's sitting position on the log was now lower than that of Peabody and he believed that was to his benefit. He knew this little man needed to feel powerful; that was why his behavior was so loutish. He prayed his uncouth manner was no indication of his level of common sense. "Yes, Mr. Peabody," he began, "Mr. Bell told me yesterday he sold a slave named Sula tuh yuh. Ah come tuh offer tuh buy hur from yuh at a profit."

"She ain't fer sale!"

"Now, Mr. Peabody, Ah was told yuh paid five hundred dollars for the gal." Jacob tried to keep a stern business face, but he was ready to knock the little man off the stump. He stood from the log and paced in front of Peabody. "Was that yuh woman Ah met before yuh come along?"

"Whut's it tuh yuh?" His eyes met with Jacob's and he turned away.

Jacob stood as close to the man as he could and spoke quietly. "Ah will buy the slave gal from yuh today and yuh will sell hur tuh me willingly. She is my wench and was sold away from me out of spite. Ah will not have yuh treatin' hur worse than yuh treat yuh woman who is disgustin', filthy and fearful of yuh. Ah will pay yuh eight hundred dollars for my wench and yuh will give me a bill of sale. If yuh do not agree tuh my generous offer, you and yuh women will not see the light of tomorrow's dawn. Do Ah make myself clear?" Jacob stood over the little man and his unblinking blue eyes gazed down on him like they carried the weight of two anvils.

Peabody's whole body began to shake. "Yuh . . . yuh gone give me eight hundred dollars? Why didn't yuh say that befo'," Ol' Peabody spoke jovially. "Ann! Ann get out here!" he yelled out.

Jacob turned to Miles and Juke and waved for them to join him up at the house. He turned back to Peabody. "We're all goin' tuh the courthouse in Jonesville tuh register the sale. Have yuh woman fetch Sula and Ah'll pay yuh when the property been registered," Jacob demanded. Then he pulled a stack of folded money from his pocket, counted out eight hundred dollars and fanned it out at Peabody before stashing it back in his pocket. He smiled.

Peabody's eyes widened and then he protested. "Ah jes left that courthouse."

Ann Peabody quietly appeared on the porch and when Jacob looked up, Peabody jerked himself around. "Go fetch that new nigger gal. Make sure she got all hur stuff and bring hur here."

Sula followed Ann Peabody from behind the house carrying a small bundle with her personal property. A strip of potato sack covered her head and an additional bag had been cut open and used as a blanket in an attempt to keep her warm. Her eyes were dazed and she stumbled when she stepped on a sharp rock with only the rags that covered her feet. She didn't look at Jacob or

Juke. She appeared to be alive, but walking in a fog tunnel, her movement only accomplished through rote memory and only breathing because the Lord had not yet taken away her final breath.

Jacob wanted to kill Peabody at that very moment. He wanted to pick up that little man and break him in half. He loved Sula, Juke and Miles and he reminded himself of his responsibility to them. If he could not shake his need for revenge, he knew he would come back for Peabody later. He reached for the jacket in the back of the wagon and ran toward Sula. "Damn you, man!" he yelled at Peabody, "where are hur shoes?" He quickly wrapped the heavy coat around her shoulder and swept her up in his arms. Her teeth chattered in his ears and he rushed her to the back of the wagon where Juke and Miles helped him wrap her in the blankets. Jacob removed the scarf from his head and covered her head, neck and mouth with it, only leaving her nose and eyes free. She continued her daze, blank stare, not responding to anyone.

Jacob stormed back to Peabody and snatched him up by his shirt collar. "Where are hur shoes? You done almost killed hur in one day! If she dies, Ah'm coming back tuh kill you!" He slammed the little man to his dirt yard and stood over him. "Tell yuh woman tuh get hur shoes!"

"Ann!" Peabody screamed, "Ann, yuh hear me woman! Get dem shoes and bring 'em here!"

Ann Peabody showed up on the porch whining, "Yuh said them be my shoes!" She flung the black lace-up ankle boots in the yard and stormed back into the house.

Ol' Peabody retrieved the boots and handed them to Jacob. "She is an ungrateful wench," he said of his wife.

Seeing the shoes angered Jacob even more. "Yuh're a scum bastard, Peabody. Yuh do what yuh want tuh do wit' yuh own wench, but yuh damaged mine. Now yuh gone free hur for four hundred dollars or yuh be dead by tuhmorrow. Ah'm gone send my men on their way. Just you and me goin' tuh the courthouse tuh register hur emancipation. Yuh see, Ah don't want 'em involved should Ah have tuh kill yuh along the way or later, but they will be back after Sula is safe if things don't go right."

"Not a problem. Uh . . . four hundred gone be just fine. Yeah, that will be jes fine," Peabody sang out. "Yuh say yuh want hur free? Yes sur! Yes sur!

Ah can do that! She gon' be yours if that's what yuh want and Ah can do that. Ah don't want no trouble."

"Then there won't be any trouble if you do what you're told. Here's yuh money in cash, but yuh gonna write eight hundred dollars on the papers. Yuh see. Yuh wasted four hundred of yuh money by not caring for yuh property," Jacob ordered. "Now write out a pass so Sula can go with my men, then yuh gonna have those freedom papers written out and registered in the courthouse!"

Peabody stared up at Jacob, took a deep breath and nodded in defeat. He prepared the pass and handed it to Miles who read it, found it to be acceptable and nodded his approval. Juke drove the wagon and Miles sat in the seat next to him. Jacob rode Nutmeg and Peabody quietly rode beside him until they reach the main road. Juke cracked his whip over Red's head, guiding him to turn left and he broke out into an even trotting pace toward Clinton while Jacob and Peabody galloped off to the right toward Jonesville.

Jacob held the door for Peabody when they arrived at the courthouse. "Eight hundred and don't try anything stupid," he reminded Peabody when he walked past him.

"Yuh back here again?" the clerk asked Peabody.

"Yes sur, Charles, got me a sale for that slave gal. This man has paid tuh have hur freed. We need the papers and we need tuh register it."

"All right, sur. Uh . . . yuh freeing da niggah," Charles slurred at Jacob. "Is that yuh bastard she got in hur belly?" He turned and began searching for the right binder while Peabody gave Jacob a sly smirk.

Jacob felt his muscles flex. He felt like a restrained jack rabbit. He clenched his jaw at the same time his knuckles went cold from the tight fist he held. Peabody cowardly turned away. *Peace be still. Even white men go to jail, Jacob. Peace be still. Thank you, Mrs. Morton.* The Lord placed her words in his head just when he needed her calming influence. *Thank You, Lawd.* His lips were tight and his breath shallow, but he held his peace.

"Okay, Peabody Ah found yuh property list." Charles turned around to find Jacob smiling and Peabody standing with a bowed head and hands clasped in front of him.

"Yes, Ah got it, Uh . . . here it is," Charles sang out. "Says here yuh recorded a sale this morning. Five hundred dollars paid for the purchase of a slave gal name, Sula."

"Yeah, well now Ah just sold hur for eight hundred dollars to this man, Jacob Natty. Made me a nice little profit, too. Would yuh register this here as an emancipation sale for this gentleman?"

"Ah thank yuh if yuh would register her name as Sula Natty." Jacob said.

"Sure will." After a few minutes, Mr. Charles made the entry to the county record and handed the freedom document to Jacob.

ঌৄৄ

Index Number: 1223
Free & Freedom Paper: Sula Natty

State of South Carolina, City of Jonesville

Benjamin Peabody Deed for Sula Peabody.

Know all men by these presents, that I Benjamin Peabody of Union County, in the aforesaid state, in consideration of the sum of eight hundred dollars, to me in hand paid by Jacob Natty from motives of benevolence and humanity have emancipated and hereby manumit and set free from slavery my negro girl Sula Peabody, formerly known as Sula Dillard, from the County of Cherokee and state aforesaid, but at this time residing in the City and territory of Jonesville, County of Union, in the aforesaid state. She being a single brown skin girl about seventeen years of age and short black kinky hair and near black eyes and standing five feet and four inches high.

Jacob Natty has the owner's right to emancipate and on this condition he has given her the sir name of, Natty. As an emancipated woman Sula Natty is hereby granted all rights, titles and claims of, in and to, the estate and property which she may hereafter acquire or obtain.

In Witness whereof I, Charles John have hereunto set my hand the seventeenth day of December A D 1860. : County Clerk *Charles S Johns*

I the said B. Peabody do likewise release all claim whatsoever. And I do hereby give, grant and release unto the said, Jacob Natty, all my right, title, interest and claim of, in and to Sula (Peabody) Natty's person, labor and service and of and in and to the estate and property which she may hereafter acquire or obtain.

In Testimony Whereof, I Benjamin Peabody have this day hereto set my hand here on December the seventeenth A. D. 1860.

Seller: *Benjamin Peabody*   Benjamin Peabody

Buyer & Emancipator: Jacob Natty   Jacob Natty

Witness present: Charles S Johns: *Charles S Johns*

Recorded December seventeenth A.D. 1860

ᔕᗒᔓ

Jacob held the bill of sale and emancipation documents in his hand and carefully read each of the two pages while Peabody looked on. "Well, Ah see everything is in order and he continued to glare at Peabody sending him warning signals.

"Sure do and thank yuh, Mr. Charles," Jacob replied. He held out his hand and shook Peabody's and their business was done. He shook Charles' hand. "Uh . . . Mr. Peabody, would yuh follow me out?" He tipped his hat to Mr. Charles and left the building. Now standing on the courthouse steps, he tipped his hat to Peabody and reminded him saying, "The deal is done. Pray yuh never see me again, but, if my Sula is hurt, you will feel the pain, yuh might even die. Good day." He smiled, mounted Nutmeg and rode off without looking back.

chapter 19

It was late afternoon by the time Jacob arrived home. Mrs. Morton was in his cabin nursing Sula with a warm hearty soup. Juke and Capers had moved Jacob's bed closer to the fireplace and Sula had been swaddled in a bundle of blankets. Light flickered from the oil lantern on the table and blended with the remainder of the day's light that shown through the single window. Sula's eyes continued to hold that fixed gazed, her ebony colored skin appeared ashen and she still had not spoken a single word.

Tears flooded Jacobs's eyes and he spoke softly for anyone to hear him. "From the first day," his words came through his cracking voice, "Ah promised hur, Ah promised hur, Ah'd always protect hur and Ah didn't. This is all my fault."

"This is not yuh fault, Jacob," Mrs. Morton whispered sternly as she placed a small amount of soup against Sula's lips. Then she handed the soup bowl and spoon to Juke and pulled Jacob from the cabin. She pulled her shawl tight around her shoulders. "Oh Jacob it's cold out here," she complained.

Jacob nodded in the direction of Juke and Cappers' cabin. Oak embers smoldered in the fireplace and Jacob fed it splintered logs to force a blaze and push more heat into the small room. He lit the lanterns hanging on two opposite walls and a soft amber glow soaked the cabin. A wooden table and three handmade chairs had been placed in the middle of the room and two beds lined the outer walls. Jacob pulled out a chair for Mrs. Morton before taking a seat across from her.

"Jacob . . . this is a brutal world, especially the south. Negroes will always be treated like property here, free Negroes or not."

"Yes ma'am." He dropped his head into his hands and wiped tears from his eyes.

"Listen son and keep yuh wits about yuh." She reached and grabbed both of Jacob's wet hands and held them tightly.

He tried to pull free, but she held to him. If he pulled harder, he would have pulled her from her seat.

"Come here, Jacob. Bring yuh chair over here next tuh mine. We need tuh pray tuhgether. Then Ah will say what Ah have tuh say."

Jacob did what he was told and Mrs. Morton took hold of his hands again. She began. "Dear Lord and Father God. Bless this man and our families. Keep him safe and guide his thoughts and behavior so he may remain rational for the good of everyone he loves and who loves him. Show him the light, Lord and keep him safe. Bless his beloved Sula and heal her so she may be Jacob's life companion. May peace be still, Lord. In the name of Your precious Son Ah pray. Amen."

"Amen, Lord." Jacob responded. He opened his eyes and stared directly into Mrs. Morton's eyes.

She knew he was asking her for the information she promised. "Jacob, Ah asked the Lord tuh grant you rational thoughts and behavior. Ah asked that peace be still."

"Yes ma'am." He nodded and his body language screamed, TELL ME NOW!

"Sula was raped and beaten; not beaten with the whip, but with the closed hand and her mind has been beaten."

Jacob sat still for a moment; his mind and body seemed to require time to reunite with the words he didn't want to hear. Suddenly he yanked his hand away from Mrs. Morton. He leaped from the chair. "He hurt my Sula!" He cried out and began to pace the cabin. "He hurt my Sula!" he screamed a gut wrenching scream.

Mrs. Morton ran to the cabin door yelling, "Peace be still, Jacob! Peace be still!" She blocked the door, stretched out her arms and pushed her palms outward creating her own force field. She knew he would never touch her, to move her from the door, to push her from his path. And she was successful at keeping him in the cabin.

Jacob was physically and mentally repelled from the door and he collapsed into a ball on the floor; his blind rage surrendering to uncontrollable sobs.

"Peace be still, Jacob!" she continued, but now in a sing-song chant that seemed to pull the fire from his heart.

He could feel her bending over him rubbing his back and shoulders and making every attempt to comfort him. Tears ran down her face and she let them fall. "It's not okay, Jacob, but the Lord is gonna make everything all right. Ah believe the baby is all right. Ah want yuh tuh hold on and be strong for Sula. She needs yuh now more than ever."

Jacob's face was wet with tears when he lifted his head. "Ah wanna go after that little man and beat him like he hurt my Sula. Ah wanna burn his shack of a house down and run off his slaves. Sula was his slave; he didn't have tuh hurt hur. He only had hur one day. He took hur clothes and hur shoes. He beat hur and raped hur. And yuh tell me, 'Peace be still!'."

"Yes Jacob. They will know it was you and the law will come after yuh," Mrs. Morton whispered softly. "Yes, they think yuh are a white man, but the law comes after white men, too. So don't make it worst on yuh family. Leave it alone! Sula will heal!"

Jacob's spirit calmed, but his breath still quivered when he exhaled his sorrow. He opened himself up from that knot on the floor and sat holding his knees to his chest with his head bowed. Mrs. Morton returned to the chair at the table. She sat tall, clasped her hands in her lap and was quiet as she watched Jacob rock himself into a more controlled state. It was only after he returned to his place at the table did she break her silence. "Tuhmorrow morning Ah'm having Miles go for the doctor."

"Why would the doctor help Sula?" Jacob asked. He wiped his face with the tail of his shirt, but when he blinked new tears fell.

"Because Ah sent for him and he will be paid. Now, Ah want yuh tuh go tuh her. She needs to be reassured that she is safe. Ah've bathed her and put her in clean, fresh and warm clothing. Stay with her and keep telling her she is safe. Ah have tuh go home now. Have Capers or Juke walk with me."

"Yes ma'am," Jacob said. He hurried to the door, holding it open for her.

chapter 20

Jacob laid under the covers, his clothed body touching and holding Sula. The warmth of his body continued to warm and reassure her of her safety. He prayed she would return to him. The crescent moon moved down from midnight toward dawn and she stirred several times before uttering a tiny moan. He opened his eyes when she turned to face him, her eyes blinking, focusing and her voice making a murmur of sounds. She trembled like a strummed harp strings and he held her, placing her head on his chest, rubbing her back, her coarse hair, the side of her face and kissing her forehead. "Ah'm so sorry my love," he told her. "Rest now, yuh need yuh rest. Don't yuh worry no more. We're gonna be tuhgether until God separates us. Sleep my love."

Jacob woke to Sula placing wood on the smoldering embers in the fireplace. "Sula," he called out.

She turned. She smiled. Her complexion had recaptured its glow and her eyes shown bright against the shimmering flare of the fire. Her dark brown hair crowned her head in tight coarse ringlet down to her shoulders. Jacob stood. His approach was slow. He wanted time to absorb her beauty before wrapping his arms around her. He wanted to hear her voice. He had heard her cry, but he had not heard her speak.

"My lovely Sula, how are you?" he asked. "Do yuh forgive me?" He wrapped his arms around her and whispered in her ear, "Do you forgive me for not comin' for yuh sooner?"

She was quiet. She held tightly to Jacob. She kissed his cheek and held his face in her hands while staring in his eyes. She rubbed his hair and a tear travel down her face. Her lips moved, but sound escaped her. She placed one hand on Jacob's lips and another on her own. Fear crept over her expression. A flood of tears filled her eyes and she moaned out her cries. Jacob tried to hold her, but she pushed him away. She patted her throat like she was trying to wake it up. She took a deep breath and pushed out a coarse deep throaty sound, "My voice," she bellowed out in a static deep bass tone. Her eyes widened, but they couldn't hold the flood of tears that followed.

"That's okay, Sula. Yuh have a voice. It's gone all comeback tuh yuh in good time." He kissed her lips. "Ah'm gonna make yuh smile and jump for joy."

Sula moved her lips and mouthed, "What?"

"Yuh a free woman." Jacob reached for his jacket and pulled a rolled document from the breast pocket. "This be yuh freedom paper. Ah bought yuh freedom from Peabody. Now, it says right here," he pointed to the words as he spoke, "Sula Natty has been granted hur freedom from hur owner, Jacob Natty, this day, December 17, 1860. She is hereby known as the free woman, Sula Natty. There be more written here, but Ah done told yuh the important words. Yuh be a free woman, Sula. Nobody owns yuh, not even me. My lovely, this is a legal document and it is registered in the courthouse." Jacob told her the information written on her emancipation papers in words she could understand.

A loud ruptured sound rushed from Sula's mouth and she froze in place. Her eyes were wide and her breath quivered. Staring at Jacob, she mouthed the word, "Free?"

Jacob nodded. "Yuh be a free woman, Sula," he whispered.

Sula wrapped her arms around him and buried her head in the nape of his neck. Jacob didn't know if she was crying or laughing, so he just held her until her body stopped vibrating before placing her freedom papers in her hand. After a while she gently kissed his cheek.

Sula had no idea how the words read, but once accepting her papers, she stood and danced around the cabin holding it high above her head before caressing it gently against her chest. Sula spun and danced until she tired and the tears that had glazed her eyes were now gone. After returning to the table she stared at the words before finally realizing she was free. She inhaled and gestured for Jacob to read her freedom words to her again and again.

"Sula, Ah will teach yuh tuh read many words, but the first thing Ah'm gonna do is tuh teach yuh tuh read every word on this paper."

She smiled and again gently rolled her papers and held them to her chest.

"Do yuh want me to keep yuh papers with mine for safe keepin'?"

Sula smiled, nodded and then held her hand out gesturing for Jacob to wait, to let her hold it for a little while longer.

Jacob smiled, "Okay, yuh hold it as long as yuh want and give it tuh me when yuh be ready." He cupped her face in his hands, kissed her lips and then every part of his face smiled.

Sula took his hand and placed it on her stomach.

"Ah know. Our baby will be born free," he whispered.

Sula flung her arms up and spun around.

"Yes, Sula, yes, but now, Ah have tuh go tuh Mrs. Morton's house tuh tell hur you be better befo' she sends Miles off tuh fetch the doctor. Yuh can stay here where it be warm or yuh can walk across the field wit' me."

She held out the flannel nightgown she was wearing and turned searching for her slave clothes. Jacob told her about the gift of clothing from Mrs. Morton, but she continued searching for her slave rags. "Stop, Sula! Yuh not a slave now! Yuh be free. Yuh got different clothes now and yuh be sure tuh thank Mrs. Morton for them. Ah burned yuh slave clothes."

At first Sula appeared bewildered, then she smiled, unrolled her freedom paper and stared at the illegible lettering. Her heart pounded wildly as she held it to her chest. While her chest was still heaving she handed it to Jacob for safe keeping. Turning toward the bundle of clothes, her smile grew even brighter; she lifted each article up to Jacob: a gray Princess Ann cotton dress, a blue and white checkered dress with a white lace collar, a brown polished cotton shoulder sash, a white cotton petticoat, two pairs of flesh colored stockings, two camisoles and two pairs of bloomers. Her legs weaken; she collapsed down on Jacob's bed and cried and laughed and cried some more.

"Ah will go tuh town and buy yuh some new shoes, mittens and a warm coat," Jacob whispered. "Everything gonna be just fine."

Sula stood and held the gray dress against her and spun around. She kissed Jacob, handed him his coat and hat and guided him to the door. "Wait for me," she mouthed and she hurried to dress.

Once dressed, she opened the door for Jacob to return to the cabin while she put her shoes on over the thick stockings. Then she took the shoulder sash and ripped it down the middle and wrapped it neatly around her head.

Jacob removed the wool blanket from the bed and wrapped it around her shoulders, before wrapping the remainder of the scarf around her neck.

Sula stood near the front porch and refused to enter Mrs. Morton's home until Jacob took her to the back kitchen door. As soon as she stepped into the room she squeezed a hand full of material from the sides of her dress, bowed her head and took a small curtsey.

"She is tryin' tuh say, thank you," Jacob said. "She's a lot better Mrs. Morton, but she has trouble talking."

"Well, yuh welcome, Sula. Ah'm so happy tuh see yuh better. Now we need tuh fix yuh voice."

Sula stood frozen in place. Still afraid of change and distrustful of white people. She clung to Jacob as he led her by her elbow to the chair close to the table. He sat next to her and Mrs. Morton sat facing her.

"Sula, darling," Mrs. Morton began, "Ah need to ask yuh some questions about yuh voice that may bring back unpleasant memories. Would that be all right?"

Sula nodded, but she was fascinated by the lace window curtains and a matching tablecloth. She had seen such in the large mansion, but this was a smaller house and the ensemble was more intimate. She needed to see beauty while answering questions about ugly memories. So she let her eyes follow the swirls and curves of the lace as Mrs. Morton spoke. She wondered who this white woman was. Why was she so nice? Could she trust her? Could she sell her away from Jacob? When Jacob stood and walked toward the door, Sula pushed her chair back and hurried to his side.

"It's okay Sula," he said, "Ah'm gonna stay right here." He walked her back to her seat. "You can trust Mrs. Morton. She's like a mother tuh me. She takes care of all of us. Yuh safe now." He kissed her forehead and returned her to her seat. "Let hur try tuh help yuh."

Sula nodded, tilted and lowered her head. Now she was only looking at Mrs. Morton with her peripheral vision.

"Oh Sula, you may hold yuh head up and look at me; Ah'm yuh friend. Now, Ah do need tuh ask yuh some questions, okay?"

Sula lifted her head, stared cautiously at Jacob and when he smiled at her she appeared to relax and then she turned toward Mrs. Morton again. Jacob returned to his seat hoping she would feel more comfortable.

"Okay now, were yuh screamin' hard when that man hurt yuh?" Mrs. Morton's face held a soft relaxing smile and she hoped to remove the bite from her blunt question.

Sula shifted her eyes between her and Jacob. She nodded and then shifted her focus away, now staring at a picture on the wall.

"Is that when yuh voice went?" Mrs. Morton pushed on and reaching to take hold of Sula's hands, to comfort and reassure her.

Startled, Sula pulled back, slipping her hands from Mrs. Morton's grip.

Jacob sprang lively, wrapping his arms around Sula's shoulders and nodding gently to Mrs. Morton. "It's all right Sula. It's all right," he whispered. He nodded for Mrs. Morton to try again. She did and when she took hold of Sula's hands for the second time she could feel her hesitation. Sula's eyes widened and shown like black pearls on a bed of cotton. Her lips were absent of a genuine smile, but gently curled. Mrs. Morton could see she was secretly crying for Jacob to rescue her. "It's okay, Sula," Mrs. Morton whispered softly, "Jacob is right here and Ah'm right here, too. Ah just want tuh help yuh tuh talk again. Ah'm not like other white people; Ah won't hurt yuh." Mrs. Morton began rubbing the back of her hands and at the same time Jacob was rubbing her shoulders and upper arms. Sula inhaled slowly and her eyelids closed pushing teardrops down her cheeks. Then more tears came and Mrs. Morton reached over and wrapped her arms around her. "Cry child. Yuh have so much tuh cry for. Cry as much as yuh want while Ah hold yuh."

Sula cried. She allowed Mrs. Morton to hold her and she sobbed in her arms like she was one of her children. Jacob turned away and continuously wiped away his tears. His core shook with anger from the sounds of her anguish. When he had last seen her, she was smiling. He couldn't help remembering his promise to keep her safe. He believed it was his freedom, lust and broken promises that caused her so much pain. He was feeling his heart breaking for the unimaginable suffering he had caused her. His pain was uncontrollable and when he took that deep breath, in that moment, his pain reinforced the hatred he had for Jackson, Peabody and the overseers at The Dillard. Mrs. Morton's words returned to him, *Peace be still.* He realized he couldn't allow anger to dictate his actions. He took a deep breath, *Peace be still,* sounded in his head and he wiped away his remaining tears. He turned to face Sula and smiled, knowing in his heart somehow he would make it all right.

In time, Sula regained control of her emotions. She turned to Jacob and nodded while Mrs. Morton was still holding her. Jacob touched the back of Mrs. Morton's hand to get her attention. "Thank yuh ma'am. Ah believe she's much better."

Smiling and sitting back in her chair, Mrs. Morton lightly cleared her throat and smiled at Sula.

Sula nodded and gave Mrs. Morton a gentle smile and used the sash from her dress to wipe her tears.

Mrs. Morton dabbed at her own tears with the corner of her apron and returned Sula's smile. "Now Sula," she began again, "Ah believe yuh have strained yuh voice from screamin' and that's why yuh can't talk."

Jacob held tight to Sula's hand. "What does that mean, Mrs. Morton? Will she get better?"

"Sure! Sula just needs tuh rest hur voice," She spoke to Jacob, then shifted her attention back to Sula. "Yuh should not try tuh talk for a few days. Drink warm tea three times a day and continue tuh wear a scarf around yuh neck tuh keep yuh voice box warm." Mrs. Morton pointed to her own throat. "Ah believe yuh should rest yuh whole self. Stay in bed for a few days. You and yuh baby have had quite an ordeal. A few days of bed rest will be good for yuh." She smiled at Jacob and continued, "Yuh not a slave now, Sula. Yuh can let yuh man take care of yuh."

"She's right." Jacob looked at her. "Let me take yuh home and put yuh tuh bed."

Mrs. Morton pushed herself up from the chair. "Just wait one minute, Ah have some hot grits, ham, eggs and hot biscuits ready and yuh can take that first cup of warm tea right here. Jacob yuh know yuh boys been takin' yuh meals over here. Sula is welcome, too. It's time for yuh two tuh eat. Yuh brothers and my youngungs have already had breakfast."

Sula stared at Jacob. She had never been served by a white person. She was confused; her world had flipped. She wanted to do the cooking for Jacob and for Juke and Capers, but there was no food in the cabin, or pots and pans, or kettles. Even the clothes she wore were strange; they were warm and soft and comfortable. She had slept in a flannel gown, a garment that she never knew existed and now she was told to rest in bed for a few days. *How does a person rest in bed unless they are near death?* She thought. She sat at Mrs. Morton's table and was served breakfast by her on matching dishes. She smiled and mouthed a timid, "Thank yuh," and then she returned to the common posture of a slave.

chapter 21

Jacob and Miles rode into Clinton to pick up the finalized deed for the fifteen acres of land purchased from Mr. Haynes. It was Tuesday morning; a day that dictated the two main streets, wooden sidewalks and merchants should only have a low volume of visitors and customers. Instead, Clinton could have been mistaken for the bustle of a Saturday afternoon shopping day. Men congregated in clusters, cursing the new president and the union of the American states.

"Who da hell do dey think they are? Dem damn Yankees voted in that Lincoln as president and he was never on da ballot down here in our southern states!" a man shouted and waved up a crumpled newspaper. Ain't we 'pose tuh be part of these United States?

"Dey don't want us in da union, we don't need to be in da union," another man yelled out.

"Each state su'pose tuh make dey own laws," someone else scream.

"Yeah!" the mob of men yelled.

"Slavery is our right!" "Dem damn republicans can't change our laws!" "We gotta do somethin'!" "We gotta fight for our rights!" "Yeah! Dey ain't gonna get away wit' it!" the spontaneous shouts riddled throughout the crowd.

Miles was at a loss while Jacob sat tall with an outward expression of awareness. "Stay here Jacob, Ah'm gonna find out what's goin' on." Miles dismounted and handed Jacob the reins' to Red and quickly disappeared into the throng of men.

Jacob watched as the men continued yelling out. The men shouted two and three at a time, all speaking at once; their arms flailed, their heads bobbed and their legs stomped the dry dirt street. Occasionally, Miles could be seen, but he didn't seem to utter a word. His head was constantly nodding and shaking and he turned from man to man, trying to attend to each conversation. Minutes later he waved his hand and walked from the crowd, returning to Jacob. He mounted Red and they decided not to discuss the issue until they were on their way out of town. They rode over to the courthouse to pick up the land deed and had to endure more anti-

Yankee rhetoric. There was much of the same talk while at the mercantile, when purchasing the shoes, coat, mittens and scarf for Sula. There was no doubt that the men of Clinton had a hunger to voice their opinion and hatred against the northern states. Miles engaged the shop owner a little longer while Jacob busied his wife with showing him their quality, light-weight fabric that Sula could use as dress sashes and head wraps, a special gift to help put that twinkle back in her eyes. Then they were on their way home.

With the town miles behind them, so went what appeared to be the caviling of angry men. Miles spoke first saying, "They're talkin' war. Can the leaders of South Carolina breakaway from the United States without everybody saying so?"

"They want to get some other southern states tuhgether and form a union of Confederate states," Jacob responded. He tightened his scarf over his head and across his face to block the cold December air, before returning his hat to his head. "That's the way Ah read it in the newspaper," he added.

Miles sat tall in his saddle. By 9:00 A.M. the sun had already warmed the air and the deep breath he took was exhilarating. "They said the new president, a Republican named Lincoln, wanted them tuh end slavery."

"Yup . . . read 'bout that, too. It's gone tuh start gettin' crazy 'round here." Jacob announced.

"Yeah, this guy Lincoln wants tuh end slavery," Miles began explaining. "And those men say they'll go tuh war tuh stop that from happenin'. But, from what Ah know, most of them ain't slave holders. They're willin' tuh fight and die tuh benefit the wealthy slaveholders. If there weren't no free labor, there'd be more paid labor for everyone, colored and white. Why are they so willin' tuh die for the rich?"

Jacob stopped Nutmeg and while his horse pranced in her steps, he spoke frankly to Miles. "Ah'm a Negro man! Ah ain't fightin' tuh hurt my brothers. Ah think it be time Ah take my family north befo' things get real sour 'round here. If war comes, Ah be fightin' tuh free my brothers. Ah want yuh tuh get yuh mama and family outta the south too, befo' you, Evan and Robby get pulled intuh their southern army and yuh mama be left alone tuh hurself and yuh baby sistahs."

Miles stared at Jacob. He tilted his head to the left and their eyes met. He knew Jacob meant what he said and he knew his timing was right. "How would yuh go? How do yuh know where tuh go? How do yuh know so much 'bout all this?"

Jacob leaned over his saddle bit and held the reins in one hand. "Ah read everything Ah get my hands on. Every week Ah get da newspaper when Ah'm in town and Ah been lissenin' tuh da town folk. Ah know when it be time tuh leave this place."

"Yuh knew all 'bout this, Jacob?"

"Ah knew."

"Then why did yuh buy the land?"

"At the time Ah needed a place for me and Sula. And we still have a place tuh comeback tuh," Jacob said. "The land is not important now. Ah been readin' 'bout this stuff, but Ah ain't seen no real crazy signs of it 'till tuhday. Still, Ah been planin' if it do happen. It ain't jes 'bout slavery, but that be da main reason. If there be a war, it be too late tuh leave then."

Miles stared off in the distance while fear of the unknown drained the pinkish tint from his cheeks. "Will yuh come tuh the house so we can talk tuh mama?" he asked.

"Ah'll be there as soon as Ah talk with Juke, Capers and Sula." Jacob responded and then he nodded and made clicking sounds signaling Nutmeg to make speed.

Miles nudged Red with his heels and the horse began to gallop.

Jacob held a newspaper with a headlines describing South Carolina's discontent with the northern election, the president and the principles of the new Republican Party. The second page had news of slave and livestock auctions and sales, mercantile sales and such, as well as information on crop shipment and passenger travel by coach, train, steamboat and railroad.

He entered Mrs. Morton's kitchen wearing an apologetic expression. Sula, Juke and Capers stood behind him on the back porch waiting to be invited in. "Ah beg yuh pardon, Mrs. Morton, but Ah took the liberty of having my family come along since this involves them too."

Mrs. Morton held up her arms and beckoned all of them into the kitchen. "We need four more chairs," she said to her sons.

"Ah can help, ma'am," Juke said and he followed the Morton boys.

As soon as everyone was seated around the table, Jacob began. "Mrs. Morton, Ah feel da hairs on my arms tinglin'. Ah pray a lot. Ah ask God tuh guide me and be my light. Now, Ah hear him tellin' me tuh take my family and go north. He has blessed me with enough money so we can make a good start and Ah can help you too if yuh be needin'."

Miles stood, walked behind his mother and massaged her shoulders. "We will always own this property, Mama. We can come back one day." He pulled his chair back from the table and took his seat.

Mrs. Morton removed her handkerchief from her sleeve and dabbed at her eyes before rubbing Miles hands. Miles had briefed his family on the dilemma. Then, her eyes met with Sula's and they gave each other an understanding smile before she shifted her gaze toward Jacob. "We have also been blessed, Jacob. Thank yuh kindly for yuh offer." Turning back to respond to Miles, she said, "Ah understand that we may return, son." She looked over at Jacob again and mustered a smile. "Mr. Haynes spoke briefly of this dilemma last Sunday, of course from his point of view. Tell me yuh plan, Jacob." She returned to dabbing at her tears knowing that even if they fled, her sons could still be pressed into service. They could even place rifles in young Evan and Robby's hands. It pained her that they wouldn't be fighting for what they believed in. She wept and continued to listen.

"Well, ma'am," Jacob spoke in a level tone, first to Mrs. Morton and then he shared his attention with everyone sitting around the table. "Ah know there's a train leavin' Clinton at seven o'clock Thursday morning. From my studyin', it seems tuh be best tuh travel up tuh Wilmington, North Carolina. There be steamships there that will take us tuh any free state on the northeastern coast. Ah been readin' 'bout New York or New Jersey. They seem like they be good states for startin' a new life. Now tuh escape a war we could travel through New York as far north as Canada, but all those northern places be mighty cold in da winter. Now that jes be da price for freedom. We can decide how far north we go later."

"Yes, that's right, but Thursday! My Lord! So soon!" Mrs. Morton murmured. All she knew would be left behind in less than two days and she didn't know if she would ever return to the land she and her husband struggled for and he gave his life to.

"Yes, ma'am. The train only leaves on the Clinton line on Tuesday and Thursday. Anything can happen before next Tuesday." Jacob stood from his chair and ran his fingers through his hair. "Ah know it sounds bad, but it be bad, ma'am. Everybody done gone crazy and Ah don't want tuh stay for a war tuh catch us in da south. We are free. We don't have tuh stay here. My family can't leave without me. Freedom papers don't mean nothin' unless they have a white person wit' 'em. So, Ah jes have tuh be white a little longer."

Mrs. Morton patted the table, making a repetitive drumming noise in her attempt to beat out her frustration. "Well, Ah guess five more white people will help if yuh can count the twins."

"Yes, ma'am . . . the twins count," Jacob responded in a softer, more humorous tone.

"Please continue with yuh plan," she said.

Jacob smiled and remained standing. His eyes saddened when he addressed his family. "I have tuh go back tuh The Dillard for Tillie and da chillen. Ah can't leave 'em behind. All of y'all gone have tuh ride in a separate train car 'cause they don't allow Negroes and white folk tuh sit tuhgether. Y'all just make sure yuh keep yuh freedom papers on yuh. Ah got a plan for Tillie 'cause she ain't got no papers." Jacob turned and addressed Miles and his mother. "We," pointing to himself, Miles and Mrs. Morton as he spoke, "we are gonna express tuh the train conductor that our people are our personal servants and we expect the best treatment for y'all. Either Miles or me will stay with y'all during da travel tuh be sure yuh safe."

Capers interrupted. "Uh . . . Jacob . . . Ah don't wanna go."

Jacob froze. He inhaled deeply and stared at Capers with fiery eyes. He wanted to yell, to order him to obey, to control and protect him until he was sure he was safe, but he was a man. He covered his eyes and allowed a calmer side of himself to emerge before addressing Juke. "And you?" he asked.

Juke shifted his eyes between Capers and Jacob, while Sula's eyes remained fixed and lowered. "Ah don't wanna go either, Jacob. When da war comes, it gon' be everywhere. Ah be lost in a new land. Here . . . now, Ah got new friends and we know dis land," Juke explained. "We could help y'all get away and take care of da land 'til yuh get back," he explained. "If war comes, da white man be too busy fightin' tuh bother wit' us. But, Ah agree wit' yuh, Jacob; if war do come dey spec you, Miles, Evan and Robby tuh go fight. Y'all be needin' tuh go away."

Jacob covered his face with his hands and everyone was quiet for a moment. It wasn't just the war, it was also Jackson and Sula and real freedom. It was the dangers of the south. It was false freedom and real fear. It was that very moment he wished he had never asked his brothers to leave The Dillard. Having their lives in his hands was more oppressing than the oppression of slavery. He pressed his hands down on the table and stood staring intensely at his brothers. "My brothers, my blood," he pleaded, "please come along. This be a horrible land. Ah believe the good Lawd has forgotten this place. You'll never be free here. Ah promise yuh, y'all will find happiness."

The visual fix Jacob had on Capers didn't deter his decision to stay. "We ain't goin', Jacob!" he declared adamantly. He sat back in his chair and shook his head as he spoke. "We be happy here. Massa Haynes lets us visit his plantation. We made friends. We met women we like. Bad things gonna happen everywhere if war comes," he repeated.

"So yuh put yuhself back in slavery?" Jacob shifted his eyes between his brothers and angrily paced the sidewall area of the kitchen.

"No, Jacob!" Juke added. "We can leave whenever we want and he feeds us and treats us good."

"Ah understand, but watch out for Jackson. Word might get back tuh him that Ah got Sula and yuh know how he hates me. He's gone hate me more 'cause Ah'm goin' after Tillie, Jenny and Simon. Take care of the livestock, then, spend yuh time over at The Haynes'." Jacob turned away from his brothers and the unbearable pain of losing them caused him to feel unsteady. His chest was pounding from the pain of holding back his heartache and tears. Mrs. Morton reached for and held his hand, then gave him an approving nod. Jacob returned to his brothers and wrapped his arms around them. "We'll be tuhgether again. Ah understand yuh meaning."

"Thank yuh, Jacob," Capers replied and Juke nodded and smiled.

Miles placed his hand on Jacob's shoulder. "Ah don't know Tillie and da children," he said, "but if they're important tuh yuh, then they're important tuh all of us. Ah'll be helpin' yuh protect them all."

"Well, Tillie be still back on da Dillard Plantation and now she be carin' for da twins, Simon and Jenny. They are my ten year old brother and sistah. Ah can't leave them behind."

"Is dey gone let yuh stay wit' dem? Ah thought colored and white can't be in da same train car tuhgether," Capers asked.

"Oh, it's okay if da white man wants tuh be with his servants, but da Negroes can't want tuh be with da white," Miles explained.

Sula, Juke and Capers each expressed an understanding smile.

Then, Jacob sat to reassure Sula and Mrs. Morton stood again. Jacob had never seen her heavy with thought. "There is so much tuh do tuh get ready," she whined. "We're gonna need traveling bags. Ah don't have enough for everyone. What will we do with the farm?"

"Mama, Ah know yuh don't approve of fibbing, but that's what we're gonna have tuh do. Why don't we just tell Mr. Haynes we have tuh leave tuh go help yuh family down in Florida, in Jacksonville, if he ask where," Miles suggested. "Ah'll say we'll be gone 'til plantin' time. We'll tell 'em Juke and Capers will be carin' for the horses and livestock 'til we return."

"Very good Miles. You can drive me tuh the plantation in a little while. We're gonna need Ol' Blue tuh get tuh the train station so Juke and Capers don't get lost." Mrs. Morton exhaled and smiled. "Ah'll tell Mr. Haynes," she said.

Sula leaned closer to Jacob and he rubbed her arm. "Okay folk," he continued, "When we sail, we will all want tuh stay together." He looked to Mrs. Morton for confirmation. She nodded and he continued. "We'll book first class passage, two large adjoining staterooms. Sula and Tillie and Jenny will act as the personal servant tuh Mrs. Morton and the twins. Me and Simon will stay wit' Miles and the boys in the adjoining stateroom. We'll act this part 'til we get off the ship." Jacob took Sula's hand in his.

"How'd yuh know all 'bout this stuff, Jacob?" Juke spouted off.

Annoyed, Jacob laughed. "Ah read, man. Da newspaper," he shouted and then he turned to Mrs. Morton and spoke in a softer tone. "Ma'am, now 'bout Tillie."

Mrs. Morton nodded.

"Well ma'am, Ah just can't leave dem behind. Mammy Pearl and Ollie are safe on the Bell Farm. Ah want tuh go for Tillie and da twins tuhmorrow afternoon. Ah'll reach the plantation by nightfall and have 'em back in time tuh travel with us Thursday morning." Jacob faced Mrs. Morton with a pleading expression on his face. "Ma'am, Tillie will need forged freedom papers. Can yuh help me wit' that?"

Mrs. Morton smiled. "That will be my pleasure, Jacob."

Jacob exhaled. "Oh, thank yuh, ma'am. Can yuh have the papers ready before Ah go after hur tuhmorrow? Her name can be Matilda Morton and yuh can say she was freed on July 25, 1855."

"Oh Jacob, this is exciting," she let out a chuckle, "Ah finally get to free a slave."

Everyone in the room laughed along with Mrs. Morton.

"Ah'll write up the papers and Ah have a seal," Mrs. Morton announced. "She is your family and we can't leave any of them behind no more than we could leave Evan or Robby."

"Thank yuh . . . thank yuh, thank yuh," Jacob said as he patted her hands. "Now Ah need tuh buy Tillie some clothes. The chillen have clothes. They worked as house servants, but they might need coats and hats and mits. Dey 'bout the size of yuh boys."

"Jacob, yuh take care of Tillie and dem chillen, we know how tuh take care of ourselves," Capers said.

Jacob stood and walked tuh the kitchen door. "Mrs. Morton, may we take our leave for a few moments?" His eyes addressed Juke and Capers and they followed him into the yard. He kept his back to the house and as soon as his brothers approached he began to speak. "What will yuh do when Jackson comes and yuh know he gone find this place?"

"Brother don't worry. If Jackson comes here, we be taken off through dem woods. Rusty will let us know if anybody be comin'," Caper replied.

Juke ran his hand through his hair before massaging the back of his neck. He exhaled slowly and spoke with his head held low. "We feel safe when we be at the Haynes' quarters. Our people be there. Massa Haynes be good tuh us. Jacob, we just settled in, now yuh want us to be scared again."

The blue in Jacob's eyes appeared to fade. He had loss this battle. He knew they meant to stay behind. Defeated, he nodded his head and returned to the kitchen and sat next to Mrs. Morton.

"All right, now, Tillie and the chillen . . ." he continued. He knew he had to put Juke and Capers decision aside and move on.

"Ah'll go tuh town with yuh, Jacob," Mrs. Morton began, "but Ah want tuh stop at Mr. Haynes' first."

Sula wrapped her arms around Jacob's neck, when she noticed tears had settled in his eyes.

"Ah really love you, Sula," he whispered and he fought to give her a tiny smile. "Now remember, you are supposed tuh be restin'. So Ah'm gone take yuh back to the cabin and put yuh tuh bed while we go back tuh town."

Sula returned his smile and nodded.

"Robby, go hitch the carriage for me," Mrs. Morton said. "Now, Ah want you and Evan to take care of the girls 'til Ah return." She turned to Miles. "Son," she spoke softer, "It might be best if we ride down tuh Martin's Depot to shop when we leave Mr. Haynes, so we can buy the tickets. It's closer and Ah think we should board the train over there so no one knows our business. While we're there we need tuh book our passage on that steamer too; they can send a telegraph for the booking. Only Blue, Capers and Juke will know we left out of Martin's Depot and they won't say anything. Then, Ah'll shop for clothes for Tillie and the children," Mrs. Morton added.

chapter 22

Jackson returned to the Yorkville Depot at 6:00 A.M., Wednesday morning. His trip to Columbia had been a success in spite of having to wait to seek out Jacob and investigate the true cause of the fire. He managed to order a complete line of clothing suitable for a southern gentleman, engage an architect, employ a contractor and submit the requisitions required for the building materials. But, Jacob continued to be his constant haunt for three days and caused him to have fitful nights.

After retrieving his horse from the stable, he rode off on the three hour journey to the Bell's farm in Jonesville. He would have no rest until he could settle his suspicions concerning Sula and if it held true, he would hunt Jacob down. He was ready and anxious to give his soul the thrill of revenge.

His horse was well rested and that was good, because Jackson had no mercy on the poor creature. The only reason he pulled back on his speed was to spare himself the possibility of his own ill fate along the roadside should the mare drop beneath him. By late morning, he stepped down from his horse and stood before Mrs. Bell with his hat in his hand. His eyes were searching the porch and yard for signs of the slave women.

"Who are yuh?" Mrs. Bell shouted with an unrefined tone that bruised Jackson's ears like course sandpaper.

Some people are more suited tuh be slaves than slaveholders, Jackson thought. "Hello ma'am," he responded, addressing her as politely as possible.

"You ain't never said who yuh are. Now, what be yuh business here?" She reached across her threshold and picked up her shotgun before closing the door behind herself. The house curtains shifted and swayed at closed windows that were absent of breezes.

Jackson's eyes were attracted to the movement of the curtains. Mrs. Bell raised her rifle and cocked it. The click attracted his attention. "Ah'm waiting. Yuh better start talkin' or yuh better start gettin' off my land, mister," Mrs. Bell warned.

"Oh . . . yes ma'am. Ah'm the man that sold yuh husband the slave women."

"Oh, yuh the highfalutin slave holder. Dem gals be my friends now and yuh want 'em back. Ah don't cotton tuh slave holdin'. Get 'fore Ah lite up yuh britches!"

"Yes ma'am." Jackson mounted his horse and rode to the end of the path. He turned and stared back at the house and Mrs. Bell was still standing on the porch. He thought he would ride down the road and check the nearby fields when he noticed a small store off in the distance. He decided to stop and make a few inquiries. Just then Mr. Bell drove up in his buck wagon with his sons.

"Well, howdy, Mr. Dillard. What brings yuh over this way?" Bell asked, greeting Jackson and wearing a broad smile. Before Jackson could reply, he turned and began introducing his four sons, including details about their ages, their likes and dislikes.

Jackson's face held a coy, uninteresting, but polite smile. He nodded pleasingly as Bell spoke and he tried to get a word in when Bell was completing his say about the fourth and youngest.

Jackson tugged at his hat. "Huh, Mr. Bell, Ah see yuh're very proud of yuh sons and yuh should be, they're somethin' tuh be proud of." He saluted each one with a slight tug to the brim of his hat and a smile and then directed his attention to Mr. Bell. "Uh, Mr. Bell . . . Ah came by tuh see yuh because Ah had a little trouble at my place and Ah'm tryin' tuh investigate the source. Ah thought maybe yuh could be of some help."

"Yes sur, whatever Ah can do tuh help yuh." Bell responded.

"Well, sur, do yuh still have that slave gal called, Sula?

"Oh no! Ah sold hur right off. Made a good profit, too. Sold hur tuh a small farmer named, Mr. Peabody; sorry tuh say he is a nasty little man in more ways than one."

"Can yuh tell me where tuh find this man?"

"Pretty much so. But yuh the second man come askin' 'bout that gal. Just this Monday, two white men and a high yellow negra come a askin'," Bell offered.

Jackson sat taller on his horse and angrily exhaled. "Tell me, did one of the white men have blue eyes and blond hair?"

"Yuh right 'bout that. He was the one doin' all the talkin'. He even took a particular fondness tuh my other slaves, Pearl and Ollie. He said if Ah ever wanted tuh sell 'em, Ah should contact the other white man." Bell pushed his hand under his hat to scratch his head. "Ah . . . Ah got the man's name and town writ' down at the house and Ah can almost remember it." He continued scratching his head and squinting his eyes.

Jackson appeared to sink in his saddle. The last thing he wanted to do was return to Bell's house where his crazy wife was.

"Miles Morton, Daddy. That's whut his name is," Bell's oldest son called out.

Jackson sat at attention.

"Yeah! He lives over in Clinton," Mr. Bell spoke up. "That's it, Miles Morton from Clinton. Do yuh still want tuh know where The Peabody farm is?"

"Sure do." Jackson fought to keep a straight face, to hold back his scowl of anger and his restless need for revenge. He felt heat rising in his body with beads of perspiration collecting under his clothing. If he were at The Dillard, Tillie would feel the wrath meant for Jacob. He knew she wasn't responsible for his actions, but she was the only person he had left that was like family to him and he needed a receptacle for his anger.

Mr. Bell gave Jackson directions to Peabody's farm and Jackson was off.

ॐ∾ॐ

Mr. Peabody stepped out on his front porch and waited for Jackson to approach. "Who are yuh?" He yelled out in an ungentlemanly manner.

Jackson stopped and stared at the shack of a house. "My goodness," he spoke to the wind, "if Ah didn't know better, Ah'd believe Ah was ridin' up tuh my slave quarters." He continued his approach. It was not his manner to scream out his name or business. At the appropriate moment, he responded. "Good afternoon, Mr. Peabody. Ah'm Jackson Dillard, owner of The Dillard Plantation in Gaffney. Ah understand yuh acquired a slave name, Sula a few days ago."

Mrs. Peabody stood in the opened door and watched as her husband moved to the edge of the porch. The corner of Jackson's eye caught her image. He stared at her high-top, ragged and twisted over shoes, her dusty cotton dress with the greasy peasant collar. Her skin was so cracked and soiled dirt settled in the crevices giving her neck and face the appearance of a crude road map. Her eyes met with Jackson's and he quickly looked away.

"That wench caused me nothing but trouble," Mr. Peabody scowled.

"What did yuh say?" Jackson asked, startled by his statement. Mrs. Peabody's appearance was so shocking he had never seen a white woman so poorly kept.

"The wench . . . Mr. Jackson, that wench, man . . . Ah paid five hundred for that wench, only tuh be forced tuh sell hur tuh that blue eyed devil for four hundred. That bastard threatened me, then made me go tuh town with him tuh register the sale." He spat a hunk of mucus that lay on the dried dirt, wiped his mouth with the back of his hand and stared up at Jackson. "That damn man," he cursed, "do yuh know what he did next?"

Jackson stared at the disgusting little man without registering a response.

Peabody didn't care that he didn't respond. His only intention was to blow off his anger. "That bastard set hur free!"

"He set hur free?" Jackson repeated his lips curling down into a frown.

"Sho-nuff. Wrote out the freedom papers and filed a copy in the courthouse."

"Jackson started laughing and couldn't stop. Tears came to his eyes. He laughed so hard he had to dismount his horse and sit on Peabody's lower porch step. He laughed at Peabody. He laughed at his living conditions. He laughed at his filthy wife and home and then he laughed at himself; he laughed hardest at himself.

Peabody picked up his rifle and aimed it at Jackson's back. "Yuh laughing at me, Mr. Dillard?"

"No! No!" Jackson lied as he continued to chuckle. "Ah'm laughing at myself." He howled out a cackle and slapped his leg. "That damn Jacob got me again."

"Yes! Yes! That's his name, Jacob Natty." Peabody uncocked the rifle and walked down from the porch.

"Well, now yuh can start laughin' 'cause that dam, Jacob Natty is a nigger, a mulatto and he made yuh sell him yuh property," Jackson managed to say. "He burnt up part of my house and stole thousands of my money and when Ah catch him, he is a dead man."

"Well, Ah'll be dammed!" Peabody flopped down on the step next to Jackson. "Can Ah ride with yuh? Yuh can do the killin'. Ah'll help if yuh need me, but Ah can be satisfied just tuh see the look on his face."

Jackson stood and stretched. He was exhorted and exhilarated at the same time. "Ah'll be leaving for Clinton this afternoon. Ah'll be at the saloon while my horse is watered and fed. Meet me at 1:00 o'clock sharp. We will arrive in Clinton before nightfall to gather information and by tuhmorrow first light, Ah shall be hanging Jacob Natty."

"We are able tuh accommodate yuh here, Mr. Dillard," Peabody waved his hand offering his home. "Why sur, yuh could get a little rest, my woman would feed yuh and my niggers will take care of yuh horse. Be my pleasure, Mr. Dillard, sur."

"Ah do have some business in town so Ah must decline yuh offer." Jackson mounted his horse as he spoke pulling at the reins and jerking his horse's head around. "1:00 o'clock." He rode away.

The Lord blessed Jacob with a full moon while traveling to The Dillard. He led Nutmeg by the reins, pulling the small carriage all the way up the slave path, a thousand or so feet from the line of cabins. "Steady girl," he whispered. He patted the horse's neck and hitched her to a tree before stealing off to fetch Tillie and the children. The cabin was still warm from the dying embers of an untended fire, but it was empty. He realized the children were still over at the mansion helping Tillie with the completion of her duties. Jacob began collecting their clothing and placing them in one of the two small carpetbags he brought along. He would allow Tillie to gather her own belongings for the second bag, but their time would be limited. He wasn't sure of Jackson's whereabouts, but he prayed he was away trying to make arrangement to rebuild the mansion and his life. It was after nine that evening when the trio returned home. Jacob sat on the floor behind the bed curtain. He heard their tranquil, but exhausted voices as they entered the cabin. He spoke softly so as not to startle them. "Miss Tillie, it's me Jacob," he whisper-called.

"Jacob?" Tillie responded. "Where yuh be, child?"

"Ah'm here ma'am. Ah come tuh get yuh and da chillen." He turned to the children and told them to get their freedom papers.

"Where we goin' Jacob?" She knew the answer. She knew he was taking her away from the plantation. She knew she would be a runaway, but she trusted him. She knew he wouldn't put her life in danger, but she was still frozen in place at the thought of freedom.

"Away from here, we goin' north," Jacob stated as a matter of fact and he left no room for Tillie to object. It was a surprise to her. She would have to leave on a moment's notice. No time to say good-bye to those she called family, to those she had come to love. But the ones she loved the most had already been taken from her. Jacob had come for her and the children. He told her to leave everything and steal away with him. She searched her small and neatly organized cabin and every keepsake she owned was associated with slavery. She removed her two hand-quilted blankets and placed one in the carpetbag and folded the other to use later for warmth during their travel. She was ready with only the clothes she wore and a shawl as her only barrier against the elements. Jacob picked up both bags, grabbed hold of Tillie's hand and they ran off behind the row of cabins, into the dense forest to the waiting surrey. The children followed close behind and were so quiet Jacob turned several times to make sure they were still there. As soon as they reached the wagon, Jacob gave Tillie her new travel clothes, including a new stylish heavy coat. He and Simon turned their backs while she dropped her slave garments and dressed in her respected disguise. Her old clothing were carried along and discarded hours later. She placed the bonnet on the seat of the carriage, but wore the disguising veil, then wrapped a woolen blanket over her head. She placed the heavy quilt around the children to ward off the wintery night air. It would be seven hours before they would be missed for their early morning duties at the mansion. They were due to arrive in Clinton by 2:00 A.M.

Soon it was that time in the morning when the chill of the night was at its greatest, before the new day glowed on the horizon and while the full moon continued to light the sky. Sula hurried to greet Tillie and the children. The men swiftly loaded the bags on the wagon. It was agreed each person would carry two small carpetbags. Two additional larger bags had been packed for Tillie, the children and Sula that contained sitting pillows and blankets to add some comfort in the segregated train car. Jacob insisted that everyone pack a very warm winter outfit, including mitts, wool sox, heavy hats and scarfs. "Ah read it be real cold up north," he warned.

Blue arrived from The Haynes Plantation with travel passes for himself, Juke and Capers. He was surprised that they would be driving down to Martin's Depot to board the train. Juke and Capers would drive all the men in the wagon and follow Blue, who would be driving Mrs. Morton, Tillie, Sula, Jenny and the twin girls in Mr. Haynes' large surrey. All Blue knew was that everyone was traveling by train to Charleston, then taking a steamer and travelling down to Jacksonville, Florida to help Mrs. Morton's family with their crops. They would all return before planting time in the spring. He did question that story when he saw Tillie, Simon and Jenny.

"Jacob, Ah's really proud of yuh." He walked close to him, his flannel jacket pushed back and his hands tucked deep in the pockets of his coveralls. He beckoned Jacob to the side for a private word. "Ah be lookin' out fer Capers and Juke don't yuh be worryin' none 'bout dem," he began. He held his head down and a little to the side, smiling. "Ah's gon' say my goodbyes now, 'cause when Ah leave y'all, Ah know dat be my last time seein' yuh." He held out his hand and Jacob accepted it. "Yuh be a good man, Mr. Jacob Natty. May de good Lawd be always smilin' on yuh." They pulled each other into a final hug.

"Ah would've never made it without yuh," Jacob said, affectionately. "Thank yuh for taking care of me and my brothers. Ah've had tuh do things tuh protect my family and they don't know nothin' 'bout it. Ah just want tuh say thank yuh and take care of yuhself, too."

"Da pleasure be mine," Blue whispered and he gave him an understanding smile.

"Oh, Blue," This time Jacob whispered softly. He stood close to his friend with his head lowered and his hands positioned on his hips. "Would it be all right if my brothers stayed up on the plantation for the next few days? If Jackson Dillard comes lookin' for me and sees Juke or Capers, it might get real bad. See, the old woman is a runaway. Ah just couldn't leave hur behind. Ah thought the brothers were leavin' with us."

Ol' Blue smiled broadly. "Sure thing, Jacob, Ah be talkin' tuh them. Now, don't yuh worry. Dere be an empty cabin up dere and Massa likes da boys." Blue assured him and patted his back.

"Is everyone loaded?" Jacob called out. He mounted Nutmeg and then turned when he noticed Robby running toward the barn. "Where yuh goin', Robby?"

It was 6:00 A.M. and Miles sang out, "All in!" He watched as Jacob closed the surrey door. "Let's move out!"

Robby hugged Rusty then ran and leaped on the bed of the buck wagon and they were off.

ॐ∞ॐ

Peabody and Jackson arrived in Clinton at 6:30 P.M., on Wednesday evening. The same evening that Jacob was racing toward The Dillard to fetch Tillie and the children. Night had fallen and the territory was unfamiliar. Every store and establishment in Clinton was closed except for the saloon and there was a small glow outlining the cracks of the door frame of the livery stable.

"Ah need information and a warm bed," Jackson barked at the bartender. Traveling with Peabody had not been pleasurable for him, but it was purely a reflection of his own prejudice. The little man had made every attempt to be an exceptional companion. Jackson glared over his shoulder at Peabody; his body language spoke of his irritation and his mind whispered, *do whatever yuh want tuh do.*

Peabody ignored Jackson's arrogance and approached the bartender more cordially. "Whiskey," he requested. When the tall, burly man with the thick mustache turned reaching for the bottle, Peabody asked, "Yuh wouldn't happen tuh know a man called Morton, would yuh?"

Jackson gritted his teeth and sucked in a swoop of air, angry that the bartender would wait on Peabody first and ignore him.

The bartender filled the shot glass and held tight tuh the bottle. "Yep, but it won't do you no good tuh know him, not now Ah reckon."

"Yuh can leave the bottle," Jackson directed. He slapped the bar's counter three times and nodded at the bartender, flipping a dollar on the bar. "Oh yeah, how's that?" he asked, this time he had tucked away his attitude.

"He's dead. Died and buried back . . . um . . . back last spring." He nodded his head knowing what he spoke was correct.

"The man Ah saw was young. Ain't near see his twentieth year," Peabody added.

Jackson pushed his hat back and nodded with more respect for Peabody.

"Morton had a family . . . had a wife and some boys. Yuh might be lookin' for the oldest boy."

Jackson chugged his whiskey glass to his mouth. "Could be," he said. "Mind tellin' us where they live?"

"Ah'm sorry mister. Morton weren't no drinkin' man. Only knowed of 'em and heard the news 'bout his passing. Now, if'n yuh wait 'til morning yuh could find out more from John Baker down at the feed and seed store. He shuts down at six and won't be open again 'til mornin' at six."

"That man, uh Baker," Peabody began, "does he live in the back of his store or over his store?"

"Sho do. He, the wife and girls live up top, but good luck. He ain't been known tuh do business after hours," the bartender warned. He stopped wiping down the bar, threw the towel over his shoulder and placed the palms of his hands on the smooth rolled edge of the counter. "Say, if'n y'all need rooms for the night, Ah got a couple upstairs."

"Yeah," Jackson replied, "two rooms 'ill do. We can see this Baker guy in the mornin'. It's too dark tuh go lookin' for the Morton place tuhnight anyway." He picked up the half-filled bottle of whiskey, his shot glass and walked toward the table. "Oh add this tuh my tab. And do yuh have any grub?" He toasted the bartender with the whiskey bottle just as he plopped in the chair.

"How's fried catfish and cornpone? The kitchen's 'bout closed so the pickin's is near 'bout tuh none."

Jackson saluted him again with his shot glass. "Man, you are a miracle worker!" he yelled out."

Peabody waved his hand and sat at the table.

శ్రీజ్ఞ

Peabody and Jackson took the east road out of town and traveled for several miles until it intersected with a road that spread from north to south. They were following the directions described to them by the merchant, John Baker. Fog blanketed the land in layers, stealing the visibility promised by the dawn and its mist clung to their skin and clothing making them feel clammy and uncomfortable. They were met by a cloud of dust from south bound wagons that had previously passed and cleared the bend. Now particles of dust raining down on them like drizzle rain.

"Got-damn-it," Jackson yelled, "Ah can't see a damn thing out here."

The horses pranced and stepped high and Jackson and Peabody held tight to their reins. "Whoa, whoa there," Peabody called out.

They continued holding their horses in place for a short period before making the turn north. Soon they allowed the horses to trot slowing along as they aggressively search the foggy mist for the pass to the Morton's farm. An hour later they trotted from the wall of fog to a clear morning where the sun rested higher on the horizon than they wanted it to be.

Jackson rode his horse several feet away from the edge of the fog and stopped; Peabody pulled up beside him. "Man, look at that wall of fog. If Ah were a praying man, Ah'd believe God hid that pass in that fog. But, if they had a God, they wouldn't be in this mess," he stated, but without conviction. He pushed his hat backup off his brow and stared at the fog wall. He chuckled lightly.

Peabody glanced at Jackson, wondering if he believed the Almighty was protecting Jacob somehow, because in spite of him, he did believe in God.

Jackson was first to jerk back on the rein of his horse, causing the poor creature to snort and hiss. "Damn it!" he scowled, "Look there. We have tuh go back! Came tuh far."

Peabody, although a man of limited manners, wasn't a fool; he knew when to allow the more dominate Jackson to rule. "Yep," escaped his lips just audible to a whisper.

"Ah know that place," Jackson said and he nodded in the direction of the large mansion house. "Mr. Haynes and my daddy were good friends."

Peabody didn't speak, but waited for Jackson to take his next move and when he pulled his horse around to backtrack down the road, Peabody followed.

The sun had risen higher and burned off most of the fog, its position indicated it was closer to 9:00 A.M. and he scowled again in his attempt to hold in his disappointment. For fear of wasting more time, they traveled slower than before, searching both sides of the road.

"Ah see it! That narrow road curvin' out from behind dem trees!" Peabody called out. "Looks like they pulled a branch from that tree down tuh hide the road."

Jackson leaped off his horse and inspected the camouflaged road. "Yuh damn right, man. They got this branch tied down with rawhide straps." *How cleaver*, he thought.

The men made their way through the pass and were met by Rusty barking at their horses' hoofs. The house was locked up tight, but the barn and cabins were accessible.

"They ain't here, but it looks like they gone be back."

Jackson looked over at Peabody. "We could wait 'em out or Ah could ride up tuh Mr. Haynes and inquire about Jacob." Suddenly, without signaling his companion or attempting to inspect the cabins, he turned his horse again and galloped up toward the pass. "Ah'm heading back tuh The Haynes Plantation. Maybe Ah can get me some answers there," he called out.

Peabody followed along in his dust.

�🙞🙜

The horse boy hurried to gather the reins of the horses as Jackson and Peabody dismounted in the front drive. The large white house reflected its brilliant hue in the cool December morning. Jackson allowed his eyes to take in the entire scenery and he couldn't help thinking of how large he remembered the house being as a young boy. Now it was just a large white house to him, much smaller than his own.

"Stay here," Jackson flashed an order to Peabody and the little man stopped as if frozen in his tracks, before backing up to stand near his horse and the boy.

By the time Jackson reached the front porch, Mr. Haynes was standing in his open door. "Is that you, Jackson Dillard?" The elder gentleman said. "Well, looka here! What brings yuh a callin'?"

"Yes sir, Mr. Haynes. Ah ain't seen yuh since my daddy's passin'. It's good tuh see yuh, sir," Jackson smiled and extended his hand as he spoke.

Mr. Haynes responded, accepting his hand and stepping out onto his porch. "It's good for me too, young man, but Ah know this is not just a cordial visit so early in the morning. It's a half days ride from yuh Dillard. Would yuh like tuh come in out of the morning air?"

"No sir, it's just fine out here." Jackson replied. His smile now turned to a more business expression. "Yuh see, sir, Ah'm lookin' for one of my ex-slaves. Daddy freed him, but that didn't stop him from creatin' a great deal of mischief. Ah have good evidence that he near 'bout burned down my house and stole thousands in gold from me. He even forced that man that rode up with me tuh sell his prize slave tuh him for near nothin' of hur cost."

Haynes walked over to his rocker and stood twisting at the corner of his long white mustache. "What's the boy's name? What does he look like?" he asked.

"Ah hate tuh tell yuh this, but that mulatto bastard looks just like me, blue eyes and blonde hair and the likes. Goes by the name of, Jacob."

"We'll, Ah'll be! Jacob been passin' for white. The sins of the father really do come back tuh haunt yuh," Haynes laughed loud and hard. Then he took in a deep breath and shook his head as he spoke. "Yuh know Ah asked that boy about that and he said he was as white as he could ever be. He didn't lie, sho-nuff didn't lie." Then he continued with his hearty laughing. He plopped himself down on his porch rocker while he caught his breath and his smile remained on his face. "Yuh lissen hear boy, now he may have caused yuh some misery, but he sure saved a white family down these parts from starving. It was like the good Lawd just dropped that boy out of heaven. Listen Jackson, Ah understand how yuh feel. Now, did anyone else take advantage of yuh?" Mr. Haynes sat forward and interlocked his fingers around his moderately pot belly.

"No sir, but Ah do need to catch that Jacob." Hatred and vengeance laced his words, beaded his eyes and forced his posture to go ridged.

Mr. Haynes eyes narrowed. *He has no need to know of Capers and Juke. Seems they have done him no harm. The Morton's will need them when they return*, he thought. "Looka here, Jackson. Ah know it's not my place tuh tell another man how to conduct his business. Ah hear yuh daddy freed all his mulattoes and Ah hear yuh have tried tuh re-enslave 'em. Yuh daddy didn't raise yuh that way. Yuh may not like me speakin' my peace, but Ah don't give-a-damn, Ah always say my mind. Now, Ah'm gonna tell yuh what Ah know about Jacob. Then, Ah don't want yuh back here 'til yuh are the man yuh daddy raised yuh tuh be. 'Cause Jacob may be yuh daddy's nigger bastard, but he's more man than yuh could ever be."

"Ah beg yuh pardon, sir!" Jackson sprang from his chair and glared at Mr. Haynes.

"We'll yuh not getting my pardon. Sit down and listen or get out, now!"

Jackson eased himself back into his chair and listened while Mr. Haynes told him that Jacob was assisting the Morton family, on that very morning, to make the trip to Jacksonville, Florida. He explained that they were traveling to Charleston by rail and then by steamer south. "They will be returning tuh their farm in time for the spring plantin'." Mr. Haynes only reluctantly shared this information because he didn't believe Jackson could catch up with him. It was all he would share with this son of a man who was once his dear friend.

Jackson stood and offered his hand as a gentleman's custom, but Mr. Haynes remained seated and only nodded his head. Jackson withdrew his hand, nodded and thanked the elder man for the information. Mr. Haynes didn't have to say what train they took. Jackson had just returned from Columbia and was familiar with the train schedules. He also knew Columbia was the junction hub for all the train connections for the region.

"Let's go!" Jackson shouted and Peabody was mounted before Jackson reached his horse. "We gotta try tuh catch that train before it leaves Columbia!"

"Man, are yuh crazy? Ah ain't gone kill my horse! That train left at around seven this morning." Peabody spoke out. His horse danced with the anticipation of impending speed, but Peabody held tight to the rein.

"Ah know an overland trail that will shorten the distance," Jackson said. "Ah know that train only runs at a top speed of ten miles per hour. There's a way-station in Alston where we can get fresh horses. Then it has a two-hour layover in the Columbia hub. We can catch up with them there."

Peabody's mouth dropped and he just stared at Jackson.

Jackson jerked his horse's bridle to the left, gave his hindquarters a kick and he didn't spare the poor creature his whip.

Again, Peabody rode off in his dust.

chapter 23

The Union & Spartanburg Railroad train arrived in Columbia from Martin's Depot and all other western stations on that line. Those passengers continuing on toward Charleston would remain on the train and later make additional transfers and connections to other rail lines before reaching their destinations. But Jacob, Miles and their families would change to the northbound Wilmington & Manchester Railroad train which sat on a neighboring track also facing the same direction. Once leaving the Columbia station, both trains would travel south-east until passing Gadeden, South Carolina; then the Charleston train would turn due south and the Wilmington train turned north bound.

Jacob was reassuring his family that their long journey would be over soon as they all sat together in the train's segregated, separation car. He looked up and through the cloudy window and recognized Jackson and Peabody racing into the depot.

"Ah'll be right back," he whispered in a calm tone before leaving the women and children. As soon as he reached Miles in the white passenger car, he beckoned for his attention. "Peabody and my old master are here lookin' for me. Can Ah count on yuh help? Brother Jackson doesn't know yuh, but Peabody does. If he sees yuh, he'll know Ah'm about."

Miles, who was sitting with his family, nodded, gave his mother a brief explanation of what was happening, before he and Jacob hurried from the car.

"What yuh got in mind, Jacob?"

Jacob looked over at the livery stable. "Keep 'em in yuh sight. Ah'll be right back."

Five minutes later and Jackson and Peabody were riding down one side of the Charleston train looking in each window. When they reached the end they turned their horses, crossed over and rode back up to the front and between, the Charleston and the Wilmington train. They rode slowly looking and searching in each window.

Tillie saw Jackson looking in the train windows and her heart raced. Adrenaline pumped through her veins and she went into flight mode. She grabbed the children and Sula's arm and pulled them to the floor before they had a chance to object. "Shush, it be Massa Jackson!" she held her hand sideways to her own mouth. "Jackson be searchin' out dere! Scramble yonder behind dem totes and be quiet," she whispered.

Sula's eyes widened and the women scurried out of sight. Simon piled the suitcases and carpetbags around them and then slid under the bench.

Tillie peeked out from between the separation of the stacked luggage and there was the ghostly image of Jackson's face searching the train car through the cloudy window and then he was gone. They all decided to remain in their hiding place until Jacob return to them.

Jackson and Peabody continued up the tracks searching the windows of both trains as they went along. They stared in the faces of the Morton family. Mrs. Morton gave them a casual glance and a sweet smile. Jackson tipped his hat and the men moved along. Mrs. Morton exhaled and continued praying and thanking the Lord for his blessings of safety.

Jackson and Peabody reached the front of the train, this time they dismounted and boarded the Charleston train to do a more thorough inspection.

Jacob returned and patted Miles on the shoulder. "Let's go. We gone get on that train at the second car and when they see us they gone give chase." He handed him a small hard club. "We gone run through the livery stable and get 'em. We ain't gone hurt 'em, just gone stop 'em. They can't know we ain't on that Charleston train."

Jacob and Miles stood near the end of the passenger car and pretended to walk toward the front. At the same time, Jackson and Peabody were making a slow and methodical inspection of all the passengers they encountered as they stepped toward the back of the train. Jackson looked up and saw his half-brother staring at him from the next car. He tapped Peabody's shoulder and the men gave chase. Jacob and Miles leaped from the train and ran into the barn of the livery stable. Just as their pursuer approached the entry to the barn, the blacksmith led two horses pulling a large rig and blocked their path. Jackson stumbled back, his arms flailing, he fell, knocking his smaller companion to the muddy ground along with him.

The blacksmith stopped the rig and ran to the aide of the men. He took his greasy rag from his back pocket, just as Jackson leaped to his feet. The blacksmith attempted to brush away patches of mud from Jackson's coat while blocking his ability to chase Jacob and Miles into the barn. While the two large horses and buck wagon held Jackson at bay, the blacksmith pulled at Peabody's arm, to hold him still while he brushed his coat and hampered his ability to stand.

"Move this damn wagon, boy!" Jackson yelled. "Get yuh ass up, yuh sorry specimen of a man!" he yelled at his companion.

The blacksmith deliberately caused the horses to rise up on their hindquarters before settling them down; they startled Jackson and Peabody again and pushed them back a few more feet. The black man's eyes jumped with laughter while his face wore an expression of fear, concern and reprisal for his apparent blundering and clumsiness against the two white gentlemen.

Finally, the entrance to the stable was cleared and the pursuers raced in only to be met with sharp blows to their heads, which rendered them unconscious. The blacksmith handed Jacob wet rawhide traps with which to tie their wrist behind their backs and secure their ankles.

"When that rawhide dries, it's gone tighten and gone take 'em longer tuh get loose," Jacob said. He pinched the side of Jackson's cheeks causing his mouth to pucker open so he could stuff a burlap knot inside and secured it with a section of rope. Miles did the same for Peabody before they loaded their packages onto the wagon bed and drove them into the woods, two miles away from the edge of town.

"Ah want tuh get this wagon back tuh the livery before we're missed." Jacob said.

The rig was returned to the livery stable and Jacob handed the blacksmith $10.00 for his troubles. The blacksmith gave Jacob and Miles a nod and they hurried to board their train. The southbound Charleston train had cleared the station and the conductor was calling for all to board the Wilmington train in anticipation of its departure.

&∾&

Peabody moaned and stretched out his legs. He wriggled and scooted over to Jackson and used his head to butt into his chest in an attempt to wake him. His mouth was dry and the burlap knot in its cavity was scratchy and irritating; he moaned louder. He watched the sun set above the horizon.

His fingers tingled from the restricted circulation caused by the rawhide trapping. He butted Jackson again. His head felt explosive and he gave out a loud throaty moan.

Jackson's eyes opened slowly before stretching wider and searching his environment; the unfamiliar area was startling. He was panicked by his inability to speak and move freely; he moaned and wiggled aggressively.

Without the ability to communicate and in an attempt to gain freedom, Peabody rolled backward over Jackson. It was his intention to reach the gag in Jackson's mouth, but his hands were tied behind his back. Jackson's confusion, anger and superior ego caused him to reject the little man's attempt and he bounced him away. But before Jackson had a chance to object a second time Peabody flung himself backward over Jackson's face again and grabbed hold to the mouth gag. He pulled it from Jackson's mouth just as Jackson vigorously flipped him sideways, dumping Peabody to the ground. Jackson spit out the burlap knot.

"Uh-uh!" Jackson yelled out. He spat. "Damn!" He spat again. He never bothered to thank Peabody only saying, "Come, let me pull that gag from your mouth." He turned his back to Peabody and did so.

Peabody wasn't too proud to use his teeth to free Jackson's hands from behind his back, but Jackson used a sharp rock to slice away at Peabody's bindings. Hours had slipped away and only the moon granted them the light they needed to find their direction. Jackson knew when he caught up with Jacob, he would just kill him on sight. Peabody was just tired; Jacob didn't mean that much to him anymore.

There was no hurry. Jackson knew all the trains were away from the hub. There would be no other trains arriving until the next morning. One hour later the men were back in Columbia and their horses were still tied up at the depot.

"Ah'm gone get me a room for the night and in the morning Ah'm gone ride back tuh that way-station for my own horse," Peabody announced. "This is yuh fight and Ah ain't yuh slop boy."

"Now, yuh gone leave?" Jackson muttered. He kicked at the dirt and balled his fist tight. "Then go! Ah don't need yuh!" He flipped his arms up and turned his back on Peabody.

"Tuh hell wit' yuh, Jackson Dillard. Ah'm gon' home in the mornin' without yuh. Good night and goodbye!" He untied the reins securing the horse and led him to the livery stable where it could be fed, watered and blanketed in a warm stall for the night. In spite of all that happened, he didn't give the stable worker a second thought about their unfortunate incident. He brushed past Jackson on his way to the rooming house without giving him a glance.

త్రా

It was a twenty five hour train ride to Wilmington, North Carolina. Mrs. Morton met the challenge with mourning for the life she was leaving behind. However, the murmurs of her fellow passengers' discontent with the northern political position were more disturbing. She removed her lace handkerchief and dabbed the tears welling in her eyes. She prayed for her children, for herself, but most of all for Jacob and his family. She and her children had the luxury of appealing accommodations, even though she had selected the moderate passenger car instead of the lavish comfort of a private cabin. Their seating was well cushioned, the floor was carpeted and red velvet drapes framed each window. The two wide sofa like benches were spacious enough for three adults and allowed for the twins to stretch prone for slumber. They wore their coats, knit caps and mittens and Mrs. Morton covered them with a single woolen blanket for warmth. Heat was the only amenity unavailable to the white or black passengers. Miles sat across from her, his head resting against the cloudy window, his hands and arms enveloped around himself and his feet spread apart stabilizing him on the cushioned bench as he slept. A tiny smile curled Mrs. Morton's lips to see Robby and Evan flopped over each other and tangled in their separate blankets. *They don't seem tuh be cold. Everyone is comfortable*, she thought as her eyes eased closed; she sighed softly. Sleep eluded her while prayer remained on her heart. *Oh, gracious Lawd, My family is warm and comfortable. Ah hope Ah don't sound insensitive, but Ah know yuh know what's on my heart. Lawd, Ah pray the hardships of slavery have prepared Sula and the elder Tillie for the merciless conditions in that horrible compartment car. If Ah could offer them any more comfort, Lawd show me.* Her inner prayer reached her lips "In Jesus' name Ah ask this of You my

Lawd. Amen. Oh, thank Yuh Lawd," she whispered. She stood and removed the woolen blankets from both of the boys and then recovered them using only one blanket. She folded that blanket along with her blanket and then she reached over and woke Miles. "Honey," she began, "Ah hate tuh wake yuh, but Ah must use the latrine and Ah need yuh escort."

Miles eased to his feet. "Yes mother. Would yuh like me tuh wake the girls and take them along?"

"Oh no Miles; Ah had them relieve themselves after we ate and before we left the last stop. They will be all right until morning."

Mrs. Morton carried the folded blankets close to her chest with one hand and pressed her other hand against the wall of the moving train to stabilize her unsteady gait. Miles smiled, her motive didn't escape him. Traveling between the train cars was treacherous, but Miles held his mother's arm until she had passed from one car to the next.

Jenny and Simon never flinched from their cuddled position on top of the carpetbags when the loud sliding door opened at the far end of the car. They shared the warm quilt Miss Tillie brought from the slave cabin. Mrs. Morton and Miles entered almost as quickly as the cold wintery air and the door slid shut making a startling clashing sound. Jacob grabbed Sula and pulled her closer to him while Miss Tillie stood at attention. She peeked around the locked baggage cage, but relaxed when she recognized Mrs. Morton and Miles approaching them.

"Ah'm so sorry," Mrs. Morton, whined. "Ah just wanted y'all tuh have these extra blankets. It's so much colder back here."

"Yes ma'am," Tillie answered. She hurriedly reached for the blankets, shook one out as a second cover for Sula. She fanned out the other and positioned it to cover Jacob, but he waved it away.

"Ah be okay," he whispered. "Miss Tillie, do yuh have a soft cushions and a warm blanket?"

"Yes Jacob." Tillie refolded the blankets and returned them to Mrs. Morton. "Jacob be right," she said. "Yuh be very kind."

"Mrs. Morton," Jacob said. "Ah checked all the blankets and cushions before we left. There ain't no need for yuh tuh be going wit'out yuh own blanket. We are jes fine."

"Mama," Miles said. "No Mama! Jacob is right. They're gonna be fine. Now let me walk yuh back up tuh the latrine."

Mrs. Morton stared at Jacob. "Are yuh gonna be all right? Do y'all have enough food and water for the morning?"

"Yes ma'am," Jacob answered. "Sula is sittin' on cushions and Ah'm holdin' hur tight. We're gonna all be tuhgether soon. Please don't make yuhself sick worrying about us".

"All right then. See yuh in Wilmington," Mrs. Morton said. She waved at Sula

Sula smiled and waved back.

⊱⊰

By daybreak Friday morning, the train crossed the border into North Carolina. There was no difference in landscape or the way the sun peeked over the horizon. The conductor crept quietly pass Miles and his family and smiled.

Miles corrected his posture and greeted him, whispering, "Mornin' sur."

"And a pleasant morning tuh you," the conductor responded softly while tapping the visor of his cap.

"Uh . . . where are we, sur?" Miles asked.

The conductor bent over slightly and surveyed the landscape. "Well, Ah'd say we're 'bout an hour into North Carolina." He stood and stabilized his balance from the train's motion by holding to the top of Mrs. Morton's seat. "We should be comin' intuh the Grist's Station Depot in about thirty minutes, sir."

"How far is that from Wilmington?"

"We should pull into tuh Wilmington 'bout noon, sir. Would be sooner, but the law always inspects the train for runaways at this first stop. Sometimes, they hold up the train for almost an hour." Yuh got some coloreds travelin' wit' you, don't yuh?" The conductor stared directly into Miles' eyes looking for any signs of anxiety. "Oh . . . and Mr. Morton, an important piece of information came over the wire. Ah got the news at the last station. Yuh fine state of South Carolina succeeded from the Union yesterday. They are tryin' tuh get other southern states to follow and when they do, we gone have us a war."

Miles sat tall and pulled the palm of his hand over his face. Everything he had heard about war was coming to pass. He would never fight for the south and he wasn't ready to die for the north either.

"Well, good morning, sir," Mrs. Morton sang out. She reached across herself and touched his arm as she spoke.

Miles stood wondering if the conductor had upset his mother because his causal talk of war had certainly upset him.

The conductor turned. "Oh, good mornin', ma'am. Ah hope Ah didn't wake yuh." He tipped his visor again.

She smiled up at him, then lowered her head and winked at Miles. "Oh no sir, this is my normal wakin' time."

"Well, y'all have a nice day. Ah must be gettin' on now." He moved down the train and into the next car.

As soon as the conductor had cleared the passenger car, Miles asked his mother if she heard about South Carolina's secession.

A tiny smile appeared on her face when she looked up at Miles. "No, Ah've not heard that, but it was inevitable," she whispered. "Why do yuh think Ah was so willing tuh leave everythin' on a moment's notice, from a man Ah've only known less than a year?" She sat up and patted the space next to her. "Come over here, Miles," she said. After adjusting her shawl, she continued. "The call for this convention went out several weeks ago and the event commenced on December 17th. Honey, that was the same day you all went off to fetch Sula. Ah knew all this would result in a war and Ah refuse tuh lose even one son tuh this cause. Ah haven't told Jacob yet, but Ah intend tuh move my family all the way tuh Canada on this journey and he should do the same."

"Mama . . . when were yuh gonna tell me? Ah'm a man. Ah should've been in on the decision making and Ah do agree which yuh." Miles stood, kissed his mother's cheek and left her side, heading toward the compartment car. He needed to talk to Jacob, but his most pressing issue was Grist's Station and he was still in possession of Tillie's papers. Jacob held the papers for Sula and the children. It was Miles intention to discuss the South Carolina issue and his mother's decision to relocate to Canada at a later time. The train jerked as the breaks were applied, then it coasted into Grist's Station.

"Jacob," Miles whispered. "The sheriff and his men are gonna do an inspection at this station. Ah was told they always check for runaway slaves here."

Sula clutched Jacob's arm and Tillie stood and held tight to the luggage cage. "Oh Jacob," Sula whispered.

Jacob kissed Sula's forehead, then hurried to kiss Tillie's cheek. "It's gone be all right." Before he could comment on anything else, he noticed several armed men standing on the platform ready to board the train.

Jacob could feel his heart pounding; he gritted his teeth and told himself to calm down. *Too many lives dependin' on me*, he thought. He smiled and rubbed Sula's arm. "Ah want you and Miss Tillie tuh just sit here and remain calm. Y'all chillen get up here on this bench and be still." He reached in his breast pocket and retrieved a stack of neatly folded papers. "Sula, Ah be givin' yuh, yuh papers. Just wrap 'em in yuh kerchief and tuck 'em in yuh bosom. Yuh know whut dem words say, so don't yuh worry. Them men gone be askin' 'bout yuh papers. Yuh pull 'em out and hand it tuh dem tuh read. They'll read 'em and give 'em back tuh yuh. Ah'm gone hold da chillen's papers."

Miles held to the luggage cage as the trained swayed and jerked to a halt. "Miss Tillie," he smiled as he spoke to her. "Now, Ah'm gone hold yuh papers. Yuh are still a slave and we have yuh belongin' tuh my mama. Yuh are hur personal servant so if they ask yuh anythin' yuh just tell 'em yuh been with Mrs. Cecilia Morton for twenty years."

Jacob searched the area for the food basket. "Simon, put that basket over here and y'all reach in and take out a ham and biscuit sandwich. Pour yuhself some tea in dem jars and look like yuh havin' yuh breakfast. Act surprised when dey come in here."

Miles and Jacob stood, one against the outer wall of the train and the other against the luggage cage. When the compartment car's sliding door slammed open, three white men entered. They all wore law enforcement badge, two carried rifles and had an additional pistol holstered to their hips. The third only wore the one holstered pistol, but he appeared to be the leader.

"Well! Well! Well! What have we got here?" The first man to approach announced. He walked like a turkey with his neck jerking his head back and forth with each step he took.

"Niggah! Niggah! Niggah! Looky here! We got us some Niggahs!" The second man yelled out.

"Ah beg yuh pardon! These people are our responsibility and property. There will not be any trouble here!" Jacob shouted as he approached the men, with Miles close behind him. They blocked the aisle, on the far side of the ten foot long luggage cage preventing the lawmen's further approach to Jacob's family.

The first two men stopped shoulder to shoulder and faced the unmovable Miles and Jacob. The third man, who appeared to be more level headed and in charge pulled his men to the side and stepped in front of them. Jacob and Miles allowed him closer access to Jacob's family, but blocked the other two men; psychological restraints were sufficient to hold them at bay.

"Who are those people?" the third man asked.

Jacob placed his hands on his hips and stared directly in the man's face. "All but one are free human beings and they all have papers," he responded.

"Those people are employees on our plantation back in South Carolina. And the other is the personal servant tuh my mother, Mrs. Cecilia Morton, who is presently in the passenger car. Ah have hur papers, but Ah don't have tuh show yuh nothin'," Miles snapped.

The dominate man pushed his wide brim hat back on his head. "Yuh're right, Mr. Morton. Ah'll take yuh word, but Ah wanna see the freedom papers for dem others." He placed one hand on his hip and lifted his arm pointing toward Sula and the twins. Sula set her biscuit in the food basket and reached into her bosom. While she was retrieving her documents, Jacob handed over the papers belonging to the children. The lawman inspected them and returned them to Jacob and then he accepted Sula's paper.

"Yuh just got yuh freedom this week," The lawman said.

"Yessum," Sula whispered in a slow drawl. She was so frightened her hands were trembling. Her voice had not fully returned so she couldn't speak above a whisper even if she wanted too.

"Who freed yuh?" the lawman grumbled.

Before she could answer, Jacob stepped in front of her, met the man eye to eye and spoke up. "Ah did!" he responded in a gruff tone. "And Ah have the papers tuh show hur freedom is registered in the county courthouse of Union, South Carolina and is legal and binding. Ah also have the contact for Mr. Samuel Wilson, my attorney, in South Carolina and who has affiliates here in this fine state should any laws on my behalf or on the behalf of my associates be violated." He removed the document from his breast pocket and held it up in front of the lawman like a poster. "Now, Ah don't have tuh answer any of yuh questions. No one here has broken any laws." He re-folded his papers and returned them to his pocket and all this while he never removed his stare from this white man.

The lawman stepped back, "Y'all folk have a nice day." He turned and walked between his other two men. "Everything is in order here," he announced. His men followed him from the car.

Jacob hurried to Sula. Her eyes held a frightful stare and her complexion had turned ashen. She leaned on Jacob, still trembling and then her tears came.

"Ah know how scared yuh be Sula, but we be goin' tuh a place where yuh will never feel that kinda fear again." He placed his hand on the side of her face and kissed her forehead.

Miles stared at Jacob and he appeared to be thinking for a long while. "Jacob," he began, "Ah saw yuh go up against Peabody, but that was nothing. Jacob, who was that man Ah just saw?"

"A frightened man," Jacob answered. "Ah be so scared Ah started tuh sound like you, Miles."

"Me!" Miles said with a chuckle. "Yuh sounded like a lawyer."

Laughter appeared on Jacob's face; his lips curled and his eyes sparkled, but he was quiet. He had an understanding smile. For the first time in his life he had discovered that he had it in him to be assertive, quick wit and the ability to speak properly; knowing that fear and desperation brought out this behavior, but not knowing until then how it would be received. He realized that repressed memories from his formative years had surfaced, that learned behaviors from his relationship with his father and his associates and from Jackson, Maynard, Moore and the many overseers. He learned from his books and later Old Blue's instructions for him to study the whites; to stand tall and look another man in his eyes when speaking, to imitate the way they spoke to each other and their mannerisms. It was only during his periods of freedom had he realized the power his appearance afforded him if he learned to wield it correctly and maintain a confident stance. When comfortable and relaxed he spoke in the colloquial tone of his youth, but this episode and the earlier experience with Peabody, taught him that he must continually perform in a poised manner to ensure the protection of his family. Mrs. Morton had always corrected his grammar and he needed to heed her instruction. He was moving his family to a new place, for a new life, there was no reason they should not have every opportunity to fit in and prosper, even if it meant he would have to remain white in the white man's world.

"Jacob," Miles called. "Jacob!" he called again, trying to get his attention

"Yes Miles," Jacob responded. He chuckled. "That was something. Ah was just thinking. That felt very good." He stared out the window and wrapped his arms around Sula and they watched as the lawmen walked down the platform.

Miles smiled.

"All aboard," The conductor sang out. The train jerked forward and the whistle blew.

Miss Tillie smiled. "Thank yuh, Mr. Miles and Jacob. Ah ain't knowed what tuh do. Y'all be som'n' else. Lawd sho' be good! Thank yuh, Jesus!" She rocked away her anxiety, took a deep breath and appeared to be rejuvenated. "All right y'all, we cain't be wasting' no food. Eat up!" she commanded after turning her attention to the children.

"Miles, yuh should go back tuh yuh family. Thank yuh for yuh help. Now, yuh mama may be needin' yuh," Jacob said.

"Lissen Jacob, Ah'm gone leave, but Ah need tuh tell yuh somethin'. It can wait, but Ah can't wait tuh give yuh this news." Miles tilted his head and took a deep breath. He waited for Jacob to acknowledge his need to continue.

Jacob returned to Sula's side and signaled for Miles to join him. Miles pulled up a crate to sit on. "It came over the wire . . . South Carolina has broken away from the United States. Mama says as soon as they get other states to do the same there will be a war between the northern and southern states."

Jacob wrapped his left arm around Sula and gently rubbed her upper arm. He clenched his lips, closed his eyes and nodded his head. He chuckled three times and the smile remained on his face. "It's happening." He raised his head and continued to hold to Sula. "It's so cold in the north," was all he murmured.

Miles stared at Jacob. He waited for his dear friend's response. He knew he would have to go along with his mother, because she needed him and his family was his responsibility, but he wondered what strategy was his friend planning.

Jacob opened his eyes and stared at Miles. "Well, Mr. Morton, did yuh know that our ship will docks in New York Harbor? Now, that is the mouth of this waterway called the Hudson River. Ah read that there be a place in Canada called Saint Catharines. A lot of runaway slaves make it there and their massas can't get them back because there is no slavery in Canada. If yuh live in Canada, yuh don't have tuh fight in a war for the United States, but if there be a war for Canada or England yuh will have tuh fight. There be only one problem and that be in the gettin' tuh Canada in the dead of winter."

Miles' mouth dropped open. "Damn Jacob! Mama said she wanted to go to Canada. So we'll be going tuh Canada."

Jacob removed his arm from around Sula and sat forward, closer to Miles. "Lissen Miles," he continued, "The farther we go north, the colder it's gone be. It be close tuh the end of December right now, so we might make it up the river before it freezes over. Then, we'll have tuh stay in this town called Albany, New York. We might have tuh stay there until spring because it's too cold tuh travel overland tuh Canada. We just have tuh pray real hard that a war don't start before spring and that no one tries tuh send my family back tuh slavery."

Miles sat back and combed his fingers through his hair. He was astonished and bewildered by the amount of knowledge Jacob had. "How do you know so much?"

Jacob chuckled again. "Ah was a slave, Miles. Most white men believe their slaves be ignorant. Most plantations have a system of communication.

We take in every nibble of freedom information. All information is passed on even when you don't understand its meanin'. When Ah needed tuh know more Ah studied maps and waterways. Because Ah was allowed in my father's company, Ah heard of the frustrations of his acquaintances when they loss their property tuh the town of Saint Catharines, in Ontario, Canada. In 1850, a law was passed; The Fugitive Slave Law and it say there is no safe place in this country for a Negro person even in the north. If a fugitive slave is living in a free states and a white person knows about it, that white person must tell the law or he can be put in prison. Hell . . . Miles, the white man can even re-enslave the free Negro person, that's why the slaves try tuh make it tuh Canada."

"We will get tuh Canada, Jacob," Miles stood as he spoke. He understood that Canada was the key to their survival.

That same Friday morning, back in Columbia, South Carolina, Jackson stood in the rooming house window and cursed himself as he watched Peabody ride his horse out of town. He didn't care for him, but the separation was difficult. Peabody was company, he was innovative, he never complained and other people liked him. *Damn that man. He even knew when Ah didn't want him around and he seemed tuh make himself invisible,* he thought. *Ah should go after him.* "No," he spoke aloud. *He has tuh get back to his spread. It ain't me. The man just got tuh accept his loss and get on home,* he reasoned. He grabbed his coat and went looking for the telegraph office.

He needed to send a telegraph to book passage on the steamer to Jacksonville before boarding the train to Charleston. The office opened at 8:00 AM. and as soon as Jackson entered the tiny room he noticed that an entire wall had been dedicated to information concerning the shipping industry. There were hand printed, pin stick cards, listing all of the shipping lines, including the dates and times for the cargo and passenger ships in the coastal regions of the United Stated, Caribbean, South American and for Trans-Atlantic vessels. There was a steamship leaving Charleston on Saturday morning for Jacksonville, Florida. If he boarded the southbound train departing at 11:00 AM., from Columbia, he would arrive in Charleston late Friday evening. He would then board the steamer bound for Florida on Saturday morning. But, of more interest to him was the S.S. Sparlding Steamship departing Charleston two hours after the train's arrival and docking in Wilmington, North Carolina early Saturday morning, then with a scheduled departure for several ports north at 5:00 PM.

An elder gentleman sat at the bland table monitoring his iron-base telegraph contraption that clicked and clacked away continuously. He manned and deciphered the sounds, wrote out messages and then placed them in separate envelops, before pinning them to a delivery board in a specific locations. As soon as the clerk had a moment of quiet from his noisy machine he asked Jackson if he could be of service to him.

Jackson held his hat in his hand and tried to remember the gentle and humble way Peabody spoke to people. It seemed to encourage them to want to help him more than whenever he asked for help. "Uh, yes sir. Ah really hope yuh can help me if yuh have the time."

"Yes sir. Ah'll do my best. How can Ah help yuh?" the clerk responded.

"Well, my cousin told me he booked passage on a steamer and Ah can't remember if it was the S.S. Sparlding or some other Atlantic steamer. Ah must apologize, sir. Ah was a little drunk at the time and it was most un-gentlemanly of me." Jackson pretended to be a little embarrassed and he rubbed his hand down his face before continuing. "Ah'm not sure if he booked the passage or if the family he was travelin' with booked it." He smiled sheepishly at the clerk. "Is it possible tuh telegraph these shippin' lines and have their manifest checked for the names, Natty and Morton? As soon as Ah locate the ship Ah'll be able tuh book my passage and board the appropriate train tuh that seaport."

"Well sir . . . Mr. . . . ur?" The clerk glanced up at Jackson for a formal name.

"Oh, yes sir . . . Dillard . . . Jackson Dillard, sir."

Before Jackson responded the clerk began tapping away, sending the telegraph for the inquiry. "All right, Mr. Dillard, Ah only had tuh send one telegraph, it was addressed tuh both steamship companies. Each one has its own telegraph office, so the response should be comin' in within the hour. You can wait or you can tell me where the delivery boy can find yuh."

"Thank yuh kindly," Jackson responded. "Ah'll be down at the rooming house. How much do Ah owe yuh?"

"We'll settle up when our business is complete, Mr. Dillard." The clerk smiled and gave Jackson a farewell nod.

Jackson smiled, tipped his hat and left the small office. His struts toward the rooming house were quick and spry expressing a confident march. He could've hired the slave catchers to hunt down Jacob and Sula, but he had a burning desire for personal revenge. He dreamed of the torturous death he had for his little brother and his slave gal.

The rooming house had a small dining room attached to the side of the building, but Jackson entered the structure through the main foyer. He was directed into the dining room by an elderly woman and elected to take a seat at a table by the window. There was no menu; only one breakfast meal had been prepared for all of the roomers. Soon after settling in, he was served a breakfast of scrambled eggs, grits, two slices of smoked ham, two hot biscuits, butter, grape jam and hot coffee. His mind continued to be plagued with hatred for Jacob. He shut out the rest of his surroundings while leaning over his plate to satisfy his stomach's grumbling expression due to its lack of nourishment.

"Ah came back, Mr. Dillard."

Jackson looked up slowly. He knew it was Peabody before his eyes set on him. Not wanting him to know how pleased he was to have him back, he composed himself. "Oh Peabody, my man," he cocked his head to the side and looked up. "Have some breakfast, man. Yuh know it comes with the room. Just let the old lady know yuh here and she'll bring yuh a spread."

When Peabody returned, Jackson explained the situation with the steamship companies and the telegraph office and his belief that even if the Morton family traveled south, he believed Jacob may have traveled north.

At the appropriate time, Jackson and Peabody returned to the telegraph office and the clerk had two envelopes prepared for him. "Thank you, sir," Jackson announced. "What's my tab?"

"That's gonna cost yuh forty cents Mr. Dillard. Ah hope the information is helpful," the clerk responded.

"We do too." He tipped his hat and he and Peabody left the office. They began walking toward the train station, but stopped after taking a few steps on the planked sidewalk to open the first envelope. Jackson smiled, "North! Ah-ha! Ah thought so!" he shouted. He handed the paper to Peabody along with the second envelope. "We need tuh get tickets to Charleston and then board the S.S. Sparlding steamer for Wilmington, North Carolina. Ah believe Jacob is gonna board that northbound steamer there and ship out tomorrow at 5:00 PM. That snake. He thinks he's so smart! Ah'll get that bastard yet!"

Peabody stared at and held up the second envelope and while Jackson ranted, he tore it open. "Well, Ah'll be!" He began to laugh in a loud chuckle. He walked beside the gloating Jackson holding the second telegraph in front of him. "Hey Dillard, riddle me this!" he taunted "This telegraph says that Jacob Natty, the Morton family and party, are on the manifest for the southbound steamer out of Charleston, too."

Jackson snatched the telegraph from Peabody's hand. He read it and crumpled both papers into tight balls and slammed them to the ground. "Damn! Damn! Damn!" He kicked the dirt. He punched the air and then he stomped off toward the train depot.

Peabody took a deep breath and followed several paces behind Jackson. He didn't know where he was going; Jackson's personality was peaking again and he didn't feel the need to share his next move.

The train depot was in view and Peabody continued to drag behind, making no attempt to keep up with Jackson. By the time he reached the ticket window Jackson was questioning the ticket agent as to what passengers purchased tickets on December 20th. for the Wilmington & Manchester Line and on the Charleston & Hamburgh Line.

"Sir . . . Ah only have information for passengers that purchased their tickets at this depot. If they boarded the train at another station or just transferred trains here in Columbia, Ah can't help yuh." the ticket clerk explained.

Jackson's white skin began to spot cherry red as his anger level rose. He was ready to release his annoyance on the agent, but Peabody arrived just in time to intervene. He thanked the poor man for his help and Jackson stepped back from the window and took a deep breath. Peabody turned and whispered for Jackson to return with him to the boarding house's dining room where they could decide what they should do next.

chapter 24

"Burgaw Depot! Burgaw Depot!" The conductor called out. The loud whistle blew several times and the train coasted into the small station. Fifteen minutes later the whistle blew again and the conductor called out, "All aboard!" and the train pulled off.

"Next stop . . . Wilmington!" the conductor walked through the passenger car shouting. "Wilmington in fifty minutes! Last stop on the easterly run!"

Miles leaped from his seat and returned to the compartment car. When he arrived, he realized Jacob and his family had no idea they were so close to the end of the line. As soon as he gave them notice, they began folding and packing their blankets and organizing their bags. It was Jacob's intention that they be the first to exit the train in Wilmington. They wanted to be completely out of the way when the baggage handlers arrived to remove the white passenger's luggage.

While Sula and Miss Tillie packed the blankets, Jacob walked off to the side and spoke privately with Miles. "We do have tuh acquire a carriage that will carry our families, but let me remind you, the drivers may take on yuh family, but they are not gonna take mine. Ah'll have tuh rent a carriage from the livery for my family."

Miles acknowledged Jacob's point and nodded his head. "We can't leave 'em alone. Ah'll hire a carriage and have the man drive me tuh the livery stable. Then, Ah'll rent a rig for you and yuh family and inquire about lodging. Ah'll tell the man tuh have the rig ready upon my return. Then, Ah'll leave my family off at the rooming house. Don't worry Jacob; there must be a Negro rooming house somewhere in Wilmington."

Jacob knew he would face this dilemma and had prayed for a solution. It was colder in Wilmington than in Columbia. As a last resort, he knew he would drive his family into the Negro section of the area and beg for someone to shelter them for the night. He also knew money would buy them warmth and even the meager bed at any Negro household.

"That's a good plan Miles. Even if you can't find lodging for us, we will have a wagon and Ah can go lookin' for myself. Now, Ah think yuh should return tuh yuh family. See yuh soon," Jacob said.

It wasn't long before the station signs came into view. Jacob's family gathered their bags and were standing and waiting to leave the train. Jacob was first to step off the train and before long, they were all walking toward the tall oak tree near the station house. The frigid air off the ocean met them with an unforgivable chill and they pulled their coats tight against their necks.

Tillie retrieved the blankets, handed them out and they all, except for Jacob, cocooned themselves against the elements. They watched the white people hurry into the warm station house and while the children continued to stare, she and Sula attended to each other with a perceptive nod. Mrs. Morton pushed her young ones ahead of herself and she looked over at Jacob, her expression being that of hopelessness. Jacob smiled and waved his hand. Mrs. Morton could only dab her handkerchief to her eyes. Her children were in the building and only Miles stood by her side.

"My family is warm," Jacob called out to Miles. "Settle yuh family in the depot then secure the transportation."

Miles nodded and guided his mother into the building.

Tillie was looking away from Jacob; her eyes met with Sula's and they both turned to stare at the chocolate colored man sitting on the driver's seat of the double rigged buck wagon. The man, who was located about a hundred feet away from them, stood when he noticed he had their attention, but returned to his seat and tucked his head when they turned to attend to Jacob. While Sula's attention clung to Jacob, Tillie realized that he was the wedge holding the man at bay; she believed he could offer the help they needed. She waved her arm at the man and smiled broadly before turning back to Jacob.

"Jacob . . . yuh gotta walk away," she ordered. "Don't look up, just walk away right now! Dat Negro man got a fix on us; he be scared a you. Go 'way! He got a wagon and he might can he'p us. So go 'way!" Tillie whispered adamantly and she held a rigid attitude in her posture.

Jacob hurriedly walked inside the depot and stood monitoring the situation from the window. Miles and Mrs. Morton rushed to his side and he explained Tillie's strategy.

Again, Tillie smiled broadly and waved her arm. "Hello Mister!" she called out while Sula and the children looked on.

The man waved back with hesitation. He smiled and surveyed his surroundings.

"Can yuh he'p us?" Tillie called tuh him. She began walking in his direction.

With Jacob out of sight, the slight built black man stepped down from his wagon and approached Tillie. He was a middle aged man with mixed gray hair and beard and he wore a tattered wool three quartered coat, gray plaid flannel shirt and faded, but clean bibbed coveralls. "Howdy ma'am! Y'all be travelin' long?" he asked. "Y'all woman and chillen all alone?"

Tillie didn't answer his questions. The man had been watching them since they got off the train and she believed he knew the answers. She knew he was wondering about the white man and she would explain as soon as she found out if the man could help them. "Well, we sho be needin' a ride and roomin' fer da night," she responded.

"Who be dat white man? He ain't gone make trouble is he?" He glanced off toward the depot and then back at Tillie.

Tillie smiled. "It be fine, kin yuh he'p us?"

"Sho-nuff, ma'am. Dat's whut we do. Mah name be Clappy Mann. We got us a lil' house and we try tuh keep up fer our travelin' folk. Ain't nut'en in town fo' us. Somebody be here tuh meet every train and we take 'em in if'n dey in need and if'n' dey kin pay or not. Ah be from da New Hope Baptist Church, dat be just outta town a bit. Now the church be keepin up just a lil' 'ol' one-room house out back fer our travelers, but it be warm and got clean beds and good food."

Tillie pulled her blanket tighter around her shoulder and sighed. "Yes sur . . . we sho be in need, Mr. Clappy Mann. Ah be called, Tillie." her voice squeaked with excitement. "Now, dat white man . . ." Tillie smiled and turned toward the depot building as she spoke. "Well, he be my sister's boy, Jacob; he be colored. Now, dere be a white family we be wit', but they ain't got no problems; dey be just worried 'bout us. Dat gal back dere be Jacob's woman and Ah know he be wantin' tuh stay wit' hur. Jacob . . . he be payin' yuh real good fer our keep."

Clappy Mann looked toward the depot and then back at Tillie. "It be my pleasure helpin' y'all, ma'am. May Ah he'p yuh tuh get on da wagon, den we be gettin' da rest of yuh family and yuh stuff?"

Tillie raised her head, "Oh thank Yuh Lawd . . . thank Yuh Lawd!" she called out before accepting Mr. Mann's assistance at boarding the wagon.

A carriage driven by a white man drove up and stopped in front of the depot to transport Miles and his family to their rooming house, but Miles refused to leave until Jacob gave the word. They all breathed a sigh of relief at watching Jacob's family boarding the double rigged wagon. Mr. Mann refused to approach the depot as long as the white driver was present, so Jacob and Miles walked back to the oak tree.

Clappy Mann lowered his wide brim hat and tucked his head so low his chin was almost laying on his upper chest at the sight of Miles walking in his direction.

"Miss Tillie, yuh said yuh people, Jacob be coming. Who dat odder man?" Ah don't cotton tuh whites. Dem white drivers be tryin tuh stop us from helpin' our kind. We gotta keep our house quiet and hidden."

"He be Miles. He be our friend." Miss Tillie grabbed Mann's trembling hand. "He be okay, he be just fine." Clappy Mann was new to her and it was improper for her to touch a man's hand like that, but she understood real fear. She knew it was necessary and she realized she might never see him again their two days stay in Willmington.

Clappy Mann remained as silent as a mute when Miles and Jacob reached the wagon. Tillie reached over and whispered the situation in Jacob's ear. Jacob turned and asked Miles to walk with him while he explained Mr. Mann's fears. Miles stood back, about twenty five feet from the wagon. He waited for Jacob to approach him with information about their accommodations and the time and place of their meeting before their sailing.

Miles waved at Jacob and his family as his carriage was driven away to their rooming house. Clappy Mann waited until the white carriage was out of sight before turning his rig in the direction to be traveled. He then headed off down a dirt road that appeared to take them away from town and farther away from Wilmington. Everyone in the wagon was quiet. Jacob and Sula sat on a bale of hay directly behind the driver's seat while Tillie sat next to Mr. Mann.

Clappy Mann was ready to release his tongue and everyone was ready to listen to what he had to say. "Ah know yuh be thinkin' we goin' away from town," he began, "but Ah jes travelin' outta da way tuh hide my tracks. Yuh know how it be . . . white folk don't want us tuh have nothin'. We gotta protect our travelers and keep da house a secret. Dey let us have a church. Dey scared of da Lawd, so we build da travel house ontuh da back of da church. Da church be set back off the main road by a mile and dat be a mile outta town. Dey think we be takin' travelers tuh our homes and we will if'n we be needin' tuh. Tuhday dere be room in da church-house."

"Ah don't know what we woulda done wit'out yuh, Mr. Mann," Jacob said. "This is for yuh hospitality." He placed fifty dollars in his hand, smiled at him and patted him on his back.

chapter 25

As the rooster crowed back on the Morton farm, so did the loud blow-horn of the S.S. Sparlding steamship in the Port of Wilmington, North Carolina, on that cold December morning. It was very early Saturday morning when Robby and Evan hurriedly dressed and were eager to escape the confines of the boarding house. Breakfast would be served between 7:00 and 9:00 A.M., but the sun had only cast its glow on the horizon. With Miles permission they ran off hoping to watch the tall ships dock. The day before they stood in awe, admiring the Atlantic Ocean and the ships at sea. They had only seen lakes, ponds and streams in their lifetime and on Friday morning they watched the sky meet the water on a spectacular horizon. Such a phenomena had only been experienced in their world through books.

"Oh no, Robby, they already tied hur down," Evan whined. He pointed to the long sleek ship and the thick ropes that tied and anchored the S.S. Sparlding securely to the dock.

An early morning fog hovered low under the gray sky as the winter's sun rose ever so slowly. It was a chilly damp morning, but not enough to send the boys back to the warmth of the rooming house. They pulled their knit caps down over their ears, fastened the top buttons of their coats and shoved their hands deep in their pockets. A large wooden crate set abandon and empty. "Perfect!" Robby called out. "Come Evan. Help me push this up tuh the building."

Evan's eyes widen and he turned searching for its owner. "It ain't ours, Robby. We can't touch it."

"Ah'm cold. So we're gonna move it and climb in to keep warm. If anybody tells us tuh stop, then we will," Robby explained. His hands were already in position to move the box.

Evan gave him a coy smile and assisted with the movement. They crawled inside the large crate and pulled one of the side flaps up. The remaining upper flap was pushed back, leaving a small window for the boys to see all the activities that revolved around the ship and the crate protected them from the wintery elements. The workers loaded and unloaded the ship, hauled large and small boxes and barrels. They stacked them on the dock and deck of the ship, all while other men worked feverously loading and unloading wagons. More than an hour slipped away and the steady labor of the men continued. The boys weren't sure of the time, but prayed they had not missed the breakfast curfew set my Miles. They agreed to crawl from their shelter, but pulled themselves back into hiding when they recognized Jackson and Peabody standing at the top of the gangway. They watched as the men argued, shouting at each other, face on face and then turning to maintain their balance as they navigated the slope of the plank. They never ceased their verbal confrontation, but the boys couldn't make out what they were saying. Within minutes, Jackson and Peabody were standing in front of the crate where the boys were hiding.

Jackson hooked his right thumb in his gun belt and allowed his other hand to flail and emphasize his spoken words. "It's still early and this ship doesn't sail until later this evening," Jackson yelled out.

"Ah shoulda gone on tuh my spread like Ah had a meanin'. Lawd only knows what's happenin' tuh my property while Ah'm chasin' 'round the country wit' you."

"Look, we should search the rooming houses around town. If they're here we'll find them. There is a 1:00 P.M. train back to Columbia, South Carolina. If we don't find them by then . . . then, Ah promise yuh, we'll be on that train." Jackson announced.

"Why don't yuh search and I'll guard the ship so they don't slip on board? Ah ain't ready for 'nother attack."

"We can do a better search if we work together," Jackson wolfed.

The boys watched as the men disappeared between the many wagons. As soon as they believed they could get out of the crate unseen, they ran as fast as they could to their rooming house.

"We saw those men . . ." Robby could barely speak he was so winded. He placed his hands on his knees, bent over and fought with his body to catch his breath.

Evan did not try to speak, but lay curled on the floor with his arms hugging himself.

"What . . . what did you say, Robby?" Miles questioned. He heard Robby, but had difficulty understanding how Jackson and Peabody knew to travel to Wilmington.

"Those men . . . the ones you and Mr. Natty stopped in Columbia. They got off the Sparlding ship." Robby took a deep breath, stood tall and continued.

"What!" Miles asked again. His face was twisted with concern.

"Yeah! They are going tuh go tuh the rooming houses and search all around lookin' for y'all. We all need tuh hide until they leave."

"Jacob," Miles whispered. "He's bringing his family tuh town this morning. I have tuh warn him and, yes, we do need tuh hide."

"We heard them say if they don't fine y'all they will take the one o'clock train back tuh Columbia 'cause they don't really know if y'all went north or south," Robby said.

"Okay, you boys did good. Now get some food. Tell Mama to take the girls and all y'all go to the room. Stay outta sight 'til Ah come back. Ah gotta find a way to warn Jacob." Miles hurried off to the kitchen where he knew the Negro help worked. Two women and one man stopped what they were doing and froze, their eyes fixing on him.

"Please forgive me," Miles began.

The Negro workers shifted their eyes between themselves and Miles and didn't speak a word.

"Excuse me, please," Miles began, "but does anyone know a man named, Clappy Mann?" Miles stood staring at the workers and they just stared back at him. He knew they knew this man. He could see it in their eyes, but protecting their kind was more important than responding to a strange white man. "Please . . . Mr. Mann is helping my friend and his family. Yuh see . . . there are two white men here in town looking for them. Ah need tuh get tuh them. Tuh keep them safe."

"Yessum boss, Ah be knowin' Clappy Mann. Ah know where they be, but dat place be a mile off." A middle aged black man named, James spoke up. "Sorry, sur. Ah cain't take yuh tuh dat secret place."

"Can yuh take a letter tuh my friend?"

"Sho' can if'n yuh ask da boss lady fo da use of hur buggy?" James replied. "She be all 'bout money, yuh hear."

"Ah understand and Ah'll pay hur for the use of your time, too."

"Thank yuh, sur."

෨✥෨

Miles secured the small carriage, wrote the letter and handed it to James for the delivery. The letter explained that Jackson and Peabody had arrived in Wilmington on the S. S. Sparlding steamship, but would return to Columbia on the one o'clock train if they didn't find evidence that they were in town and traveling north. He asked that they remain in their secret place. He also wrote, "Be very careful; Jackson could change his mind and remain with the ship. We should meet behind the rooming house at 2:00 P.M. I am praying both men board the train and leave Wilmington, but beware."

Miles folded the letter and handed it to James who stuffed it in his front trouser pocket before climbing on the wagon.

"Ah thank you kindly, James."

The men saluted each other by nodding and James rode off.

෨✥෨

Miles returned to his mother's room and stood surveying the street below. He stepped back behind the sheer curtain when he noticed the two men walking toward the depot. Their eyes were searching, examining the buildings and establishments, scanning for the evidence they sought; this was just a first run, a more thorough investigation was planned on their return.

"Mama, there they are," Miles whispered. He waved his hand, gesturing for her to join him at the window.

"Yes, the one that looks like Jacob's twin. Ah remember him from the train station in Columbia."

"Yes Mama, the evil brother. Ah don't know why God made them tuh look so much alike. Jacob is a free man; why does Jackson pursue him so?" Miles continued whispering.

Mrs. Morton patted Miles' hand. "Honey, Jacob is a very private man. There are a lot of things about his life he hasn't shared. In time he will, it's just his way."

෨✥෨

James tapped the horse's ass with the reins and it trotted inconspicuously along the coble road right past Jackson and Peabody, not even earning a casual glance from them. Once out of town, he drove the horse at a more punishing pace in tune with the urgency of Miles demeanor. Within the hour he had reached the New Hope Baptist Church. Clappy Mann's time with the travelers had ended and it was now his cousin, Luther Mann who was the host and driver. James entered the church and hurried to the front where he located Luther stretched prone on the pew.

"Hey Luther," James called out.

"Hey James. Whut yuh doing here tuhday? We ain't goin' turkey huntin' 'til mornin'."

"Ah know dat Luther. Ah'll be seein' yuh tuhmorrow 'bout dat. Ah need to see dem travelers. Ah got me here a message fer da head man." He dug his hands deep into his pants pockets before feeling and squeezing the breast pockets on his shirt. "Oh my Lawd. Ah done loss dat letter," he sang out; dreaded lines etched his face; his head and shoulders reacted with a frightful shiver.

Luther sat up and goose necked James. "Whut . . . you be trusted and yuh lose da message." He walked past James shaking his head and mumbling. He reached a door at the back side of the pulpit and opened it. "Uh . . . Mr. Natty, can Ah see yuh fer a minute?" he called out. He closed the door without latching it and walked back to the front pew.

James stood with his head hung and Luther sat with his arms winged over the back of the pew as Jacob approached.

"Is everything okay?" Jacob asked. His eyes shifted between the two men.

"Uh . . . dis man here be James. He works at da roomin' house in town and he got a message fer yuh."

James stared at Jacob and every word his mama and papa taught him froze somewhere between his brain and his lips. No one told him a blue eyed, blond haired, white man would be staying at the secret place. How was he supposed to tell this man that he loss the letter? How could he will himself to speak? "Uh ... Uh," were the only sounds James could utter.

Luther stood, "Uh ... Mr. Natty. Ah believe yuh appearance kinda surprised my friend."

"Yes sur. Uh . . . uh . . . Ah had a letter, but it got away from me. Ah mean . . . Ah don' loss da letter in my haste tuh get here."

Jacob took a deep breath and it seemed his eye turned bluer while his expression turned to deep concern. "Well, what did da letter say?"

James' lips held a deep frown and he continued to hang his head, twisting it slightly upward; his eyes stared up at Jacob like a naughty little boy; he shook his head. "He didn't tell me, sur."

"Don't call me, sur. Ah'm younger than you and Ah'm a Negro. You are my, sir! My name be Jacob. Please, call me, Jacob."

"Yessum."

Jacob shook his head. "Can yuh read?"

James shook his head.

"Do yuh have any idea what he was trying tuh tell me?" The virtue of patience and understanding was a gift inherited from his years of servitude. "Mr. James, can you tell me why it was so important for Miles to send yuh out here?"

James' eyes sharpened. "No one had ever called him 'mister'. Yessum. All he say tuh me is dat two white men be in town lookin' fer yuh and he be needin' tuh keep yuh safe. Now dat be all he say tuh me, but he be writin' a powerful lot in dat letter, so Ah know he say more fer you."

Suddenly the sanctuary loss the early morning light that shown through the small windows. Jacob had to get to Miles; he was no match for Jackson alone, much less Jackson and Peabody. "Mr. James, Ah need to ride back tuh town wit' you." He checked his pocket watch. "Ah'll be ready in fifteen minutes . . . will dat be all right? Ah have tuh speak wit' my family before Ah leave." Jacob turned toward Luther. "May Ah press yuh tuh have my family at the Wilmington House by 2:00 P.M.?"

Luther gave Jacob a nod.

"Ah wanna thank y'all for yuh hospitality. Ah don't know what we would've done without y'all." Jacob said as he shook Luther's hand.

⤙⤚

Thirty minutes later James and Jacob arrived at the edge of Wilmington.

"Ah seed dem men dat Mr. Morton be talkin' 'bout. Dey be walkin' tuh da depot' and Ah rode right near dem. Now, Mr. Jacob, maybe it be good if'n yuh get down under dis here seat while Ah be drivin'. Dere be a blanket back dere that yuh kin hide under."

"Ah sho' will. Now, if yuh see dem men, tell me, but keep goin'. Ah be much obliged if yuh just get me tuh the roomin' house. Ah'll wait in the carriage while yuh go in and look see if the men be in there." Jacob settled tight under the seat and his hand touched on a folded paper. He pushed back a corner of the blanket to allow for a stream of light. "Wait Mr. James," he whispered. "Ah found the letter. Drive the wagon away slowly while Ah read it."

James' face held the strained expression of disappointment and anger with himself for not taking special care with the letter. His breath quivered with relief as he sucked in the cool air of Jacob's discovery. Sitting back against the seat and without unnecessary commotion, he turned the mare and headed back out of town.

"Dear Lawd . . . Mr. James, this letter says stay away from town; that the men don't know where we are and if they don't find us they will leave on the south bound train at one o'clock."

James continued to drive the mare away from town. "Oh . . . Mr. Jacob, dere be a God and he sho be lookin' over us."

"There sho' is, Mr. James." He pushed the blanket away from his head and pulled out his pocket watch. "It be just 10:56."

"Mr. Jacob, we be back at the secret place long befo' noon."

Jacob exhaled and paused before he spoke. "Ah want yuh tuh drive me down tuh the depot, if yuh will? Then just let me off and Ah'll hide out. Yuh say the train be leavin' at one o'clock? Ah need tuh see dem men be on it befo' my family gets tuh town."

Miles had watched Peabody and Jackson walk below his window and disappear into the Wilmington Rooming House. Meals were always served in the dining room from early morning through the dinner hour. He left his room and stole down the corridor, peeking around the corner of the wall until he located them sitting at a table in the lower level. He was satisfied; they were having their meal and not searching about. He returned to his room.

James returned to the rooming house and walked around the far end of the dining room. He prayed he would not attract the attention of the two strangers as he carried a stack of white sheets and towels toward the maid's station. Once out of sight, he hurried to the Morton's room and tapped lightly on the door.

"Who's there?" Mrs. Morton sang out.

Miles had his mother respond to the door knowing Jackson and Peabody were looking for men. When James responded, Mrs. Morton stepped back and Miles cracked the door for a visual inspection before letting him in. James shifted in place and waited for Miles to speak first.

Miles stared at James and waited for an update. He tilted his head and took a deep breath; finally he spoke up. "Well, did Mr. Natty get my letter? Is he coming with his family at 2:00 P.M.?"

"Well, sur. Mr. Jacob's family will be here at 2:00 P.M. Mr. Jacob came back wit' me. He be hidin' down at da depot'. Say he gots tuh see dem men leave on dat train tuh be sho' dey gon'."

"Jacob is here?" Mrs. Morton asked.

"Yes ma'am," James replied. He took a gentle bow before leaving the room.

Miles put his arm around his mother's shoulder. "Yuh know Mama, Ah think it's good that he's at the station. This way we can be sure we're safe. Don't worry, they won't see him."

"Ah suppose so," she muttered. She patted Miles' hand and walked to the window. "Oh, Miles, they're leaving!" She turned and covered her mouth with her hand.

"Don't worry Mom, they're walking tuh the depot. It's gone be over soon." He placed his arms around her shoulders. Robby and Evan hurried to her side and clung to her long flowing skirt. "Mama, our trouble would be greater if they returned to the ship."

"Praise the Lord they didn't do that," she whispered.

☙❧

The train, with its massive engine had cooled down after arriving in Wilmington the day before and was now revved up again. It would be twenty five minutes before the 'all aboard' whistle would sound, but for the present time the firemen were feeding the boiler and pressuring it up; steam blasted from its large engine and bellowed out in thick low clouds, hissing like a dragon threatening to break loose.

Jacob could see the station and he watched the road carefully. He searched and waited for Jackson and Peabody to walk by. The road was open and clear and the forest offered concealment in all directions. *I can drop Peabody first*, he thought. He pulled up his trouser leg and retrieved his pistol. *I'll hold Jackson back with my gun to his head and order him to pull Peabody's body off into the forest, that insignificant little rat.* He held his small derringer loaded and ready to fire. *The only reason Ah'm even considerin' sparin' Jackson is for the sake of my family. Ah would've done him in a long time ago, but he is the only heir tuh The Dillard. If he's dead, they'll sell that place and all my people will be scattered. Ain't nothin' can stop me from cripplin' him fo' sure. He can't hunt me no more.* Anger screamed in his head and his body rocked, ready to leap. He held his small pistol in his hand as he heard their loud voices echoing off the trees. The sounds of their footsteps seemed to amplify in his head; they crumpled the hard clay road. His hatred now controlled his animation, he was ready.

Suddenly he saw his gun leave his hand and he felt a heavy weight pulling him into the dried leaves. "STOP JACOB!" Miles voice sounded in his ears. "STOP, NO! We need yuh! Yuh can't see the future! Let them leave and it'll be over," Miles whispered his yell. He held Jacob from behind, his arms and legs wrapped tightly around him with one hand covering his mouth. "Sorry Jacob, we must be very quiet," he continued to whisper before slowly removing his hand.

Jacob lay still without trying to shake himself loose. From between the breaks in the white birch, oak, evergreen, shrubs and other such forest growth of winter, they could see Jackson and Peabody walking less than a hundred feet away. Their breathing and eyes were involuntary, but their other body movements were frozen less they would break a twig, crumple the dry leaves or ripple the wind. Even the slightest interference with nature might insight the smallest creatures and stir the senses of their pursuer. This would only force Jacob back to his original course of action, of which the future could not be predicted. So the young men lay still, entwined in each other, their earth colored clothing blending with the hue of the forest and praying that not even a bird stirred to attract attention in their direction. They only heard the voices of their enemies as they argued how their decision to sail the north bound Sparlding had delayed their pursuit. As their sounds grew dimmer, Jacob and Miles resumed a more amicable posture. Miles apologized and Jacob expressed his thanks.

Jacob and Miles welcomed the sweet crisp air surrounding them because their lung heaved with the anxiety to be filled and replenished several times before their strength could returned. Jacob nodded at Miles and this was accepted as his apology. Miles brushed the dried leaves from his pants, made eye contact with his friend and returned his nod.

"Now let's steal down to that depot and witness their departure," Miles announced.

A one horse carriage was driven down the road at a trotting pace. Both men crouched down and Jacob noticed James was the driver. Miles ran ahead and flagged him down. James had a female passenger from the rooming house aboard.

"Howdy, ma'am." Miles tipped his hat. "Oh what a lovely bonnet you're wearing. My dear mother would love tuh own one so beautiful." He smiled. "May Ah have a word with yuh driver; it will only take a few seconds?"

"Most certainly young man," the older lady responded. She smiled and lightly touched the side of her bonnet.

James turned and received her approval gesture before stepping down from the carriage.

Miles gave the lady a broad smile. He tipped his hat and they turned away from her and whispered to each other.

As James climbed back into the driver's seat, Miles was again attending to the lady. He was careful not to make too much of an impression on her because she would be riding the same train as Jackson and Peabody; it was possible that she might casually mention the young man that stopped her carriage and spoke to her driver while she was traveling to the depot.

Jacob remained in the forest until the carriage was out of sight and then he joined Miles and they sat on the bank along the roadside.

A moment passed before Miles broke the silence, "We'll wait here for James to return with the carriage. He's gon' tell us if they left on that train. Then we can ride back with him."

Jacob rubbed his hands together anxiously and nodded his head. His chest heaved slightly, heavier than required for normal breathing. An uneasiness appeared to sting him like honey bees. He felt the sweetness of freedom from Jackson's evil for himself and his family, but he also knew the sting of oppression and racism would always remain. The chill of the long winters and frigid weather would be an unequal and challenging exchange and he didn't want to leave the warmth and beauty of the south. He thought about Mammy Pearl and Ollie, all of his family at The Dillard and he wondered if he would ever see Juke and Capers again. He had done some bad things, but they needed to be done. Miles would never understand the walk he had walked, but he loved Miles like he loved his brothers.

"Miles," Jacob began. He pushed his hat back and allowed his hands to support his head.

"It's okay Jacob. Speak if yuh have to, but Ah already understand."

Jacob smiled. *If yuh understood my pain you would have a hole in yuh heart.* He turned and stared at Miles and chuckled lightly.

"James gone be here soon and it'll be over," Miles said. He rested his elbows on his knees and stared forward.

Suddenly, a shadow rose over Jacob and another over Miles. "Stand up . . . stand up slowly both of you." Jackson's voice was deep, cold and without emotions.

Jacob and Miles stood and raised their hands over their heads without the order to do so. Peabody took a step backward, but held his gun pointed at Jacob. Miles notice this and also noticed this to be true for the sight of Jackson's gun. He locked eyes with Jacob and by the time his heart beat four times he had communicated this to his friend.

Jacob heard the rambling words of Jackson, but he concentrated on signaling Miles to back away from the line of fire.

"Get over here! Yuh a dead man. Yuh one niggah that won't step over the line again," Jackson yelled.

Jacob bowed his head and pointed inconspicuously to the ground. He watched as Miles eased himself to a prone position. He removed his hat and stepped in the space that lined up between Jackson and Peabody.

Peabody moved closer to him, waving his gun as if it suddenly made him a taller man. "Ah ain't never had no niggah do that tuh me!" He stared at

Jackson as he spoke. Staring like he was requesting his permission to fire his gun.

"Ah told yuh he was mine!" Jackson screamed, giving the little man his attention.

Jacob flung his hat toward Jackson's face, then dropped to the ground and rolled at a tumbling speed. He heard one shot and felt a sharp pain in his neck.

"Jacob!" Miles screamed. "Oh no, Jacob, Jacob!" he cried out.

"Oh!" Jacob moaned. "Ah think Ah got hit in the neck."

"Let me see." Miles whined. He turned Jacob over and examined his neck. "Yuh have some nasty scratches, but I don't see any bullet holes. Can yuh move yuh head?"

Jacob continued to lay on the ground; he examined his own neck and then massaged it before moving his head around. "Ah'm okay Miles, but what happened?"

Miles pointed to the two men slumped over on the forest floor. "Well, they tried to shoot you, missed and shot each other. Ah think they fired at the exact same time, because Ah only heard one shot." He chuckled, an ironic soft chuckle. He took a deep breath and exhaled forcefully. "Everything happened so fast, but Ah think yuh rolled yuhself into this tree." He patted the tall pine tree and helped his friend to stand.

Miles rushed over to Peabody. "Well, this one is real dead. Shot right between the eyes. Brother Jackson is a pretty good shot; no . . . Ah don't believe so, he was aiming at you, Jacob."

Jacob stumbled over to Jackson. A small pool of blood covered the leaves surrounding where he lay. "Oh Lawd, he can't be dead. Please don't let him be dead, Lawd," he whined. He placed his ear to his chest. "Ooooh! Ooooh! Oh thank Yuh Lawd! He ain't dead."

"Why don't yuh want him dead, Jacob? The next time he will kill yuh."

"It's not about him, Miles. It's about my people. Ah'll explain later." Jacob began to examine his head. "There is no bullet hole in his head, but he's out cold. He must've hit his head on that rock." There was a small pool of blood near his head and on the side of that large rock, but a larger pool was soaking the ground from under his lower back.

Miles tilted Jackson up sideways and then quickly lowered him. "Ah don't know how, but Ah think he caught a bullet in his back. Sorry Jacob."

As the train chugged away from the coastal city the whistle blasted. Black smoke bellowed and polluted the air as it hovered low in a trail over Wilmington. "Well, he missed his train," Jacob murmured and shook his head. He stood looking down at Jackson. "Lawd, please let him live," he prayed.

"And he is gonna keep coming after yuh," Miles reminded his friend.

"Well, by the look of his injuries, it won't be no time soon. I just pray he lives. Once we get on that steamer he won't know where we're gettin' off."

"Well, just tuh be sure Ah'm gone tie his hands behind his back. That should slow him down a bit."

"No, Miles. Right now it just looks like a shootout between two men. If we tie his hands then it'll appear as foul-play."

Jacob began walking toward the road. "James gone be comin' soon, so let's go. Don't tell 'em nothin' about all this, then he won't know nothin' if he's asked."

"Ah see yuh point." Miles shook his head and followed Jacob through the forest. They reached the road a mile away from where the incident occurred and continued walking toward the rooming house.

James drove up and stopped the carriage near Miles and Jacob. As soon as he knew the men were seated he began with his update. "Ah declare, Mr. Jacob. Ah had dem men in my sight. Dey be standin' just tuh da side of da baggage cart and dat lady Ah be drivin' . . . well, she be havin' a word wit' 'em and she be fixin' wit' dat hat she be wearin'. When Ah turn back, dem men be gone."

"Gone?" Jacob said. "You ain't see 'em get on the train?"

Miles looked at Jacob. "Well we didn't see them come back this way so they must be gone."

"Lissen Mr. James, yuh did yuh best. Let's get back tuh the boardin' house."

"Thank yuh, Mr. Jacob."

chapter 26

Lester arrived on schedule at the rooming house along with Jacob's family, but before they left for the ship, it was time for a meeting. Jacob, Miles and Mrs. Morton sat with the families to discuss a few issues. Using a charred clump of wood-ash that had fallen on the fireplace hearth, Mrs. Morton drew a crude map on a page of old newsprint. She pointed out their current location and the distance they had to travel.

"We will continue to travel up north and we must be diligent to protect ourselves from a cold and chill like nothing we have ever experienced." Her finger moved from what she had designated as Wilmington to the place she marked as New York Harbor. "When we reach this place we will have traveled about 600 miles at sea. We will be on this ship for more than a week." She smiled at Sula and Tillie. Robby and Evan were holding tightly to the rambunctious twins and then she smiled at them. She thought of how the sea might make any one of them sick, but held that thought to herself. *Dearest Lord, spare us from this malady. Please Lord, in the gracious name of Yuh son, Jesus, Ah pray. Amen.* "We will dock in many ports along our journey and Jacob and Miles agree with me." She paused and directed her attention toward them.

Tillie held Jenny and her smile was the reassurance the child needed. Simon sat close to Sula holding her hand. The concept of the distance to travel in miles had little meaning to them, but a week at sea, where the sky met the horizon and after that the earth appeared to fall away, was terrifying. This price they were paying for freedom was the most frightening thing they had ever experienced.

Jacob stood, nodded and continued speaking where Mrs. Morton left off, "Yes, we do agreed. When we dock, my family is tuh stay in the cabins, except for Simon. Ah want him tuh go tuh Robby and Evan's cabin and stay there until Ah tell him he can leave. Do yuh understand? Stay in the cabins where our white family be." Jacob stared at his family and waited several moments for each person to acknowledge his order. "Ah love yuh so much, so don't worry. Ah promise tuh keep yuh safe." He continued smiling at them and then he returned the meeting to Mrs. Morton.

"Thank yuh Jacob. Now, we will all meet in my cabin every morning for prayer and devotion and Monday morning will be special . . . it will be Christmas. Our love for each other will be the only gifts we need. We will celebrate with our special devotion and prayers of thanksgiving."

Christmas was a holiday having a dual meaning for a slave and a white person. They all smiled, nodded at each other and rocked with joy. They knew very little of Mrs. Morton's God, the deity who gave her so much strength. The only God they knew was the one that was preached about to reinforce their servitude and obedient to their master. They had heard of the man called, Jesus, but they were never told He would save them; they were never told He would keep them in His mercy and love them. They were never told He was preparing a better place for them in His Heavenly Kingdom. Christmas was a time of holiday for their master and a labor free time for them. Jacob was the only savior they knew and he was just a man who could bleed and die just like them. He had done more for them than any man they knew, so they placed their faith in Jacob and respected Mrs. Morton's God. But Jacob knew the Lord. He was taught the bible stories and of the most precious gift ever given to mankind. He listened to Mrs. Morton and knew it was his duty to deliver the good news to his family in a manner suitable for their understanding.

Mrs. Morton pointed to her map and called the place New York Harbor. "When we arrive here, we will get off of the S.S. Sparlding steamer," she continued, "we will be in slave free territory, but everything will not be what it seems to be. We will still be in the United States and we want to travel to Canada." Mrs. Morton went on to explain the ferry trip up to Albany, New York and then the overland trip to Saint Catherines, Ontario, Canada. She explained The Fugitive Slave Act and continued relentless pursuit of Jackson. For the sake of herself and her sons, she explained South Carolina's secession from the union, the call for other southern states to join them and the possibility of war. She knew it wasn't time to tell them of the treacherous mountainous passes they would soon face, the bitter cold and dangers of the slave hunters they might encounter along the way. She wanted time to pray on that. "Now, before we leave for the ship let us pray," she said.

"Oh, Gracious Lawd, our Father, You have been so good tuh all of us. You gave us the signs and You are removin' us from harm's way. We have come so far and we still have so far tuh travel. We ask that Yuh continue tuh watch over us and remove all danger that threatens our journey. Traveling by Your great sea will be a first time for all of us. Dear Father, Ah asked that You remove our fears and allow us tuh trust that You will deliver us safely. Many obstacles may threaten our travels Lawd and You know what they are. Please Lord, clear a path for us and bestow mercy on Yuh servants. We ask all these blessing in the name of Your Precious Son, Jesus Christ. Amen Lawd . . . Amen, Amen, Amen"

And they all repeated, "Amen."

ॐॐ

Tillie and Sula listened while Mrs. Morton prayed. They didn't bow their heads or close their eyes.

Tillie turned to face Sula. "All of us?" Tillie whispered to Sula. "Dear God gone take care of all of us? She pray fer all of us."

Jenny and Simon looked up at Miss. Tillie as she began to walk toward Mrs. Morton. Sula hurried to her side.

Mrs. Morton turned and gave the ladies a gentle smile. "Is everything all right?" she asked.

Tillie smiled. "Ma'am," she began, "yuh prayed fer all of us. Yuh God gone take care of all of us?"

Mrs. Morton took hold of Tillie and Sula's hand. "He is not just my God. He is Lord of All. He blesses you, too."

"Where's He been? If'n He be fer us too, den where's He been?" Tillie asked.

Mrs. Morton paused. She inhaled, closed her eyes and stopped moving. *Lord what answer do Ah give them*? A few moments passed as if the Lord had answered her. "Let's get on the ship and we will have plenty of time tuh learn more about the Lord and his works. But for now yuh just remember, God loves you too and He will keep yuh safe." She kissed Tillie and Sula on the forehead and then did the same for Jenny and Simon.

The four of them caught their breath at the touch of a white woman's lip against their skin and then they smiled and were quiet.

❧❧

One carriage and a buck wagon were driven away from the Wilmington Rooming House that afternoon. Mrs. Morton insisted all of the women and girls ride in the carriage and the men and boys ride in the buck wagon along with their luggage and bags. Mrs. Morton, Miss Tillie and the twin girls rode in the back under the canopy while Sula and young Jenny sat up on the driver's seat with James.

While Jacob and Miles took care of all the passenger check-in information, Lester and James carried the baggage to the cabins. One cabin was booked in the steerage section to satisfy the segregation issue and three large cabins were booked on the upper deck. Mrs. Morton insisted that her personal servants were close by to answer her calls and to meet her needs. Miss Tillie, Sula and Jenny were assigned an adjoining cabin to Mrs. Morton and the girls. Miles, Robby and Evan moved into the third cabin and Jacob and Simon bunked in the steerage compartment.

Miles, Jacob, Evan, Robby and Simon stood on the deck watching the men hoisting up the gangplank. They jerked themselves in the direction of the large whistles and looked up as the boiler blasted and blew out gushes of white steam. The engines rumbled and the ship moaned a harmonious hum. The anchor was pulled through a large opening in the side of the hull and the boys ran to the bow, climbing on the railing to get a better look. The deck filled with excited passengers and the dock gave way to standing room for friends and family wishing 'bon voyage' to the travelers. Everyone waved and the sendoff was merry.

Tears fell from Jacob's eyes. *Dear Lawd, keep us safe during our travels and in this unknown land.*

EPILOGUE

Sunday morning church service at the New Hope Baptist Church was scheduled to begin at 11:00 A.M. so Luther and James had to be home by 10:00. Wilmington was still asleep during the pre-dawn hours when they entered the forest on the west side of town. They carried their glowing lanterns and hoped to kill turkeys to place on their table for Christmas dinner. Luther was a terrible shot, but he had the eyes of an eagle, even in the dark. James could kill a fly on a leaf at twenty paces, so they were perfect as a hunting team. They found a clearing and baited the turkeys with dried corn kernels before stepping back behind the tree line deep in the woods. After removing their gear they positioned themselves on the ground, on a blanket of dried leaves, then they waited for the dawn to wake their pray. Turkeys sleep in trees and they knew it was pointless to go searching around for them in the dark. All they had to do was wait for the sound of their flapping wings, when the turkeys would be lowering themselves to the ground in search of food. The men knew they would wait until the hungry birds located the free meal.

James and Luther had hunted turkey together several times over the years and they were two of the best. Their rifles were old and would only fire one shot at a time before requiring a reload, so their plan had to be calculated to the second. They were as quiet as a whisper and always downwind of their pray. As soon as the birds began to feed, James took aim. Luther stood in position. James fired, tossed his rifle aside, reached and caught Luther's rifle, took quick aim, fired and the men yelled out triumphantly. The sun was still resting on the horizon and two turkeys lay dead. Luther immediately beheaded the turkeys and strung them up by their feet on a tree branch to drain their blood.

It was early and the men still had time to hunt. Perhaps a deer might be grazing in the early morning. That would be a wonderful gift to the church. Luther was first to shimmy up the oak tree and as soon as he was secure on a solid branch he gave James a boosting hand, assisting him to position himself on the opposite branch. They were searching for deer, but in the distance Luther recognized two men lying on the forest floor. James didn't see anything, but he believed Luther and they climbed down from the tree and hurried off.

Luther stopped twenty feet from the two white men and James came up beside him. "Oh Lawdy, is dey dead?" Luther asked. He stepped closer to get a better look.

"Don-know," James responded as he tipped closer behind Luther. As he got closer he recognized them and instantly decided not to acknowledge that fact.

Luther stood over Jackson. "He don't look dead." He held his fingers against his temple on the left side of his head. "Naw, he ain't dead, but he look lak he be hurt real bad."

James stood over Peabody. "Well, dis one be real dead, gots a bullet in his head."

The men backed up until they had backed into each other. "We gone get help den we's gone get on way from here. Ah don't want nothin' tuh do wit' no white man's troubles,' Luther said.

The men ran all the way to town, to Sheriff Bennett's home. After telling him of their findings, the sheriff hurried to Doc Wilder's home. The sheriff saddled his horse and the Doc hitched his wagon. Luther and James rode in the back of the doctor's wagon to the edge of the forest and then they had to trot at least a half a mile on foot, while the Doc and sheriff rode double on the sheriff's horse.

As soon as Jackson and Peabody were located, Luther and James were allowed to go on their way. They retrieved their turkeys and were at the New Hope Baptist Church in time for the 11:00 A.M. service.

త్రాఙ

Peabody's body was buried in Wilmington, North Carolina. His wife never heard from him again. Jackson was moved to Doctor Wilder's home where he remained for one month. Peabody's bullet had shattered his second lumbar vertebrate, but it did not injure his spinal cord. Jackson's pain was unbearable with every move he made. The pain would prevent him from walking, sitting, or any movement. The Doctor explained that he would have been better off if his spinal cord had been severed. Jackson begged the Doctor to operate on him and sever his spinal cord. Doc Wilder responded saying, 'That would be unethical."

The only pain management for Jackson was the new medication, Cocaine, whereas he was trained to give himself regular injections. He was then returned to The Dillard Plantation.

෨෧

Two weeks after setting sail from The Port of Wilmington, the Mortons and Jacob and his family arrived north of Albany, New York, where the mouth of the Mohawk River emptied into the Hudson River. A week into January and the weather in the northern region was surprisingly mild and Mrs. Morton reminded the families that the Lord was constantly blessing them. Jacob and Miles rented a large and crudely furnished log built house. It was located north of Albany on a lower wooded plateau of the Catskill Mountain overlooking the Mohawk River. It was not home, but it was as if the Lord compensated for that with the breath taking beauty of the surrounding landscape. Their needs were many, but most of all they were all ready to hibernate until spring.

They had calculated that they would be in the region approximately three months, or for the time it took for Sula to deliver her baby and regain her strength. The men rented a horse and rig from the livery and purchased food staples, plates and eating utensils, bowls and cooking pots, axes, saws, hammers, nails and lanterns from the general store in Albany. They also purchased animal traps, fishing hooks and twine and two rifles, with ample ammunition for protection and hunting, Early each morning Jacob, Miles and the boys searched the surrounding forest for dead dried logs suitable for heat; then they hauled and chopped the wood daily. They needed more blankets, pillows, water and wash basins and towels and Jacob knew that most of what they acquired would soon be left behind when they continued on their journey. The mattresses in the house were old, dusty and filthy. There were three full size beds and Jacob and Miles figured they needed four new mattresses; one bed would be for Mrs. Morton and the twins, a bed for Miss Tillie and Jennie and Sula, one for Miles, Robby and Evan and he would quickly build a bed for himself and Simon.

Sometimes Mrs. Morton went to town with Jacob and Miles and whenever they made the trip they purchased supplies, enough to last for a month. The men and boy hunted, trapped and fished for their meat and the families kept to themselves.

৵৽

March 19th, 1861, Sula called out for Miss Tillie. She was reaching to stack the dishes after diner. "Oh Aunt Tillie, something is happening! Mah clothes, everythin' be wet . . . Ah'm so sorry." She stood holding to the back of a chair, looking down at the puddle of fluid on the floor.

"Oh chile, it be yuh time." Tillie hurriedly placed her arm around Sula's waist and led her to the bedroom. "Mrs. Morton!" Tillie called out. "It be Sula's time. Ah be needin' yuh!"

Everyone leaped to their feet. Mrs. Morton rushed to the room and then she turned and looked back. "Y'all sit down, this is woman's work. Oh Jacob, help Jenny to get a good fire going. Ah need her to bring in the hot water. She's a little woman." She entered the bedroom and slammed the door behind her.

As soon as the water was hot Jacob helped Jenny carry the bucket and kettle to the bedroom door. He stood at the door as Jenny entered the room carrying the kettle. He peeked over her head trying to get a glimpse at Sula, but Mrs. Morton appeared at the door and shoed him away.

The time was unmeasurable for Jacob, but when he heard the first cry of the child of his blood his tears flowed like a steady rain. He stood in his track unable to move. He heard Mrs. Morton calling him, but he just stood at the side of the open door. Miles placed his hands on his shoulders and guided him to Sula's side and he lowered himself to his knees. He kissed her forehead and his tears dripped onto her face.

"We have a son, Jacob," Sula whispered.

They laughed. He pulled back the blanket covering his tiny son and he cried and laughed. "You are born free my son. You are the first in our families to be born free. Sula . . . Ah want to name him Franklin. The name means 'free man'," Jacob whispered a pleading request to Sula.

"Yuh not gone give him yuh name?" She asked.

"He can have my name in the middle. Franklin Jacob Natty should be his name." Jacob smiled and wiped the tears from his eyes with the back of his sleeve. He looked up at Miles. "My son, Miles, this is my son, Franklin Jacob Natty."

Miles smiled, "He is a handsome fellow, Jacob."

Mrs. Morton stood back smiling as everyone had a chance to see the baby. Jacob and Sula beamed with joy as new parents should. Then Miss Tillie sounded off. "Jacob, you can stay in the room if yuh be real quiet. Sula be needin' her rest."

Mrs. Morton laughed, "Miss. Tillie is right, everybody out. He is the cutest little thing with them blue eyes like is daddy."

Miss Tillie followed Mrs. Morton from the room laughing and added. "Well, Ah know his hair ain't gon' be much lak his mama's 'cause his head is as bald as his behind. Ah know he gon' be a brown skin boy too, dat be by da color of dem ears."

"How can you tell all that?" Mrs. Morton asked.

"Ah don' birthed Negro babies and white babies. Negro babies be born with a head full a thick pretty hair; most white babies be born bald. Negro babies can be born almost any shade, but their fingernail beds and ears give away dey true final shade." Tillie smiled as she spoke. She went about fiddling and fixing in the kitchen, while Mrs. Morton stood listening, appearing perplexed and thinking about what Tillie had said and the things she had never thought about.

"Miss Tillie, thank you," Mrs. Morton said. She smiled because of the new information.

Tillie smiled and nodded her head.

꙳꙳

Jacob and Miles had inquired and were put in touch with an Indian guide who would deliver them to Saint Catherines, Canada in the Province of Ontario. They had secured passage on a riverboat to take them up the Mohawk River, beyond Rome, New York and then onto the Oneida River and later onto the Oswego River. The guide explained their entire journey, even the facts of the Fugitive Slave Act; a law that Jacob was well aware of. He explained that the Mohawk River Route was frequently watched by the slave hunters so documentation always needed to be available. Jacob asked how many men usually traveled in a hunting party. And when told there were usually three or four, he just nodded his head. Miles stared at him and knew Jacob was not going to allow anyone to hurt his family and neither would he. The guide warned that there were three sections of the rivers where they would have to travel overland and on foot because of the rapids and waterfalls. He informed them of the secret shelters at these locations where the families could rest as long as they wanted before continuing on. Once they reached Oswego they could book passage on a ship to cross Lake Ontario. The guide continued telling them that all of the ships docked in the Port of Oswego were British and once on a ship everyone would be in British territory and free of the laws of the United States. The ship would dock in Toronto, Canada in the Province of Ontario. He informed them that Toronto was a very nice town. "You may remain there if you want or you may decide to purchase a horse and wagon and head south-west to Saint Catherines. I will stay with you until you reach your destination," he said.

They all settled in Toronto, Canada on April 11, 1861.

The United States Civil War began April 12, 1861 with the Confederate soldier's attack on Fort Sumter, South Carolina. By April 19, 1861, President Lincoln called up 75,000 Union soldiers.

The End

Made in the USA
Charleston, SC
16 July 2016